D1125973

		DATE DUE	

Fame and Fortune

By the same author

Novels
Obbligato
The Earlsdon Way
The Limits of Love
A Wild Surmise
The Graduate Wife
The Trouble With England
Lindmann
Darling
Orchestra and Beginners
Like Men Betrayed
Who Were You With Last
Night?
April, June and November
Richard's Things
California Time
Heaven and Earth
After the War
The Hidden I
A Double Life
Coast to Coast

Short Stories
Sleeps Six
Oxbridge Blues
Think of England
The Latin Lover

Biographies
Somerset Maugham
Byron

Translations
(with Kenneth McLeish)
The Poems of Catullus
The Plays of Aeschylus (2 vols)
Euripides: Medea, Bacchae
Sophocies: Ajax
Petronius: Satyrica

Essays
Cracks in the Ice
Of Gods and Men
The Necessity of anti-semitism
The Benefits of Doubt

Autobiography
Eyes Wide Open
A Spoilt Boy

Ancient Greece
Some Talk of Alexander

Notebooks
Personal Terms
Rough Copy
Cuts and Bruises

Screenplays
Two for the Road
Oxbridge Blues

Fame and Fortune

Frederic Raphael

BOOKS

First published in Great Britain in 2007 by JR Books,
10 Greenland Street, London NW1 0ND
www.jrbooks.com

A catalogue record for this book is available from the British
Library.

ISBN 978-1-906217-34-1

1 3 5 7 9 10 8 6 4 2

Typeset by SX Composing DTP, Rayleigh, Essex
Printed and bound in Great Britain by
Cromwell Press, Trowbridge, Wiltshire

For Sarah

I

On election day, May 3rd 1979, Adam Morris walked from his house in Tregunter Road to John Sandoe's bookshop in Blacklands Terrace, Chelsea, to collect a book he had ordered about the Jesuits in Paraguay and also – but as if it were not at all his purpose – to check whether copies of his latest novel, *The Vulture's Portion*, were suitably displayed.

In the improbable hope of seeing someone actually buy a copy, and perhaps even wanting to have it autographed, Adam loitered among the paperbacks at the top of the stairs. He heard the ting of the bell as someone came into the shop.

'Good morning, John.' The low voice lent seductive grace to routine greeting.

'Good morning, Francesca.'

She cleared her throat. 'Have you got this novel Julian thingy wrote that review about, called *The Vulture's Potion* by any chance, in the *Sunday Times*, was it?'

'*Vulture's Portion*. Yes, we do. Over there. We also happen to have the author.'

'Do you? Where?'

'Up here,' Adam said. 'But he can easily remain invisible, if not immortal or wise. Please don't . . . feel obliged to . . .'

He came down, head lowered, as if shy, buttoning his chapped suede jacket, a show of paperbacks badged against his chest.

'You haven't changed, I see.' She was a fine-nosed, fair-haired, blue-eyed woman in her middle-thirties. The voice seemed taller than she was. She wore a grey pinstripe trouser suit and a white silk shirt.

'Have I not? From what?'

1

She was turning the pages of Adam's novel. He suspected that she would wear the same expression if she were interviewing a prospective servant. 'From when you were younger.'

Adam chose to do his modest chuckle. 'And I'm equally sure you haven't,' he said.

'But I have,' she said. 'In many ways.' She looked up at him with a smile. Her face was sweetly oval; nice lips. 'However, I still wish you were dead.'

Adam said, ' "However", do you?' He put the three paperbacks he had chosen on Sandoe's table. 'You seem to have taken against my novel with remarkable celerity.'

'Still using long words when short ones would do, I see.'

She was standing in the narrow alley between the centre table and the window, taking off one of her white gloves.

'Am I to assume from the rare charm of your tone that we've met before?'

'What I really wish,' she said, 'is that you were *dying*.'

'That's very flattering of you. Meanwhile, I'm trying to remember where I've heard those high-heeled vowel sounds before . . . Or is this your usual tactic when picking up stray authors? If so, excuse me –'

As he made to pass her, she raised her ungloved hand and slapped his face. Adam blinked and looked round, as if someone else must have been the target. John Sandoe had gone into the inner room. When she raised her hand again, Adam grabbed the woman's wrist and held it tight. 'What the hell's the matter with you? And what the hell do you think you're doing? I now wish I was Jimmy Cagney and had a grapefruit with me – because I should take great pleasure in squeezing it right in your not unbeautiful puss.'

'You always have to be charming, don't you? Is that supposed to be an American accent? I remember you were quite an actor. Or thought you were.'

'Sadly, you're safe. I have yet to go to the fruiterer's this morning.'

'Meanwhile, you're hurting my arm.'

2

'Am I? Good.'

'Do you like hurting people then?'

'You slapped my face, for Christ's sake. And looked likely to repeat the dose.'

'That's exactly for whose sake I slapped it.'

'Gentle Jesus meek and mild, did you really? Are you sure He'll be pleased? What exactly is this all about? Or even approximately what?'

'That novel of yours.'

'*That* novel? Which one was that? There have been several.'

'As if you didn't know. *An Early Life*.'

'That was five years ago. What was wrong with it?'

'The way you wrote about Donald,' she said. 'What's wrong is a world in which shits like you get away with writing books, and people like Donald die.'

The bell tinged as another customer came in. He took off his flat cap, glanced at the couple, and went quickly into the back room.

'*Francesca!* Of course. Got it!' Adam said. 'You're Donald Davidson's pretty, vicious, little sister. The one with the horse. Nelson, was it?'

'So it's all coming back now, is it?'

'I'm not sure it ever went away.'

'You put us all in a book. Talk about vicious!'

'I was doing my modest best to remember Don as he was when we were all . . . young and . . .'

'You think you have the right to use real people and . . . make money out of them.'

'Money had nothing to do with it. I waited more than twenty years. And I thought Donald . . . deserved to be remembered . . .'

'So you dug him up and made a book out of him.'

'I don't think that's what's upset you. If upset is what you are. I think it's what I remember about you, and you know I do. Calling me "Jew" in that charming way you did, when we were looking for a tennis ball which you'd hit into the long grass.'

'*Weren't* you one?' she said. 'A Jew? *Aren't* you now? I can still

3

see the look on your face. Fancy you remembering Nelson! It doesn't upset me at all.'

'Look . . .' Adam lowered his voice as another female customer came into the shop: 'Donald died. I didn't kill him. You didn't kill him. You could always have a word with your merciful God and see if He knows who killed him, or millions of others . . .'

A man came into the shop. 'Adam,' he said, 'what are you doing here?' It was Bruno Laszlo, producer of *The Woman in Question*, for which Adam had won an Oscar a decade earlier. 'I've been calling your agent for a week. What are you doing at the moment?'

'At the moment I'm having a private conversation with . . .'

'Of course. How do you do? Do you have a few minutes possibly? We can have a coffee round the corner.'

'What do you think?'

Bruno was wearing a blue silk suit, a pink shirt with the top button undone under the narrow blue woollen tie. He looked at Francesca and then at Adam. 'I understand, but I have this very important idea I want to talk to you about. Right up your avenue.'

'I'll call you,' Adam said.

'I interrupt you.'

'It is your habit.' Adam looked back at Francesca, almost as if he was afraid that she might have gone. Bruno patted Adam's elbow and went to ask John Sandoe about a novel whose title and author he couldn't exactly remember, but it sounded interesting.

'You haven't changed, have you?' she said.

'Yes, I have. No, I haven't. Isn't that true of all of us?'

'You're still glorying in it . . .'

'In what am I?'

'You lived and Don didn't.'

'I'm a writer. All I've done is my possibly unworthy best to . . . immortalise Donald by writing about someone, all right, very like him. It's the only resurrection I can supply.'

'You got your own back. On all of us. Saying the things you did.'

'No, actually: saying the things *you* said. And putting them on paper. I'll tell you the truth, Francesca –'

'The truth, will you really?'

Bruno Laszlo came back with two large art books. 'Adam, listen, now you're still here, I take two minutes of your time. Two minutes.'

' – *and* buy you a cappuccino,' Adam was saying to Francesca, 'if you feel like it, and that's as far as it goes.'

'If you want,' she said.

'I'll call you tomorrow, Bruno. Promise.'

'But will you do it? How is your wife?'

'I will. Even though I promised.'

Adam eased Francesca towards the door, a courteous hand on her elbow. She was still carrying a copy of *The Vulture's Portion*.

'Are you stealing that book,' he said, 'or shall I put it back?'

'I'm stealing it.'

'Then I'll put it back.'

'You don't have to play the policeman. John puts things on my account. Automatically.'

'Very wise of him, I imagine.'

'Imagine, do you? You don't have to do this, you know. Just because I slapped your face.'

'Well, I seem to be doing it, don't I?'

They went to a coffee bar at the corner of Flood Street.

'So. Round two. Seconds out.' Adam clinked his transparent spoon against his plastic cup. He tore open a packet of brown sugar and spilled the grains on to the puckering froth of his cappuccino.

'Was I really as beastly when I was a little girl as you made me seem in your novel?'

'No. You were much worse. And also much more attractive, of course. You weren't *that* little. Oh those shining, pink, lightly flossed adolescent shins! No wonder *Lolita* sold millions.'

'Don't you? Sell millions?'

5

'Ha! Tell me . . . how are your . . . parents?'

'Daddy died. Mummy's in South Africa.'

'Best possible place for her, I imagine. Is she all right?'

'She was. Until I told her about your book.'

'Nice of you to do it then. I admired her. Eventually. Her dignity. And her courage, when Don was . . . dying and she . . . still wanted him to come on holiday with me and Barbara.'

'That's why you had to make her out to be some kind of a Nazi, is it?'

'The kind you find only in the top drawer. Next to the Londonderries. What about . . . the place . . . in the country – Gifford's End – you had?'

'Sold. To some ghastly developers from the Lea Bridge Road.'

'Long noses? Bound to have had.'

'Probably. They divided it into flats, built dozens of perfectly vile little houses in the grounds, and . . . made tons and tons of money.'

'That's all they care about it, isn't it? Of which no doubt you received your . . . vulture's portion.'

'I've watched your progress.'

'All the way from A to B. *Almost* to B. My progress is an exercise in slomo. Slow motion. Technical term from the despicably long-nosed movie business.'

'You seem quite concerned with noses. Why is that?'

'Do you still play tennis?'

'Not since I had my children,' she said. 'I bet *you* do.'

'Not as well as my son Tom. How many children do you have?'

'Two. Daughters.'

'And are they as beautiful as you . . . *were*?'

'You couldn't resist it, could you?'

'Unworthy. I apologise. And untrue. If a question can be untrue.'

'You always did, didn't you? Apologise. More than was necessary.'

'Really? Oh! And I always thought I was very . . . outspoken. As beautiful as you *are*, I should've said, but I wouldn't want to do a nice thing like that, would I?'

'You never *really* want a fight, do you? You prefer laughter and applause.'

'Every time,' he said. 'Do you want another coffee?'

'You never tried to kiss me. Why?'

'I mistook you for the Holy Grail. Untouchable. Too late now.'

'Are you still married to her?'

'Barbara? Yes, so far as I know. Yes. It's not *that* long, you know. I am and I'm glad I am. Are you not still married to . . . him? Whoever he is, or was. Presumably. Assuming you're still . . .'

'Dominic? Of course, officially. I'm still a Roman. He went off with a very young girl when I was in the nursing home having Claire, but that doesn't really −'

'A little thing like that! Why ever would it? What does he do? Dominic.'

'He's got pots of money. He does what he likes.'

'And do you hate him too?'

'Hate Dominic? Not at all. We're very . . .'

'My script has . . . "good friends", but you're not going to say that, are you? Or "close"?'

'*Together*, I was going to say, in certain ways, still.'

'Should I be curious?'

'If I told you, you'd only put us in a book, I expect.'

'That does seem to be my ugly habit.'

'He thought you were picking me up, didn't he?'

'Did he? Who was that?'

'That wop or whatever he was in Sandoe's.'

'Bruno. I expect so.'

'Do you have a card at all?'

'Card? Oh, *card*! No. I associate having cards with people who sell insurance to people.'

'I have one. But I'm not selling anything.'

7

'I can't imagine your ever having to.'

'Write your number on one of mine, if you feel like it. You're not in the telephone book, are you?'

'No, as a matter of fact not.'

'No one is any more, are they, you want to talk to?'

'We're all afraid of getting wake-up calls from burglars, aren't we? Wanting to know why we're still there when they have work to do.'

'Is that it, do you think?'

Her eyes were on his hand as he wrote his telephone number under hers and then swivelled it for her inspection.

'God knows why I'm giving it to you,' he said. 'Or why I wouldn't really.'

'You owe me a slap, don't you?'

'Do I? I don't slap ladies as a rule.'

'Not even if they ask you nicely?'

He pushed back his chair, but he didn't get up. He swallowed what was left in his cup and said, 'I must go and . . . write a sentence or two before lunch. Have you voted yet?'

'Of course. But it won't put the clock back, will it?'

'Oh for the good old days! How we hated them!'

'Did you? I didn't. Will you put me in a book now, do you suppose?'

'And press the pages very firmly together afterwards? I might, if you're very good.'

'And if I'm very bad,' she said, 'what will you do then?'

ii

Barbara Morris was making a heap of all the obsolete flared jeans in Adam's and their son Tom's cupboards, with a view to handing them to Oxfam, when the telephone rang.

'Hullo.'

'Is Mr Morris there, please?'

'Who am I to say is calling?'

'This is Mike Clode. Quick as you can, dear. It's a little important.'

'Mike Clode! Surely you mean it's a *big* important.'

Mike Clode said, 'Hullo! Is that . . .? It is, isn't it? Barbara.'

'*Dear?* Alias the girl! Yes, it is. Are you duly embarrassed?'

'Barbara, darling! I didn't recognise your laryngitis. Can you hear me grovelling? I grovel. But if . . .'

'He isn't. He's gone to buy his new novel into the bestseller list. He'll be home any minute now with two thousand copies. Oh hold on . . . Any minute has arrived, because here he is.' Barbara covered the receiver. 'Mike.'

'What does he want?'

'You.'

Barbara handed Adam the telephone and he blew out his cheeks as she went up the stairs. 'Sir Michael.'

Mike Clode said, 'How did you know?'

'How did I know what? The Greek alphabet? The Lord's Prayer backwards? Shit from shinola? What?'

'You know bloody well what. The knighthood. It's not supposed to be out yet.'

'Oh the knighthood. I didn't know. Do I now? Oh my Lord. Correction: oh my *sir*. My Lord will come a little later in our island story, I presume.'

'If *Private Eye* finds out about it prematurely, they'll blow me out of the water.'

'You're out of the water already, chief. Look around you. And high on the hog. You're not going to call yourself Sir *Mike*, are you? It sounds a bit like a holiday-camp tycoon. With braces and a tie-slide.'

'Never mind all that dated banter. It's not what I want to talk to you about.'

'Let me guess. You've got the money. For a movie I almost certainly don't want to do. And you don't want me to tell Bruno Laszlo about it because you and I are going to produce it ourselves this time, apart from me.'

'Who told you that?'

'You did. Your voice. Plus the Pavlovian saliva which, to my shame, I detect on my usually caustic tongue.'

'Could all happen one day soon, but that's not actually it at the moment. When can we have lunch?'

'The song the sirens sing!'

'It really is time we gave them all hell again! And made a movie that knocks their eyes out.'

'Of course it is. Having just published a novel that takes bite-sized chunks out of the movie world, what better time to plunge boldly back into the midst of the midden? Good timing too, just when Mrs Thatcher's promising to reduce income tax in genuinely undeserving cases.'

'She's not going to get in, is she?'

'Ask Jim. That's the man who lives in Number Ten, where the knighthoods come from.'

'How about a week today? For lunch. Denis Porson's got this new place everyone's going to. One o'clock unless you hear to the contrary. Two by Two.'

'Sorry?'

'It's called 22, Greek Street. Keep it to yourself, won't you?'

'It can't be much of a secret if everyone goes there.'

'The knighthood, mate.'

'I promise you it will come as a huge surprise. You're the last person, I will tell them, that I ever expected to call sir.'

'The last word's very much your line, isn't it? So I'll leave you with it. Till next week then.'

iii

Earlier in the year, the Prime Minister, on his return from an international conference, had been asked what he proposed to do about the crisis in Britain. Jim Callaghan's alleged reply – 'Crisis? What crisis?' – was answered by sustained strikes which left mountains of garbage in the streets, the dead unburied in icy cemeteries, sewage untreated and provoked Alan Parks, on his

10

twice-weekly chat show, to put it to the Home Secretary: 'Prime Minister? What Prime Minister?'

Parks was, of course, the number one wandering reporter in the BBC's coverage of election night. Still *terrible*, if no longer *enfant*, the burly Aussie polymouth, as he cleverly styled himself – 'thus proving that prophylaxis has its place in public life' – was now among the most conspicuous of Adam Morris's Cambridge contemporaries to have gained metropolitan media fame. 'Put it this way: I get delivered to your lounge or living room, depending on your high or low estate, ready boxed, but without ribbons and with increasingly less on top.'

On election night, Alan was posted in Smith Square. In leather trousers, check yellow and brown woollen shirt, cowboy boots and a fringed leather jacket, he gave the impression of having been called at short notice from a poker game in the nearest saloon. He ambled towards camera with an air of – as he had put it in one of the challengingly allusive articles he sometimes wrote for *The New York Review of Books* – 'a space-traveller stuck with how to make human beings seem even vaguely credible to the grown-ups back home on Mars'.

As his shoulder-loaded cameraman, The Great Sid, and his wired producer, Fiona Maclean, backed away from him, Alan was preparing to be suitably spontaneous. When Fiona mouthed, 'And . . .' and pointed her forefinger at him, he was plumb on cue: 'Here I am in one of the more vibrant centres of political activity, outside Transport House, Labour Party head-quarters, as we observe the hindquarters of the Callaghan government scurry into history, if not obscurity. And I happen to have with me – through sheer luck and a rare capacity for wrestling famous men to the microphone, when they least want it . . .'

Alan leaned out of shot and hugged the smiling figure of Ronnie Braithwaite, Callaghan's Minister of Higher Education, into a tight two-shot.

'Why would I not want it, Alan? Always a pleasure to put you right!'

11

'. . . the Right Honourable Ronnie Braithwaite – who, I imagine, is about to tell us that the country has made a tragic mistake in evicting our natural lords and masters, the Labour Party, and electing the upstart Mrs Thatcher. Am I right, Ronnie, or are you still arguing the toss when the game's already in its closing overs?'

'I shall tell you no such thing, because it hasn't necessarily happened yet.'

'So what do you suggest we do, Ronnie? Give it ten minutes? And then you can throw in the towel after one more mop of that famously high brow of yours?'

'You will have your fun, Alan –'

'Fun? Will I really? One day? Can you put a date on that possibly, Ronald? Seriously, you're not about to say it's too early to say what the result is, are you? Because it's a quarter to three in the a.m. and every swingometer in the land now shows that the Tories are in, and well in, and scoring all round the wicket. Isn't it about time you told us the one about how sorry we'll all be one day soon and, God willing, and the electorate forgetting, you'll be back to mess things up again another day?'

'Did you always want to make a living by putting words in other people's mouths?'

'It's a service I render to a select few.'

'I will say this –'

'Aha! And in your own words, is this going to be?'

'It does look as if it's going to be, all right, a very close-run thing.'

'No, it's in the Duke of Wellington's words. After Waterloo; a famous battle, as all you clued-up commuters have already clocked. Wellington did actually win, however, according to the latest intelligence. Which leaves me hazarding the guess that this is the first, and last, time that Jim Callaghan gets cast as Napoleon the Great. I daresay he'll find St Helena can be a very pleasant place for a weekend break. Cape Town and straight on; you can't miss it, Ronnie, if loyalty has any place in politics and a visit to the vibrant Jim rates among your future plans.'

12

'You know what you are, Alan –'

'I wish I had time to find out, Ronnie, but unfortunately, for some . . .'

On his earpiece, Alan had heard the studio anchorman saying, 'Sorry to cut in, Alan, but we've got another result coming up. South Suffolk . . .'

'Another surprise, I shouldn't be surprised,' Alan said. 'And so away from dreary old London, and Ronnie Braithwaite's straight talking, let's hear it from pulsating Suffolk, South, shall we?'

As the lights went off above The Great Sid's camera, Alan smiled at Ronnie Braithwaite as if they were both in the same joke and pointed to the boxed monitor in which Fiona was now scanning the black-and-white scene in Staunton town hall.

After a double tap of his index finger on the microphone, a local dignitary read from a shaking piece of paper. 'I, Fred Stanley Goodenough, as returning officer for the South Suffolk constituency, announce that the following votes have been cast for the candidates in the parliamentary election in the consti-tuency of Ipswich East and Staunton.'

Alan and Ronnie Braithwaite might have been two actors in the same charade, waiting for a joint cue to resume their parts. 'We're off the air now, Ronald,' Alan said, in an everyday voice. 'You can dare to tell the truth knowing that no one's ever going to hear it. You never seriously expected your tired old comrades to keep the red flag flying yet, did you?'

'Samuel Robert Beddowes . . .'

'The incumbent Labour MP,' the youthfully grey-haired anchorman whispered in the studio.

'Thirteen thousand four hundred and eighty-one.'

'What did I tell you, Ronnie? Labour's manifestly clapped out and longing for the ref to stop the fight. Deny it and I swear I'll never call you an honest man again.'

'Quite honestly and totally off the record . . .'

'Yes, indeed. And what a conveniently lonely spot that can be when the truth will out!'

'. . . there was a certain feeling that something had possibly changed. Jim himself acknowledged that privately.'

'Like acknowledging that an elephant has just left a major *stronzo* on the front doorstep.'

'I don't stretch to Spanish I'm afraid,' Ronnie said.

'Spoken like an Oxford man. Let's put it subtly: you all knew Labour was stuffed.'

'It's been a long run and we've done a lot of things to be proud of.'

'Not least you personally. Six years in a chauffeur-driven limousine spent wondering what more comrade Ronnie can do for the workers before they decide to be ungrateful enough, as they evidently now are, to usher you to the nearest bus stop. Brutal times these, for those without the foresight to book a cushy billet in private industry.'

They waited for the Conservative figures while the returning officer read out a list of minor candidates and the votes they had culled. Alan continued in the quiet tone which promised that he was not being paid to employ it and that Ronnie's confidences were safe with him. 'Is it true you've got your hat in the ring for Master of a famous Oxbridge college? Or is it two?'

'You know your trouble, don't you, Alan?'

'Of course: I can't always get an erection. But that's nothing we have to handle right now. Because, apologies, and here we go. Fiona is signalling frantically. And . . . cue elderly poop with the big news.' Alan snapped experienced fingers as the returning officer came to the name of the Conservative candidate.

'Timothy Gerald Harvey Dent. Twenty-eight thousand nine hundred and sixty-nine.'

'Which proves, conclusively, Ronald, as widely forecast, that *your* big trouble is that your party is run by a clutch of put-the-clock-back trade unions and you're *never* going to get it up again.'

'One minute to go, Alan, they're telling me,' Fiona said, 'and we're back on you again.'

'You think you can say anything you want,' Ronnie Braithwaite said, 'to anybody you want to.'

'That is my overpaid job, Ronald. Power without responsibility. The role of the harlot down the ages. Uncle Rudyard
was right, and it's just the part I always dreamed of playing. Your
goose is now just about as cooked as it can get, I'd say, wouldn't
you, Ronald?'

Fiona was indicating that they might not be back on air for
another three or four minutes.

Ronnie said, 'Not much point in me hanging around, Alan,
is there, any longer?'

'Not in the hope of high office, I don't suppose, Ronnie.
Even the spud-bashers are turning their backs on the socialist
millennium. But give it a minute.'

'They may yet be sorry. The spud-bashers.'

'Indeed. Meanwhile they're cheering their empty heads off, is
that what you're saying?'

Fiona pointed to the monitor where the studio anchorman was re-affixing his earpiece. 'And now back for some
reaction to Alan Parks who is still, we hope, with Ronnie
Braithwaite –'

'Ronnie,' Alan was ready to say, 'as you were very forth-
rightly conceding off the record just now, the party's pretty well
over. The Labour Party, that is –'

'Alan, you really do think you can get away with murder,
don't you?'

'And you're not all of you as sorry as you'd have to pretend
to be if the loony left was sweeping back into power with plans
to make Liverpool the new capital of the country, even though
they'd have to find an ideologically correct substitute for
"capital" – or do you deny that and also maintain that the earth
is still as flat as it ever was?'

'This is the last time I take part in any interview you're likely
to conduct. I'm serious. I've had enough.'

'Ronald, to be brutally frank – no, to be brutally Alan Parks
– I can confirm to you that ex-Labour ministers are unlikely to
be as much in demand in studios and places where they sing as a
recently rodent-nibbled biscuit –'

'Is there anything in the world you wouldn't twist for a cheap laugh?' Ronnie said.

'There absolutely is, but I can't show it to you now, Ronald. There are ladies present.'

'And thank you very much,' Fiona said, as the light went off above the camera.

'You're an impossible shit, Alan Parks,' Ronnie said.

'Um, excuse me interrupting –'

'Excuse you?' Alan said. 'I invite you.'

'Only I'm from, um, Tory Central Office,' the girl said, 'and they want me to . . .'

'And who could blame them when you look like you do? Am I right, Ronald? You know the ex-minister, don't you?'

'Veronica,' the girl said.

'And why not?'

'They want me to take you to –'

'– the pinnacle of the temple? A place I've always wanted to see. How are the cities of the plain looking these days?'

'– talk to . . . um . . .'

'*Her?* Speak up, Veronica. You mustn't be shy. It frightens the horses.'

'I can't promise.'

'Lie to me then. Not that you have to. I'm yours anyway. Have a great time in the wilderness, Ronald. And now . . . Rule, Britannia, cleverly rescripted to read Rule, Maggie Thatcher, and the devil take the Trade Unions and Allied Trades, preferably high in the fleshy part of the ample left buttock. Veronica. What do you do in the daytime, as if it mattered? Lead me to it, or her, or whatever the buffet offers.'

iv

In Medlar Cottage, two miles from the steel and concrete campus of Staunton University, Gavin and Fay Pope watched the slow nails being driven into Labour's electoral coffin. Timothy

16

Dent, who had just won the constituency in which they lived, was a local entrepreneur whose benefactions to the university, a few years earlier, had inflamed Gavin's radicalised sociology students, for whom chanting hosannahs to Chairman Mao and demanding increased grants were compatible substitutes for academic diligence. They had denounced a 'capitalist takeover', but – after a preliminary 'as seen on television' strike – few were now showing any reluctance to use the new Media Complex.

'So, *Sic transit gloria* Thursday, it looks like being! Master Dent is among the prophets.' Gavin was looking left and right for a glass or bottle with something in it. 'Will Madame Thatcher grace him with instant office, do you suppose, *cara mia*? Is there lower yet to sink? I'll drink to that. Or I would if I wasn't holding an empty glass. How can such things be? Bottles seem to have legs in this house. You haven't been muttering "Quick march" under your breath, have you, Fats?'

'I don't care what you say to me any more, Gavin, but if you don't change your ways, and very soon, they're going to take your chair away.'

'Then I shall sit on the floor and contemplate the stars.'

'Your own vomit is a likelier prospect, if you don't choke on it first.'

'You have a tongue tonight, little wife. In a strictly metaphorical sense. As regards "little", I mean.'

The studio anchorman on the BBC was nodding at what he was hearing on his earpiece. 'Our latest projection, I'm being told, gives Mrs Thatcher and the Conservatives a clear majority . . . Oh, you can see it up there, of between thirty and fifty.'

'Well, there it bloody well is,' Gavin said, on his hands and knees looking to see if a bottle could have rolled under the prolapsed belly of the sofa, 'we're in for a decade of mother knows best. And the worst of it is, perhaps she does. He added *sotto voce*.'

'Are you sure that shouldn't be *blotto voce*?' Fay said.

'Tim Dent MP. *Omoi peplegmai chairian plegen eso*, as Agamemnon said in a not dissimilar situation.'

17

'Did you put your hand up her skirt, Tim Dent's wife? Once upon a time. Jeanne?'

'The frog lady? No, *hélas*, not even as often as once. Not one terrified finger did I insert between those far-from-loosening thighs, *je t'assure*. Bird's nest soup is not a French dish, at least not one that I ever got to lap.'

'Only I was looking over some of my old diaries,' Fay said. 'You'd be amazed at some of the things I found.'

'Christ, you're not going to publish them, are you?'

'What would "The Queen of Mashed Potatoes" or "The feminine for elephant" want to do a thing like that for?'

'I never called you those meaning anything –'

'Yes, you did. And worse. And often, and in front of other people. And you know it.'

'Not with any intention of . . . hurting you. I was making light of – what was not. Come on, Leah mine, you know my nasty little ways.'

'Fatso,' she said.

'Christ, I'm thirsty. You're the only woman who's ever meant anything to me, Fay. You know that.'

'That's what you've got against me, I presume.'

'Got it. The venomous new light in your eye, reason for: you voted for the bitch, didn't you? Thatcher.'

'It's a secret ballot.'

'And – more important in the shabby, domestic scale of things – you voted *against me*. And all I hold dear, if, dear, I do. You don't love me any more, and tonight's the night to break the news, is that the brief motto in your outsized cracker?'

'It's not a cracker I'm going to pull, Gavin. Certainly not with you, and certainly not tonight.'

'But lo! What sidles here with timely tread and modest words all set to be unfolded on just such an occasion? Our heroic new MP, with loving Madame Ooh-là-là nailed to his mast.'

Tim Dent, in a chalk-stripe blue suit and non-denominational tie, leaned to shake hands with a yellow-rosetted opponent, the very shaved face shining with generous victory. Then, with a

18

becoming squeeze of his wife's hand, he addressed the electors. 'I am now not only a Conservative member of Parliament, and very proud to be so, I am also the representative of . . .'

Gavin said, 'each and every one of you –'

'. . . each and every one of you . . .'

'And,' Gavin said, 'I should just like to take this opportunity to say –'

'. . . and,' Tim Dent said, 'I should just like to . . . take this opportunity to say –'

'He's Mr Unpredictable, this one!' Gavin said.

'– that the result of this historic election means that we have the chance of –'

'Will he dare to venture a new start?'

'– a new start in this country . . . perhaps our *last* chance . . . to modernise Britain and work together towards renewed prosperity and pride restored!'

'An elegant chiasmic pair,' Gavin said, 'rarely seen in public these days. Mark my words, madame, the price of clichés is set to rise.'

'And now,' Tim said.

'– on a more personal note, if I may –'

'– on a more personal note, I should like to thank my wife Jeanne . . .'

'. . . who cannot get enough,' Gavin said, 'and certainly not from someone as busy as I'm going to be now –'

'– who has done so much to support me –'

'Did nobody ever advise him to take the weight on his elbows?'

Tim Dent was saying, 'As for my principal opponent, the out-going member – who – no, no . . . who fought a very fair and honourable fight and who I know will –'

'Oh shut up.' Gavin reached and clicked off the television. 'Christ, I hate magnanimity at times like this. Why can't he behave like an honest Christian and piss on the buggers below? I should've stood against the sod. He wouldn't have been nice about *me*. I could have beaten the bugger, bet you.'

'Gavin Vincent Canute, could you really?' Fay said. 'You flatter yourself. The blue tide would still have come in. I'm going to clear up and go to bed and you can do what you like, as if you were ever going to do anything else.'

'Oh God,' Gavin said, 'here comes the washing-up revenge again! You'd even've voted for him against me. Your own wedded hubby. You minx. You *mountain*. Where do women learn to make clearing a few glasses and things into a major work of art and a protest movement all in one, or two, or three?'

'If you really want to know, yes, I did. Vote for him.'

'You voted for *her*. The original tracked vehicle steered by its own tracks. Want to know something you may not know? I rather look forward to my sociology seminar in the a.m. and the long faces of the youthful comrades as they face a future without cabinet members that picket British industry in the interests of the yobboes and the Luddites. Tomorrow just may be a day worth living for, thanks to the grocer's daughter. But she must never, never know.'

v

'Rachel, breakfast's on the table,' Barbara called up the stairs. 'As if there was any point in saying so. Again.'

Adam was watching the mini-TV on the counter in the kitchen.

'In my wild flights of non-partisan fantasy,' Alan Parks was saying, 'I have, of course, been expressing only my own personal and overpaid point of view, as well as reflecting that of the now vast majority of voters for whom the red sunset is even now turning into the buh–buh–bluest of the day . . .'

'Enough already. How does the bugger do it? Alan's managed to talk all night and there isn't an ahem on his vocal cords. While I can't even say good morning without sounding like a scratched seventy-eight.'

'When you're really only a scratched forty-seven.'

'Who's counting? Don't count.'

20

'Sorry,' Rachel said.

'So young, so beautiful,' Adam said, 'what's to be sorry about?'

'Being late. I was revising.'

'Something dull and not relevant to today, I hope. That's what I'm paying fees for.'

'The Radical Enlightenment, actually.'

'*Viva* Spinoza. The Jew that's underneath the lot, with or without a majuscule. Do I intrude an unwelcome Semitic note?'

Barbara said, 'Isn't that your favourite activity?'

'Mummy's home! Yes, it is. As you should know, my sweet princess.'

'Did you vote for Thatcher, Daddy?'

'I didn't have to, luckily. The Tories always win in Chelsea anyway. So I stuck to my principles and wasted my vote.'

'Why does he always pretend to be so cynical?'

'May I answer that one, madame chairman?' Adam said. 'Or am I supposed to say Madame *chair*?'

Barbara said, 'Is there a known way of stopping you?'

'Then I will tell you. For the simple reason that in this country people like me always have to pretend to be something, because –'

'– otherwise they guess you're Jewish,' Barbara said.

'They've all guessed already,' Rachel said.

'Only because they're anti-Semitic,' Adam said.

'Or,' Barbara said, 'because you keep batting on about it?'

'It sometimes comes out inadvertently.'

'Ever considered checking your zip, Dad?'

'Sixteen years old, a schoolgirl even, and already she uses words like . . . *zip*!'

'I read your books, don't I?'

'You're going to be late, Rachel. And your father's dialogue is not a good excuse.'

'But it is a living,' Adam said.

'I'm only missing prayers. Ben Blotky's coming by for me in a tick.'

'Blotky already! One of your people? One of *my* people?'

'No idea,' Rachel said. 'Never asked him.'

'So what was his name before he changed it? Not Kelly by any chance?'

'Is this what they call "*schtick*",' Rachel said, 'what you do all the time?'

'As opposed to *shikse*, which means –'

'A girl who isn't Jewish –'

'So count your blessings.'

'He calls me Rachel and then I'm not supposed to be Jewish.'

'*We* called you,' Adam said. 'Your mother had the casting vote. Why else would you be so beautiful?'

'That's what they call *schmooze*, Raitch,' Barbara said, 'if you're looking to widen your vocabulary . . .'

'. . . and narrow your horizons. With all the noses in her family tree, she has one like yours? *Shikse* has to be right. So which prayers are you not going to as a matter of interest, Jewish or . . . what's the other thing?'

'Didn't I tell you?' Rachel said. 'They have special agnostic prayers now.'

'And what do agnostic prayers pray, pray? Or do they only threaten to go back and believe in God unless their just demands are met?'

'We have sensible talks about . . . you know . . .'

'*You know?* My voist fears are confirmed. First thing in the morning you're *sensible*?'

Barbara said, 'You're not *talking*, Adam; you're *writing*. I can hear the typewriter clacking behind every word.'

'Contraception? Is what you're sensible about possibly?'

'Sometimes.'

'Contraception *sometimes* is, believe me, by no means often enough. Ben Blotky, is he someone – ?'

'He's a friend.'

'I was a friend of your mother's once. And now look at us.'

'That was before he knew he was going to be a success.'

22

'And then when I was, you and Tom turned up. Asking to be privately educated.'

'We never asked to be. I certainly didn't.'

'If you hadn't been, you would've, believe me. One thing no one will ever, ever say in this country: I wish you'd sent me to a Comprehensive. That can't be the postman. He's on time.'

'That'll be Ben. See you tonight.'

Rachel kissed Adam's cheek, smiled at Barbara and went skipping out. Barbara collected the empty grapefruit halves and put them in the bin.

'I meant it,' Adam said. 'About why she's beautiful.'

'You think too much about noses.'

'And not enough about . . . what, are you saying?'

'I'm not saying.'

'I can still hear you. Ba, could you possibly put a stitch in the pocket of that leather jacket that I should have junked years ago? Please.'

'First you put the boot in, then you expect me to help you do up the laces.'

'I have to go and do some work. Are you here at lunch time?'

'Why?' she said. 'Are you going out and someone's delivering something and you want someone to be around?'

Adam caught her as she came for his Grape-Nuts bowl. 'We ought to have a holiday together. You and me. Soon. Alone. Venice or somewhere.'

'Don't worry about me, Adam,' she said. 'It makes me feel inferior. Go and do some work.'

'We can go out to lunch, if you'd like. Together. Celebrate the victory of everything I have long detested but just may come round to, if the promised tax cuts materialise.'

'It'll be ready at one as usual,' she said.

'She's got your eyes too, I realise. Rachel. Both of them, lucky girl.'

'Telephone.'

'The hell with it.'

'He lied. Do you want me to – ?'

23

'It's OK,' Adam said.

'I thought it would be.'

Adam leaned against the sink to answer the wall phone. 'Hullo. Tom! It's Tom!'

'Is he all right?'

'Is everything all right, your mother wants to know? At once! Because it's an unusual hour . . . Shouldn't you be asleep in someone's lecture by now? Or don't they still have lectures in Cambridge?' Adam looked at Barbara. 'In my day, you know. What? That's wonderful. Meaning you'll definitely get your Blue, right?' Adam covered the phone. 'He's definitely in the six, he's been told.'

'Tell him "wow".'

'Your mother says "wow", which is not a common occurrence. Of course we'll come. And abuse the umpire if he calls anything out he shouldn't. Terrific news. Aren't you lucky you didn't inherit my second service? Say hullo to your mother.'

'That all sounds wonderful,' Barbara said. 'You've made your father's day. That's right, first Mrs Thatcher and now this . . . His cup runneth over.'

'And on to my clean trousers, as usual. No two without a three, so what else can go right? *I* can go write, he punned cleverly: some lousy movie. How low can a man get at the peak of his powers?'

Barbara was saying, 'I know, but he'll get over it. Bye, darling.'

'What will I get over? Because I'll be the judge of that.'

'Knowing that Tom can do a few things you can't.'

'Three times a night, I shouldn't wonder. Please God making a living will soon be one of them.'

'You've got more money than you know what to do with. And please don't say what you're thinking of saying.'

'And the accountants' bills to prove it, I wasn't going to say. I hate it, Ba, you do know that, don't you? I dream of a cottage somewhere. France maybe. And . . . never again having to wonder whether the cretins or the critics − where there's a difference − like what I've done.'

'Dream on, as Rachel would say.'

'What do you dream of?'

'You. Happy.'

'Do you? And what do I look like when I'm happy?'

'Unrecognisable, don't you?'

'I *am* happy. Truly.'

'See you at lunch then. After I've called you to come and have it for the third time and you've only got this one call that you really have to make first.'

vi

Professor Pope walked, with the usual slump of books and folders under one arm, the hand in his corduroy pocket, across the campus of Staunton University towards seminar room C: 'One of the great battlegrounds of the ongoing Civil War,' as the vice-chancellor had more than once described it. The concrete of the recently new buildings was striped with long black stains. As Gavin had remarked, to no loud laughter, in Council, 'The award-winning architect had not, it seemed, been advised that it frequently rained in equatorial East Suffolk.'

As he glanced through the window, Gavin saw that this year, yet again, his students were expressing their individuality by conforming to radical type: tank tops, undone laces, flared jeans, aggressive hair, Trotskyite spectacles.

'Well, comrades!' Gavin said, as he came in. 'Or should I say well, well!' He tilted a spill of books and papers on the lectern desk. 'The people have spoken, the General Will has generally willed and what have we here in England's once red and litter-strewn land? Glum faces? The people have let the People down, do I infer?'

'Don't do it, Gavin,' Jonty Logan said, from his left-wing position in the front row, 'because we were all betting you would.'

'Spare the bookies and spoil the children! So, the big topical question all are burning to confront: what are the lessons to be

25

learnt on this apparently counter-revolutionary May morning? Have we a suitable slogan? No enemies on the Left, shall we try? And not many friends either, is that the sadly decimated size of it? Yes, Henrietta. As I am always willing to say at the drop of a . . . whatever the freckled beauty cares to drop.'

'He has to do it,' Jonty said. 'He has to. Sexist crap, and he thinks it's clever.'

'What future do you honestly see for the Left now, Gavin? Jonty thinks –'

'Jonty is here present –' Jonty Logan said.

'As is widely recognised, if not applauded –'

'– and can say what he thinks himself. Personally, I see a serious split.'

'A serious split is not to be sniffed at,' Gavin said. 'Except among consenting adults, of course. But I digress. All right, you want to be serious, Jonty? In that case, look at the facts and their woefully unpalatable, democratically arrived at consequences –'

'Look, we're all bloody well aware of the weakness of bourgeois democracy. You've only got to read Gramsci –'

'Among other good things, comrade, if you want to be educated at all and please your mother. Bourgeois democracy as opposed to what? The strength of the *people*'s version? As seen in Hungary in 1956, Prague in 1968? What would Signor G. have to say if he could be with us here today, with a satchel of hindsight on his back? That what we really need now is a spot of Soviet intervention? Thanks for the memory?'

'He never said that.'

'He died too soon, poor Antonio. The poet says the same of the late J. Christ Esquire, who should have hung around a bit and had a few kids. That would've taught him. But yet again I digress, were you about to remark?'

'The weakness of bourgeois democracy,' Jonty said, 'is that the voters don't know what the consequences *are*, of anything. They need to be educated. Would be Gramsci's point.'

'Bloody reactionary rabble with false consciousnesses, all of them. But they're also the salt of the earth, the vessel of salvation

26

and what else have you got in the hitch-hiker's guide to the higher crap?'

'You think you're some kind of Socrates, Gavin, don't you?'

'Better looking though. Much. Longer in the shank, surely. As Henrietta presumably has her hand up to say.'

'Actually, I was going to ask, where does this leave the Left, Gavin, then, in your opinion?'

'I would hazard tied securely in a black plastic bag awaiting collection. Groan if you must. And apparently you must. But my crystal balls tell me to expect a brief period of shocked intro-spection, a rash of *mea culpas* hotly followed by a sharp attack of the neo-Trots. For which not even the renowned Guava supplies a reliable cure.'

'We all knew you'd be bound to draw the wrong conclusions.'

'Pray draw me some right ones, master Logan. In clear, bright colours, if you have your agitprop chalks to hand.'

Ben Pinto said, 'How about if what the electors really wanted, and were never offered by the bourgeois Left, was a much more radical kind of Socialism?'

'With higher taxes that would lead the multinational monsters to transfer what's left of their operations in this country to some benighted oriental corner of the globe?'

'Seriously, wouldn't Workers' Control cut out the non-productive bourgeoisie and the parasitic middlemen?'

'And leave the world to darkness and to me. All power to the Soviets! Why did nobody think of that before? Oh but they did, and what followed was the bloodiest tyranny in the as yet unended history of man and its concomitant rivers of blood and tears. So why not let's try it again? Any ideas on a postcard at all?'

Jonty said, 'You're really revelling in this, aren't you?'

'As revels go,' Gavin said, 'it's a little short on wine, never mind women, which it's not easy to do with breasty Ginny in our midst. Yes, I noticed you were here, braless in Gaza at the mill with the rest of us. We have to bite on the bullet, dear comrades, when there's nothing tastier on the menu. Thatcher

27

touched a chord and we must live with its twang and learn our lesson. Which is?'

'We didn't get our message across clearly enough?'

'Note the statement that is also a question. A modern sonic phenomenon. Or might it just be that "our" message – yours and mine, dear Hetty – was entirely *too* clear, and the voters tore it into little pieces and threw it in our faces? *Or* then again – yes, nicely spoken, allegedly hyphenated David? Speak up!'

'I didn't say anything, sir.'

'Time you did, was my point.'

'Perhaps people want a holiday from policies, is what my father was saying.'

'Jesus Christ on a bicycle.' Jonty Logan slid horizontal behind his desk. 'And while they're on holiday, what's going to move into Number 10?'

'A reactionary government, with an avowedly right-wing Euro-programme of disempowering the working class. Do I take the words out of your mouth? And what then?'

'You tell us. What do you recommend we should do in the meanwhile, Gav?'

'You and I, Hetty? While the Treaty of Rome burns. Do what Nero did, and fiddle our taxes, those few of us who pay them. Oh, I seem to be alone in that department. What an overpaid lackey that makes me!'

'Seriously, are there lessons to be drawn?'

'And quartered, I would say, Benjamino. We could acknowledge, not to say anticipate, the cold snap about to chill the darling buds by scrapping make-believe degrees in pseudo-academic subjects, inter-disciplinary lack of discipline served up with the mushy peas of received ideas.'

'Meaning what exactly?' Jonty was looking around him like a commander about to rally his men for one last charge.

'Oh, am I going too slowly for you? Personally, I confess to having gone along for much, much too long with the Rousseauesque delusion –'

'Rousseauesque! Bloody hell!'

28

'Jean-Jacques not among your prophets, Jonathan? Your loss! Pray check him out, by this day week, and give us a brief *résumé* – or resume if you prefer the rough, insular mode – of no more than three thousand of your own words, if you have that many, of his ideas and their influence on subsequent forms of enlightened or misguided liberationism –'

'Are you actually setting me to –'

'Do a spot of practical, dust-snorting research? Haven't I got my bloody nerve though? It'll make a healthy change for you from playing darts – left-handed to show solidarity with the toilers – and farting *à la* Cultural Revolution when visiting lecturers don't pander to the going Maoist cant. It might even be more socially useful than writing the f word in weedkiller on the vice-chancellor's lawn. I name no names, but yours does come to mind, Jonathan.'

'*Right,*' Jonty said.

'As in "This Means War"? Let me advise against it. With unprecedented firmness.'

'Where does Rousseau come in exactly?'

'Thank you, Henrietta in the blue peacekeeper's beret. He comes in as being the first to foster the idea that the young are an uninhibited fountain of natural goodness and that our old friend Higher Ed can only applaud them on their way to first-class degrees in the number they first thought of.'

'We all know one thing, don't we?'

'That in itself could be progress, Jonty.'

'I.e., the Vicar of Bray is alive and well and living amongst us in the form of Professor Gavin Pope two, the sequel.'

'Things change, my dear old Bolshevik friend. Grant-assisted wassail will, no doubt, continue in some quarters, for a while, but if you look at the wall, you will see the writing on it. And what it says – to quote the original Aramaic – is "Time To Get Some Proper Work Done". Shock, horror and go to it! Di-is-miss!'

Adam's old Cambridge friend Denis Porson had made such a success of *Bumpkins*, his Suffolk country house hotel-restaurant that he had expanded his gastronomic empire to London. Adam walked into Two by Two to find whitewashed brick walls, a black leather bar and a black and white tiled dining room with buttoned banquettes, second-empire light brackets and black bentwood hatstands with very few hats on them.

'Adam, my dear!'

'The very same. Roughly. Master Clode hasn't called to say how late he's running, has he?'

'Not yet. Can I tempt you to a small glass of reheated shampoo while you wait and wait and wait? Shipments of the blushful Hippocrene have yet to materialise.'

'I've got this ostentatiously new book, thanks, Denis, I'm supposed to be reviewing. I'll sit and scribble fierce things on the comp. slip. You've certainly done this place up. I remember it when it was nothing but a yellowing hotbed of second-hand Hungarian goulash. Whereas now —'

'It's your inferior decorator's gallimaufry, dear, I confess it freely, long before you twist my arm.'

'No, no, it's tremendously —'

'Find the right adjective, and two weeks in Tenerife could well be yours. So be warned!'

'Tremendously *vous*,' Adam said. 'And you look to be doing very, very well. Every other table fully equipped with a commissioning editor and people eating out of his or, more often, her hand.'

'Early days. For the restaurant, dear, not for us. Old time is still a-flying, the bitch!'

'Speak for yourself, Denis.'

'There has rarely been a nobler cause. I must go and reduce a *sous-chef* or two to tears or what's a heaven for?'

Adam read his book, made sighing notes — desiccated was spelt, as so often, with two s's and one c — and wondered at the coincidence that Mike Clode's ex-wife, Jill Tabard, was sitting, also alone, at a table next to the biggest aspidistra in the room. When he looked directly at her, Jill was not looking at him; and when she looked at him, he smiled at his book.

At twenty-two minutes past one, Mike Clode, bearded and cloaked in a swirl of Douggie Hayward's tweed, hurried in, wearing the expression of someone whose patience had been sorely tried. The cloak removed, he scanned the room in his black corduroy suit and black turtle-necked sweater.

'Adam!'

Adam had made sure that he was the only person who did not look up at Mike's entrance. 'Mephistopheles, I presume! With you in a moment, squire.'

Adam left Clode standing while he added another caustic comment (and page number) to the tally on the compliments slip. Mike scanned the room, in case there was someone who had missed his entrance, and — with a little lurch of surprise — caught sight of Jill.

'Adam . . . listen, old son, terribly sorry, but . . .'

'Is this a still small voice I hear?'

'Slightly embarrassing booboo time.'

'You've forgotten your credit cards.'

'Worse than that.'

'There isn't anything.'

'Give me a minute or two, mate, will you?'

'Are you about to be in my eternal debt, mate, do I gather? Could this be a moment to treasure?'

'Small case of double-booking. Jill's here. I need to —'

'Go to it, squire. I'll sit and read on and wonder if you're ever coming back.'

'I will. I promise.'

'That rarely shortens the odds by a great deal.'

Mike crossed the room, sideways this way, and then sideways that, touching any number of shoulders, and sometimes tipping their owners with a fond word or two.

'Jill! Darling!'

31

'Hullo, Mike. I was a little early. And you weren't.'

'You look wonderful.'

'And aren't I?' she said.

'Of course you are. Here's the thing –'

'So I notice. *Tout de noir vêtu*. Not in mourning, are you?'

'Do you remember Adam Morris?'

'Not dead, is he?'

'Of course not. He's sitting over there.'

'I know that. I did observe him actually, looking too clever by at least a quarter for the rest of poor suffering humanity. So now let me guess. Got it! The work of a moment. You've promised to have lunch with him, having completely forgotten you were having it with me. And now I'm Scylla and he's Charybdis. And never the twain shall meet.'

'Totally not true. Well, not entirely. Look, I won't bore you with how much of a total no-no my new secretary has been.'

'Are you now about to tell me that you asked this soon-to-be-ex-secretary to phone your ex-wife to cancel our lunch and she phoned the wrong ex-wife?'

'Funnily enough –'

'It's not funny at all. Your beard is though. You always were an absolute bog-brush, and now you've got the bristles to prove it. The king of double-dealing, aren't you?'

'I've had worse notices. Much.'

Adam closed his book and went across to the window table.

'Listen,' he said, 'excuse me – hullo, Jill, how are you? – but I'm just going to pop out and buy another book because I've actually now finished this one. Including the disappointingly inadequate index and the non-existent bibliography.'

'Adam,' Jill said, 'what a nice surprise! I didn't see you. What're you doing here?'

'What indeed?' He bent down to kiss her cheek, and then the other one. 'I loved you in *Miss Julie*. Why don't you stab Mike for an encore?'

'Good idea,' she said. 'I'll need a fish knife though.'

Mike snapped his fingers. 'Got it! Obviously. Why don't we all three have lunch?'

'What about?' Jill said.

'Why does having lunch have to be *about* something?'

'If it isn't I'm going,' Adam said.

Jill said, 'Because you can't get it off tax otherwise.'

'Has to be the right answer,' Adam said, 'and gets the prize. Listen, seriously, darling, I don't care about lunch. Bold plan B: I'll go and half-finish something disgusting at my incredibly unsmart club, and you and Mike can —'

'I don't care about Mike all that much.'

'In that case,' Adam said, sitting in the chair opposite her, 'how about even bolder plan B2: you and I have lunch and Mike can go to *his* club?' He leant, through Mike's large shadow, across the table. 'What do you suppose Mike wanted to talk to me about before we dumped him?'

'Very funny,' Mike said. 'Highly risible. Denis!'

'Sir Michael?'

'Can we get possibly a third chair up to this table, do you suppose?'

'The work of a moment!' Denis lifted a bentwood chair high above a neighbouring diner's head and set it between Jill and Adam. Mike sat down.

'Hul-*lo*!' Adam said. 'Mike Clode! Can it be? Do join us! Of course you're interrupting something. But do cut in to tell us many of the things you've been doing recently and why we should give a damn.'

'Why does Adam always have to go that little bit further than the occasion demands?'

'Because I'm a Putney train,' Adam said, 'that has to get to Wimbledon. What I need is a good stationmaster. Hard but fair. Are you up for it?'

Jill said, 'He's up for pretty well everything in my experience.'

'Only if it's pretty enough, darling.'

'So, that apart, why did he want to have lunch with you, Jill? Any idea?'

'He just might have heard rumours that I was going back to the National to do *Hedda*.'

'*Again*. Which he now hears isn't true anyway.'

'Hence the cancellation, no doubt,' Jill said.

'Never cancel, darlings, always postpone. That way Christmas will always be there when you need it.' Mike leaned back, tilting his chair slightly. 'Menus would be a start!'

'Menus and champagne,' Denis said, unloading a silver tray, 'and *quelques amuse-gueules*, and amuse boys, if that's your bag. Never as easy as they think, some of them!'

'What's good here, Denis, any idea?'

'Let me save the court's time, if I may, and bring you a lunch you'll enjoy all the more for not having to choose it.'

'Great idea,' Mike said. '*Etonne-nous!*'

Denis made eyes at Jill. 'I'll try. Mustn't make a Cocteau of it, though, must I?'

'Here's to it, children,' Mike said. 'Whatever it may be.' He reached to clink his glass against Jill's. 'We should regard this as an omen.'

'This being . . . ?'

Mike sneezed twice. 'Bubbles up my nose. Sorry about that.'

'Ominous indeed,' Adam said, mainly to Jill. 'An eagle sneezing twice, to the left. What is it warning us about the wishes of the gods?'

Mike said, 'Adam . . .'

'That sounds very like his coming-to-the-point voice. Little children may well die in the streets.'

'OK, yes. Television. Adam, are you with me?'

'Still here.'

Jill said, 'I don't think I am though, am I?'

'Jill . . . this could interest you too. Marginally.'

'The margin isn't my favourite spot on the stage. Seeya.'

'If that's the way you feel, darling. I'll give you a call. Can't tomorrow. Monday. And we'll fix something.'

Adam said, 'You can't let her go. *I* can't let her go.'

'Sit down,' Mike said. 'She wants to go. Let her go. Because I really do need to talk to you.'

'I'm ashamed of myself for not . . . About what? If it's television, I don't want to do it. Almost certainly. I'm too old to be nice to script editors.'

'Hold your fire. And your wet blanket. Because this could be your big chance to put your mouth where somebody else's money is. We're talking about control here, not . . . writing silly bloody plays.'

Jill Tabard walked through to the now empty bar. Denis, in unlikely spectacles, was sitting at a table in the window with a folder of bills and documents.

'Jill dear, something wrong?'

'Mike wants to talk business. I totally don't. So I'm doing a bunk. Ay've got my pride same as anyone, not that it shows.'

'You've still got to eat. How about getting your remarkably even teeth into a drop more champagne? Come into the office and I'll bring you some caviare to wash it down. No one need ever know.'

'You are a nice man, Denis.'

'When I have the time. Come on.'

He unlocked the door next to the long zinc bar. The office had a Venetian blind on the street, a big desk and businesslike steel cabinets on the short wall. Denis pushed things aside and sat Jill in his black leather swivel chair. He held up a hand, indicating that she should wait there, and came back very quickly with a flute of champagne and an eggcup of caviare.

Jill said, 'Denis, whatever you do, don't tell Mike I'm in here, will you?'

'Our little secret, darling. The first of many. I should be so lucky!'

'I'm putting this syndicate together,' Mike was saying, 'to be in place, with a full game plan, by the time the Orwell TV franchise comes up for grabs again in eighteen months. I want you on side, Adam, to help kick the present people off the park.'

'What makes you think they can be shifted?'

35

'They put on total catchpenny crap.'

'And what makes you think they can be shifted?'

'You know your trouble, mate? You lack faith.'

'Faith in what?'

'OK, we can't move mountains. We can move molehills.'

'And make mountains out of them? I can well believe it.'

'I need you on board, Adam. Not because you're easy, and not because I like you . . .'

'It's because my middle name is Jonah, isn't it?'

'Is it? No, because you're well known, but not very. You seem a little bit dangerous, but you're actually a play-safer . . . You pretend to be snarly and up-market, but your presence'll impress the ITV board because you once won the stupid Oscar and you can also spell Wittgenstein with your tongue tied behind your back.'

'Enough of zis foreplay,' Adam said. 'How many shares do I get for doing what?'

Denis Porson knocked on his office door and went in. Jill was sitting with his spare glasses on reading a copy of *Gay Times*.

'I 'ave 'ere,' Denis said, 'with the condiments of the chef, an *île flottante* on a sea of *crème anglaise*. Just the stuff to give the droops.'

'I'm not drooping at all now,' Jill said, 'but I'll still scoff it. You are sweet, Denis.'

'I'm sweet and this is pudding.'

Jill said, 'Mike always does things like this. By mistake on porpoise.'

Denis sat on the corner of the desk. 'Why did you come?'

'Because he whistled, didn't I? Because I'm still a bloody fool. Same thing, right? I want him . . . to say he was wrong. I don't want *him*, I want *that*. Don't smile. Not that *that*. Him being a little bit . . . human.'

'Never wait up for them to be that, dear.'

'I do wish I'd had his child though.'

'Just as well you didn't in the circs.'

'So I could hurt him about it. I'm not a totally nice person, Denis.'

36

'Show me one, dear. And it's two dream weeks in Tenerife and all the gazpacho you can swill.'

'This rag of yours is a bit saucy, isn't it?' she said. 'I had no idea how explicit the smalls could be.'

'Wait till they get bigger, dear.'

The door opened and a stocky man in chef's whites walked in without hesitation. 'Denis, I 'ave to tock to you . . . oh sorry!'

'Gianni, this is Jill Tabard. Star of stage and . . . what else do you do, dear? She's a wonderful, wonderful actress. This is my partner and *very* close friend Giancarlo Luchese. The big white hat, on the big white head, tells you what he does in his spare time.'

'Spare time, I don't 'ave. But I 'ave to go out. The boys can clear up. Back about six, Denise. They all know what to do.'

'I do want you back though, Jankers. We've got that restaurant critic lady coming. The bitch's office booked her in incognito so we can be sure to recognise her.'

'I said I'd be back, *caro*, I'll be back. Unless you ask me where I'm going.'

Jill called out, 'Thank you so, so much for my lovely food.'

'*Gran piacere, signora.*'

Denis said, 'He leads me a dance, dear, and I very much suspect it's the *pas de trois*, but what can you do?'

'Don't ask me, will you, Den my love? You know the worst thing about being unhappy about a shit? It's so . . .'

'Addictive, dear, is the word that wins the prize. Is it not? I mean, take me. *Please*. And leave me somewhere I'm not likely to find me.'

'You're just trying to be one of the girls, Denis, because you're fine. You're great. Look at how well you're doing.'

'Doesn't show up in the mirror, dear. And what's it all for, finally? The bubble reputation? Because at any moment – pop! And you're a wet drop on the world's dirty floor. They mop you up and shake you out of the window and *ecco tutto*.'

'Oh shut up, Den. There's only room in here for one long face, and it's mine.'

'It's not long at all. Can chins be pert? Advise me.'

'God, yes. They can also quiver.'

'*And* be pert?'

'Can be done,' she said. 'Needs talent though.'

Denis opened the office door and then shut it again, quickly. Mike and Adam were just leaving the restaurant. Denis dropped his jaw and popped his eyes and Jill laughed and reached for his hand. 'One thing I've always wanted,' she said, 'and never had.'

'It can't be success then. How many letters?'

'Children.'

'Oh honey,' he said, 'me too. Dirty secrets time!'

'Are you serious?'

'Of course. Always did want to be a mother. All soft spots, dear, me. If you look closely. Probably the problem. Have another drop of Armagnac. Saves wondering what to do now.'

Jill said, 'Do you want to get married, Denis?'

'Of course. Sweet dreams of permanence. But Giancarlo doesn't. Not the type of moth to have only one flame, that one, alas!'

'Bloody good Armagnac this! Married to me, I meant.'

On the pavement in Greek Street, Mike said, 'I'm truly glad you're on board, Adam. Jonah or not, as the future will show. Do you want a lift at all?'

'Thanks all the same, I'll take the stairs.'

'Take the stairs? Only I've got Percy with the Rolls, if you want dropping somewhere.'

'Lift . . . stairs; forget it. I still feel bad about Jill.'

'Well, don't. Some people are never so happy as when they're re-opening their old wounds. She's a scab-picker, that one, from way back. How's your brother these days?'

'My *brother*? That's a bit of a long shot, isn't it? I didn't know you knew I had one.'

'Very bright, I gather.'

'Derek? A pillar of fire by night.'

'And doing very well by day, I read somewhere.'

'True. He's waxing mightily. In fact, he's now older than I

am. He overtook me on the last bend. I'm understandably choked, but at the same time happy for the lad.'

'He's got this big place in Norfolk, I hear.'

'He has indeed. It's so big it's practically two places.'

'In the Orwell TV catchment area, it has to be.'

'Do I smell something in the wind, and it isn't flowers?'

'He's got financial clout, and savvy and –'

'– unfortunately he couldn't do lunch, is that it?'

'Never asked him,' Mike said. 'I couldn't get a number for him.'

'And that's why you asked me. Tell you what: I'll see if I can get it for you.'

'Your own brother, and you haven't got his telephone number?'

'I was defending Thermopylae,' Adam said. 'But I can always stop. Call me Ephialtis. And I'll give you the number.'

'What you like is when only eight people in the whole bloody world know what you're talking about. By the way, I've got new offices. This is my direct line. By-passes the girl.'

'I'm honoured. What do I dial if I want the girl?'

A white Rolls-Royce came alongside them. The chauffeur got out and opened the door for Mike.

'You do too many auditions, Adam, anyone ever tell you that?'

'Everyone does. But I still seem to do them. What should I do, do you think?'

'Grow up might be an idea.'

'That's the English for have an affair, isn't it? I don't think Barbara would like that. I'll just have to stay as sweet as I am.'

'She might welcome it. You'll probably find she's been having one for years. You never know with the sex.'

'Get in your big white car, Sir Michael, and go on your big white way.'

Gavin Pope was walking back to Medlar Cottage, reading the *New Left Review*, and smiling at the sustained absence of jokes, when a large blue Rover slowed up beside him.

'Professor Pope.'

'The same.' Gavin walked on. '*Almost* the same. A few more scratches on the bodywork.'

'Tim Dent.'

'MP. I know.'

'I was hoping to see your wife.'

'You're unlikely to need a microscope. Why?'

'To thank her. For her contribution to my campaign. Funnily enough though, I also wanted to see you. Do you have a moment?'

Gavin folded the *New Left Review* and thrust it into his jacket pocket. 'If it's about joining my adult education class, I'm afraid I've already drawn the line. Well above your head.'

'You're a very amusing chap sometimes. Only I've been handed what could be a hot potato. By the Prime Minister.'

'Really? And is it nice to have a cook with metal hair?'

'Which means I could do with your help. If you could contrive to be somewhat serious for a minute or two.'

'Do you want some tea?' Gavin said. 'Goes well with a hot potato. And I've been advised to drink more of it. Funny stuff. So far I've only discovered that it goes very badly with ginger ale.'

'OK, if I park here?'

'Until you bring in some legislation to stop you. By all means. I don't run to a barouche.' Gavin unlocked the front door of number 14. 'Fay? Visitor! *Fay?* She doesn't seem to be around. But come in anyway.'

Gavin boiled the kettle and, as if he were unsurprised, did what Fay usually did for him and his visitors.

'Why would I want to help the Tories?' He carried the tray into the front room. 'I leave that to my wife. She's got the hats for it.'

'I've been reading your book on the *Myth of Equality*.'

'Have you just? Seminal, but flawed, they tell me. Like so many of us with the stains to prove it.'

'The PM has these friends –'

'It must still be fine weather. Wait till she turns her back.'

'– who want to finance a think-tank. We'd like you to head it up.'

'Kindly omit the "up" if we're talking halfway serious turkey here, or English for that matter. "Head it *up*" is what third-rate Ipswich forwards do when faced with open goals. I should prefer simply to head it, if I do anything to it at all.'

'This is a moment that may not recur.'

'They all are, my dear old Carian friend.'

'It's your big chance to do something practical for education in this country. Now or probably never.'

'You know what Jesus said on a roughly comparable occasion? "Get thee behind me, Stan".'

'I thought it was "Satan",' Tim Dent said. 'Look, I'm offering you the chance to influence policy, five, ten, fifteen years before the Socialists have another opportunity to do the utterly ruinous things you talk about in your honestly very . . . all right, outspoken book.'

'I was winding up the comrades, you know that. *Advocatus diaboli*, that's me.'

'And now you can give the key one more twist and actually do something.'

'Frightening,' Gavin said. 'You're asking me to turn my back on a lifetime of commitment to Socialism and all the complimentary waffles I can eat.'

'There's a moral issue here, Professor Pope.'

'Oh indeed. But putting that to one side, what about the screw? Presumably I'd have to resign my professorship, and thirty pieces of silver doesn't go all that far these days.'

'Double your present salary. London allowance. Index linked. Help with accommodation.'

'Pension plans respected?'

'Plus car allowance.'

'Don't drive. How about a secretary called Emma?'

'If that's what you're sticking out for.'

'She can drive,' Gavin said. 'It's a wind up, isn't it?'

'Question of who's winding whom rather, isn't it?'

'The very one Comrade Lenin was still asking when I bumped into him recently.' Gavin put his bottom lip over his top one and looked at his tea. 'The National Union of Mineworkers have sold their South Wales library and installed a bingo hall in its place, did you know that? Well, they have. They used to call anti-Semitism "the Socialism of the stupid" . . .'

'Did they?'

'I think it features in my index, if you check. And now . . . Socialism is. But what's the alternative? Mrs Thatcher's brave new market economy, which amounts – among the darker necks in the woods – to putting the B stream, as wide as it's shallow, out on the streets with nothing much more to say than "Hullo, sailor" and small prospect of a rich and imaginative inner life, if any.'

'Unless we can educate them, Gavin.'

'We as in you and me and Mrs T. with her big blue pencil? By increasing unemployment even as we squeak?'

'By revising the curriculum and renovating the places it's taught in. I hoped you'd be tempted. You truly should be.'

'And I truly am, old cock. But "lead us not into temptation" is one of the many requests made of the Lord by those of my faith. And yours, perhaps, before the C of E became a buggers' bingo hall. Thanks but no thanks, the children say these days.'

'You're missing a yuge opportunity,' Tim Dent said. 'If you ever feel like changing your mind, believe me, I shan't think any the less of you.'

'That's yugely reassuring,' Gavin said.

After Tim Dent had left him with a long face and a regretful handshake, Gavin walked into his study. An envelope was propped against the space bar on his Olivetti. He looked at it,

42

without opening it, and went into the downstairs lavatory and threw up, and then he did it again. 'Bloody tea. Hate the stuff.' He walked through the empty house to the kitchen and drank a glass of water, staring out at the uncut lawn. He went and made another attempt to vomit, and then sat at his desk and opened the unsealed envelope.

'Enough is enough, Gavin, and in your case, no one can say there hasn't been a good deal of it. I've found a place I want to live while I write my novel and lose two stone. I shall let the children know and make sure they don't bother you, as usual. I expect you'll convince yourself that I've done something cruel and unreasonable, and I must say I hope so. As you always say, this has got nothing to do with you; it's got to do with me. Don't shout, don't plead and don't pretend that you're broken-hearted because it'll only be vanity and you know it and I know it. F.'

Gavin took a new bottle of whisky from the locked cupboard beside his desk, unscrewed the lid and went with it into the bathroom. He looked at himself in the mirror and raised the bottle. 'Here's to you, Fay!' As if enjoying every drop, he poured the contents of the bottle slowly into the bath.

'Canossa here I come,' he said.

ix

By half past six that afternoon, the Armagnac bottle was below halfway full when Giancarlo came into Denis's office.

'*Ciao, buona sera!* Still here?'

'Seem to be rather,' Jill said.

'We're just going to switch to a drop of fizz, Gianni, if you'd care to join us.'

'What are we celebrating?'

'All right, if you must know: Jill's asked me to marry her.'

'And what have you told her?'

'I'm going to do it.'

'Are you sure you can? This is a joke, yes?'

43

'This is a joke, no. Thing is, as you know, because we did talk about it once, I always did want to have a child. And so does Jill. Furthermore –' Denis twisted the cork and eased the fizz out without a pop.

'Furzermore what, for God's sake?'

Jill said, 'We think we can love each other, Giancarlo. If you'll let us. Please.'

'And what about me? Will you let me? And him? Love each other? I don't want champagne now. I've gotta work to do.'

'Why not? You know what they say? It takes three to tango!'

'One glass,' Giancarlo said, 'why not? And to hell wiz it!'

'Make the sign of the cross over us, Gianni, and we shall bless your name for ever.'

'You are both completely mad.'

'And very happy,' Jill said. 'Thanks to you.'

'Completely.'

x

Adam had walked up South Moulton Street to buy Barbara a birthday present at Brown's. Afterwards he walked down to Brook Street. There were always cabs at Claridge's. He stopped to look in a shop that sold antiquities and, reflected in the window, he saw Barbara, in the frogged suede coat he had given her the previous Christmas. She had just been to her hairdresser in order to be smart for the première he thought they really ought to go to the following evening. A small smile on her lips, she looked so beautifully alone with herself that she might have been with someone else. He remained where he was, mouth slightly ajar, thinking that they could share a cab home. He was hesitating, because he didn't want her to see the Brown's bag, and then she glanced at her watch, checked her step and, with one elegant skipping motion (it reminded him of Rachel) turned and went into Claridge's. The cockaded doorman leaned on one foot to push the rotating door behind her.

'Taxi!' Adam got in and sat there, in the traffic, till the driver turned his head. 'Can we go to, um, just a second – here we are, I've got it – 74, Regent's Park East, please?'

They went up Portland Place and into the park. Adam scratched the back of his neck. The cab pulled up in the private drive outside the renovated Adam terrace. Adam sat there for a moment.

'This what you want, guv?'

'Seems to be,' Adam said.

He rang the bell and waited. When she opened the door, she smiled, quite as if she had been expecting him.

'I don't know what I'm doing here,' he said, 'but . . .'

'Am I alone?' Francesca said.

'Was almost certainly my next question.'

'I am, as it happens.'

'Are you now going to slam the door in my face?'

'What if I did?'

'It might well come as quite a relief.'

'You haven't brought me a present, have you?'

'What? Oh this, no. Actually it's something for . . . someone else. I probably should've . . . but I seem not to have . . .'

'In that case,' she said, 'you'd better come in.'

II

He walked into Francesca's house like a patient honouring an appointment with a specialist which it would have been cowardly, but tempting, to duck. The high hall had a black and white marble floor and tall flowers on the spread-eagle console under a convex gold mirror.

'Christ,' he said, 'you've actually got a lift.'

'I don't use it,' she said. 'It's useful for what Dominic calls clobber. Do you call things clobber?'

'Not a lot.'

As Francesca climbed the wide, easy stairs to the first floor, he went after her with a smile that doubled for a shrug. He chose to have no choice. Why should he not look at that shifting behind in the white cotton trousers? Where did she get those wedge-heeled pink espadrilles? She was a woman he could do what he liked with. He stopped and took a deep breath and looked through the big sash window on the landing on to a professionally trimmed garden with a clematis-trellised brick wall behind it.

'Are you coming?'

The L-shaped drawing room had three similar windows, with dark blue silk curtains, gold-banded at the waist. There were Augustan busts in sconces on each side of the Adam fireplace.

'It looks as if David Hicks has passed this way,' Adam said. 'Very handsome pad, as they say these days, some of them.'

'Do you like Alsace?'

'I've never been there.'

'The wine.'

'The wine. The wine I like.'

She left the room. She looked very neat from the back. He

46

told himself to look at the pictures. It was his business to notice things. One was of a man, carrying a briefcase and wearing steel-rimmed spectacles, looking at a folded map in a dark wood where the tree trunks were black columns supporting a roof of evening foliage, as if in a natural cathedral. The man's face was pink and shiny with sweat, although the wood seemed cool. Above a desk between two of the high windows was a Whistler etching of a boy looking out from a doorway. Adam thought he recognised the desk – Regency or very early Victorian – as the one at which Francesca's mother, Lady Davidson, had been sitting when he said goodbye to her at Gifford's End twenty-five years earlier, after visiting the dying Donald for the last time. Barbara had been with him. How sad it all was, and how happy they had been to get away!

'You can pull the cork, if you don't mind. I hope it's cold enough.'

'I was wondering if you'd have green-stemmed glasses.'

'Oh, God, were you? And I did. We seem to have them. Do you consider them appallingly naff?'

'Appropriate. Did you paint that one over there?'

'Yes, I did.'

'It's very –'

'Oh don't hunt for adjectives.'

'– despairing,' Adam said. 'Dante-esque even!'

'Try "pretentious", it's a better fit.'

'I don't think so, at all. Has it got a title?'

'*Some Hope.*'

'Is the title?'

'*Appropriate*, don't you think?'

'Is he anyone in particular, the man? Boy. He is, isn't he?'

'It wasn't meant to be Don, but . . . I suppose it is, now I look at him again. Took you being here . . .'

'Do you really believe in life everlasting?'

'I don't know. I certainly don't care.'

'I still think about him. Donald.'

'Do you? What is there to think?'

47

'I should never have known him if it hadn't been for the pure chance of sharing rooms at Cambridge, and yet – it's very nice this Alsace – when I look back he seems to stand for ever in a patch of light, sentenced to eternal youth. Inspiration, threat, reproach, warning. Something.'

'Sounds a bit poetic. I didn't have all that much to do with him, you know.'

'That's not how it seemed at the time.'

'I was quite angry with him actually.'

'For dying?'

'For being so important to everybody. I was hoping to take Nelson to Badminton that summer and instead – it was all Donald. I'm not proud of the fact, but there it is. I hate tragedies. I was also jealous while we're at it.'

'Were you? What of? And what are we at?'

'She was so smug. The girl you were with. So cat-with-the-creamy! She was also a lot more . . . attractive than I would have wanted.'

'Barbara. I married her, you know. Do you still paint?'

'Sometimes. I have a friend who does it better. I realised I was imitating her. Stalled me rather. Do you want to go to bed with me?'

'I don't trust you, Francesca, a bit.'

'Very wise,' she said. 'That way I can't disappoint you, can I? Or do other things to me? They don't have to be horizontal.'

'I don't even trust your question. Your motive for asking it.'

'I thought it'd save time,' she said. 'A lot of men would've come to the point already. But you're . . .'

'Modest.'

'You think things matter.'

'And don't they?'

'Are you bothered about fidelity?'

'I don't think it bothers me the way infidelity would.'

'So you don't go to bed with other people?'

'I seem not to. I flirt, I suppose, but . . .'

'Does she?'

'Do what? Flirt?'

'Go to bed with people.'

'Barbara? I doubt it. She doesn't flirt much either. That I know of.'

'Do you wonder?'

'I wonder everything. I write, remember?'

'God, yes. Are you afraid she'll find out?'

'If I sleep with other people? I expect so.'

'Then why are you here?'

'How about curiosity?'

'How about you're angry with me?'

'Possible. I don't get my face slapped by strange women all that often.'

'And anger makes you want to do things that desire doesn't? A bit of luck then, was it?'

'I don't think I'd say that.'

'That's why I thought I would,' she said. 'It makes me responsible, doesn't it?'

'For what?'

'You fucking me. You don't have to have a conscience. Will that make a nice change?' Her neck seemed longer as she sat sideways on the triple sofa and looked across at him. 'Jewboy?'

He said, 'It's a bit of a victory for you, isn't it, that I came here like this?'

'And now you wish you hadn't, is that where we are at the moment?'

She sat quite still now, in profile, looking at the man leading the oxen between the dark trees.

'Of course I want to go to bed with you.'

It was convenient to make pleasure into a duty. Doing what he wanted became a matter of courage. He put his glass soundlessly on the polychrome intaglio table. He saw her smiling at his fear of seeming clumsy. The smile was an incitement not to be kind to her.

He went and stood in front of her and pulled her up towards him. She was smaller now. The pale pink lips came slightly apart when he kissed her. He did it nicely, remembering how an actor had once told him that the way to find new values in a scene lay in avoiding the obvious. Her face was so close to him that the proud chin was the only feature in focus. Leaning away, he smiled at the way the white throat seemed to lengthen as she reached for the longer kiss which he didn't deliver.

'You ought to be Alice really. Not Francesca. You have the neck. Does your hair . . . come down?'

'It can. I don't want to have a name at all really.' He had his hands on her shoulders. He could hear the slide of breath in her nostrils. 'That was a very . . . careful kiss,' she said. 'More goodbye than hullo. Should you really be going, was it meant to tell me? Can that be the time?'

Adam said, 'Take your clothes off.'

'Don't you want to do it for me?'

'When I tell you,' he said.

'You're very . . . abrupt suddenly. Want to get it over?'

'Would you sooner I went?'

'Is that what you want to do?'

'Does it feel like it?'

'What do you want to do to me?'

'I don't know. Yet. Something.'

'You can. Whatever it is. Hurt me, do you? Aren't you going to, undress?'

'Do you want me to?' Adam said. 'Hurt you?'

'Depends how clever you are,' she said. 'That's only where I had my appendix out. Do you ever go with whores?'

'I don't actually,' he said.

'"Actually" meaning you'd like to?'

'I remember sitting in the car, his car, with Donald, looking at the whores in Curzon Street back in the days when they still paraded up and down . . . He was fascinated by them. But then so was Flaubert.'

'And that makes three of you. There you are. This is the front and this is the back. What do you think?'

'You're very beautiful.'

50

'Almost like new,' she said. 'Golden delicious Dominic says they are, when he does. He loves bums. Is this what you like: me naked and you dressed?'

'Seems to be,' he said.

'Do you want to do anything particularly? Do you want to *command* me to do anything at all? Undress you, sure you wouldn't like me to?'

'Not a lot,' he said. 'I never had a nanny. Sit down in that chair. The upright one. Don't cross your legs. Just sit there. Finish your wine. It's too good to let it get warm.'

'You're not going to get out of this house without doing *something*,' she said. 'Don't think you are. You wouldn't like to offend me, would you?'

'You've got quite a short fuse, haven't you?'

'How about yours? I haven't seen it yet, have I? I hope I'm going to. I suppose you were cut, weren't you? Don't worry, so was Dominic.'

'You're right,' he said. 'There are things I'd like to do to you, that you deserve.'

'Six or twelve?' she said.

'What?'

'Do I deserve? I used to love it when I used the whip on Nelson. I never did it hard, but I could feel him shiver, when I touched him even. I imagined the sweat. It made me sweat imagining him. You're sweating yourself, aren't you? I am.'

She stood and came across to him and held out a hand so that he could help her down. Then the front door banged.

'Anyone at home at all?'

'Dominic?' she called out. 'That you?'

'Of course. Where are you, scrumptious?'

'Up here. Drawing room.'

'For God's sake put your clothes on,' Adam said.

'It's only Dominic.'

'Put your fucking clothes on,' Adam said.

'These are my fucking clothes basically.'

Dominic came up the stairs and into the room. 'Hullo. Oh,

51

hullo! Sorry if I'm untimely.' He kissed Francesca on the cheek and held out his hand to Adam. In his long hound's-tooth tweed jacket, fawn twill trousers, brown shoes with gold buckles, russet woollen tie, graph-paper shirt and bone-buttoned camel waistcoat, he reminded Adam of the Young Conservatives who, in 1950s Cambridge, used to frequent the Pitt Club. Had he left his period flat cap in the hall? Dominic looked both young and old, town and country. Francesca said, 'This is Adam Morris, the writer. My husband, Dominic.'

'How are you?' Dominic said.

'I'm on my way,' Adam said.

'It certainly looks remarkably like it.'

Dominic appeared as unsurprised by Adam's presence as he was by his wife's nakedness. The long thin nose, bunched red lips and wrangle of fair hair gave him the air of a brazen angel with not much further to fall. Sitting back now, wine glass between her pale fingers, Francesca seemed to be West End-tailored in her uncreased skin, the trim apron of darker than expected pubic hair neat between her legs like a couturier's clever accessory.

'Do you want some Alsace, Dom? There's some left.'

'I'll get a glass. On no account go away. I want to ask you something.'

'You knew he was coming,' Adam said. 'Didn't you?'

'What does it matter? He isn't bothered.'

'I'm bothered. Didn't you? Know?'

'You really should come in a green-stemmed glass,' Francesca said, 'you're so irredeemably middle class. He was due, grant you that.'

'Do you do this a lot, you and . . . Dominic?'

'We do it sometimes. We do what we want when we want. If you really want to go, you always can.'

'And you and he can have a good laugh.'

'We might well. Or he might turn nasty. Possibly very. He might give me six; he might give me twelve. I never know really. That's what I like about him.'

Dominic came back with a glass and poured himself some Alsace. 'I don't know where you keep the fancy glasses. I'd sooner have a tumbler anyway. Don't go off the boil on my account, you two, will you?'

'Seriously time I went,' Adam said.

'Must you? I do hope you haven't taken offence.'

'Offence, no.'

'Then perhaps I shall. I wanted to ask you how much of that book of yours I read that Francesca gave me was true.'

'Jesting Pilate had the answer: what is truth? I can't improve on it. And anyway I very much doubt if you did, want to know.'

'That's a bit rude. I come home and find my wife naked in your oddly dressed company —'

'I don't think I'm oddly dressed.'

'That's between you and your tailor — and you treat me like an affronted, all right, dignitary.'

'I'm affronted or you're affronted?'

'What do you imagine will happen when you've gone?'

'No idea.'

'Have a punt. What do you?'

'I imagine laughter.'

'Has she told you what she likes to have done to her? Specifically. Hasn't shown you the arsenal yet, has she?'

'Can I get a cab, do you suppose, at this hour?'

'She was hoping you'd guess. You're feeling a bit let off, in truth, aren't you? What would you do in similar circumstances: if you'd come home and found your wife flaunting her fanny to the company?'

'No idea. This really and truly isn't my territory, I'm afraid.'

'No? But you still think you can come up here and strip my wife naked and I don't give a damn? I'll have a civilised glass of crappy Alsace with you and you can walk away feeling like a man who's had a lucky escape, that how it is? With his virtue intact.'

'Nothing wrong with the Alsace,' Adam said. 'Hugel's a very good shipper.'

'Up in the world, are we? We're not divorced, you know, the lady and I. I could cite you in court, if I felt like it. Or – better – talk to some of my chums in the press. Everyone I was at school with seems to be a journalist these days. Do you think you're famous enough to rate the front page as a serial shagger?'

'I doubt it. And where do you get "serial" from? You flatter me.'

'Find it hot, do you, in here, suddenly?'

'I find it – all right – set up, is what I find it. And now I'm going to go home.'

'You'll think about her though. You'll think about her all the way. What you missed. That hairless arse of hers. And when you get into bed with your wife tonight. You won't be able to help yourself. And what you could have done to her – what we both could – if you'd had the balls.'

Adam said, 'Is this seriously something you do a lot?'

'We do it when we do it, don't we, ladyship? Sometimes it's serious. And when we don't, we do something else. We keep ourselves amused, and sundry others at times, don't we, scrumpsh?'

It was raining when Adam left the house. There was little prospect of a taxi, so he started to walk across Regent's Park, relishing the rain on his hair and face, a shower after the game. He did turn and look back at the lights in the Adam terrace after he could no longer tell which was theirs. The rain tasted sweet. As he came into Baker Street, a cab came along with its light on and he had to have it.

ii

He paid off the cab and stood in Tregunter Road and looked at the lights in his own house as if strangers lived there. It was almost a surprise (but then again no surprise at all) when his key fitted the lock. He looked up the stairs. He could hear *Sultans of Swing* coming from Rachel's room. Presumably she had somebody up there with her. Adam hung his coat over the boss of the banisters.

'Hullo.' He cleared his throat. '*Hullo-o!*'

Barbara came up from the kitchen. 'What happened to you?'

'Very little, very slowly. Hair looks very nice.'

'I told you I was having it done.'

'And I'm telling you it looks very nice.'

'I wasn't sure what you wanted to do.'

'About what?'

'Dinner. You said something about going out possibly.'

'Did I? In that case, how about Chinese? There's always that place in Horrywood Load.'

'I've done a shepherd's pie now.'

'Which I would much prefer. We're out tomorrow night, now I come to think of it, aren't we? That bloody première.' He followed her down to the kitchen. 'I'm sorry if I'm later than you expected. Rachel's in, I gather, from the sound effects. Is she going to eat with us?'

'She's got somebody upstairs.'

'Master Blotky again?'

'French this time. From the Lycée. Jean-Yves, I think his name is. They have this exchange arrangement.'

'I have little doubt.'

'The schools. You seem . . . not quite as usual. Who've you been with, because you haven't quite got rid of them yet, have you?'

'I went to a balls-achingly boring Private View and saw absolutely no one I know, which left me feeling . . . diminished. What about you? Did you see anybody at all today?'

'Not unless you include Gerald, who said my hair needed a little more body.'

'Don't we all?' Adam said. 'He's certainly given it some.'

'I never see anybody, you know that.'

'People see you though, don't they? And a very pleasant sight it is too. With body.'

'You sound . . . pissed,' Barbara said.

'*Pissed*, do I? As in drunk? Because that's . . .'

55

'As in displeased,' she said. 'Out of humour . . . and trying to hide it.'

'Oh! *Pissed*. I'm not pissed. In that sense. At all. Except that I'm home later than I wanted and now I've made you feel . . . How do you feel?'

'Hungry!'

'I've made you feel hungry.'

'No, no,' she said. 'Something's odd. You didn't kiss me, is what. It doesn't matter, but I realise now.'

'You're right,' he said. 'And it does matter. Fortunately, I have a remedy.' He kissed her and held her against him. 'I'd really like to take you to bed. Now.'

'Wearing an oven glove?'

'Can't it come off?'

'Alsace.' She put her tongue out and in again. 'You've been drinking Alsace.'

'Yes, I have. Can you give it a year? And a bottler perhaps? I told you I went to a Private View.'

'Funny wine for a Private View.'

'You should've seen the pictures. Views of Crete that suggested that the island was composed mostly of string and plentiful squeezes of Gibbs SR.'

He watched as she took the shepherd's pie out of the oven and got in her way while she drained the broad beans. When he took off his coat, he realised that his shirt was wet between his shoulder blades, sweat not rain.

'Won't be a sec.' He ran upstairs and washed and dried himself. Dire Straits seemed a well-chosen accompaniment, though the best directors might think the irony plonking.

'The nearest I can come to a new man,' he said, when he took his *Champs* T-shirted place at the table again. 'Do you mind what they're doing up there, Rachel and . . . *monsieur*?'

'I don't know what they're doing and, no, I don't mind. Do you?'

'Wonderful shepherd's pie. Probably not. As long as it's what she wants.'

56

'I don't think anything much'll be happening unless Rachel wants it to.'

'She's your daughter then, is she? I used to know how often we'd made love, you and I. Precisely. I lost count after thirty-one. You don't look any different.'

'You wouldn't say it unless I did.'

'True. You look even better, more . . . *cachée*, as Jean-Yves would say, if he said it. Rachel would probably say it too by now.'

'I don't actually think she fancies him.'

'What's so amazing about women is, you never know . . . the things they do, or the things they don't. *Cachées*, aren't you, all of you?'

'Nothing much hidden about me, apart from a wrinkle or two if I can't find the stuff I need.'

'You don't have to wait for airports, you know. Which reminds me, I did mean it about going away somewhere, you and me.'

'You always do,' she said, 'but we still don't go.'

'How about Venice?'

'As you have so often said before.'

'What would *you* like? Pick a card.'

'Venice would be lovely.'

'The Lido. I know you too well, don't I?'

'In other words, I always do what you expect, and you wish I wouldn't. And if I *didn't*, do you think you'd like that?'

'I expect so. Until I didn't. Or you didn't. What were you doing at Claridge's?'

'So that's it. Who told you what? And what are you hoping?'

'I'm not hoping anything. I'm just asking because . . . I happened to see you as a matter of fact. Going in.'

'Suppose I was . . . seeing somebody. Isn't that what they say? On *The Coast*. Suppose that. Would you think more of me? You don't know what you want to be true, do you?'

'Who was it?'

'Have you been spying on me for long? Is this a little . . . foible of yours now, keeping an eye on me when I'm out?'

'I was coming out of South Moulton Street and there you were – fresh from Gerald, presumably – and I was admiring you as you walked along, like a stranger, this lovely look on your face, and then I saw it was you, and I was going to suggest we got a taxi together only I was carrying something . . . I got you . . . and I hesitated and then suddenly you went into Claridge's.'

'News just in,' Barbara said. 'I'm alive all the time you're not with me. Does this come as a shock?'

'I haven't the smallest wish to control what you do, Ba. I trust you –'

' – to do nothing you wouldn't want me to. Just like Rachel.'

'Nothing like Rachel. I was childishly curious and I shouldn't have been and I'm sorry. Where's the dog house? And why are we doing this?'

'I went into Claridge's to have tea with Shirley. Shirley Parks.'

'Shirley Parks! Did you really?'

'Am I lying, do you mean?'

'I mean I didn't know you were friends.'

'Well, you don't know everything, as you so often say.'

'But always in the hope of being contradicted.'

Barbara said, 'She asked me to have tea because she wants me to get involved in this charity for mentally handicapped children she's the chair of.'

'Is theirs still alive?'

'And very voluble. He was with her. All six feet of him.'

'She took him to Claridge's?'

'The woman evidently has no shame.'

'Good for her. How old is he now?'

'Sixteen. He has a name and everything. Donald.'

'What does he talk about?'

'What does anyone?'

'How many Jews there are in the government, don't they? Old Estonians, as that poop Macmillan called them. The Queen's Jews; it's a very old number. Things go wrong; it's all their fault. Things go right; what've they got to do with it?'

'You slightly wish I'd been having an affair with some close friend of yours, don't you? Or would you prefer someone famous? More creditable in a way, that, wouldn't it be? A Jew or not a Jew?'

'Classy Gentile, preferably. Then I could hate you both.'

'Please don't clear the plates.'

'Haven't you finished? If you did, who would it be with? If we're going to do this.'

'Who've you got?'

'Is Mike a friend?' Adam said. 'I don't like him all that much. I don't know who I do like really. We probably ought to see more people or find some new ones.'

'I ought to give dinner parties, you mean, and ask smart people to them and butter them up so they say nice things about you in the newspapers and slip me their daytime phone numbers in case I want to go to their black leather pads and discuss Proust for starters. Seriously, I've deprived you, haven't I, of society? People who'd look good in the index when you do your autobiography.'

'Does Alan still live with them? Shirley and the kids?'

'Some of the time, I gather. The twins are pretty well grown up. Alex is a trainee cameraman. Focus puller, is that the technical term?'

'Bound to be. What's Tom going to do, do you suppose? Please God he doesn't want to be a professional tennis player. We'd have to spend our lives watching him play and chewing our nails. Mike Clode thinks you're very attractive, you know that, don't you?'

'Of course.'

'But you've never been tempted.'

'Not if you say not.'

'By Mike, have you?'

'One speculates sometimes, about people. What they'd be like. I don't much like the beard.'

'Right. I'll tell him on no account to shave it off.'

They heard footsteps on the stairs, coming down, and then in the hall.

'*Bonsoir, les jeunes.*'
'*Bonsoir, monsieur, bonsoir, madame.*'
'Jean-Yves's just going. I'm walking him to the bus.'

When she came back, in her green mackintosh, and fresh lipstick, Rachel sat with them in the sitting room while they watched the boring news. After she went upstairs, Adam and Barbara smiled at each other.

'I'm going to have a bath,' Barbara said.

'I'll have one after you.'

'With me, if you want.'

'Never really room, is there?'

'No.'

'I love you, Ba,' he said. 'We could always get a bigger tub.'

'And then we'd never do it,' she said.

He kissed her and he went into his study and shut the door and took his squared notebook out of its drawer. Barbara went downstairs to lay the breakfast and, while she was there, she called Shirley Parks and then she went upstairs and ran her bath. Adam's ear told him all of these things.

When she came out of the bathroom, he was already sitting on his side of the bed, reading his new book. Their brief smiles were the smiles of familiar strangers. As Barbara lifted her white cotton nightdress over her head to put it on, Adam saw only her shining body, the head veiled, and then she dropped it.

He lay in the bath and damned Dominic for being right, as he was bound to be. When he came back into the bedroom, Barbara's bedside light was on. Up on one elbow, she was reading an old Penguin of Joyce Cary's *Herself Surprised*. Adam turned out her light and was grateful for the upward flash of hostility. He pulled at her nightdress and covered her face with it again.

'Are you smiling under there?'

'I might be.'

'And what about?'

'That'd be telling,' she said, 'and I don't like telling, do I?'

She smiled as if she almost knew something, and he smiled

too, as if he did, and then they made love for much longer than they had for many months.

In the morning, she stood and looked at herself in the wardrobe mirror and said, 'That was a bit different. I don't know what Gerald's going to say.'

'You don't tell Gerald about what you do in bed, do you?'

'About my hair. I might as well not have gone to him.'

'It's still got body. So have you.'

iii

Dan Bradley, who had been the leading Cambridge actor of Adam's generation, until he decided that he had no taste for the limelight and wanted to be a schoolmaster, had worked for several years in a state boarding school for problem children. After his wife left him and became Joyce Hadleigh, the television presenter who specialised in serious family issues, he found a new job in London. His and Joyce's children lived most of the time with him, first in Camden, where he had been an assistant headmaster and then, until they went to college or to work, in Wandsworth, where he was now a headmaster. Joyce often worked nights and, as she became 'sincerely quasi-ubiquitous' (the *Observer*), travelled more and more frequently on television assignments. She liked to think that she and Dan were very civilised with each other about things.

Dan's hair was finer, but he still had the handsome, honest style of a man who was glad to do what he did, and did it as well as he knew how. When told that an Inspector Knox, and Detective-Constable Capel, had arrived at the school to see him, he tried to guess which of his pupils had done something silly, again.

Knox wore a tightly belted blue mackintosh and a brown hat. Capel looked around the study and made Dan wonder what kind of crime he might have committed without knowing it. Everything, he realised, could be evidence of something.

'How long have you been headmaster here at Disraeli Road,

Mr Bradley?' Knox took off his hat and began slowly to circulate it between his wide hands.

'Coming up to six years it has to be now. Seven nearly, God help me.'

'And before that?'

'May I ask what this is about, because I do have people . . . ?'

'Bear with me, Mr Bradley, if you would. And before that?'

'Heavens! I taught in Camden for several years. Then I came here. That's about it, I think. Do you want dates?'

'We have them,' Knox said. Capel nodded. 'And before that, you taught in a special school, didn't you, in?'

'North Essex, yes, I did.'

'Middleford House.'

'Was indeed what it was called.'

'For disturbed children, I believe.'

'Children with problems of one kind and a mother, as we used to say, very much among ourselves.'

'In other words with no father, would that be?'

'Usually not. Sometimes preferably not. "One kind and a mother" was one of those in-house jokes that probably doesn't travel very well. I expect you have a few of them yourselves.'

'Graham Moony.'

'I'm sorry?'

'Name mean anything to you?'

'Graham Moony, does rather. Why, I wonder?'

Capel said, 'A one-time pupil of yours, sir, could he be?'

'A footballer,' Knox said, as if Capel had said the wrong thing. 'That you took a particular interest in possibly.'

'*Graham*. Of course. Got it now. What about him?'

'You do remember him now, do you, sir?'

'Of course. I got him a trial with . . . Arsenal, wasn't it? He was very talented as a lad. And very . . . attractive.'

'You obviously liked him.'

'Yes, I did. I did. Up to a point.'

'What point was that, sir?' Capel said.

Knox was scratching his eyebrow as he looked at Capel, and

then at Dan, as if he expected the headmaster to understand what he was thinking.

'He had a violent side,' Dan said. 'Graham. I got him a trial and he deliberately fouled the goalkeeper. Unnecessarily. For the hell of it, I felt it was. Fouled me too somehow.'

'But you liked him.'

'Not at that moment, a lot. Generally speaking, it was my job to like him. If you give yourself the luxury of not liking your pupils, you never get through to them.'

'And you felt you'd . . . got through to him, did you, sir?'

'Until . . .'

There was a double tap at the door and a woman in a long grey skirt and pink blouse walked in. 'Oh I'm sorry, headmaster, I had no idea.'

'Tell them to start the meeting without me, Alice, would you? And I'll be there as soon as I can.'

When she had gone, Dan stood up. 'Do I gather that Graham Moony has done something that brings you here this morning? If so, kindly be good enough to tell me what it is and how I can help you. Or has someone done something to him?'

'What would you say if I told you he was being held on charges – among others – of rape, and causing grievous bodily harm?'

'I'd say I was very sorry to hear it. Has this somehow got something to do with me? Has he asked for my help or something?'

'You're married, I believe, Mr Bradley. Your wife is Joyce Hadleigh, is that right, the TV personality?'

'He hasn't done something to Joyce, has he?'

'Not at all, sir. Why would you think that?'

'So what exactly has she got to do with anything? Who did he . . . attack then, Graham?'

'The female's name is Vera Purchase, it seems. She's a prostitute. Master Moony's a pimp among other . . . activities.'

'When did this happen? And where?'

'Paddington. About ten days ago. It was in the papers. And on the London news. You didn't read about it, didn't ring a bell at all? She was very badly mutilated.'

'See this stack of stuff? That's what I read. And the one you can hear now is the only bell I hear. *Mutilated?* Whatever did he do to her? And why?'

'He and a friend tortured this girl till she very nearly bled to death. He believed in black magic, or so he's said.'

'And now he's asking to see me, is that it?'

Knox said, 'Why do you imagine he might want to do that?'

'It doesn't require much imagination, does it?' Dan looked at his watch. 'He's in trouble. He has no family. If that's not why you're here, perhaps you'd now be good enough to tell me why you are, because I do have things I'm supposed to do.'

'Since Graham's been in custody, Mr Bradley, he's been interviewed by a number of people –'

'My imagination does stretch that far,' Dan said. 'And?'

'– including a psychiatrist,' Knox said. 'You no longer live with your wife, I believe.'

'That too was in your paper, presumably. Journalists. I'm sorry to be . . . impatient, but I am supposed to be at quite an important weekly staff meeting.'

'Still on good terms with her, would you say? Your wife?'

'We like to think we're civilised people. We have our children to think of. And, to tell you the truth, which I know you want, I don't quite see what it's got to do with anything you could conceivably –'

Knox said, 'Did you ever give Graham Moony money, Mr Bradley?'

'Money? For what?'

'Would very much be my next question.'

'I haven't seen Graham in . . . it must be eleven or twelve years.'

'It's ten, sir, actually,' Capel said.

'If it's ten, then it's ten. I'm sorry to say I haven't given him a thought since. If you're hoping that I can tell you something relevant about him you aren't in a much better position to find out for yourselves, I'm afraid I'm going to disappoint you.'

'This money you gave him —'

'I was probably very foolish. Inspector . . . Knox, isn't it?'

'Knox it is, sir. You remember doing that now then, do you?'

'Yes, I do. I was annoyed that he'd . . . made a mess of the chance I'd bothered to get for him. I took him out for a meal afterwards and then —'

'You're a very forgiving sort of a man then, sir, do I gather?'

'Not especially. I'd brought him up to town. It was supper time. While we were eating, I think it was, he told me he wasn't going to be a footballer after all. He'd make more money doing something else. Plumbing, I think it was. And he was going off to do that. I was . . . disgusted, to tell you the truth.'

'And that's when you gave him money, is that right?'

'Right? Oh in the sense that I did it. Yes. Inspector, you're supposed to be investigating this . . . rape, is it?'

Knox said, 'What makes you think that, sir?'

'Well, if you're not, hadn't you better tell why you're here exactly? You've been giving me the impression —'

Capel said, 'How much money did you give him, Mr Bradley?'

'Too much. Ten pounds possibly. It was a lot then.'

'Too much? For what, would that be?'

'His own good evidently. I was angry, now I look back.'

'With Graham?'

'You keep calling him by his first name. I find that oddly . . . callous. When you think of the girl he apparently . . .'

'You called him Graham yourself, sir.'

'I knew him as Graham. It doesn't matter. Question of . . . style, I suppose. And that was before . . . you're totally sure it was him who did what you say he did?'

'I only know he's been charged. Him and his friend, Patrick James Doyle. Do you know him at all by any chance, this Doyle?'

'Why on earth would I? Does he claim I do?'

'We have to make sure of things, sir,' Knox said. 'You said you were angry. With Graham.'

'And myself, because I'd allowed him to make a fool of me.'

'How exactly had he done that?'

'I'd gone to some trouble to fix for this Arsenal trial, through a friend of mine, journalist. I told them how promising he was and he deliberately . . . did what he did. And instead of really facing him with his stupidity, I . . . punished myself. By giving him more money than I could afford.'

'And was that the first time you did so, sir? Gave him money?'

'First and last. What is this? What are you implying? What are you implying? Please put that hat down and tell me.'

iv

Adam had been commissioned to write a screenplay about a once famous black singer, Leda Lemaine, whose early recordings had led critics to compare her with Ella. Bill Savage, a television journalist, traumatised by having seen, and been forbidden fully to report, terrible things in an African civil war, becomes addicted to her few records when he is lent a cottage in Menton by a successful friend. While he is in the cottage, there is a telephone call, for its owner, a professional biographer of famous people, from a very rich man, one of his subjects, whose yacht has come into Villefranche: will he come to dinner? Bill explains that he is not the man who owns the cottage, but the rich man asks, will he come anyway? Bill says he doesn't have the right clothes. 'There are no right clothes any more. Only right people. Come however you are is fine.'

One of the people at dinner on the *Argo* is, of course, a black woman who Bill becomes convinced is Leda Lemaine. She is remarkably beautiful and, though she seldom speaks, her voice is enchanting. Bill falls in love and becomes convinced that Leda has been sequestered, for his private pleasure, by the rich man, whose interests include the arms trade. Conviction becomes a dangerous obsession and so the story develops.

66

He had told himself, in his notebook, that it was no more disgraceful to fabricate a *pièce d'occasion* concerning a milieu of which he knew almost nothing than to construct a baroque palace or write *Trimalchio's Feast*. He wished only that he believed it. Sometimes it was an irritating relief when the telephone rang.

'Hullo.'

'Adam? It's Joyce Hadleigh. Am I disturbing your work?'

'Yes, thank you. What can I do for you, Joyce? Is something wrong?'

'It is rather. I'm in Harrod's.'

'Bad as that?'

'And I was wondering, can I jump in a cab and come and see you?'

'Of course.'

Adam rolled back the page he had just typed, sighed, and reached for the telephone.

'Mike Clode's line.'

'My clothesline? I don't think you should say that, you know. Or is that where you hang your friends out to dry? Can't you just say "hullo", as it's your private line?'

Mike Clode said, 'What can I do for you, Ad?'

'Listen, this Orwell TV franchise thing. Have you asked Joyce Hadleigh to join the syndicate by any chance?'

'Not a bad thought. At all.'

'By all means make it your own then. Only she called me out of the blue and she's on her way here so it occurred to me that it's possible she's fishing.'

'Well, she might be useful. Throw a little bread on the waters, only don't make the bait bigger than the fish, will you? Is she still joined at the hip with Alan Parks?'

'Alan comes under Any Other Business these days, I think, with madam.'

'Because A.P. *would* be a catch. I dined with your brother Derek last night. Did he tell you?'

'The news hasn't trickled down yet.'

'Der reckons we could go public within three years of start up.'

'Der, eh? You're down to the short strokes already.'

'We could be looking at paper worth something like two million posited on any given stake of twenty-five grand within three years of start up.'

'Where's the rest of the working capital coming from? Like fifteen million at least. Before we can start positing.'

'Der knows a raft of people that's chicken feed to.'

'The raft's not called *Medusa* is it? Doorbell, Mike. Got to go and let Joyce in, while Der goes to feed them chickens. Butler's day off. I'll let you know how it goes with Joyce.'

'She could be decorative, but we don't need her. Remember that. *Medusa* meaning what exactly?'

'Footnotes later, squire.' Adam hung up, pushed back his desk chair and put on his loafers, and went to answer the door.

Joyce said, 'Dan – *Adam*, sorry! So sorry. I'm in a state, because have you seen the morning papers?'

'I get up, have breakfast and go to work. Papers are a distraction. Why, what's happened?'

'Have a look at this and you'll know.'

'Come on in. Barbara's somewhere. Do you want some coffee?'

'I've had it.'

Adam walked into the sitting room, frowning at the newspaper Joyce had given him.

'"WANDSWORTH HEADMASTER FACES SEX ABUSE ALLEGATION. Daniel Bradley, 48" – God, we are getting old, aren't we? I suppose he has to be – "has been suspended from his duties as headmaster as a result of . . . The accusation dates back *ten years* . . . Bradley, who is married to Joyce Hadleigh, the television presenter" – they had to get you in there, didn't they? Probably wouldn't have been in the paper otherwise, would it?'

Joyce said, 'That's why I feel so terrible. Partly.'

'I don't believe a word of it, do you?'

'They must have some evidence, I suppose. No, of course I don't.'

'This must have been while you were still . . . together . . .'

'Of course. In that bloody awful cottage in Middleford. I can't imagine what the kids are going to feel.'

'It's ludicrous. Isn't it? Some bloody yobbo who's been charged with some kind of GBH and God knows what connected with black magic. Black magic! They're never going to believe him against Dan.'

'Why would he make it up? After all this time. Look at this one.'

Adam read: ' "The accused man claims to have been regularly and systematically abused during his time at Middleford Special School." ' Adam bunched the paper between his hands and threw it across the room. It unfolded as it flew. 'How many oiks use adverbs like "regularly and systematically", unless they've been spoon-fed with questions expecting the answer yes? With a hey nonny-nonny and a hotchacha! Why would he make it up? To look like a victim of the vile middle classes, wouldn't he?'

'What do you think I should do, Adam?'

'Inspector Adam of the Yard for the moment, OK. Because did Dan ever give you reason to . . . think anything like this was going on? Is what they're going to ask you. Did Graham ever . . . come to the house?'

'Cottage. Yes, he did. Several times. Dan was a big believer in one-on-one coaching. Very pretty boy now I think about him.'

'Then don't,' Adam said. 'Tell them about his acne and his appallingly unappetising socks. And forget about one-on-one. *Please*. He loved you, didn't he, Dan?'

'Loved me, pitied me. Loved pitying me. That was another life, thank God.'

'You do still see him.'

'Not much. I used to a lot more. At the changing of the guard: when the kids were small and had to be collected. You're lucky you never had to do that stuff.'

69

'Has he got a woman, I hope?'

'No idea.'

'Look here, you don't *believe* this shit, do you, Joyce? You had three kids with the man.'

'Two actually. Peter's . . . someone else's.'

'Oh yes, you mentioned that, didn't you, on the box, wearing your Sunday specs?'

'I believe in honesty.'

'We all do. As long as it's what the viewers really want. You don't seriously imagine he sexually abused small boys, do you?'

'Abused, no. Sexually, no.'

'That shouldn't leave much, but it seems to somehow. What?'

'They were horrible, some of those boys. You can't imagine. Dan loved them, or tried to, but they didn't love anyone, and they never could. They were capable of . . . all sorts of things.'

'Seducing people, for instance?'

'Dan had to be so . . . available. He'd come by the cottage sometimes, this Graham we're talking about, when Dan wasn't there, and there'd be such a gleam in his eye . . .'

'Did you ever ask him in?'

'But I did dream about him once, I remember.'

'Dream what?'

'I was giving him a bath. I was in it with him. It's OK, I had my clothes on. Most of them. He was white all over, as if he'd been bleached, but he did have this ginormous –'

'– pustulant sore on the end of his nose, I hope you'll tell the court. He had quite a reputation as a cocksman, Dan, didn't he, at Cambridge? Shirley always looked very . . . sated.'

'He was a different person then. He was an actor. That was before he turned into a sort of frockless priest wanting to save people. Me especially. Sex was never a big thing with us. Except one night I remember when he really hated me. It was wonderful. At least twice. Generally, he tried to combine it with being nice and that never works, does it?'

'I always admired him for turning his back on showbiz and

fame and . . . all the stuff that really matters. Why are you here, Joyce, exactly?'

'You obviously liked him.'

'And you didn't?'

'I probably didn't like myself. For marrying him the way I did. I don't know why we were all so keen on it. Marriage.'

'I put it down to Dr Leavis,' Adam said. 'And D.H. Lawrence. "Look, we have come through!" Which very few of us have, it now seems.'

'*You're* happy, aren't you? You and Barbara.'

'Absolutely. Tell your friends. Ruin their day. She must've popped out, as people always say. Funny word "pop". Nurses tell you to pop your things on the chair, do you find that? Talking of marriage, have you too received the most improbable invitation of the century?'

'Denis Porson and Jilly Tabard? I couldn't believe it.'

'They put him in clink, you know. Years ago. For goosing a copper in Leicester Square.'

'That was B.W. Before Wolfenden. Different world.'

'Do you think Jill knows what she's getting into? She must.'

'Don't men dream of converting lesbians to the true faith?'

'The theory of the big bang. I have heard of it.'

'Why shouldn't women ditto?'

'Women fancy a bit of ditto too, do they, on occasion?'

'And we often wipe our own behinds. Sordid, isn't it?'

'You never forgave him for coming to your rescue. Dan. And now you're going to come to his, is that it? Ditto ditto. Are you?'

'I always think of you as someone who knows what to do.'

'Dear God!' he said. 'Do you really?'

'Why else am I here?'

'I was wondering. Look, you've got to absolutely make it publicly obvious that you don't believe a word of this stuff. Be seen smiling with Dan, if you can fix it. Enjoying a joke, as the *Tatler* used to say. Tell your chums on the newspapers how ridiculous it all is. Because it is, isn't it?'

Joyce said, 'He could always have been a *bit* queer, for all I know. A lot of people are, aren't they? Not that . . .'

'Not that, of course! Is the bit I agree with totally. Keep that in!'

'What gives you the right to despise people?'

'A brief interview is usually sufficient. Why did you leave him?'

'I didn't want to live in a tatty little cottage and wash and cook and bear witness to his saintliness for the rest of my life. Am I the bitch of all time?'

'What about the children?'

'You're quite right.'

'Remind me,' Adam said.

'I didn't want to spend my life looking after them either.'

'I always thought women liked being wives and mothers and that was why they did it.'

'Underneath all the cynicism, you're very romantic, really, aren't you? Karl says it's basically what's wrong with your novels.'

'You must write one sometime and I'll be the first to tell you what's wrong with it. Promise. You'll find you appreciate it enormously.'

'Oh would you really do that? Because actually I've been asked to. Write one. Stella Briggs wants to publish it.'

'Before you've even done it? Lucky you.'

'I told her the general idea and she loved it.'

'. . . all you have to do now is add boiling water, stir and serve. Not about Dan, is it?'

'Who'd want to read it? About the television world and what really goes on. Life with the piranhas on the sixth floor.'

'She's right, Stella. Everyone will want to read that.'

'Do you have an agent at all I could talk to?'

'Jason Singer will ask you to dance without a doubt. Put me in it, your book, and I'll sue your boots off. Very nice boots incidentally. Pussy in boots, what could be better? No creases in them either. How do you do that?'

72

'I only bought them this morning. You're not really *in* television, are you?'

'Funny you should say that, because I may be about to be dragged in, some of the way, by Mike Clode.'

'I love Mike. He's so . . . so . . .'

'Is he not? He's made so-so into an art form.'

'. . . *energetic*,' she said.

'He's roped me into this syndicate that's hoping to get the Orwell franchise next time around. The present lot get rotten ratings and they haven't got a duke on the board, which Sir Mike seems to think he can manage. In a meritocratic, egalitarian, first-past-the-post society, even the dimmest duke makes all the difference apparently. You didn't come here just to pass the parcel, Joyce, did you? Dan done up in brown paper?'

'You know, Adam, you're being so . . . nasty to me that if you were anyone else, I'd think you fancied me.'

'The whole world fancies you, don't they? All that nicely spoken cleavage and husky sincerity, with just the hint of a provincial accent creeping in to reassure the proles about which side of the tracks you came from? How's Alan Parks these days? A panjandrum, I gather, but still carrying that banner with the strange device, Excelsior. Which being translated means "Up yours, I'm in the lifeboat".'

'I don't see Alan all that often these days.'

'You're a true Wittgensteinian under the skin, Joyce, aren't you?'

'Never been accused of that one before.'

'Once you've climbed the ladder, you throw it aside.'

'You really *are* being remarkably unpleasant. Why?'

'Possibly because, much as I welcomed it, you've punctured my morning so that I shan't have done my conscientious eight pages by lunch time. Meaning I shall have to do them this afternoon instead of playing middle-aged soccer in the park, and —'

'I think I'll go before the and bit, shall I?'

'— and you'd really love Dan to be guilty, wouldn't you? Which is more likely, as a reason —'

'I'd love him to be *human*. I'd love him to have done *something* in the last hundred years that wasn't the right thing. But I certainly don't want *them* to . . . do anything to him.'

'How about send him to prison for five years and ruin his life for ever? Not in favour? Very Christian of you, Joyce. In the great tradition, I would say.'

'I've actually *defended* you to people,' Joyce said, 'can you believe that?'

'If I close my eyes very tightly and clasp my hands devoutly together. To whom, for instance, have you? Defended me?'

'Karl, Terry, Jack, Jonathan, Philip. Lots of people. You know Middleford, where we used to live?'

'Do I? Why?'

'Only I bought a cottage not far away. Just occurred to me to mention it. It's actually well in the Orwell catchment area. So if . . . you wanted me . . . you know, in your syndicate. I do sort of qualify.'

'As a tempting local morsel.'

'I have been approached by a few other people.'

'Never doubted it. Form a queue this side, I imagine. I'll mention it to Mike. He'll almost certainly call you like a shot – no, I did *not* say "like a shit" – and ask you to stump up twenty-five grand. Meanwhile, I'll give Dan a ring, if you've got his number, and tell him that we're all on his side, some of us. And I'll alert Mike to get busy.'

'I did hope you would. It'd be such fun.'

'On Dan's behalf. All *you* have to do is say how totally upright, in the non-ithyphallic sense, your admirable ex has always been.'

'*Iffy-phallic* would be nearer the mark, in my experience. But then being sorry for a woman never was much of a turn-on, was it? Have you got Mike's number?'

'Of course. But I'll call him, promise, and tell him about Dan –'

'Only then I could get on to him about . . . this TV thing.'

'I'm sure he'd be dilated if you got on to him. Here's the number. Somewhere. Here.'

'Sorry about . . . puncturing your morning.'

'Oh I've got a kit,' he said. 'Little thing like that.'

Before he opened the door, she put a hand against it and kissed him on the lips, with a light lift of her new heels. He smiled his married man's smile and wondered whether he had made the little pilot light in her loins flare a touch more brightly than usual on a Wednesday morning.

v

Denis finished checking how many acceptances he and Jill had had so far for their reception and sat for a minute, before twitching his shoulders and deciding to go and do what he knew he had to.

Giancarlo was sitting on a plastic dustbin, in his unbuttoned whites, and his chef's hat, smoking a *cigarillo* while the boys swabbed the work-surfaces and returned the kitchen to disciplined order.

'How many covers do you think we did for lunch today?' Denis said.

'Ninety-five?'

'A hundred and two. And guess how many people are coming to the wedding?'

'The same?'

'And counting,' Denis said.

'Aren't I lucky to have the chance to make a cake that big? Am I?'

Denis said, 'You do understand, don't you, Gianni? Don't light another one of those things now. You hate it when anyone else smokes in your kitchen.'

'Of course I understand. You're punishing me. For that boy on the beach at Diana Marina. Right?'

'Wrong. In spades. I never expected fidelity. I only promised it.'

'And now look what you're doing.'

'I love you, Gianni, and you know it. To the hilt. Not to mention further on suitable occasions, weather and the pot of Vassili permitting. But there's one thing you and I can't do, and can never do, and that's make babies. Granted?'

'You should 'ave been a woman,' Giancarlo said.

'Play it as it lays, dear, that's the way of this bordello of God's creation, isn't it? What *was* She thinking of? You're supposed to be Italian, says so in your pisspot. You know all about sons and heirs. I shall think of him as *ours*, you know, when he's born. Yours and mine as well as hers.'

'Have you thought what you're doing to 'er? You make 'er a laughing stock. A star like that with a fucking faggot.'

'I should be so lucky. One thing at a time, however. She's had a horrible time and I want to see if I can make her happy.'

'She's a desperate woman. She needs a real man, but she also fears them.'

'And that's why she's marrying a poof. Hole in one, dear. We all know that. It doesn't matter. We like each other and we understand each other. Just like you and I do.'

'*Nussing* like you and I do. You're doing this to me, is the truce of it. And she's doing it to *him*. To Michael . . . he doesn't eat oysters.'

'Clode. Very possible,' Denis said. 'We talked about that. The whole thing's against the odds, in spite of, nevertheless *and* notwizzstanding. So bloody what, angel?'

'It's not a real wedding; I don't care how many people come. It's a choke.'

'If it's a choke, please don't laugh at it. Because they're still coming. Gianni, I love you. And I need you on our side. Desperately, duckie.'

'A hundred and two covers at lunch. Not bad, uh?'

'Fucking marvellous, *cazzo mio*! She's not going to make any difference to us, and she knows it. I hope you do.'

'*Zuppa inglese*,' Giancarlo said. 'De new recipe. You, me and a woman. Stir and serve.'

'Not necessarily in that order.'

Adam had just realised that, for the story to work, the rich man had to know that when he called the cottage it would be Bill Savage who answered the phone. That way the discovery that Leda Lemaine was still alive was not a coincidence but the bait in a trap. It meant going back fifteen pages, but it had to be done. He hated sending scripts to producers with even the smallest correction written in by hand. How he wished he never had to work with other people! But when the telephone rang, he wondered if it was Bruno Laszlo.

'Hullo.'

'Are you still angry with me?' she said.

'Angry?' Adam said. 'No.'

'Because you don't have to worry.'

'Do I not? Meaning you're going to pay my income tax, and the school fees and . . . ?'

'Meaning I have no wish to ruin your life.'

'Then why have you called?'

'I want to see you. Is *she* in the room with you?'

'This has gone far enough, Francesca, really it has.'

'You think nowhere is far enough? I don't. No one's going to find out. I love secrets. Dominic thinks you're a coward.'

'It's a view.'

'Because you went home. He thought it was my fault. Shall I tell you what he did when you'd gone, to me?'

'No.'

'I thought writers were interested in people. And what they did. Especially Old Etonians. He told you he loved bums, didn't he? He does.'

'Look, Francesca, it's very nice of you to call, possibly, but don't do it again. Please.'

'Then come and see me. You don't have to stay longer than you want. Call me and I'll tell you if it's convenient.'

'Will you just? Who for?'

'Dominic needn't come into it, if that's what you prefer. I

want you to come because . . . I want you to. I hate just dreaming about people. Simple as that.'

'Simple can get very complicated I find, and I don't want it to. One bit.'

'Yes, you do. Listen, if you don't want me to call you, you'll have to call me.'

'Is that a threat?'

'You can do things with me that you can never do to her. There's no heaven, Adam, and there's no hell. You taught us that. So why not do what you want to do?'

'Francesca –'

'I'm willing to be patient. But not for ever. Remember that.'

vii

'The whole thing is absolutely ridiculous,' Mike Clode said. 'I think Dan is probably the most *manly* man I ever met. I'm going to call Wally Burleigh, who's just about the brightest brief I know.'

'That means the most expensive, doesn't it?' Joyce said.

She had called him from the corner of the Fulham Road and he told her to jump into a cab and come up to the Barbican. His new offices were in a penthouse with black tables and white leather upholstery on the chairs and the window seat, from which Joyce could see how big the cross really was on top of St Paul's.

Mike said, 'I can always get him to overcharge my company for some opinion I never asked him for and that way we can shag the chancellor. You still love him, do you, Daniel, darling?'

'Do I? I'm more concerned about the children honestly.'

'Truth is, you never loved him, did you? Not like he deserved. You were wrong.'

'You can't be right or wrong about love. You love someone or you don't.'

'Shall I tell you something? Avoids awkward silences. OK then: I don't think I ever loved anyone as much as I loved Dan.

78

Not embarrassed, are you? You're looking over the tops of your glasses at me.'

'I'm not wearing glasses,' she said.

'Apart from that you are. Sex didn't come into it, of course. With me and Dan.'

'It didn't with me either, really. Because when we were at the May Ball and I was telling him about being pregnant, and what a pillock Alan Parks was being, I thought he was just this dishy bloke to talk to and totally committed to whatsit. Shirley. And then suddenly he was being . . . a saint, really, unfortunately.'

'You never spotted the shining armour till it was too late. What a Coriolanus he would have been today! Better than Larry. Hang on, I thought you had kids with him.'

'I did,' she said. 'But not sex. He served me right and that was it. Why do you really want to run a TV company?'

'You know the answer to that one. Because I believe we can render a public service and prove that intelligent programmes and grown-up drama don't have to be elitist or over people's heads.'

'Do you really?'

'How about I like power, money and women, and that's the way to get them? How else would I get you up here in your shiny boots? Got the spurs with you at all? I'm sure you've won them.'

Joyce said, 'Adam Morris honestly seems to believe . . .'

'And essential that he does. He's my beard. *Our* beard. Yours and mine and who all else's. I reckon he'll want to do programmes that're really intelligent and cultural. And he might even convince the bloody commission that he means it. We just have to hope that he doesn't walk away in disgust after eighteen months of frustration, don't we? After we've stopped him doing a thirteen-parter about Heidegger and Hannah Arendt, whoever they may be. Once we've got the licence, they can't stop us printing money till seven years have passed. By which time we shall all have better things to do, and – with a bit of luck – the moolah to do them with.'

Joyce said, 'All sounds very alluring.'

'I'm just so glad that I had the idea of asking you to come on board.'

viii

Adam had not seen Dan Bradley since they were at Cambridge together. Yet as he drove across Wandsworth Bridge in his grey Alfa Romeo, with the lid folded back, Adam felt himself to be honouring an antique loyalty.

Dan seemed neither surprised by nor grateful for Adam's visit. His handsome face, the good jaw gleaming with coppery stubble, seemed amused, if not puzzled, by Adam's uneasy handshake. He wore a black donkey jacket, fawn cords, short green rubber boots, and black work gloves.

'As soon as Joyce told me about . . . what happened,' Adam said, 'I thought I'd see if there was anything I could do.'

'You do a lot of journalism, don't you?' Dan led Adam through to the back garden, where he resumed digging out an elder bush with a shiny-tongued spade.

'I do very little,' Adam said. 'Good God, you don't suppose that's why I'm here, do you?'

'Amazing how polite and sympathetic people are,' Dan said, 'when they're hoping you'll say something that they can twist into a headline.'

'Dan, look, sorry, but I can make more money in one week rewriting a Hollywood movie than you make in a year. Journalism is pennies. I hope that's a convincing argument in Madame Thatcher's New Model Economy. I just want to help if –'

'If I'm innocent?' Dan said. 'If I'm guilty? What's your guess?'

'He's lying, isn't he? The boy. I didn't believe a word of it. Nor did Joyce, come to that.'

'No? It did happen, you know. That kind of thing. At Middleford. It just never appealed to me. There were staff though who . . . did take advantage of the boys and I never did

80

anything about it . . . except hint to the Head, who may have been one of them, now I think about it. And then again – I don't know why I should say this now – maybe some of those – so-called corrupt relationships –'

'– were what the boys looked forward to more than the loveless lives they had when they were at home.'

'If they ever were,' Dan said. 'Here's what I actually think about Graham Moony.'

'He was disappointed you didn't try to do the things you didn't do, and this is his revenge.'

'Might not be far from the truth.'

'Then on no account tell it,' Adam said, 'will you?'

'Instead, I paid him off. I gave him some money when he said he wasn't coming back to school – more than I could afford – and I bet he knew it. He knew damn well it was done in anger, resentment, possibly, because he didn't care for me enough to do what I wanted him to do. Make a good impression. Behave himself. Become . . . more like me. I could swear I wasn't remotely interested in him . . . physically, but it's still possible that I did . . . all right, corrupt him.'

'It's also bollocks. You did your best for him. You would. You do it for everybody, don't you, from what I hear? And now you want to be a martyr, just like you were with Joyce. And be punished for it. Martyred twice over in other words.'

Dan bent both hands to the trunk, as far down as he could reach in the hole he had dug. Adam guessed that Dan wanted to show how superfluous his visit was. He strained and looked at Adam and then he was tottering backwards with the uprooted bush.

'How much do you make writing films?'

'*Re*writing,' Adam said, 'is where the money is. I have known it to be thirty grand. A week. Talented people get more. I think the kid was coached. Asked a lot of leading questions anyway, by the cops. Don't fold your arms and wait to be crucified, Dan, will you? Because you will be. You used to be an actor. Be one now. Act innocent.'

81

'I *am* innocent, you bastard.'

'That's better,' Adam said. 'Keep that in.'

Dan pulled off the green gloves and lobbed them, one at a time, into an empty tub on the square of crazy paving by the back door. 'Much it matters,' he said. 'My career's shot anyway, you know that. I'm not even angry about it. If you want to see how funny everything is – justice, the whole bloody world – be an innocent man.'

'Think of your children,' Adam said. 'Think of them.'

'I will. I do, thank you very much. How are yours? You do have them, don't you?'

'And the bills to prove it. Wonderful actually. Our daughter's very bright and very beautiful. Tom's at Cambridge, about to get a tennis Blue. Time flies. I wish it wouldn't do that, but . . . Don't feel sorry for the little bastard, Dan. Think of that poor bloody tart he did all those things to he probably got from some sick comic book. And don't wonder if you're not somehow responsible. You're not. He is. And his friend. And now if he can hurt you, he'll do it, gladly.'

'*Why?* As you seem to know it all.'

'It's *fun*, Daniel, hurting people. It's power. It's a stick in God's eye.'

'And that's what you had to come haring across London to tell me, is it? Why did you want to do that?'

'I probably always wanted to be one of the boys,' Adam said. 'But I don't suppose I ever shall be. What do you think?'

'Very nice of you anyway.'

ix

'So,' Gavin said, 'let me see if I have the picture. It seems to be that no one has done any work since the last time we met and now Jonathan is making the brave proletarian gesture of lighting a gasper. What exactly is this?'

'How about we're drawing the line?' Logan said.

'In the sand with which your ostrich heads are filled.'

'After you insulted us.'

'Inadequately, it seems. I can do better. And I shall, depend upon it.'

'Accusing us of all copying out more or less the same essay.'

'Is there not a word of truth in what is manifestly the case? Less or more. Henrietta, do you happen to have a stack of Bibles with you? Because pray swear on them that everything you did in the last three weeks, not to mention the last three terms, was your own personal and unaided work.'

'You could say we were taking industrial action,' Jonty said. 'In response to deliberate provocation.'

'I could, if you'd ever show the slightest signs of being industrious. Anyone who did a proper job of work would say, with the far-famed modicum of working-class bluntness, that you're a spoiled, privileged sub-class of skiving adolescents –'

'He has to do it. Treat us like children. He has to.'

'Treatment you're very lucky to get, because you're actually lager-fattened semi-adults who're defrauding the taxpayer and deluding yourselves and also – the supreme sin within these four off-white walls – proving to me how *fucking* stupid I've been all these . . . years, now I come to think of them.'

'Something achieved,' Jonty Logan said. 'And now what about us, Gavin, you poor, sad, alcoholic wanker?'

'You were stupid when you got here and you're insisting on being even more stupid when you leave.'

'And whose fault is that?'

'I have a list of suspects, Benjamin, and I don't deny that I am on it. Quite high in the rankings or, as you are no doubt whispering under your beery breath, Jonty, the wankings. It takes all sorts to make a world unfortunately. You may remember – though I wouldn't put any money on it, even if I had any – that Socrates considered that only the examined life was worth living. When I examine mine, I see smugness, conceit and absurd credulity in the basic decency of the young. Socrates –'

'Who Gavin presumably thinks he is –'

83

'But on no account ever imagine yourself to be anybody's first choice for Alcibiades, will you, Jonty?'

'What does that mean?'

'Look it up, sonny, in your spare time. A, l, c, i – industrial action, eh? Do you have your non-negotiable demands with you?'

'We do, actually.'

'Then by all means let's not negotiate them. Picket the faculty offices, burn your books and your boats, it's all the same to me. Because – being less fond of you than your furtive little vanities may still want to imagine – I shall now bid you all a brief and final farewell. You've had enough of me? Ditto I of you, more than, and there's an end on't. I am, as our cousins say, out of here. For good. With a spring in my step.'

'Looks more like autumn to me,' Ben Pinto said.

'He'll be back,' Jonty said. 'Autumn?'

'You bloody fool, Jonts, aren't you?' Henrietta ran down the lecture room steps and went out, leaving the door open. Gavin heard her coming after him on the composition stone pavement. 'Gavin.' He did not slow down. 'Gavin, please, hang on a minute . . .'

'Rely on them to send the pretty one.'

'We thought you'd . . . take it as a sort of joke.'

'And so I do, Hetty; the sort I never propose to laugh at again. You've had your fun and I don't deny having some myself, but suddenly, it's enough. You know what Noël Coward said about the tyranny of tears, don't you?'

'Not really.'

'Then you can guess. You have heard of him presumably?'

'He was gay, wasn't he? I did write something actually, of my own, on Ramsay Mac, started something anyway, but . . . people felt that we ought to – you know –'

'God, yes: show solidarity. You didn't want to be a scab. So you stopped thinking for yourself. Just what universities are there to get people to do, isn't it?'

'You're not really going, are you? You're the best lecturer we've got. We all know that really.'

'You're a very nice girl, Henrietta Gibson. You may not want to be, but you are. Pretty and adequately bright. If you want to work, work; if you don't, who can blame you? Sooner or later – unless your parents are rich –'

'Which they are certainly not.'

'– you'll get a job, if you're lucky, and if you're luckier, find someone to make a life with. You'll still discover that life is more questions than answers, whatever the Little Red Book says.'

'I do know that, honestly. I wish you'd come back.'

'My days of Bill Baileydom are well and truly over, Hetty.'

'What're you going to do now then?'

'Regroup is the term that comes shambling to mind. I'm going to regroup.'

'I did love you teaching us,' she said.

'Don't cry. It makes your freckles run.'

'Oh Gav.'

He touched her arm, went back and kissed her on both cheeks and tasted the salt on them and then he went into the faculty office. As he dialled Tim Dent's number, he looked down at his grey jumper and picked with his thumbnail at the clot of ketchup on the hem.

''allo.'

'That has to be Mrs Dent. This is Gavin Pope.'

'Oh yes! 'ow are you?'

'Fine. Thriving, like the new Britain. Sleeves rolled up and looking for work. I was hoping to speak to your husband.'

'I call him.'

'Professor Pope. You just caught me.'

'And you me,' Gavin said. 'If the offer's still open.'

x

Adam and Barbara had planned to drive up to Cambridge to watch Tom play tennis in the one remaining match before the Big One, against Oxford, but on the previous evening, Barbara's mother had another heart attack. Barbara had to go to

85

Macclesfield to see her. Adam drove to Cambridge alone, in the Alfa Romeo which had been paid for by a two-week rewrite on a movie that was never made.

As Adam walked through the college courts which he remembered so well, he allowed himself all the feelings of privilege and pride that had become disreputable during the quarter of a century, and more, since he was an undergraduate. Tom had rooms in a new complex which covered what had been the Fellows' croquet pitch. Morris, T.A., was stencilled by the door. In Adam's day, there were no such doors. You had to walk down from your rooms and across the courtyard to the loo. Now all the students (not a description that Adam's generation of undergraduates ever applied to themselves) had their own bathrooms. He could not remember having had a bath during his entire time at Cambridge.

'Tom? It's me.' Adam waited for the door to be unlocked. 'Are you all right?'

'Yes.'

'Sure? Nervous?'

'Not really.'

'What time's the match?'

'Two-thirty. Only I'm not playing.'

'Not playing? You were definitely in the six, you said. What happened? Not injured are you? They haven't dropped you?'

'Why would they do that?'

'I was just thinking about something that happened to your Uncle Derek years ago. Much it matters. So what's . . . the problem?'

'No problem,' Tom said. 'I've dropped myself. I'm not going to play tennis any more.'

'What's happened? Something has. What?'

'Tennis was a way of vanity for me.'

Adam said, 'Oh for heaven's sake.'

'Exactly so. I don't expect you to understand, but something very important has happened to me. Do you want to come in?'

'Come in? Of course I do. You haven't found Jesus or something, have you? Nice rooms.'

'You want that to be nothing, don't you?'

'Tom, will you please explain what's – ?'

'Yes, I will, but you're not going to laugh and you're not going to nod and pretend to understand, because I doubt you ever will or ever could.'

Adam said, 'Is it OK if I sit down?'

'Because Jesus is exactly what I've found. Or rather, He's found me, because of course He was always there.'

'And He doesn't want you to play tennis? Are you sure? Have you *checked*? You can't imagine how proud I am of you, how *jealous*. So's . . . your mother.'

'You see?'

'No. And you know I don't.'

'It's all got to be about what you feel. I don't come into it.'

'Who's been . . . working on you, Tom?'

'I think you have probably, don't you? Over the years.'

'I don't think so. Can I . . . sounds silly . . . can I have a glass of water?' Adam sat and looked at the empty bookshelves. He saw none of the things that he and Barbara had given Tom. He sipped the water Tom brought him. 'If this is all because of something I've done, for God's sake tell me what it is. You can't imagine how . . . thrilled I was . . . we were when you told us you were getting your Blue.'

'Vanity,' Tom said. 'Why did you call me Thomas?'

'Perfectly good name. Have you actually told them you're definitely not playing? Please God you haven't, because if you're doing this to . . . do something to me . . . consider it done.'

'Not at all,' Tom said. 'I recognise your disappointment, obviously –'

'And it's obviously making your day, isn't it?'

'You're so full of anger.'

'I don't know about anger. Frustration maybe.'

'We don't believe in anger. It leads to war and the rupture of

87

the One. You named me Thomas in honour of doubt, didn't you? Doubt is your god, really, isn't it?'

'We named you Thomas because of Thomas Mann, I now remember. We were reading *Felix Krull* and we somehow hadn't clocked that the old boy was gay as a bird. Thomas Mann, I'm talking about. Too late to be sorry now.'

'It's never too late, is the beauty of the Lord Jesus. You think it's funny, don't you?'

'That must be why I want to cry. Which presumably . . .'

'You can't bear anything not to be about you, can you?'

'What does Christine − isn't that her name? − think about this? Very pretty girl.'

'Christina. It was hard for her.'

Adam took a breath, looked for humour in Tom's eye and didn't find it. 'I've got this new car in Chapel Court,' he said. 'I thought would impress her, and you. You've dumped her for Jesus, is that now the situation, do I gather?'

'I knew you'd be like this.'

'What else do you know? I could do with a prompt or two.'

'I should've told you not to come. I have to find my own way, Adam. Try to see that.'

'I do. Is this it? Your own way?'

'Through the dark wood. And seek out the path of inner grace.'

'Some hope!' Adam said.

'The *only* hope, and I only wish you could see that I have to take it. Instead of which . . .'

'I've done what?'

'It's your . . . *attitude*,' Tom said. 'You think you talk to other people, but you really only ever talk to yourself.'

'You're throwing your whole life away, for Christ's sake.'

'That's exactly for whose sake. Didn't He say . . . ?'

'He said a lot of things. *C'était son métier.*'

'Here we go.'

'What particular, um, *brand* of Christianity have you been persuaded to embrace exactly, and who by, if I may ask?'

'The Redemption Church of the Lord Jesus, the Sun and the Moon. Under the inspired teaching of the Reverend Miguel Sung. Go ahead, make your famous effort to keep a straight face. I expected that.'

'Christianity with a twist. I can't believe it.'

'Can you hear yourself?'

'Where does he come from this Miguel . . . what's his name?'

'The Reverend Miguel Sung. What difference does it make? Where do we come from? He was born in China but then he went to Peru. He speaks nine languages.'

'And says the same things in all nine presumably.'

'If this is how it's going to be, and I might have guessed, I truly think you should go.'

'He *doesn't* say the same things in all of them? What've you done with your rackets and things? Tom . . .'

'OK, I didn't need them any more.'

'Get thee behind me, tennis, is that the new − ? And what about the new record-player Ba gave you? And the Bach? Has all that gone too, do I tell her?'

Tom said, 'Why do you care about money so much?'

'Who are these people, Tom, and how did you get mixed up with them?'

'Wrong. I *was* mixed up, and alone. Like the wandering Jew. What kind's this new car of yours?'

'It's that Alfa we saw in that mag. Every wanderer should have one.'

'You're so proud of it, aren't you, turning your back on the truth? Suppose I asked you to give it to me, the car. You did offer me one once.'

'And I will again. When you promise me you won't give it to the Reverend Miguel Sung. I read about him in one of the colour supps, didn't I? And his money.'

'You really don't know which wall to punch, do you? They all lie about him. They have to.'

'Think about yourself, Tom. Think about why you want to hurt people this much.'

'I know it's hard for you. And I'm sorry, but I'm going to leave Cambridge at the end of this term.'

'That's why you didn't tell me not to come. So you could see my face when you told me. Leave without taking your degree and you're going to regret it for the rest of your life.'

'Because then I won't be any of the things you're always pretending you don't care about. A Blue. A Cambridge man.'

'A Jew. Is the point, isn't it, that we haven't come to?'

'It always has to be with you. But then what kind of a Jew are you? What kind of anything are you?'

Adam sat with his feet apart and his hands over his ears. 'Kill the father! Every Freudian's ambition!'

'Perfect example: you always say you don't believe in Freud and yet you do. You don't even believe the things you *do* believe in are true.'

'And which are those?'

'You're so afraid of what you're going to have to tell people, Barbara included, about me, aren't you? Imagine if she backed me up.'

'If she does, she does. Up to her.'

'You're busy wondering what story to tell people about why I'm dumping Cambridge. Deny it. What will you?'

'You're being very clever, Tom, and very cruel. Shaking your head is all part of it. I don't know what all this has to do with Jesus, or His old dad, but doubtless you do. You're also right, I am wondering what to say. To myself first of all.'

'Tell yourself that I have a Master I respect and is leading me to Christ along the path of Truth and Purity. I may change my name, by the way.'

'You're afraid of being called a Jew, is that it?'

'No, no, that's you. You always call yourself a Jew before anyone else does. And then you get out of it by saying you don't believe in it.'

'I have only one thing to ask you, Tom. Oh, that's the name you're changing, is it? Two. Don't try and hurt your mother with this. More than you will anyway. And don't try to convert Rachel. Leave Rachel alone.'

'Now we're coming to it!'

'To find her own way to whatever she wants to be. And don't gloat too much over what you're doing to . . . us.'

'What can I? You're rich and famous.'

'Ask the first hundred people you meet if they've ever heard of me. If you want to be famous in today's England, you've got a better chance doing the weather forecast on the box.' Adam stood up and put one white hand on the window-sill. 'Tom, these new-fangled churches that try to cash in on old credulities – and I do mean cash in –'

Tom said, 'Admit it. If I'd become a Roman Catholic, at least you wouldn't be so embarrassed, would you?'

Adam looked out of the window. 'Extras punting on the Cam,' he said, 'there always are, aren't there? Not a trouble in the world, it seems, any of them. I'm very sorry, I truly had no idea how unhappy you were.'

'Me neither, Dad. And then I realised. And now I'm not. And you're still sorry.'

'I don't know who's done this to you, or why you've fallen for it – and I only hope that when you realise what they've done, you won't be too proud to come back to us. Because . . . because, *because*! Just don't come to me for money. I won't give it to you.'

'I wouldn't do that,' Tom said. 'I know how much it matters to you.'

'Forgive me, Lord, but I do not wish to contribute to the Rev Miguel Sung's next caddy but three.'

'You believe anything that suits you. I could give you the truth to read, but you wouldn't do it, would you?'

'Live it through, Tommy,' Adam said, 'if that's what you really want. Imagine that God is good and man is made in his image. I wish I could.'

'James,' Tom said, 'is the name I've chosen to be baptised in.'

'The brother of Jesus.'

'I'm surprised you know that.'

'I went to boarding school,' Adam said. 'I'm going to go now before I embarrass you, which I probably do already. I'm not going to try and . . . embrace you or anything, because I don't want you to push me away any more than I am now. I'll say just this, if I can and then I'll . . . Come back to us, if you want to. One day. Don't be too proud to do that. Please.'

He stood on the landing, not believing what he believed. They were still punting on the Cam. Girls were laughing. Adam sniffed and sniffed and then he walked back to Chapel Court, where the porter had said he could park the Alfa. He sat in the car for a while, wishing he could weep, or laugh, wishing that he felt less and also that he felt more. He thought of many things that he might do and knew he would not, and then he backed, carefully, and drove out of Chapel Court and through Cambridge to the A11. He stayed well within the speed limit, hoarding the speechless solitude.

Barbara was not at the house when he got home. She told him on the telephone that her mother was not too bad, but she was going to stay overnight. When she asked how Tom had got on, he said that he would tell her all about it when he saw her again.

Rachel had gone to a party. Adam tried to read a book about the Sixties that he had been sent for review, but after a few pages he closed it. He called his brother Derek's London house, but the message was that he and Carol had gone to the country. He went and sat in the Alfa. After a while, he started the car and drove, as if with no destination in mind, through the hopeless streets. People were still playing tennis in Regent's Park, badly. Adam sniffed and drove round to Regent's Park East.

There were flashing lights: an ambulance and police cars. He stopped short of Francesca's house and watched as a reporter quizzed one of the policemen on guard.

As the reporter was raising his knee to make a note in his black book, Adam contrived to get next to him. 'Excuse me, but . . . what's happened exactly? Did the copper tell you? I'm not press or anything, but . . . it just could be to do with someone I know vaguely.'

'Woman's been murdered apparently. Francesca Fairfax. Her and her fancy man, the both of them, the copper says. Blood everywhere, he was glad to tell me. They're looking for the husband. Dominic Fairfax, mean anything to you?'

'Not really,' Adam said.

'I checked him out in the morgue before I left the office.'

'Sorry?'

'What we call the cuttings department.'

'Oh yes, of course. How did you know to do that before you even got here?'

'Got the word from one of the coppers on the switchboard, didn't we? Quite well known, it seems he was, this Fairfax character, in the society fun and games department. Look at the place. Those people. All that money and they do things like that.'

'Christ Almighty,' Adam said.

III

Adam drove back to Tregunter Road and closed himself into his study, his spiral-bound squared notebook open in front of him. He wrote in his notebooks in ink; his pen, he thought, was more sincere than his typewriter, and sometimes more intelligent. He wrote nothing about Tom. He had to tell himself how shamefully relieved he was that he had not been the man who was with Francesca when Dominic chanced to come on them, if chance it was. He had left Tom with the feeling that he had died but that no one, including himself, had yet noticed it. But his imagination had to return and play with what the scene might have been at Regent's Park East, if he had been Francesca's lover. Could he, by some clever ploy, have survived what killed another? What if Dominic had been killed? Possible plots proliferated on the squared page, and over. He heard the front door open and then shut and female footsteps on the parquet.

'Anyone around? Daddy?' He closed the notebook and put it in his drawer and then wondered why he would be sitting there like that. He heard Rachel calling upstairs and then her footsteps came to his door. He swivelled to face her as she came in. 'There you are. Didn't you hear me? Are we playing hide and seek or something?'

'Something,' Adam said. 'How are you, Raitch? Are you all right? Good party?'

'I'm absolutely fine,' she said. 'Excellent party. Shall I turn a light on? It's a bit Valhalla-ish in here. Are you aware?'

'Very aware.'

'Come on, what's wrong? Something is.'

'Yes, it is. Quite a lot actually.'

'Did Tom not win his match?'

'No.'

'Oh dear.' She looked at him again. 'Grandma — ?'

'— is fine. As fine as can be expected. Your mother's coming home tomorrow. Tom didn't play his match, is what happened.'

'I was afraid of that,' she said.

'Were you just?'

'In the sense that . . . I knew he was going through a few changes.'

'One bloody great change, it seems. What did he tell you, when? Why didn't you tell me that something was up?'

'Promised not to. He kept wanting to talk to you but he was afraid.'

'Well, he managed it today. What the hell is he doing, Raitch, doing this?'

'His own thing, is how he sees it.'

'He's sold all his possessions, pretty well, did he tell you? And given the Rev Sung the money. I'm ashamed at how much it hurts.'

'It's nothing to do with you, is what you have to realise.'

'That's what married people always say when their husbands or wives have been to bed with other people. And it always always is, something to do with them. Rackets, record-player, records, everything. I wish I liked whisky. Because I'd have a whisky. I lack vices, really.'

Rachel said, 'How about a cup of tea?'

'A vice to conjure with. Should I do something? Does he want me to do something? Scream, shout, plead?'

'Try suffer,' she said.

She made herself busy as Barbara so often did: cups, milk, biscuits, tea. He sat in a cane-seated steel chair just by the wall phone on which he had heard the news of Tom's selection for the university six. He wished it did not occur to him that that was just the shot he would have specified in the screenplay.

'What have I done to him, Raitch? Hit me.'

'You're too much. Don't drink it while it's too hot. You fill

95

the room. You breathe all the oxygen. You're too clever, you've done too many things –'

'And so few of them worth doing. If I'd had the chance to play tennis for Cambridge . . . I'd've known it was a very bad year . . . but . . . goodness . . . how I would've loved the scarf!'

'He had the one thing he knows you wanted, so he dropped it on the floor and . . . try picking up the pieces.'

'All the king's horses,' Adam said. 'I always thought we got on very well, Tom and I.'

'That's probably part of what . . . disturbs him,' she said. 'He's so like you in so many ways that –'

'I don't see that.'

'You never look like people other people think you look like. You think I'm like Mum, but I'm not, not really.'

'You can't see yourself from the back. And you've got her eyes. But I know what you mean. I was once told I looked like a very clever philosopher. He didn't think so. And I hoped not.'

'You see your weaknesses –'

'Especially on the backhand. *And* often the forehand.'

'– and he only sees your strengths. So . . .'

'He sees only . . . I've lost my son.'

'He's alive,' Rachel said. 'Drink your tea. He'll be back.'

'He hates being a Jew, I suppose. Even though he isn't one. The Chief Rabbi wouldn't have him to tea. Well, he wouldn't have *me*. He certainly wouldn't have Spinoza. He's also threatening to drop out of Cambridge, Tom.'

'I know.'

'As if it was something I made him do. You can't imagine what a thrill it was when I went up.'

'I think I can.'

'You're happy with your life, aren't you, Raitch? If you've got some secret list of things you can't bear me to do . . . You don't hate it when I call you Raitch, do you?'

'I only hate it when other people do.'

'You're a beautiful girl, Rachel. You can't imagine how

much . . . you matter to me. I know what I'm doing and so do you, don't you?'

'Finding a reason to cry.'

'An excuse is more like it. I haven't told Barbara yet. About Tom. It's like a death.'

'No, it's not,' she said.

'You're the first person I've talked to. Your bad luck, as we used to say at school. Are you learning a lot?'

'I'm learning quite a lot.'

'I don't mean tonight –'

'I know. And yes, I do want to go to Cambridge. Or . . . somewhere.'

'Whatever happens – *whatever* happens – don't ever fear to come to us. We'll always be on your side. Always.'

'You're not going to lose me, Daddy. I'm very pleased to be who I am.'

'And Tom isn't?'

'Wasn't. Maybe he will be now. And then he'll see things differently. Keep breathing.'

ii

Several weeks after his first interview with Inspector Knox, Dan Bradley was charged with gross indecency with a minor, during the time that Graham Moony was a pupil in his charge at Middleford Special School. Mike Clode arranged for Daniel to be defended by Walter Burleigh, a QC who had acted in Mike's first film, before preferring another medium in which to star.

Burleigh sat at a long walnut table in his chambers, pink-ribboned briefs echeloned at his elbow. His face seemed as consciously, and severely, creased as the striped trousers: the flesh itself was tailored to his profession.

'We have a choice, Mr Bradley. To challenge the charges at the committal stage or to reserve our defence for the trial.'

Dan had chosen grey flannels and an elbow-patched sports jacket. 'How can we prove that something didn't happen?'

'We can't. And fortunately we're not called upon to do so. The prosecution have to prove that it did: happen. I can't imagine quite how, at this stage.'

'By making this boy – this man now, I suppose – swear that it did, and him making it . . . *graphic* enough to be credible. I suspect he'll know how, Graham. Does "at this stage" mean that you think they might have a few years ago? Is that what you're implying?'

'I don't think indignation is a pedal worth pressing, least of all with me. I imply nothing. I have little doubt that this is a wicked fabrication. Fortunately for us, Master Moony is a sadistic little pimp who manifestly has everything to gain by parading himself as a victim.'

'Little doubt, have you?' Dan said. 'Meaning everyone's going to believe that what he says is true. Whatever happens. Including me, probably, in the end.'

'It's entirely natural that you should be bitter. We all would, I daresay, in your shoes. What's vital is that you – if I may say so – act as if you were nothing of the sort. Serene tolerance would be my recipe. No one can promise what the magistrates, in their infinite capriciousness, will or won't do, but I'm tolerably confident that – sooner or later – you'll walk out of court without a stain on your character.'

'Those are the ones that never come out,' Dan said.

'Is your ex-wife prepared to testify, have you discovered, if it comes to a full-blown trial?'

'On my behalf, you mean?'

'Was what I –'

'Joyce probably wishes I was guilty, but she must know I'm not.'

'Not important at this stage, but you might care to talk to her. Mention the effect on your children. You do have them, don't you?'

'They're no longer children, but yes. Three. Mr Burleigh, suppose I admitted doing what I never did –'

'Why ever would you want to do that?'

98

'– might it help his defence, in his trial, do you suppose? If I did. Graham's.'

'This young man tortured and defaced a girl in cold blood, and with a good degree of . . . pleasure, it seems. I doubt if Jesus Christ Himself would hurry to be crucified on his behalf. If you wish to go further than Our Lord, it's entirely a matter for you. For what it's worth, I think it would be a wicked thing to do. Suppose Moony gets a shorter sentence thanks to you, what will you think when he gets out and does the same sort of thing to some other wretched little drab?'

'That's quite a good point.'

'I rather thought so. Serenity and tolerance, Mr Bradley. And save charity for another time, and a better cause. I did hugely admire your Romeo, by the way, at the A.D.C. Saw it in my first year.'

iii

For the last two weeks of the summer term, Rachel and her class went on an exchange trip to Montauban, in southwestern France. Adam took Barbara to the Grand Hotel des Bains on the Venice lido. They lounged on the beach during the day, under wide umbrellas, and – when the afternoon had cooled – they took the *vaporetto* to the Piazza San Marco and went with the shuffling crowd towards the Rialto. They dined on the third night at the Ristorante alla Madonna.

'*Pronti, signore?*'

'*Prontissimi,*' Adam said. '*Due spaghetti alle vongole, e poi – poi* . . . what did we say?'

'The liver, didn't we?'

'The liver, of course. *Dunque, fegato alla Veneziana per tutt'i due. Ci sono spinaci?*'

'*Come no?*'

'*Una porzione spinaci, olio, limone, e una bottiglia di Montepulciano, c'é lo?*'

'*Certo, signore. Acqua minerale?*'

'*Senza gas, per piacere.*' Adam looked up into Barbara's straight face. 'What?'

'I didn't say anything.'

'And I heard you,' he said.

'You have to be good at everything, don't you?'

'I thought that was what your look was saying. I have to try to be would be truer, and crueller. Crueller usually is truer, innit the truth though? D.H. Lawrence called Venice "the abhorrent green, slippery city". Did you know that?'

'I didn't go to Cambridge, did I?'

'Anything for a laugh, that was David Herbert.'

'Everyone else orders in English,' she said.

'Look, I did Latin for twelve bloody years and now it gives me petty pleasure to be able to order a meal in Italian . . . I don't find that very Cambridge. Just . . . polite actually. What's wrong, Ba?'

'You tell me.'

'I asked first.'

'You're bored.'

'Meaning you are. I'm not bored. I'm perfectly happy. *Imperfectly* happy, if we must be accurate. Tom, right? Is what's wrong. And we agreed not to talk about it and not to worry about it and so we both worry and neither of us likes to talk about it, and now I've ruined the evening. Which doesn't mean you're not very beautiful. You are.'

'If in doubt tell a woman how beautiful she is.'

'And what do you tell me, if you're in doubt, if you ever are?'

'I tell you you shouldn't have married me, don't I?'

'Yes, you do. And then I say, "You mean *you* shouldn't have married *me*" and then we have a great evening. I did marry you and I still can't believe my luck. Despite . . .'

'*Spaghetti alle vongole. Buon appetito.*'

'*Grazie.* OK if I say *grazie*? Joking!'

'Tom was always afraid he could never do anything to please you.'

'And when he knew he could, he didn't. He tore Cambridge up and threw the pieces in my face. How could he? How could he, Ba? Did he talk to you about it before he did it?'

'He was probably afraid I'd tell you.'

'I have to be the villain. I wish I bloody well *was* sometimes, up to my neck. As it is, I'm permanently up to my knees. In tepid water.'

'Dive in then,' she said. 'Tell me about this woman.'

'What woman?'

'The one who slapped your face in the bookshop. That woman, with the tits like —'

'You've been reading my notebook,' he said.

'You left it open at the page, and you knew I was going to do your room, because you were on your way to some ultra-important meeting and you told me so. "Tits like special offers", wasn't that the immortal phrase — ?'

'I don't even remember what I wrote exactly.'

'Not surprising, because you . . . write in a way —'

'— that's intended for my eyes only. Yes, I do though. Remember: I said that the slap on the face was . . . "a violent proposition". Do I quote myself with narcissistic accuracy?'

'Did you see her again?'

'*Un piatto vuoto, prego*,' Adam called to the waiter. '*Per* . . . All right, yes, I did.'

'"All right" as in I asked for it, is that?'

'All right, as in she called and asked me, and —'

'You needed her permission before you dared to make a move. That's always been your problem with women.'

'Is it not? I'm a timid soul.'

'It wasn't your problem with me. Why was that? Because it didn't matter what I thought?'

'Please try not to have said that. That was . . . May I mention "love" without —'

'Ha!'

'Without "Ha!" You were a chance in a lifetime, and this is the lifetime. So far so . . . what? Good? Fairly good? *Grim?* Tick box.' Her hand was there, so he took it. 'Writing's what I do when I don't know what to do.'

'He'll come home one day.'

'Yes,' Adam said, 'and want to know where the fatted calf is.'

'You went to bed with her, is that what you're telling me, but didn't put in your notebook because you knew I'd read it?'

'Does all this tell me why you've become so . . . so *amused* in the last little while?'

'*Amused?* Have I? I hadn't noticed that.'

'I have. The little looks, the movements of the mouth, the really nice meals, the . . . the politeness. They generally mean trouble. Emotional cystitis.'

'Are you still seeing her?'

'No. No one is. She got murdered. Along with her lover. By her husband. It was in the papers. A lot.'

'He wasn't the one they found in Capri or somewhere?'

'Ischia. Was he not? He was. Floating. Face down. After which, no further questions. Case closed. Except here. I did not go to bed with her.'

'She's the girl who called you "Jew". You put her in *An Early Life*. You must've been thrilled when she . . . made contact –'

'Is indeed the *mot juste*. I was, to tell the truth – often a dubious move – considerably . . . how about motivated? I was motivated rigid. But that was all. As it happened. Or, as in fact, it didn't. Happen. Nearly isn't quite.'

'And now you're sorry.'

'Relieved. My name is Adam Morris. You – playing the part of Barbara Morris – and I have been married some years now. All because we said we loved each other and I believed it.'

'Cue tears, eyes brimming with.'

'Don't get technical with me, Ba. I've taught you all you know, haven't I? And it ain't much!'

'That's nice.'

'About showbiz, I didn't have time to say. And you've only taught me . . . how to . . . love.'

'*Era buono, signora?*'

'*Buonissimo*,' Barbara said, as the waiter took away her plate. 'Is there such a word?'

'There is now. Yes, there is. Of course there is. I won't let him ruin our lives, Ba.'

'Who are we on to now?'

'If he wants to be some kind of a crazy Christian, Tom, well, that's his bag, as they say, and he can pack it, as they don't.'

'Don't entertain me all the time, Adam.'

'Smiling gives you wrinkles, doesn't it? Isn't it flattering, that I try to amuse you?'

'You practise on me.'

'Well, you're some fiddle. I didn't go to bed with her. I don't even go to bed with you, a lot, do I, these days?'

'*Attenzione, signora. Piatto molto caldo.*'

'See? I can burn my fingers for all he cares. You on the other hand . . . are something else! A *bella donna* can always trust Italian waiters. It's in the phrase book.'

'Did you feel cheated?'

'Do I get a clue? Like . . . when?'

'When she was killed.'

'Do you want the truth? Who does?'

'I'm interested.'

'I sometimes wish we were strangers. And you'd never heard it all before. I'd find you so easy to talk to.'

'If you met me now,' she said, 'for the first time, I don't suppose you'd give me a second glance.'

'Look around the room. No, look! Who else would I be glancing at? Anyway, this isn't about glances.'

'It's about Tom.'

'She's pretty though!' Adam said. 'The Chinese girl in the corner. Unless she's Japanese possibly.'

'It's about me not being Jewish.'

'Nothing of the kind.'

'Yes, yes. It's about my not being Jewish and never really understanding –'

'– how little it means to me. You're right.'

'And how much. What're you bloody well smiling at now?'

'You. Because I love you. Hurry while stocks last.'

'Special offers,' she said. 'You bastard.'

'Writing in a notebook is like practising scales.'

'The moment they fall from your eyes. Are you trying to persuade me or trying to persuade yourself?'

'Bound to be.'

'Come on. What did she offer that I don't? A Get Out of Jail Free card, could it be?'

'Whenever I played Monopoly with the kids and had to take a Chance, I always got the one that duns you for house repairs.'

'Or is that when you play Monogamy?'

'I wish I'd said that. And don't call me Oscar! Tom once said to me, not long ago, when he was still human —'

'Don't, Adam. It'll turn into a habit.'

'Right. He said, "Dad, what did you do in the Sixties?" He hoped I was going to have spent most of the time in the great bed of Ware, rubbing shoulders — and other parts — with famous people and getting stoned out of my mind —'

'And what was I supposed to be doing all this time?'

'Looking after the kids, weren't you, in a miniskirt? Pussy pelmets, someone called them, miniskirts; no, it was not me. And cooking amazing meals and not being remotely jealous because no one ever was in those days and anyway you probably had a special friend of your own that you and your girlfriend used go and get photographed by, while topping and tailing each other on a bean bag; what else?'

'Two more ideas like that and you'd practically have a novel that says it all.'

'Now we've got Victorian values back again, everything's changed, of course, hasn't it? *Has* it? Poor Tom, he couldn't really believe it when I told him that I was perfectly happy being with you, and him, and . . .'

'Could you?'

'You're a clever girl, Ba. And not always as nice as I like to think. Which is nice to think. Shall we go back to the hotel or do you want a cassata ice cream?'

'She wanted to be killed, I suppose, didn't she? Your Francesca Fairfax. I know what cassata is. She wanted it to happen.'

'Except when it did, I imagine.'

'And you were going to be the mortal sin that made her deserve it.'

'Clever, clever you! I just thought she fancied me. Silly, silly me.'

'You seriously ought to write a novel about it. A sequel to *An Early Life*. And then you could deny that it was even faintly autobiographical.'

'I don't want to do that, and you don't want me to, do you? I do wish we were still like we were back then. When we first went to Rome. Do you ever think about Donald?'

'Not really. You were upset because I didn't want him to come to Italy with us, weren't you?'

'And I'd've hated it if he had. I felt like a shit leaving him, though, didn't you, to die like that?'

'I just wanted to be alone with you. You can have a nonconformist conscience if you want to. I don't. I don't want any ice cream either.'

'He bit his nails, is what I remember most vividly. Strange sucking sound he made while he was working at it. I should never have had anything to do with films, should I?'

'Then give them up. We can do without the money.'

'This from the girl who walked into Claridge's looking like a million dollars wearing the latest Missoni!'

'You wouldn't like it if I looked like . . . what was her name? Anna.'

'I'm surprised you even remember her.'

'She stripped off as well, didn't she? A lot of women seem to take their clothes off for you.'

'Very few. She only took her sweater off. Anna. Thank God. And didn't have a lot to show for it.'

'What's she doing these days?'

'Still swilling it down, I imagine. Last thing I knew she'd gone up north somewhere, supposedly to dry out. Here's a funny thing: I want to go back to the hotel. Very much. Why would I want to do that?'

Barbara said, 'If Tom doesn't want to see us or talk to us for a while, that's his affair. You shouldn't think about it.'

'Are you promising you won't?'

'Tom's my son. Yes, I will. But you're my life, you bastard. And it's time we went to bed.'

'*Senta, prego, il conto!*' Adam took her hand. 'Very nice of you to say so,' he said. 'The bastard part, I mean.'

Standing against the rail of the *vaporetto* that took them back to the lido, they kissed as if they were lovers who had just met and who were dreaming of what was already true, that they could be together all night and do whatever they wanted to do, and be together again the next day. They kissed until it hurt her jaw and she leaned back and gasped and smiled.

'I'd forgotten,' she said. 'You used to be quite a kisser.'

'You're all smudged.'

'You too. Should we care?'

'Twenty-five years!' he said. 'Jesus! And you haven't changed. Except for the better.'

'*Schmoozer.*'

'I'm not really Jewish, you know. I just told you I was.'

'I know. But I'll still go to bed with you. Probably.'

'*Lido! Fine del corso. Lido!*'

They walked down the long wide street from the *vaporetto* station to the beach, both smiling, not looking at each other. When they could see the sand, Adam said, 'Byron used to take exercise riding his horse up and down this beach, did you know?'

'Yes,' she said, 'and I don't care.'

'Good. Nor do I.'

They walked up the gravel drive and into the polished foyer of the hotel. The floor seemed slightly sprung. As they crossed

106

to the caged lift, the black-coated porter came out of the inner office. 'Signor Morris. There's a message for you, signore.'

'Damn,' Adam said.

'Liar,' she said. 'You love messages.'

'And pleasures postponed,' he said. 'But not for long. It's OK, it's only from Mike. Might've guessed. He wants me to call him. "Urgently" even. And you think I'm going to, don't you?'

'Think you should?'

'You go on holiday and tell them you don't want them to call you unless it's really urgent, they always do. And it never is.'

'You still better call him.'

'Anything to interrupt people who have better things to do. Tom always used to cry, or come in, when we were making love, do you remember?'

'Do I? I was always ashamed of how annoyed I was with him when he did. I love these old moaning lifts. I bet they replace it any minute now with one of those obstinate silent ones.'

'He always had to press the button, didn't he?'

Barbara said, 'I want to warn you about something.'

'If you've got the curse, I shall kill you.'

'If you call Mike after we've made love, then we're not going to make love.'

'I have a logical objection to that.'

'I knew you would have when I said it. But it's still true.'

'I never got his message, did I? I will not phone him tonight. Promise.'

Adam opened the lift gate and Barbara brushed her hand against him as she stepped out.

'*Senta, prego! Retenete il ascensore, per cortesia!*'

Adam held the door open with his back to the man who was coming along the shaded corridor. 'I don't believe it!' the man said. 'Adam, how are you?' Bruno Laszlo was wearing a grey lightweight suit, and a white shirt with the usual button undone under the off-centre black knitted tie. 'What are you doing here?'

'Holding the lift for you, Bruno, aren't I? What else would I be doing? You remember Barbara, don't you?'

She was looking back at Adam from the door of their room. She walked a few steps towards them as Bruno looked at her.

'You are here with your wife?'

'It looks remarkably like her, doesn't it, from here?'

'That's very romantic. She looks very beautiful still.'

'And she's not bad when she's on the move either.'

'Wha-at? This is very lucky, for me, Adam. And for you. Do you have time to have a coffee or a *digestivo*? We go back to the suite.'

'Bruno, the lift; the lift, Bruno.'

Bruno said, 'Only listen, I have this book I've optioned, almost, and I promise you, you are the first writer I thought of . . . How long are you here in Venice?'

'We may cut it short now we know you're here.'

'Barbara, please. Talk to him. I win him the Oscar and he treats me like I don't know what.'

'I'll say goodnight.' She walked down the corridor and opened the door of their room. 'See you in the morning, Ad.'

'Goodnight, Bruno. *A domani*, and not a minute before.'

'One minute! Just one. I give you the book, you read it, and you tell me what you think —'

'I know what I think. It's cheap and nasty and it has possibilities, unfortunately. It sags a bit in the middle and the woman's character needs to be made more interesting. And proactive. Key term. The premiss is there, it needs a lotta lotta work.'

'Exactly what I think. You see? How did you get hold of it as a matter of interest?'

'Bruno, get in the lift and press the bloody button. You've probably just blighted my holiday and wrecked my marriage.'

'Wonderful luck, I must say, running into you. I call you in the morning. We have breakfast.'

'We do *not* have breakfast.' Adam closed the lift gate and held it shut. 'Press the bloody button, Bruno.'

As the lift was going down, Bruno called out, 'Do you still have the same agent?'

'Same agent, same wife. Same Bruno Laszlo. Everything else is different.'

As he knocked on the door of the room, he wished he had not been amused, and flattered, and relieved (who ever knew when Hollywood's fountains would cease to flow?) by Bruno's urgent thoughtlessness. And what could Mike Clode want, come to that?

'Who is it?'

'It's the plumber,' Adam said.

'I don't need a plumber.'

'Issa that the lady of the house?'

'This isn't a house and I'm not a lady.'

'Then I've come to the right place. Open up. Got something for you.'

When she opened the door, she was standing there naked, one long leg crossed over the other, the breath just audible in those neat nostrils. Her face was the only part of her that looked dressed. 'Special offer,' she said.

'You thought I'd do it, didn't you?' he said.

'And I'm still somewhat hoping that you will.'

'Go with Bruno and collect this manuscript or whatever it is.'

'I'd've packed a bag by the time you got back.'

'I wasn't coming back.' He pulled her against him. 'And I would've deserved it. And where would you be going with it, your bag?'

'Oh do shut up, in the nicest possible way.'

'That may be nicer than you deserve. Do you know why I shall always want you, Ba?'

'Not really.'

'Nor do I. But I shall. And I do know really.'

'As long as it's true, I don't honestly care. Why?'

'Because, whatever happens, however much we talk, or don't, I never quite . . . know it all, do I?'

'Infinite variety, that's me.'

'And yet always the same.'

'Thank you,' she said. 'I think.'

'And not goodnight.'

The next morning, they had breakfast on their terrace and then they went to the beach. Adam lay on his mattress with the second volume of Runciman's *History of the Crusades* and watched Barbara oiling herself until she had to ask him to do her back. 'I know what you're thinking,' he said.

'And you're almost certainly right.'

'Then tell me.'

'I'm thinking you're thinking, "When can I slip away and phone Mike Clode without her being pissed off?" Do I read you like a book?'

'Probably the same one that Bruno's optioned. Almost.'

'If you want to call him, call him. Mike.'

'I don't *want* to. What I want to do, which you may not want to . . .'

'Is what?'

'Go to the Ghetto. I promised Shylock he could change some money for me.'

'I'll come with you. If you want me to.'

'I want to see the synagogues. I don't know why. I never go near one in London. We can do Torcello tomorrow. Unless you'd sooner Murano. Do we need any more glasses that look like boiled sweets at all?'

'You want to go alone, don't you? To the Ghetto.'

'Not particularly. Do you mind?'

Barbara said, 'Why should I?' She turned on her front and stretched flat with her book on the sand below her.

'You sought I was a dream,' Bruno Laszlo said.

'How are you, Bruno?'

'To tell you de truce, I don't know. They do some more tests when I get back to London.'

'You know something I've never understood. Why would an Italian like you want to live in the smoke?'

'One day I tell you. Or one day you go to Ferrara and see what you see. All right, I tell you now: because I left Italy, nineteen hundred and forty, and England was the only place I could go. Gratitude, you probably don't know about that. And now I have an English son . . . How is your son, by the way?'

'Tom's very well.'

'Look, I don't want to interrupt your holiday . . . And anyway I am going to Milan later – but this book, when can you read it? Be serious for once.'

'Leave it with the concierge, and if I like it, I'll call you when I get back to London.'

'You won't. Like it. Otherwise why would I show it to you? It needs some ideas, like we had for *The Woman in Question*. I told them you would be perfect.'

'Have you got a director?'

'We decide that later.'

'We? As in you and I? And then later than that you and he will decide that you both wrote it.'

'You know, Barbara, it's time Adam made his directorial debut. I would like to discover him in many ways.'

Barbara said, 'He's ripe for discovery.'

'You'd hate it. If I directed something. What's it called, this book, Bruno?'

'Very memorable title. I forget exactly. I leave it with the concierge. You call me when you get back to London, we have lunch, we talk . . .' Bruno went unevenly across the sand in his city shoes. His black silk socks paled over the ankle bones.

'He doesn't really mean it,' Adam said, 'about directing. They tell you what you want to hear, until they've got you . . .'

'I'm thinking of having my hair done,' Barbara said. 'Shall you mind? There's a place in the hotel.'

'You're a very nice woman,' Adam said, 'aren't you?'

'Among other things,' she said. 'You don't need to be all that nice to have your hair done.'

'No, you don't, but you are.'

Adam knew that she had chosen to do something that would give him a couple of hours, and more if he wanted it, to take the *vaporetto* to the mainland and down the Grand Canal to the

111

Ghetto Nuovo, which – as a guide was explaining to a group of tourists (three or four of them skull-capped), in the smallest and simplest of the synagogues – was actually the old ghetto.

'I love that wooden balustrade around the balcony,' one of the female tourists said. 'I guess that's where the women prayed, am I right?'

'That's where. High days and Holy Days, when they prayed all day, the women up there, they got pretty hot. It was like – forgive me – a sweat box up there. Some of them lost like eight pounds in weight.'

'Eight *pounds* in one day?' One of the larger ladies had to say. 'I should be so lucky!'

As she got her laugh, the guide was saying, 'A little like you might expect, it wasn't only with Christians that Shylock and some of the others refused to pray, it was also with other Jews. This is where the Ashkenazim prayed – the Yiddish-speakers, roughly speaking – and across the piazza we'll be visiting where the Sephardim did. The lectern in here, it was so heavy, it *is* so heavy, the floor started to give way under it, so what did they do?'

'Put a new beam underneath?'

'They moved it to another part of the floor. They weren't just Jews, they were also Venetians. In Venice, if you get asked to a dance in one of those old *palazzi*, you'll never see a true Venetian dancing in the middle of the room. Well, some dance; others pray. The Inquisition forbade Jews to use marble or gold to decorate their synagogues, so they painted the wood to look like marble. They got to be so good at it that the Christians turned jealous, till it was smarter, and also more expensive, to have fake marble in your *palazzo* than the real thing.'

'Wouldn't you know it?' the fat lady said.

Adam loitered on the fringe of the group. At once grateful for what he was learning and wishing that they were not there, he smiled to himself, and then at a girl who noticed him, and his smile. She frowned, head on one side, and came over to him.

'Excuse me, but are you in our group?'

112

'No,' Adam said. 'I'm just . . . painted to look like it.'

'I didn't think I'd seen you.'

She had black hair, in a loose bun, and green eyes and a thin straight nose. The lustrous lips seemed amused at her own nerve in talking to Adam. She was wearing an emerald-green raincoat and black boots.

The guide was saying, 'Now we go to the Sephardic synagogue which is not too far away, but you may need your umbrellas, I'm afraid.'

'Are you Sephardic?' the girl said.

'I'm mishmashic,' Adam said. 'Who knows by now what anybody is?'

'I do. You're Adam Morris.'

'That's true. According to recent reports. You're going to lose your group.'

'Promise? I saw you on TV. In New York. One time. You destroyed some stupid critic. Susie Beaumont, was it?'

'She still lived to snipe again another day.'

'You were so . . . *contemptuous*. People in America don't act that way.'

'Happens when I'm roused,' he said.

'I wouldn't like to be the person who roused you.'

'Write nice things about me then.'

'I don't get to write those kinds of things.'

'The straight face indicates that I was kidding. An old British habit. Rarely gets a laugh. Meaning you write other things?'

'I loved *The Woman in Question*. Saw it three times. At least. Short stories only so far, me. I'm Rachel by the way.'

Adam said, 'Hullo, Rachel by the way. Rachel what?'

'Mollo. Two ells. Which is a pseudonym, for Molho with an h not a second l. My father told me. My grandfather came from Thessaloniki. Just in time. The rest of his family stayed behind, and they all got murdered. Except one . . . She escaped, it's an incredible story – do you want to get some coffee?'

'Sure. What are you going to do? Wait here?'

'I meant, shall we –'

113

'I know. Let's.'

There was a café a few doors down from the synagogue. The rain brought out the drab dignity of the Ghetto.

'Did you catch the sign on the window? This is really and truly a kosher cappuccino. It really is. What's the difference, do you suppose? Five hundred lire probably.'

'You're just so like I always imagined.'

'Always is a long time,' he said. 'Who was she? This girl who escaped from Thessaloniki? Not you, was she?'

'*Me?* Come on! We're talking almost forty years ago. She was a cousin of a cousin, of a cousin. She was actually on the train to go to . . . I don't know . . . Auschwitz, I guess, and she managed to escape because some German officer, OK, wanted to fuck her. I mean, this happened pretty often, I found out, and afterwards they'd just push the women back on the train. You don't hear too much about those details because Jews being killed, people are interested in that part, but Jewish girls twelve years old being raped . . . and then dumped back on the train to go and be murdered, that doesn't go down so well with the popcorn, does it? Plus the nice neighbours who turned people in they'd known since children. Those Jews in Thessaloniki —'

'— had been there longer than the Christians.'

'Some of them. A lot. OK, so . . . listen I could tell you quite a bit about this girl and this German officer, whose name was Mikhail Winter, Vinter I guess. He took this kid cousin of mine off the train and hid her. At first he just wanted to abuse her, which is what they all did . . . but . . . turned out he wasn't entirely what he seemed because — you're nodding. Did you guess already?'

'This isn't the one about the SS officer turns out to be Jewish possibly, is it?'

'You think I'm shitting you? You think this is some Holocaust legend I'm giving you here. It's totally not. This is true, so help me. This Winter guy was partly Romanian, and he'd had this like first love affair – before the war – with a Jewish

114

girl who got murdered by the . . . what were those people called in Romania?'

'The Iron Guard?'

'Has to be it. So he had this . . . guilt . . . and . . . anyway, now he falls in love with this girl he grabbed off the train, Anya, and she survived the whole war, first with him, and then when he was sent to the Russian front, he kinda . . . bequeathed her to this other officer . . . and finally God knows how many men later, she . . . she was a survivor. At least she was a survivor. Seventeen years old.'

'Why do I feel guilty?' Adam said. 'Hearing this story.'

'We all do, and they don't,' the girl said.

'Maybe that's why. The aggression that dares not speak its name. Where did she go?'

'Back to Thessaloniki. To see what and who was left. She was one of the very few of the sixty thousand Jews who used to be in that city that ever made it back. Guess what she found.'

'Very few open arms, I imagine.'

'The Christians had stolen everything the Jews had left behind. I mean, *everything*. Clothes, furniture, houses – and it was like their owners never existed. When she tried to get her family's house back from the family'd moved in there . . . You want to do some guessing what happened? She was only arrested and accused of being a whore for the Germans. Her own best friend from school before the war testified against her . . .'

'There are lovely people everywhere, aren't there? And?'

'She was sent to jail for ten years. Which she did not survive. She got typhoid in one of those cold post-war winters, and . . . died. So what do you think?'

'We can never know what other people went through, Rachel. It's our good fortune and it's our curse. Is the best I can come up with.'

'Could it make a movie?'

'A movie! Sure. A movie they wouldn't make.'

'There must be ways,' she said.

'To tell you the truth, Rachel – which I can do because I

115

don't know you and I can be . . . brutal, if you like – I don't think we can catch up with . . . things like that by telling them again. It won't bring anyone back, it won't stop things happening again, which is what everyone always pretends, and that's not why people make movies or write books about those things, they do it to show that it never happened to them. It congratulates all of us on not being . . . *those* people. Never again always happens again and there are always people who want it to.'

'Which is your excuse for . . .'

'Not an excuse. Excuses are for not doing things that should be done. You've heard of catharsis –'

'What happens when you see a tragedy.'

'Supposedly.'

'And you're purged by pity and terror.'

'On the button,' Adam said. 'But actually – do you want to hear this or shall I vanish into the Venetian evening? – actually, I don't believe that tragedy necessarily had that effect on people, or that it was meant to, just because Aristotle said it did. Maybe the audience also laughed. Maybe they also gloated. Maybe there was more in common between the tragic theatre and the Roman circus than scholars choose to notice. You're going to lose the rest of the tour, because there they go, don't they? Do you know where you're staying?'

'You can't imagine what it means to me talking to you like this. The people on my tour – they're so . . . stifling. Do you really *like* Venice?'

'Its past I do,' he said. 'And who came here: Ruskin, Henry James, Proust, Byron, A.E. Housman . . . just the class of ghost I like to mix with.'

'I love Proust!' she said. 'Rachel-when-from-the-Lord, remember her? I guess you know what D.H. Lawrence called it, don't you, Venice?'

'Remind me,' Adam said.

'Green and slippery, didn't he?'

'You very tactfully omitted "*abhorrent*".'

116

'You are truly unbelievable. How did you *know* that?'
'A writer's life is an endless series of exams. You have to pass. Some of them. Listen, I have to go.'
'I will never, never forget meeting you like this.'
'I was working at it.'
'Truly. Are you alone here in Venice? I would do anything to spend time with you.'
'I am not. But thank you. And thank you for telling me that story. I told you it wasn't the kind of thing that could ever make a movie. So if you knew anything about movie people, of whom I am not truly one, you'd be looking out to see how soon I put your girl into a movie which owed nothing to your story. Since I'm not really one of them, I'll only steal it very slowly, if at all. Maybe in ten years I'll suddenly find the seed you set pops into life. No threats, no promises. You never know with Jews, or writers.'

They walked out into the piazza. Drops of rain seemed to be falling individually, leaving dark stars on the flagstones.

'This has been so, so great. I'll never forget this. Truly.'

She had to kiss him and try the tip of her tongue against his lips. Then he walked away through the drizzle to the rocking *vaporetto* stop on the Grand Canal. It was a relief to leave the girl, but a pleasure to think how willing she was to go with him. If her name had not been Rachel, would he have been less paternal with his kiss? It had been a soundless slap in the face, the coincidence of her name; it returned him to reality.

As the conductor unlatched the *vaporetto*'s leather strap and let him aboard, he thought about Tom. What would he have made of the little synagogue where Shylock and his tribe prayed to the God Whom they trusted with such tenacious absurdity? Adam was already thinking of what he would write in his notebook. Why had Jesus not leant down to help that seventeen-year-old girl when they crucified her? 'Father, Father, why hast Thou deserted me?' *Et toi, mon vieux, qu'est-ce que t'as fais toi-même?* All the furious *naïvetés* which did not bear public expression, weren't those the only things he really wanted to say?

117

Over dinner that night, at Corte Sconta, not far from the Arsenal, Adam did not mention meeting the girl. Why would he? He and Barbara dined at length and walked along the Riva degli Schiavoni, past the Bridge of Sighs and the Doge's Palace, with its corner sculpture of Adam and Eve being expelled from the Garden of Eden. They were easy together, but desire did not join them on the boat.

The next day, they took the *vaporetto* to Torcello. In the little Byzantine church, Barbara noticed a girl looking in their direction, and especially in Adam's. 'See the dark girl in the green mac? I think she's recognised you.'

'She's probably got a message for me from Mike Clode.'

'You never called him!' Barbara said. 'Or did you? *Did* you?'

'What do you think?'

'You did.'

'I didn't actually. I forgot, on purpose. Just what he'd do. I'm afraid.'

'She really *does* know who you are,' Barbara said. 'She wants you to look at her. Go on. Give her a thrill. See what I mean?'

'Pretty,' Adam said.

'In a way. I don't like the earrings.'

'She could always take them off,' he said.

iv

'Mike Clode.'

'Adam Morris.'

'No,' Mike said. 'You've dialled the wrong number. This is Mike Clode.'

'I know that, Mike. This is Adam Morris.'

'Why do you always have to play games, Adam? What kind of accent was that supposed to be? And where the *hell* have you been?'

'In Venice, if you must know. With a woman.'

'Does Barbara know about this?'

118

'As a matter of fact, yes; she does. She's being wonderful about it.'

'I called you in Venice, and left a message.'

'Italians!' Adam said. 'What was it about?'

'Your brother. You have to talk to him.'

'Derek? Do I? Why?'

'I detect . . . problems. On getting seed money for the Orwell bid. Which Der can help us with. You're the obvious ambassador. Have you read this book of Joyce Hadleigh's Bruno wants us to do? *The Sixth Floor.* Distinct possibilities, I thought.'

'He gave me a proof. He didn't mention your involvement. But then you seem to be involved in just about everything these days.'

'Joyce told me about it. I put him on to it. Bruno doesn't read, you know that. He sniffs.'

'And you do, do you? Read? How about my novel you promised you really really wanted to "get to", was the term, I think? Have you got to it yet?'

'Have a glance at the back burner. It's still on it, believe me. Timing's not right. Give brother Derek a jingle, Ad, and let me know what's happening on the Rialto.'

'Nicely put,' Adam said. 'I know Shylock will appreciate your concern.'

v

Walter Burleigh had his black coat on as well as his striped trousers when he and Dan Bradley walked across Marlborough Street to have a cup of tea after the preliminary hearing. The tabs of his advocate's collar fluttered as he went along. Dan was wearing a grey corduroy suit and a grey turtle-necked sweater.

'I don't think you should attach undue significance to the magistrates' decision,' Burleigh said. 'Pure formality.'

'They think I've got a case to answer. That doesn't sound exactly insignificant to me.'

119

'They're obliged, somewhat, to accept what the police tell them, since – rightly or wrongly, and I think rightly – we elected to reserve our defence. To which you agreed.'

'The way I feel now, I think I was probably wrong.'

'Discount feelings, is the usual rule. If you had been, I'd have said so. Wrong. You accepted my advice. And your solicitor's, of course.'

'They want me to be guilty,' Dan said.

'Nobody in there wants anything all that much, Mr Bradley. Except to get through as many cases as possible and have lunch.'

'The people. I can tell how they look at me. Look over there. They were in court, those two, I'm prepared to bet.'

'You were excellent in court: made a very dignified impression.'

'So did Sir Roger Casement. They still hanged him.'

'That was a long time ago, and he did happen to be guilty. In English eyes at least. No one is going to hang you, if I can help it. The important thing is to stay calm.'

'I'm sure you'll manage it very easily,' Dan said. 'How long before it comes to court?'

'That depends on how crowded the calendar is. Late autumn, would be a reasonable guess.'

'And what do I do till then?'

'Best thing would be to go back to work.'

'I've been suspended. Not by the neck, like Sir Roger Casement, but nonetheless –'

'I've got a cousin who writes textbooks. Sells all over the world. School certificate cribs and such-like. Quentin. Lives in Guernsey. Has to. Money coming out of his ears. Remembers you as Henry the Fifth at Cambridge. Better than Olivier, he says. We held our fire, Mr Bradley. Steady the Buffs, remember? When we open up, we shall blow them away. And now I must run. No, no, allow me.'

Dan said, 'It's very tempting.'

'What's that?'

'Running.'

'Good nurses don't do it,' Burleigh said. 'Nor do wise defendants. Be of their number, and call me, if you need me.'

He shook hands with Daniel, who watched him walk to the door of the café. As Burleigh hitched himself into his topcoat, he revealed that he was wearing red socks.

vi

Denis Porson was reading *Scoff*, a new food magazine, in which Alan Parks – a frequent customer of Two by Two – was taking an expensive look at the restaurant critics, not least Tamara Singer, who 'put on pounds sterling' by regular sneering at the hands that fed them. Denis knew better than to imagine that Alan Parks would remain a loyal ally, but it was nice to see Gianni well spoken of. Denis might not have brought *Scoff* to read, but it seemed tactless to read *Gay Times* while waiting for Jill to get the results of her test.

'Was I for ever?'

'And a day, dear,' Denis said. 'What's the ongoing story of the man within?'

'Heart's beating fine,' she said. 'I'm . . . everything that a good balloon should be. It all makes me want to cry. And more than a little bit nervous.'

'Me too, sweetie. But don't worry: I'm sure we're both going to be wonderful mothers.'

'I never really thought it would happen.'

'Nature's a bitch, dear, and she does like to have her way. You were very patient and very . . . thoughtful and . . . I'm thrilled beyond expression which is probably as well. Mawkish would be undercooking it.'

'You're worried about Gianni, aren't you?'

'Yes, truthfully . . . But what the hell? The hell would be if he threw a tantrum and upped sticks. But he seems somewhat to be enjoying the . . . challenge? Challenge.'

'I don't mind, you do know that, don't you? Whatever you have to do to keep him happy.'

121

'Happiness isn't all people want, is it? Tends to be the problem in my sometimes shopsoiled experience. But so far so tempestuous. At least he's not Sicilian. I don't think we need fear daggers.'

'I'm ashamed to say –'

'That usually precedes the truth. What?'

'– I shall always love you for this. It's so unlikely it's the most heavenly revenge I can imagine. Not against Mike, not against anyone. Just . . . against!'

'Which cues me, if I remember the script correctly, to say . . . Jill, dear, you've made me the happiest man in the world. Not always the first term I would apply to myself. Man, I mean. I shall have to grow up, I suppose, now. No more Peter Pan pills for Master Denis. Hey-ho! And on we go, my love!' He kissed her hand and then his own and pressed it to her belly. 'And you, in there! Who'd ever have thought it?'

'I'm going to the Beeb,' she said. 'Imagine playing Hedda with a bump! The kind they can't hear on the radio.'

'I shall repair to my lonely cell and use my imagination on the accounts for the last month. *Honi soit qui* mauls your pence, as the bishop always used to say before they caught him at it.'

'We shall have to think seriously about names.'

'Not Leslie and not Robin,' Denis said, 'are high on my list. I want us to raise a straight homophobe with a brutal way with women. That way I shall know neither of us has laboured in vain. Don't mean a word of it, dear, do I? Or do I?'

Denis walked back to Greek Street. It was the fallow part of the afternoon when the boys had cleared up and gone to play football in the park or whatever they did before reporting back for their supper. After a flick through *Gay Times*, Denis worked at the accounts. He hoped, and feared, that Giancarlo was having a good time somewhere. Towards six o'clock, he recognised the footsteps and the usual knock.

'So,' Giancarlo said.

'Come in,' Denis said. 'As if you hadn't.'

'You don't tell me things any more.'

'Gianni, I don't ask you for a full account of where you go or who you do and that's the way it's always been. What have I not told you that creases that pure Cararran brow?'

'The new house.'

'I might have guessed. Who told you about it? My money's on Patrick. Not to say Patreek, because there's absolutely no need, is there?'

'How did you know that?'

'I swore him to silence, so he's the obvious suspect. Not that he hasn't got marvellous plans for the interior.'

'I'm sure you all do. Perhaps it's time I had some of my own.'

'It was meant to be a surprise. For you. The house. It's going to look very like a warm-hearted version of Ham Spray house. Less ham, more spray.'

'I don't know what you're talking about.'

'Wasted on the desert air, that's me all over, partly. Oh come on, Gianni.'

'Imagine if I told people.'

'Please don't pout. Or else shave first. A hirsute pout is a little bit *excessif.*'

'If I told them how you managed to get it up.'

'Cheap isn't you, Gianni. And that is. There's going to be tons of room for all of us, as Patreek should have told you when he sprung his leak. Did he tell you you were going to have the closet of your dream, with garden access? You are.'

'I knew this would happen.'

'Gianni, you're the chef in London it takes longest to get a table to be fed by. I love you. Jill loves you, for reasons which it would be very . . . *low* to go into in detail. And yet you stand there like a sorry little *ragazzo* whose mother doesn't love him. When he also knows very well she does.'

'When it's born, you won't have any more time for anything.'

'Darling sweetheart, listen to mother . . .'

'I know you too well.'

'Your privilege. It's done now, dear, no putting the stuff back in the tube.'

'That I was foolish enough to squeeze.'

'*Help squeeze*. Be honest, if you must. Consider the veil drawn. Pray do not rend it from end to end.'

'I know when people have had enough of me.'

'Can we shorten the pastry slightly, do you think? Because I was actually about to offer – no, offer sounds too . . . seigneurial – about to *propose*, on bended knee, if need be, that you become joint managing director of Two by Two, with appropriate perks tailored to your own personal measurements, which I know from deliciously cruel experience to be considerable.'

'She doesn't want me around.'

'Still less does she want you a square. Gianni, for God's sake, ducky. Jill dotes on you, is the truth. *And* your *ris de veau*. Allow me to forbid you, gently but firmly, to hurt her feelings or mine by playing the part of jealous Jimmy. I don't want him in the cast. However I do warn you: I just may draw the line if you insist on us taking you for walks in the pushchair, but otherwise Liberty Hall is all yours just as much as it's ours.'

'You've changed.'

'Socks and undies. Time I did. High time. I'm getting Bernie the Bolt to draw up sheets and sheets of boring contractual papers. Solicitors are *such* fun people. But anything to help you sleep, sweetheart, that's always been my rule.'

Giancarlo said, 'Meaning what? Joint?'

'Fifty-one me, forty-nine you. Per cent. I have to think of the family. If that isn't true love, I don't know what is. Now give me a kiss, for Christ's sake. I've got books to fiddle before the quality arrives. All better now?'

'I can always get a house of my own.'

'Why not? Whenever you want to. Meanwhile, back to the kitchen, Gianni, might I suggest? *Prestissimo*. Where you belong.'

'We did a hundred and fifteen covers at lunch, while you were at the hospital. So if you've ever had enough of me . . .'

'I shall have had enough of life. I shan't. Ever. And now do shut up about it. Is that the shadow of a smile?'

124

'I'll go piss in the stockpot,' Giancarlo said.

'Probably just what it needs. How *does* she do it? Face it, the secrets of the bedroom are *nothing* compared with the secrets of the kitchen. *Ti amo, caro* and for Christ's sake don't forget it.'

Giancarlo closed the door and looked at himself in the big mirror behind the bar.

'Hullo, Gianni!' Jill said, putting her script and bag on one of the low glass tables. 'Everything all right?'

'That's what he tells me. But he tells me many things.'

'He'd do anything for you and you know it.'

'And you? And what will you do?'

'Have some orange juice. Talk, talk, talk, that's Ibsen. She's not called gabbler for nothing.'

'I like women too, you know. You do know, don't you? You and I, we are both artists, am I right?'

'Kisses'll have to do you, darling, until I shed the dome, but you're welcome to those.'

vii

Derek Morris was a member of Stags, a Mayfair club that combined expensive exclusivity with lack of snobbery. Having been both Captain of Fencing and a First in Economics at Cambridge, he now preferred the company of gamblers, property developers and stock-exchange speculators. He had explained to Adam, when he offered to put him up for his own somewhat bohemian club, that Stags had better appurtenances than a gentleman's club, in terms of service, swimming pool, good food and a central location, without the presence of gentlemen, whose bookishness did not interest him and whose horses, even if they owned them, rarely won races. Stags had contacts, whether financial or social, of a kind that might be useful.

Adam followed a club servant into the back drawing room where, even on a fine day, a coal fire burned in the small grate. Derek, in a dark grey suit, striped double-cuffed shirt, and off-white tie, was reading the *Wall Street Journal*. Adam had chosen one of his suede jackets and American trousers. He had put a college tie in his pocket, in case it was obligatory. It was not.

'Your guest, Mr Morris.'

'Sorry, Der,' Adam said. 'I was finishing a sentence. In a traffic jam. With the wind against me.'

'Do you want a glass of champagne? I seem to have this bottle here.'

'Exactly what I came for. How are you? How's Carol?'

'She's fine. Everything's fine. Nobody wants pounds, but there are plenty of dollars. How are you?'

'What's the problem then? Mike tells me there seems to be one.'

'OK. There isn't unless there is. Things are moving a lot in the communications field they tell me. A gamble's a gamble and I don't mind that, as long as I win, but . . . Ad, do you really want to be a television executive? Cheers.'

'It might be amusing. Jeers, as Alan Parks used to say.'

'And it might well not. I thought you wanted to be a writer.'

'Every writer, alone on the heaving waters riding his skimpy talents, fears the day he will be dismasted, and dreams of a safe harbour lined with cashable cash.'

'Are you going to go to an office and sit in on board meetings and listen to accountants on the weekend? You think you're not, but you will, when you least want it.'

'Enough of this foreplay, Der. Because is this all about there being a problem raising the funds? Not skint, are you?'

'In good Queen Maggie's golden reign? It wouldn't be my money anyway. No more of it than's courteous. You know me: Mr Punctilio. No, it's more that I was having a word with Monty Waring, if you know him.'

'Of course I don't. I don't even know the deputy literary editor of the *Observer*. How come you get to know people in the cabinet? You must've been at Cambridge with the right people. I wish I had.'

'Nothing to do with Cambridge. Monty and I were fishing on the same stretch of water last weekend.'

126

'One of your tiddlers, was he?'

'We were both staying with Konni Georgiadis. Which isn't really the point.'

'But you stuck it in all the same,' Adam said. 'Up to his navel in the Greek Colonels, wasn't he, friend Konni, a few years back? Papadop and Co.?'

'He'd love to meet you actually. Big, big fan.'

'He sells aeroplanes to the Arabs. And rockets. He'd sell them the H-bomb if he had it in stock.'

'Be fair, Ad. He'd sell it to anyone. Konni's all right.'

'Do you mean it when you say things like that?'

'Is that your high horse waiting at the gate? Naying as usual. One hand washes the other. Greek meets Greek and so it goes. Shall we go and have some lunch? Do you know how many Arabs are investing in Israel's Silicon Valley? Don't ask. You always want to take a moral view of the world, but the world doesn't work that way.'

'I'll make a note,' Adam said.

The panelled inner dining room was green-carpeted and had tall windows overlooking a churchyard. A many-branched silver chandelier overhung the centre table; on the sideboard, Georgian candlesticks flanked crystal liqueur decanters with chained labels round their necks. A waiter was serving roast beef from a trolley with a domed silver lid which had been rolled back. The carver's annexed wooden panel already had some silver in it.

'You can't give carvers banknotes,' Derek said. 'It wouldn't be kosher.'

'Of all the traditions the English favour,' Adam said, 'the tradition of the bogus is the one they like best. And now back to the river bank with Mole and Toady, alias Monty Waring, who just happened to tell you what?'

'We happened to get talking about the upcoming TV franchises and what the chances were of who got what. I never mentioned you were involved, or that I was . . .'

'One of those topics that comes up when the salmon won't.'

127

'Not the salmon season,' Derek said. 'I was explaining how I thought that some of the franchises looked like changing hands and I asked him, in a causal way, to give me an overview on it all.'

'That takes some casual doing, doesn't it? The beef looks excellent. Do me.'

'Oysters to start?'

'If you insist,' Adam said. 'Six Colchesters sounds ample.'

'Same for me,' Derek said to the waiter. 'When we were back indoors, he took me into the library.'

'Really? And what do international crooks have in their libraries these days? The codex Sinaiticus? In mint condition?'

'Do you want to hear this or don't you? Monty's very discreet. He simply took a sheet of writing paper and he wrote some things down on it and then he put it in an envelope and sealed it, with sealing wax —'

'Discretion itself, Monty Waring. Was he wearing rubber gloves, did you notice? Trust a sweet old-fashioned thing like Konni Georgiadis to have sealing wax on the desk. Next to the land-mine brochure, no doubt.'

'— and then he dated it and handed it to me. He made me promise not to open it until after the new set of franchises were announced.'

'But he also bet you that what was inside was exactly what the independent commission — over which he doesn't, of course, have any control whatever — would decide, come the revolution.'

'He did actually. A grand.'

'And winked at you with his glass eye. Like you or not, in other words, he was warning you off, is that the large family size of it?'

'Extra large, I would say, old son, old sport.'

'I don't presume to know much about business. You think we ought to back off?'

'Question being, are we taking part — what could turn out to be a rather expensive part — in a game of charades?'

128

'Well, it is the national game, so someone once said.'

'I thought you should know the sitch. Up to you how seriously you take it.'

'Only one thing's really serious at the moment, Der, and it's the one thing I can't do anything about. How are your kids?'

'Tanya wants to be a writer. I'm having her certified. Linda is . . . *muy Linda*. Which is a start. Carol's gone to Forest Mere to have her bum reduced. I'm on the lam, when I'm not on the beef. You haven't heard from Tom, I gather.'

Adam said, 'Barbara may have. I haven't.'

'Want Tabasco?'

'Lemon's fine.'

'He's making you sweat.'

'In the name of the Father and of the Son . . .'

'He's probably sweating himself somewhere. Wondering how he can ever get in touch again without crawling.'

'It could be a double bluff,' Adam said, 'couldn't it? What Monty Waring did.'

'Possible. But then you have to ask yourself —'

'Why would he bother to — ?'

'Exactly.'

'It's the crappiest independent channel there is at the moment. Orwell. They do *such* b. awful programmes —'

'As Dad would have said in a less outspoken era. I never see it. I rarely look at TV. Carol watches all the soaps. She says they're a lot more real than life. Her life, I suppose she means. I never know what to do about women. Money's much easier to handle.'

'How rich are you these days?' Adam said.

'Rich enough to worry about where to put it. How about you?'

'I sometimes wish I could buy a cottage somewhere in France or Spain or Italy, and have just enough left over to pay for the basics and only write what really needed saying.'

'Successful as that, are you? Impressive.'

129

'Are you and Carol all right, Der?'
'All right? Of course. Why?'

viii

Apart from casual appearances elsewhere, and her journalism, and the new novel she had promised Jason Singer, after the success of *The Sixth Floor*, Joyce Hadleigh was now hosting a brace of programmes (one on One, the other on Two) on current and social affairs. Her daughters Hannah and Carol were at Bedales, but her son Peter, who was twenty-three, and a sound man with ITV news, lived in two rooms of her flat in Albert Mansions. He travelled a lot. When Dan called and asked if he could come and see her, she said yes, of course, and then wondered what she should wear. She decided on jeans and a blue shirt and a silk Versace waistcoat with a dangly belt thing at the back. While she waited for him, she looked at the sitting room with Dan's eyes. Its two chintzy chesterfields and its Regency coffee table, the soft carpet, the Paul Klee lithographs and the Matthew Smith over the fireplace were suddenly harsh evidence against her, though she was not sure of the offence. When the entry phone buzzed, she tried to remember exactly what he looked like. He might as well have been a stranger, and was more interesting for that. He looked at her, but didn't touch her.

'Come in.'

'This is very nice. The flat. Very commodious.'

'How are you, Dan?'

'I am . . . as you see. And hear, no doubt.'

'Of course. It's ridiculous, all this. You want me to give evidence for you, is that . . . ?'

'Walter Burleigh thinks it might . . . help. Everyone all right?'

'Of course I will. All right? I think so.'

'You're very kind. Offering.'

'Meaning I'm not the total bitch you expected me to be.'

130

'I expected nothing. Coming up in the lift, I was mostly trying to remember what you looked like.'

'Don't you watch the box at all?'

'Not a lot, and anyway that's not what you look like. I didn't recognise the woman on *The Spanish Prisoner* as you, even though she was wearing your name.'

'I wish they hadn't called it that, but it seems to have caught on.'

'All that matters presumably.'

'You haven't changed, have you?'

'That's not what I came about.'

'Which was?'

'I thought you ought to know something. I've taken early retirement. Whatever happens, I've served long enough to have my pension. They can't take that away from me, even if they put me in clink, I don't think.'

'Nothing like that's going to happen.'

'No? I propose in any event –'

'Dan, don't "any event" me. Please. We were married, remember?'

'Hear me out, Joyce. I propose to make over two-thirds of it to you, for the children –'

'We don't need your money. Look around. I certainly don't need it and even more certainly don't want it.'

'I want the children to know that I –'

'That you're a saint. And can sleep like a top on a bed of nails. They do. Do you want a drink at all? I do.'

'I also took out some life insurance in their names, some time ago, so it's now . . . irrevocable –'

'Daniel, what the hell are you up to?'

'Up to? Nothing very much just at the moment.'

'Where are you living?'

'I've got a room. There's nothing to worry about. I just wanted to tell you that I fully appreciate –'

'Jesus Christ, will you shut up? Will you shut up?'

'You're tired.'

'Exhausted. The minute I see you.'

'Don't worry, I'm going now.'

'Just don't tell me that you expect to be gone for some time. You are *not* Captain Oates. You're *not*. Think of the girls, Daniel. Think of Peter. And stop thinking about me, and how you can hurt me.'

'Never entered my mind.'

'When did you last fuck anyone?'

'I'm not here to talk about that.'

'Do you want to fuck me? I don't mind. I think I'd like you to. I've got better at it. I would like you to. As long as you're not nice to me.'

'You're trying to embarrass me. You don't. I think it's rather . . . gallant of you.'

'Then hit me or something if you want to, but don't . . . please, do anything . . . to yourself. Daniel.'

'I have to try and keep sane,' he said. 'Is all I'm trying to do.'

'You won't be doing it to me. You'll be doing it to them. Your children. I'll give any evidence you like and you'll be acquitted and *then* you can hate me again, if you have to.'

'I like the painting,' Dan said.

'Matthew Smith.'

'Very colourful. I meant that one.'

'That's one that Hannah did.'

'And that's the one I like. Very much.'

'You wouldn't even kiss me, would you?'

'I'll kiss you,' he said. 'Gladly.'

There was a rap on the front door.

'How did whoever it is get in without buzzing?' Joyce said.

'I'll be going,' Dan said.

Joyce clicked her tongue and went and opened the front door. Mike Clode, clean-shaven now, was standing there in a grey woollen raglan coat. 'Bad moment? I was in the area . . .'

'Dan's here,' Joyce said. 'Do you want to funk it or are you coming in?'

'Daniel!' Mike said, in a big voice, arms out, coat open to

132

reveal black trousers, grey shirt and a maroon velvet jacket.

'Hullo, Mike.'

'Christ, I'm glad to see you, old son. Completely unchanged. Isn't he? We're all behind you, you know that, don't you?'

Dan looked at his watch. 'Is that the time? I must fly.'

'You and Peter Pan,' Mike said. 'He could still be an actor, Joyce, you know. How long's it been? You know what, don't you, looking at you?'

'I have a great future behind me, isn't that what they say?'

'I never heard them,' Mike said. 'You know what you *could* do, and that's head up our educational department, and front a proggy or three. That you really could do. Has Joyce filled you in about this Orwell television bid I've roped her into? We're pretty well a shoo-in.'

'I'm the last person you need. Thank you, Joyce, for . . . what you said you'd do. Goodbye, Michael.'

When Joyce came back from seeing Dan to the door, Mike was sitting across two of the three places on the sofa looking at the Matthew Smith. 'What you get for loving people,' he said. 'Amazing, isn't it?'

'What can I do for you, Mike?'

'Good point. May as well get to it. Alan. As in Parks. Reckon he'd climb on our bandwagon if wheeled in his direction?'

'I could ask him.'

'Next time you're horizontal together.'

'We don't actually do a lot of that any more.'

'Got a new woman, has he?'

'He's got an old wife. I.e. our age. How about I've got a new man?'

'You could always call him up, though, couldn't you? Alan. He's never been a mate of mine, but . . . he does have the right kind of voice to cry in the wilderness. I want this bid of ours to be . . . irresistible. In spite of anything that Adam Morris may do to make their nibs suspect us of being closet highbrows. I love *The Spanish Prisoner*, by the way. Very good title. I'll bet it's yours, am I right?'

'I heard loud whispers that you were being wooed by a Hollywood studio.'

'No truer than what I hear about you being up to your delicious gills with a certain famous agent gentleman. Couldn't be Jason Singer, could it?'

'You're a bad, bad man, Mike Clode.'

'And you're not an altogether nice woman. Shall we dance?'

'Mike, I'm seriously afraid Dan might go and kill himself.'

'He won't. He wanted you to think so.'

'He didn't care what I thought.'

'Probably hoped you'd fuck him.'

'I offered. He didn't.'

'What an ass. How much did you pay for the Matthew Smith, if you don't mind me asking?'

When Dan's case finally came to court, that autumn, the judge instructed the jury, almost at once, that the evidence against him was entirely circumstantial and almost certainly spurious. He was surprised that the case had ever been brought. Mike Clode arranged a party to celebrate Dan's acquittal, but Dan did not attend it. He left England the next morning and went to live in Brescia, where he became apprenticed to a shoemaker.

ix

A year later, after the Independent Television Authority had allotted the new franchises, Derek Morris was invited to lunch with the Right Honourable Monty Waring at White's. The minister suggested that Derek bring his brother, whose work he very much admired, especially that early novel; what was it called again? Adam put on his new suit and, after thought, decided against his college tie. Barbara advised a silver and black one that didn't look Ferragamo, but was.

'Set in South America,' Waring said. 'Which one would that be?'

'*The Disappearance*, probably.'

134

'Was precisely what it was. With the delicious dictator's daughter.'

'The dictator's delicious daughter might be less –'

'Grammatically cack-handed. Absolutely right. I thought we'd have some champagne, Derek, if that doesn't conflict with your religion. I remember that scene where – what was his name?'

'Bruce?'

' – realises that the place she wants him to do some mountaineering is the same room where her father's people do things to their prisoners. You don't say what, or what she wants him to do to her, but it's one of the most erotic things I ever read. Just the way she takes her shoes off, "knee to chin". No knicks, we realise somehow. Why is that?'

'Because I got your imagination to supply the details.'

'Trick of the trade? Interesting. Look, I quite recognise that you don't have all that much to celebrate at the moment, but I still don't see why we shouldn't celebrate it. How do you people feel about how the franchise business went?'

'You can probably guess, can't you?'

'On a good day, I probably can. Disappointed, I've no doubt. What does "gutted" mean that they all say all the time, these footballers and people?'

'Pissed off,' Adam said, 'doesn't it?'

'Must do.'

Derek said, 'Our friends took a lot of time and trouble over the bid.'

'And all the signs were that it was in the bag,' Adam said.

'So was the cat when they slung it in the river.'

'Shall I pour the champagne, Mr Waring?'

'We shan't find it unduly easy to drink otherwise, Morgan, shall we? Are you writing a new novel, I hope?'

'Since I'm not going to be a television tycoon, I shall have to, I suppose.'

'No cause for lamentation there, then. Not for your admirers, at least. You'll grant me that much, Derek, I take it.'

Derek said, 'Are we allowed to say cheers in here?'

'Nothing in the rule book against it, I don't think.'

'Cheers then,' Derek said. 'Notwithstanding which –'

'I'm not so sure about words like "notwithstanding".'

'Without wishing to sour the occasion,' Derek said, 'there is one thing that really needs to be mentioned.'

'Which is what?'

'Timothy Gallon,' Adam said.

'Clever chap. What about him?'

'The way he behaved.'

'Behaved? Over what?'

'He was vice-chairman on the franchise panel.'

'So he was. Never liked him. Jeremy thing got him on it. To balance that bloody awful Lady Pink-at-the-Edges person, with the dangling spectacles.'

'*Over*balance her, is more like it,' Derek said. 'He asked most of the questions. Very hostile and very sarcastic, hinting – and eventually more than hinting – *jeering* that we'd hugely underestimated the capital we were going to need to operate as we said we would –'

'Budgets, I find, have extraordinarily little to do with the number you first thought of.'

'We more than matched the incumbents.'

'And you went in to bat accordingly, presumably?'

'I didn't get much of the bowling,' Derek said. 'Gallon waved me aside and concentrated on biffing Mike Clode, our chairman to be, that eventually wasn't.'

'Mike got surprisingly rattled,' Adam said. 'Talked too much and not too well.'

'And finally rather fell over his own notes,' Derek said.

'Hadn't read his Clausewitz then,' Monty Waring said. 'Being well prepared isn't always the best plan. Frightful lottery these hearings, at the best of times.'

'I'm never too sure which those are,' Derek said. 'I brought your envelope with me.'

'Did you so? I'd quite forgotten about it. Your brother and I had a little bet. Who was going to get which franchises. Or not get them. If memory serves, Derek, you owe me a thou if my predictions were right.'

'Should cover lunch,' Adam said.

'Before I open it though,' Derek said, 'there's something I wanted to . . . mention.'

'Speak, Lord, for thy servant heareth.'

'As a member of the commission, Timothy Gallon is supposed not to have a stake in any of the companies in line for franchises, isn't he?'

'Goes without saying.'

'So why is it being said, do you suppose?'

'Do I detect a touch of asperity in your normally amiable tones, Derek? Time we had some lunch possibly.'

'I don't like being cheated all that much. Want of breeding I expect.'

'Cheated? By whom exactly? Careful how you answer, I should.'

'Here's what I've discovered since our syndicate lost the bid. Against all reason, and accountancy –'

'Assuming the two to be compatible.' Monty Waring seemed to assume some exclusive understanding with Adam.

Derek said, 'Gallon happens to be vice-chairman of Beefeater Holdings –'

'Common knowledge.' Monty Waring continued to look only at Adam, with a combination of complicity and disdain.

Derek sipped his champagne and showed no sign of feeling the frost. 'How about the fact that Beefeater Holdings has a pension fund which owns a hundred and fifty thousand shares in the current set-up of Orwell television? Which had its mandate renewed by the commission. How commonly is that known?'

'What's your point?'

'Since you're looking at me,' Adam said, 'my limited understanding is that Gallon's company stood to lose a lot of money, if we'd got the franchise. Shares in the old Orwell

137

would've gone down like a lift, wouldn't they? Instead of which they rocketed.'

'The Beefeater pension fund's a completely separate thing. Hence Beefeater itself had no direct interest in it whatsoever. Which is all that Master Gallon's involved in, that I know of.'

'You're joking,' Derek said.

'Am I? When I joke, I laugh, loudly. Often I'm the only one to do so. I'm not joking at all.'

'How about Beefeater's *indirect* interest?' Adam said.

'You're the lawyer,' Monty Waring said.

'I'm no sort of lawyer at all,' Adam said.

'Oh.'

'Come on, Monty,' Derek said. 'The pension fund actually belongs to Beefeater Holdings. Who are legally entitled to use it as collateral, whenever they see fit. No one has to be a lawyer to know that. So in effect –'

'Forgive me, but this isn't Lyons Corner House. The club doesn't go bull on people talking business in here. Especially when other people can hear.'

Derek said, 'What would you say if I told you that our syndicate is considering suing the commission? And the government, if need be.'

'I'd say, and it's all I'm going to say, that in that very hypothetical case, you would be wise to think twice, and if that doesn't do the trick, think yet again. When're you proposing to open this envelope of ours? Which I assumed to be the object of the exercise.'

'Gallon should never have been on the commission,' Adam said.

'Couldn't agree with you more. Possibly. If it's any comfort to you, he soon won't be. Bad man rather.'

'It's no comfort at all, Monty,' Derek said.

'Drop it, Derek, is my firm, friendly advice. Madame will take a dim view if it comes to her ears. So indeed might I. Persist and it'll only make you look like troublemakers. You can't imagine what long memories people can have for bad losers. Smile through your tears and all sorts of nice things might happen. Forgive me, but I'm now rather pressingly eager that we not lose our table in the luncheon room. The ravens do gather rather.'

In the smoking room after lunch, Derek broke the seal on the envelope. He had little doubt that Monty Waring's predictions of which of the various syndicates would win, or retain, the ITV franchises would be correct in every case, and so they were. Derek wrote Monty a cheque for one thousand pounds only and he and Adam walked out into wet St James's.

'Fuck him,' Adam said. 'Perfect example of see-you-next-Tuesday as father would have said. I was ashamed to eat his beastly lunch.'

'I thought it was all right, for that kind of place.'

'Burnt the *croûte* and undercooked the salmon, as Tamara Singer wouldn't fail to note, unless suitably buttered on both sides. We ought to bloody well sue their socks off. All of them.'

'Their socks don't come off, Adam.'

'You're not bothered, really, are you?'

'Not a lot. It wasn't much money and it can all be written off. And I'm certainly not bothered for your sake. You don't want to be a bloody television executive.'

'I wouldn't mind being rich though.'

'Really? I don't think there's anything you wouldn't manage to mind just a bit.'

'Bloody man all the same,' Adam said.

'Ah, here's Alfredo.'

'Why didn't he park outside the club when it's raining?'

'I don't like to give those people the satisfaction. You know what they say about Jaguars.'

'Nothing to what Jaguars say about them.'

'Is what they're afraid of,' Derek said. 'Anywhere I can drop you?'

'I'm in it already,' Adam said.

'No, you're not. And you know you're not. Business is a nasty business, and politics is nastier. If you didn't know before, you know now. High time too.'

139

Alfredo was standing with an umbrella over them. Adam said, 'You patronising little . . . Cambridge man, aren't you? What're you worth these days?'

'You know what they say in the club they'll never let us into. Rude to count.'

'They do it, all the bloody time.'

'Everybody bloody does it, Ad. Everybody. Except you.'

'Story of my life!' Adam said, and closed the door on his brother, who was already answering the telephone in the beige interior, but did wave as Alfredo drove away.

In the *Evening Standard* which he bought under the arches at the Ritz, Adam saw that Mike Clode had announced that he was so disgusted with the limited opportunities in the British movie and television industry that he was accepting a totally unexpected offer to become CEO of Transworld Pictures in Los Angeles.

Adam walked in the rain back to Fulham. He arrived with very wet shoulders and turn-ups. There were no messages worth bothering about, but while he was in the bath, Barbara showed him an advertisement she had circled in the *Spectator*: a large cottage for sale on the boundary of the Dordogne and the Lot, in three hectares of hilltop land. It had white shutters and 'huge possibilities'.

Adam said, 'Meaning it needs a fortune spent on it.'

The cottage was called *Écoute s'il Pleut*. It had woodworm and no telephone. They stayed at a little hotel in the village while Adam found an architect and a builder in Caillac. Three months later, although not as much had been done as promised, the woodworm had been purged and the roof retiled with *tuiles de récupération*, which restored the antique rusticity of the place. While Barbara dug heaps of weeds out of the overgrown garden, Adam restarted work on the novel he had abandoned six months earlier.

IV

In October 1986, Barbara and Adam saw on the BBC2 news that the Reverend Miguel Sung, founder of the Redemption Church of the Lord Jesus, the Sun and the Moon, had been sentenced, in Atlanta, Georgia, to four life terms for offences including the repeated rape of under-age girls, torture, fraud, tax evasion and drunk driving. Adam and Barbara listened to the news together, but without any common reaction. They glanced at each other, furtive with thoughts each had kept hidden from the other. Tom's long absence had held them together; it had also kept them apart, though each liked to think that the other did not realise it.

'We don't even know if he still has anything to do with those people, do we?'

'True,' Barbara said.

'He could be anywhere, doing anything.'

'Still . . .'

'Still, I don't argue with,' Adam said.

'I almost wish we'd never seen the bloody news.'

'We'd've found out sooner or later.'

'If it makes you so . . .'

'So what?' Adam said. 'Is what it makes me. So fucking what, about almost everything else that happens. What does it make you?'

'Sorry. For you.'

'Meaning you don't worry about what's happened to Tom?'

'That's something else,' Barbara said. 'And I think you know it.'

'I do, I do. Shall I say I'm sorry? I'm sorry. It's opened the wound is all it's done, isn't it? Has for me. But then my stitches come out very easily. You're looking very – what? – *cold*, can it be?'

'You want all the guilt for yourself, don't you?'

'Vanity of vanities,' Adam said, 'and fuck the preacher, it says in my text. What worries me is . . . not worth talking about, is it?'

'Rachel,' she said. 'Anything happening to her.'

'Is probably right,' Adam said. 'As of now. And how.'

'Because she's doing all the things you want her to do: being brilliant at your old college, reading Classics . . .'

'And she's very nearly as beautiful as you are.'

'Oh stop it, Adam,' Barbara said.

'I stop, you stop,' he said. 'I just hope that Tom hasn't thrown his life away for someone anyone could see was a charlatan from way back. Think we'd recognise him if we saw him?'

'I don't know. Answer the phone. Please. Answer the bloody thing.'

'Hullo?'

'Is this Adam Morris?'

'It could be,' Adam said. 'It rather depends who is this.' He watched Barbara as she squatted in front of the television and lowered the volume.

'OK. My name is Hannah Waxman. I work with Mike Clode over at Transworld.'

Adam covered the receiver. 'It's California.'

'Should I leave the room, do you mean?'

'Just bow your head'll do.' Adam took the telephone to the bay window. 'What can I do for you, Hannah, or – if my guess is correct – what can we both do for him?'

'Mike would like to talk with you in approximately thirty-five minutes from now. Is that a practical possibility?'

'Should be. If he has the strength to pick up the phone. Or does he have people to do that for him?'

'Very good to have this opportunity to talk to you. I'm only a huge, huge admirer. I loved *The Woman in Question*.'

'Yes?' Adam said. 'Ancient history's my favourite subject too.

142

If only we'd had a good director on that movie. I was definitely kidding, be sure to tell him.'

Adam walked over and stood next to Barbara. 'Sometimes I still feel like the idiot teenager who wonders why the pretty girl won't look at him. Should I?'

'I was just listening to something.'

'Other news now,' the announcer was saying. 'We're getting reports of an incident in Southern Lebanon in which an ITV camera crew have been involved in what may have been an accident or possibly a roadside bomb explosion. ITV reporter Vince Cregan is said to be safe, but a sound man is reported to have received serious injuries.'

'Don't get your hopes up,' Barbara said. 'About Tom. I'm not going to. I daren't. I wish they'd never mentioned that man.'

'I know. I do know. Do you want the box on any more?'

'You turned it on.'

'Then *con permesso* I'll turn it off. Truth to tell, if only by way of in-fill, I didn't expect ever to hear from Master Clode again, once he was translated to mega-tycoonery.'

'But you did hope,' she said.

'Strange how those girls all now make simple statements sound as if they were questions. As in, "My name is Hannah Waxman?" Who ever said it wasn't? I don't think I hoped exactly. But then again —'

'And not for the first time.'

'— in yet another low mean decade in which money is the only thing that talks . . . if we're going to do out the basement — the garden floor, as Roy Brooks would have said, in his prime — to give Rachel a flat worthy of an imminent PhD, I do wonder what cheap and nasty project Mike has in mind. Assuming he ever calls back.'

'Why else would he bother to get — Hannah, was that her name? — to phone you?'

'Because he's an archetypal Norwich man.'

'I thought he always boasted he came from Hemel Hempstead.'

143

'As if he were the only person who ever did. "Norwich" is what squaddies used to put at the bottom of their letters when writing home to their wives, on lined paper of course, during the war. Recent research reveals that it was an acronym for "Knickers Off Ready When I Come Home". Mike likes to check availabilities. Did you really not know, what Norwich meant?'

'I stop at St Alban's,' she said.

'St Alban's, really, do you? What does that stand for?'

'Try "bugger off"!'

'I might've guessed.' The telephone was ringing again. 'It's got something to do with the Quantum Theory, doesn't it? Why the phone sometimes never rings and other nights it rings again and again.'

'Seems Mike's even hotter to trotter than you hoped, or feared, or both. And if you think I'm going to pick it up, think again.'

'Hullo.'

'Is that Adam Morris?'

'You've changed accents! Clever girl. Can you do South African?'

'Sorry? I was hoping to speak to Adam Morris, if he's there.'

'He is, and he's sorry too, and who is this?'

'My name is Fiona Maclean. I'm the producer on *That's Asking*. Alan Parks's programme.'

'Of course. I'm very sorry, I was expecting – it doesn't matter. Fiona Maclean, of course. As in "the legendary".'

'I don't know if you ever watch the programme.'

Adam sat down with his legs over the arm of the chesterfield. 'Last time we did was when Alan referred to the miners' strike as "possibly the last time that brave, misguided men will go into battle for the right to cough their blackened lungs up by the time they're fifty" and Arthur thing said that Alan was a disgrace to the regiment and should be shipped home to Botany Bay as soon as transport could be arranged.'

'That was last week he said that.'

144

'Then it was last week we watched it.' Adam was watching Barbara as she picked up her book and glasses. 'Time flies, subject of course to delays due to the late arrival of the incoming aircraft.'

'You do have to entertain the girls,' Barbara said. 'I'm going to go and finish reading Proust in the kitchen while I wash up.'

Adam covered the receiver. 'Why do we have a washing-up machine? I'll be right there.'

'Alan was wondering if you'd care to be on the panel on the twenty-second. Only it's going to be in Cambridge.'

'I think that'd be . . . that'd be fine.' Adam noticed, as if he were his own policeman, that his voice changed tone when Barbara left the room. 'Cambridge is a very nice spot, I hear.'

'I know he'll be pleased. He's always saying we should get you on. Do you know Gavin Pope?'

'I know *of* Gavin Pope, and the Thatcherite noises he's taken to making. With deep self-loathing, I sometimes find myself furtively agreeing with the tart-tongued truant.'

'Only Gavin's going to be on the panel and we're hoping to get Susie Beaumont, if you know her.'

'Susie Beaumont? Everybody does. The women's woman, the men's . . . I could try bane, unless you prefer scourge.'

'Plus A.N. Other.'

'Always assuming you can get him. Or her. He said, watching his genders for fear of the feminist thought police.'

'I'll send you a contract. And we'll be in touch nearer the time, if you want to have a car to take you up to Cambridge or anything like that.'

'Thank you, Fiona. Look forward to it. My best to Alan.'

He sat there, vacantly pleased, and then he sighed at the sound of activity in the kitchen.

'Very noisy pages, he's got, in your edition, *le petit* Marcel. Let me do that.'

'It's done.'

'Master Parks want me to be on *That's Asking*.'

'I gathered. Apotheosis.'

'Not to say Apocolocyntosis, which you never would.'

'But Rachel might.'

'I could always call her. You said they ought to get me on it. I didn't realise how much influence you had.'

'When is this?'

'The twenty-second.'

'I thought we were going to France. For you to finish the novel.'

'We didn't book anything. My big chance to be *aere perennius* for five minutes. More enduring than bronze . . . It's what Horace said, in *tota modestia*, about his own poems.'

'He explained to those at the back of the class.'

'Kiss me, before you forget how. Do you despise me?'

'For quoting Horace at me? Yes.'

'For never saying no to people. I only need a month to finish *Life and Loves*. Less possibly, with no telephone. Do you think it's slightly dated, as a title?'

'Possibly.'

'Jason thinks it's fine.'

'Then don't ask me. Ask Jason again.'

'And yet I love you. OK, I'll try and think of something better. How good a title is *Middlemarch*?'

'It's been used.'

'My point being . . . OK. Look, if you don't want me to do *That's Asking*, I won't.'

'And have you languish for ever in the shade? And know it's all my fault . . . ? If it's what you want to do, do it. Only don't tell me afterwards what a total bore it was and you wish you'd never done it and you only ever do those things because I like people to come up to you in airports and tell you how much they disagree with everything you say.'

'Why do you always have to tidy things up within an inch of their bloody lives? And please don't tell me it beats listening to me talking on the telephone. Because it can't. Leave Maria to do those things in the morning. That's what she's overpaid for.'

'I remember when you thought having domestic help was

taking advantage of the working class. Now it's helping to beat unemployment.'

'We were all Socialists once. And that was quite enough. If you really want to go to France before the twenty-second, I can always remember how much I hate Susie Beaumont and bow tactfully out, probably doing my back in the process.'

'Oh Adam, really, what does it matter? If you want to be – what was it – *I.R.A. perennius* – why shouldn't you? As if any of it really mattered. It's not *my* book.'

'True. And bless you, for not being an angel. Do you think about him as much as I do?'

'But I don't blame myself as much as you do.'

'Guilt's a form of anger really, isn't it?'

'And greed. You want everything to be your fault.'

'Nothing to be done, is there?'

'Then that's what we'll do.'

'Your nothing and my nothing, they're not the same nothing, are they?'

'As long as he's alive,' Barbara said.

'The bastard's not going to call, you know, after all that. Mike, I mean, is he? What did I tell you?' The phone rang. 'It had to do that, didn't it? Or what's a Quantum Theory for? Be quite fun not to be here, wouldn't it, for him, now?'

Barbara walked over to the wall phone. 'Hullo. Yes, it is. Yes, he is. Just a second. Or less.'

Adam said, 'Hi!'

'Adam? It's Alan. Parks.'

'Alan! In that case, hullo. I just talked to Fiona Maclean, about doing the programme. Be great fun, especially in Cambridge. Susie Beaumont's such an old friend of mine. It says here.'

'Good, good. Only I'm not calling about that.'

'Oh, well, anyway, what else can I . . . sound excited about?'

'Have you heard the news this evening possibly?'

'Hard to hear anything else. Wall to wall these days. What particularly?'

'About what happened.'

'I'm glad they've nailed that bastard Miguel Sung, if that's what we're talking about.'

'In Lebanon. Who's Miguel Sung?'

'Lebanon. Some kind of explosion, was it? I gather Vince Cregan's OK. A.N. Other got hurt, they said, but . . . brave, bearded Vince is safely crouched in a ditch, no doubt, blaming the hated Jews in his usual totally unbiased way . . . Some poor bloody anonymous sound man wasn't so lucky, was that what I gathered?'

'No, he wasn't. And he's not so anonymous either. That was Peter.'

'Peter.'

'Peter Bradley.'

'Not Joyce's son?'

'Joyce's son. Among others.'

'Oh my goodness, I had no idea. They didn't give a name . . . How bad is he?'

'I just hooked up with Vince. They blew chunks out of him, the bastards. He was that side of the car.'

'Shit. What're the . . . the chances they can . . . ?'

'Nil. By the time they gathered the bits, he wasn't there any more. That's how it is when it isn't funny.'

'Have you spoken to Joyce?'

'That's the thing. I can't find her. She's doing a book signing on her new novel somewhere unpronounceable, in Wales, I think. I'm trying to discover where.'

'I thought – you and she were still –'

'Joined at the hype, is all we are these days. Things change, but fundamentally they're always shit, aren't they? In case you're the one man in London who doesn't know, which I doubt, very much, Joyce emptied her entire vitriolic vocabulary into my recumbent form. In her new so-called novel. *The Big Time*, have you read it? I'm pretty well word for word, and blow for blow, the character –'

'Craig Baloney! God, of course you are! But didn't I hear an interview in which you said you loved the book and you and

Joyce would always be the best of – I think you said "mates"?'

'I wasn't bothered being Craig,' Alan said, 'not a lot, but Joycey couldn't forgive me for what she'd said about me. Haven't spoken since.'

'Jason'll know where she is. Our mutual well-known literary agent, hers and mine. I'll get on to him.'

'You'll have a job staying on. Slippery sea monster, that Jason Singer. Why say things like that at a time like this? Because this isn't the time I want it to be. Stalling. I'd appreciate it if you could . . . get word to Joycey . . . Joyce before the *paparatsos* spring it on her. I keep reseeing that scene in *Dolce Vita*, the price of the prehensile mind, you're thinking.'

'But trying not to. Great scene: Signora Steiner, wasn't it? Who doesn't know her husband's shot himself. How about Dan?'

'Dan?'

'Bradley. Otherwise known as Joyce's ex. And Peter's father, isn't he?'

'You seriously don't know?'

'Don't I? What?'

'I'm Peter's – as they say, *natural* – father. You must know that. You still there?'

'I didn't know if I was supposed to. Know. All the same . . .'

'What does it matter? Tell me what matters, Adam, and I'll tell you it bloody doesn't.'

'He brought . . . him up, didn't he? Dan. I mean, as if . . . Well, not as if . . . I mean, he was . . .'

'You're right: too Christian to be true. He can't seriously still be being a cobbler in bloody Brescia, can he, Daniel?'

'Far as I know. After the court case he buggered off and . . . *hasta la vista*, as they rarely say in Brescia. Are you all right, Alan? Where are you? Ubiquity must take a toll.'

'There is a tide in the affairs of men which, taken at the flood, leads on to Wolverhampton Town Hall, unfortunately, for another session of *That's Asking*. Cue applause or you may not get them. A further instalment in one deluded Aussie's endless quest for fame and fortune. Fork right at Aylesbury and you can't miss it, they tell me. How are you, by the way?'

'Fine. And dandy,' Adam said. 'And wizard, no doubt. We never outgrow the comics of our childhood. I am sorry, Alan. About Peter. Truly.'

'Me too.'

'I'll call Jason *instanter*.' Adam fitted the white receiver back in its cradle. 'You know that thing on the news, about the sound man who got . . . blown up?'

'I gathered,' Barbara said. 'Horrible. Why did he call *you*? Alan. You're not exactly bosom buddies, are you?'

'Perhaps he doesn't know as many bosoms as we think he does. How horrible the way other people's tragedies make you feel so much better. Aristotle never thought of that one. Plus . . . doesn't matter.'

'What?'

'I was going to say something, but I thought better of it.'

'It must have been a beauty,' Barbara said.

'OK. *The Big Time*'ll be a shoo-in for the Dickens Prize after this, won't it?' Adam was dialling as he spoke. 'Gallant Joyce Hadleigh surfing in on a wave of informed sympathy. Is what I had the elementary decency not to say.'

'Jason Singer.'

'Jace, it's Adam.'

'You've finished it!'

'Have I? What?'

'*Life and Loves*. Great, great title. When do I get to see it?'

'How about when it's finished? That's not why I phoned. End of May, probably. I shall almost certainly have to go back and work on the beginning again, taking out the good bits. It's about Joyce. Hadleigh.'

'*The Sixth Floor*'s sold 35,000 hardback. *The Big Time*'s all set to do even better. Why don't you ever write books like that, about the movie business? *No Holds Barred*. Not a bad title.'

'*Middlemarch* is better,' Adam said. 'Joyce's son Peter, have you heard? What happened to him, in South Lebanon?'

'Been hurt, has he? Occupational hazard.'

'Hurt isn't all. Alan doesn't seem to think he's . . . survived. Parks. I was just talking to him.'

'You were lucky to get a word in. Nothing much she can do then, except –'

'It's her son, you bastard, we're talking about. Have you got a number where I can get her?'

'I didn't even know you knew her. *Middlemarch* has been used, hasn't it?'

'That's because she didn't recognisably pillory me in her book, the bitch. I was at Cambridge with her, as I'm sure you know.'

'Whatever. I have 0600 760 1449 for her. Oh something I wanted to ask you. The Dickens Prize. How do you feel about it?'

'If they ever try to thrust it down my throat, I almost certainly won't refuse to swallow, but I hope I shall also remember all the crappy books that've won it in this greater than ever decade of the English novel.'

'Being on the jury, I meant.'

'And have to read six hundred magnificent new novels in two months? Thrilled. Don't tell me you can fix it, because I know you can. Do me a favour, and don't do me a favour, Jace, not this time, OK?'

'Samuel Marcus Cohen is going to be chairman and he mentioned you might be –'

'– a likely yes-man when the time comes for him to decide the winner?'

'It's three grand. Plus whatever you get, when you sell off the books, which is tax free.'

'You have to make do with the glory, in other words. Which is not yet taxable, but Nigel's working on it. Only share-pushers, cash-only cowboys and off-shore shits don't pay tax these days. No fun, no mun, is what the Dickens sounds like to me.'

'I could always get you a Review Front, pound-a-word, now-it-can't-be told article and you can have posthumous fun telling them all what happened behind the scenes and why you never want to be on the jury again, as if you would be.'

'I'm going to call Joyce. I don't want to, but I am. Cheers, Jace.'

Before Adam could dial again, the telephone was ringing.

'Adam,' Barbara said, 'is that the Quantum Theory for you again possibly?'

'Ha! Hullo?'

'You were talking to your fucking agent. Deny it.'

'I was too. But not about you Sir Mike. And not Shapiro. The literary one in London. Should I be ashamed of myself? You remember literature, don't you? The loser's form of screenwriting.'

'Don't do it, mate. Whatever it is. Because I need you over here. You can't imagine what Hollywood's like once you're in the driving seat.'

'Do I gather you're offering me a job as a chauffeur?'

'Are you remotely capable of cutting the crap?'

'Try the mustard, old pal, old buddy. I'd sooner cut that. What's going on? Note the practical tone.'

'OK, end of foreplay. *The Big Time.* Does Bruno still want you to write it?'

'Assuming he really has got the rights. Which he swears he does. But only on the head of his son, so who knows?'

'You don't want to do a picture like that.'

'No? Last time we spoke, you were possibly certainly going to direct it. The wench is dead, it seems.'

'Adam, I have just one thing I want to say to you. *Fatso.*'

'*Fatso*, do you? Well, it's your privilege.'

'You can be so English sometimes. Fay Pope's book. *Fatso.* Read it?'

'Sounds like crap. Isn't it?'

'Golden crap. It's a cracker. It only needs salt. About this professor's wife who sheds five stone and becomes the hottest thing on the campus. Ugly duckling's revenge. My version – *our* version – you switch the whole thing to the U.S. Trendy lefty

152

professor's dogsbody wife cuts loose, starts saying everything nobody's ever dared to say before, winds up running for President of the United States. Wins. Becomes the first lady who really *is* the first lady. Declares peace on the world. I don't know how long I'm going to be in this job, and that's why I want you out here. You're on a shrinking ship, Adam. You don't know how little England looks like from here. You think it's the good ship lollyplop, I see it as the once sceptr'd isle capsizing on the horizon.'

'How can you talk like that about England? Have you ever read *You Can't Come Home Again*? Could be your story.'

'Even the coverage is too long.'

'Just think about the title then. And yours, of course.'

'I never asked for it.'

'Oh is that how you got it? I didn't know that.'

'You should've come out here, Ad, when you won the Oscar. You'd be a rich man today. How soon can you hop on a plane?'

'I don't do hopping. You need an American. To translate *Fatso*. One that can hop.'

'I had one. Nominated three times. Lazy, greedy and coked out. Which is why it's not working, the system, any more. The fees they pay people out here are bloody obscene. No wonder the movies all cost upwards of twenty-five million. We're changing that out here at Transworld. And, believe me, this town is turning in its gravy.'

'Clever stuff. Who wrote it? Charlie Bisto?'

'Slimline is the only way to go.'

'How much are they paying you not to pay people?'

'This is a once in a lifetime chance, Adam. Cut the Cambridge-style crap and come over into Mesopotamia and help me. I'll talk a deal with Ron Shapiro tomorrow.'

'What happened to today?'

'Is a point. I want you here the day after. Put it in your diary. You're fifty something. Fifty-four, aren't you? We both are. Now or never, mate. Read Gavin Pope's column in the *Spekky* this week. Old time is still a-frying.'

'You don't call Americans "mate" at all, do you?'

'Mate? They'd think I was crazy. Why?'

'Just checking. Mike, listen, I have . . . serious things I have to take care of. You remember Dan's son Peter? Dan and Joyce's son.'

'I don't believe I ever met him. Why?'

'Because . . . Not your problem.'

'Stay in England and you'll be a bloody Jew all your life imagining that nobody's noticed, and they all bloody well have. Now or never, my son. I mean it. Old time is still a-flying. And so can you, first class. I've got a call in to Ronnie. And don't try calling and warning him. My call is already in and he'll take mine before he takes yours. I know you. Twist your own arm, will you, because I'm a busy man?'

'Jesus,' Adam said. 'He wants us to go to Hollywood.'

'Are you sure that's who you were talking to?' Barbara said.

'He's going to talk numbers with Ronnie Shapiro. And the hell of it is . . .'

'You want him to. California here you come?'

'I don't want . . . not to have gone . . . and then . . . find I'm reduced to driving an English car for the rest of my life. Might it be fun, do you think? Calif., for a limited season only?'

'You'd like it to be my fault if you don't go, wouldn't you?' she said. 'And also, of course, my fault if you do.'

'Should cover it! But the fault, dear Brutus . . .'

'I don't think you're an underling exactly.'

'A ling though; I am a bit of a ling. The trouble with Mike's bullshit is that glitter of gold on the top.'

'You were going to phone Joyce Hadleigh.'

'She'll only think I'm being nice because I want to write the script of *The Big Time*, which I half do and half don't.'

'Do you seriously think she's going to give a damn about a thing like that at a time like this?'

'Am I ashamed of myself? You don't know these people. Nor do I really. Better if I give Alan the number Jason gave me and then . . .'

154

'You can sit back and wait to see who phones you next.'

'You must be the wife!'

'A small part . . .'

'But you do get the close-ups.'

'It might have been Tom, mightn't it? In Lebanon.'

'But it wasn't. Do we now believe in God? Do we now not? It wasn't. We don't. I don't.'

'And people would've been wondering who should call us.'

'To hell with life, let's go out to dinner. Get away from . . . Do you suppose Denis Porson'd still have a table? He will if I tell him it's for you.'

'You do work at it,' Barbara said.

'Thank you. But it's not a living.'

'He won't even remember I exist.'

Adam called Alan Parks and gave him Joyce's number and then he checked that Two by Two had a table and then, while Barbara did something to her hair (assuming he was serious about going out), he went into his study to put something in his notebook about Miguel Sung and false messiahs. The phone rang again.

'Ad? It's Derek.'

'I thought you were always dining with the Queen at this hour. Everything all right?'

'Not bad.'

'Only we're just going out.'

'Won't keep you. Only are you in the market at all?'

'What would a Simple Simon like me be doing there?'

'I'm talking about shares.'

'I've got some stuff. Mostly what you told me about a bit too late. Why?'

'I had an interesting talk with Konni Georgiadis this afternoon. Spare me the sarcasm. Konni thinks there's trouble coming.'

'There has to be, doesn't there, for him to make a living?'

'He's selling in a big way. So am I, bit by bit. He gives it six months.'

'Which probably means six weeks?'

'At the most. I thought you should know.'

'Thanks, Der. I will withdraw my drop from the bucket first thing in the morning. I have got a few things actually.'

'If Konni's wrong, he's wrong.'

'Shits of his dimensions rarely are though, are they? Whence cometh our salvation. I have just written down in my notebook. Thanks, Der. Just the pay-off I needed. Love to Carol.'

ii

'Bra, darling!' Denis Porson said. 'How are you? I thought you'd never grace me 'umble, but here you are, as ever was, and long will remain, I trust. Not a scratch on the paintwork, dear.'

'Advantages of having one careful owner, Denis.'

'I would never describe you as owned by anyone, Bra dear, and nor would you; still less would Master Morris, if he has his own breast interests at heart.'

'Bigger and better, Denis, aren't you, these days?' Adam said. 'Two by Two, as if you didn't know, is rated "The number one watering hole for showbiz and allied trades".'

'So the colour suppurants tell us. And who am I to say shucks? *Ever!* I don't know who half the people are, but of course *they* do, and rip off their old school ties and put on their best estuary accents to prove it. In the dear dead days, I would've shown them the door. Now it's the wine list.'

'The old guard still do survive.'

'They do, they do. In choirs and places where they swing. How are the mighty fallen? Almost certainly on their Lobb-shod feet as usual.'

Denis asked one of the boys to bring them 'A bottle of Dom's strengthening medicine' and sat down with Adam and Barbara while they drank it.

'How's Jill?' Adam said. 'Back on the boards, do I gather?'

'Playing Beatrice, in Manchester. And rushing home whenever she can to see Septimus.'

'How old is he these days?'

'All of five, dear. But big enough for seven. I'm quite frightened of him. He's got a left hook like Long John Silver.'

'Septimus Porson. Name like that, he's got to be a scholar.'

'Oh dear, must he? I hoped a hairdresser. I'm just going to go and tell Gianni he's got quality to feed. The *hoi* and *polloi* we get in here these days wouldn't have shown their heads above stairs when mother was a girl. But we must never say so, except *sottissimo voce*. That can't be right, can it? But it's still true. Be warned: I shall be back before you've finished saying "How does she do it?"'

'You see?' Adam said. 'Denis loves you. Amazing, how he beat all the odds, isn't it? He's even got a son. Who else in today's world would call anyone Septimus?'

Barbara wiped her lips. 'Where is he, Adam, do you suppose: Tom?'

'I know. Let's hope he's really . . . living somewhere, not . . . all right, chanting some happy-crappy gibberish, in a yellow nightshirt with a pigtail down his back.'

'You're really very conventional, aren't you?'

'God, yes,' Adam said. 'Any minute now I shall be writing about the nineteen-fifties as the good old days. With a quill pen, ay shouldn't wonder.'

'Because we were young. Is why they were good.'

'And wore existentialist trousers while everyone else had rolled umbrellas and bowler hats and stuck to their class-ridden ruts. We all waxed *mucho* satirical, because nothing was ever really going to change. Now the bulls are all running the china shops. But according to Derek, the bears are just around the corner. He will come home one day, Ba. For your sake at least.'

'Don't ever imagine I might be on his side, even slightly, when he does, if he does. He had no right to talk to you the way he did.'

'Kind of you to say so, but that's what sons do. Old, sad story. All there in Uncle Sigmund.'

'Please don't call me kind,' Barbara said. 'It only puts space between us. Yes, it does. Marooning poor lonely you in your private vale of tears. Only Jews allowed.'

'Hey . . . you want my troubles? Come on in!'

iii

Joyce was sitting in a country house hotel suite with 'White Rose' on the door instead of a number, watching the closing moments of *That's Asking* on a television set that slid, slightly, out of the large armoire facing the bed, when the new, flat telephone rang.

'Call for you, Miss Hadleigh.'

'All right,' she said.

'Joycey? It's Alan.'

'Just finished watching yourself on the box? You were very . . . Alan Parks. For the time of year.'

'As a matter of fact, I'm just getting into the car to drive back to London.'

'Be driven, you mean.'

'Cruelly accurate as usual. I had to call you. I don't know how to say this, because –'

'You don't need to,' Joyce said. 'In fact I need you not to. Please. How did it go tonight? You looked very relaxed to me. And I loved what you said to "Ergo-centric Enoch", it sounded like, "the classic rationaliser". Well over the punters' heads, that one, I should've thought.'

'So did Fiona. How come you were watching?'

'What else is there to do in Monmouth when you're dead?'

'What're you planning to do, Joycey, about – ?'

'They're flying me out to Beirut tomorrow.'

'I'll come with you, if that –'

'It wouldn't. ITN've fixed the flight.'

'I can squeeze in,' Alan said. 'I've lost a bit of weight. I wish I had something wise and brave and the least bit worth saying to say.'

'I'm surprised not to hear that Wittgenstein had something useful to offer for a time like this.'

'There's always, "Death is not an event of life. It is not lived through." Which I used to think sounded comfortingly painless. But the truth is, we *do* live through it, when it's someone else's. Shows what a narcissist the good Ludwig really was. Our son's, for instance.'

'I won't let you make me cry, Alan. If you want to cry, hang up and go and cry. I know . . . that you're feeling whatever you're feeling, but I haven't anything sweet or comforting to say. Hannah's driving down to collect me in the morning and she wants to come with me to Beirut. We'll fly home together with the body. I'm not going to cry. This isn't one of your TV interviews. So don't wait and wait and hope I'll crack up because I'm *fucking* not going to.'

'I love you and I admire you, Joycey. In my own unattractive way. I know it's all over, and it never properly began . . . but life's a bastard and death is worse, and on we bloody well go. What else can we do? That's the Law and the Prophets and to hell with them both.'

'You're very eloquent when you're . . . whatever you are at the moment. Wondering how you can manage to get out gracefully, would it be?'

'He did what he wanted to do. Hang on to that. It's more than most of us do. You don't think I'm human, do you, Joycey? You never did. Maybe that was what was attractive.'

'Possibly. You were very good on the programme tonight. Didn't show a thing.'

'At a time like this, there's nothing like being phoney through and through.'

'Go home to Shirley, Alan,' Joyce said, 'and be kind to her.'

'She doesn't need me to be kind to her.'

'Yes, she does. Think about it.'

Alan said, 'I've thought. You're right. As usual. Is there anything I can do?'

'Something you can *not* do, there is: call me again, ever. Or come to the funeral in a tight suit. Goodnight, Alan.'

iv

'At least do them a lobster *capucc'*, Gianni.'

'The lobster *cappuc'* isn't on tonight. Is why you're asking, when you see how busy we are. I can't stop everything everyone's doing just because you want something –'

'*Caviare surprise* then, give them that. There were two over from lunch. I saw them.'

'Your friends always have to be a special case. Why?'

'Because so they are. Apart from the fact that this does happen to be my fucking restaurant.'

'You see, what you really think? It's all yours.'

'Gianni, honey, please. Look at the contract, duckie.'

'Keep your voice down talking like that.'

'This is down. Fifty-one/forty-nine doesn't sound like it's all anyone's to me. Not worth a prolonged hissy fit, Gianni. Give them whatever seems good to you.'

'I sometimes think –'

'I know, and very hurtful it is when you do it.'

v

Alan sat in the back of the Volvo with Fiona Maclean. They were going through Aylesbury when he said, 'Are you interested in something rather peculiar, not to say distasteful, but I'd like an explanation for?'

'Not particularly.'

'Fair enough.'

'Such as what?' she said, when the town was behind them.

'You know I told you I was going to call Joyce about Pete being . . . dead?'

'Meaning you didn't?'

'No, no, I did that. I don't in the least want you to do

160

anything about it, but as a matter of interest, as I say, have a feel of this.'

'Very impressive.'

'That's not why I raised it. In a manner of speaking. Which I didn't. I can't. No Byron he; nor yet was he, I suspect. What's odd is, it wasn't brought on by any erotic idea that's going through my head. Not that I don't find you attractive, Fiona.'

'You're the most almost lovable man I know,' Fiona said.

'This isn't a pass. I make passes, they're clumsy and unmistakable. It's a physiological curiosity and I thought you might have some suitable, well all right, put-down to offer.'

'Do you want a serious answer?'

'If it fits, I'll try it. Such as?'

'Your body doesn't know how to respond to grief. There're only so many things it can do. Laugh, cry, bleed, shit itself or have an erection. The erection cures grief by demanding direct attention. Which, God knows, you're giving it. It's also comic, which is your ultimate resource, when Wittgenstein has failed you.'

'Very articulate you can be, Fiona. I'd kiss you if you didn't have something in common with the Forbidden City. Where are we next week?'

'Wisbech.'

'I know that. But where is it? You don't have to do that.'

vi

'Everything all right?' Denis said.

'That caviare egg thing was just wonderful.'

'Gianni laid it specially for you, Bra dear.'

'And I love all the white china lids.'

'And the all-together-boys disclosing of what lies beneath? Hats off time! Adorable isn't it? Frogs started it. *Un, deux, trois* . . . oh my goodness, look at that!'

'It's amazing what you've done, Denis,' Adam said, 'the pair of you.'

161

'The three of us, dear, but who's counting? Septimus probably. He does it up to twenty already. Quite enough to be going on with. What've you got there for them, Bobbie?'

'*Paupiettes de Sole Giancarlo!*'

'*Un, deux, trois* and –'

'Looks fantastic,' Barbara said.

'*Bonne continuation*, as they will say unless given a sharp kick on the ankle. Better than "enjoy" is all I can say, or will. See you later.'

Barbara said, 'If that's all cream and butter, I shan't sleep for a fortnight.'

'Funny how food's getting all *stacked* these days,' Adam said. 'Symbol of the new vertical society as against the horizontalism of Labour? Eight-hundred-word piece in that for somebody. And when did they start having polygonal plates? Not that I have anything against polygons, as long as there're never more of them than there are of us.'

Barbara said, 'Adam, have you tried it, the sole? If it is sole.'

'It said it was when it was . . . disclosed, didn't it?' He looked at her slightly twitching lips. 'Something wrong?'

'You tell me. I only know I cannot *possibly* eat it.'

'Celeriac's all right. And the fried bread, isn't it?'

'I'm talking about the fish, in a deliberately very quiet voice, because . . . taste it.'

Adam nibbled what was on his fork. 'You're right. Jesus! What is this? We can't send it back.'

'I don't care,' she said, 'but I'm never eating it. What are we going to do?'

'Smile appreciatively. For the moment. Nibble some celeriac. It seems fine. Because . . . here comes our leading lady now.'

'How are Gianni's *paupiettes*?'

'Very . . . unusual,' Barbara said. 'Very . . .'

'Tangy! Is the buzz word, isn't it?' Adam said.

'It is now.'

'We were just trying to guess what was in them. Not the celeriac but the . . . buzzy bit.'

162

'Secrets of the confessional, dear, never to be revealed. Gorge but don't . . . probe . . . as the old adage 'ad it! But Gianni does love a caper.'

A young man in very narrow black-framed glasses and a black silk suit came slimly between the tight tables. 'Denis. Someone for you in the office.' He looked down at Barbara and Adam. 'Lord Lacey. About the wedding on Sunday.'

'Damn and blast,' Denis said, 'and on my eager way!'

'I'll repeat the question. What *are* we going to do?'

'What would they do in the movie? I hate to make a . . . witless suggestion, but suppose you opened your handbag in your lap and . . . we played tip and run?'

'Do you know what you paid for it?'

'Every last shekel. But it's *sauve qui peut* time. And I do mean now, before Denis gets back to ask us how it was. You first, then me. And . . . action!'

'My best bag.'

'I know. And you're *my* best bag. As we used to say in the wonderful, wonderful fifties.' Adam turned and looked at the door. 'Oh my goodness,' he said, 'look who's just come in, the ravishing Mrs Schiff!' He turned back to Barbara. 'Quick, as all adjacent heads turn, open wide and . . . Now. Keeping your napkin . . . that's it, over the groin area . . . and . . .'

'Denis would die if he saw us.'

'Better him than us. And . . . done it! Print that one! Careful. It's quite hot. Hope it doesn't melt.'

'It will not *melt*.'

'Put it on the floor then, in case it . . . steams. Just make sure the clasp stays clasped when we make our dignified rush for the door. What a shame we have to cut such a delicious meal short, but we've just heard . . . What have we just heard? The house has been burgled. Banal but plausible everyday stuff, the mark of the telly's most successful soaps: they wash culture down the plug-hole and leave the mind soft and baby-like. But I digress. Doesn't seem unduly hot, the bag. We'd better run before it does.'

'Oh my goodness!' Denis said. 'All done? *Déjà*? How was it?'

'Gone in a trice, Denis.'

'Two trices.'

'What about a *soufflé Grand Marnier* to finish things off with the wanton ostentation only to be expected in a place that's six feet off the ground like this one?'

'To tell you the truth, Denis –'

'That has an ugly ring, but pray proceed, Master Morris.'

'We're both . . .'

'I know you are. Symbiotic. I've heard the savage rumours, but hoped as always to keep them from you. Our just desserts are justly famous.'

'And we'd like nothing better,' Barbara said, 'another time, but Adam has to get up really, really early.'

'So if we could have the bill, Den . . .'

'You disappoint me sorely, but I shall choke back the tears, dears. The champagne was *offert*, as they say, in case you're furious not to have to pay for it.'

'Denis, honestly – thank you so much.'

The young man in black was in the doorway, miming to Denis that he had a telephone call.

'I do want to meet Septimus sometime,' Barbara said, as Denis made a sorry face. 'Before he's bigger than I am!'

'It shall be arranged. I'll talk to Jill as soon as she's out of work. Bless you both. The devil's driving as usual.'

Barbara said, 'Adam, we have a problem. The best handbags may not melt, but they can leak at the seams. Small, but growing puddle on the floor.'

'Christ. Wrap it in your napkin. And we'll make a run for the door.'

'How can I? People'll see.'

'It can be done though. Catullus wrote a poem about a napkin thief, did it all the time.'

'I totally do not care what Catullus wrote.'

'I'll take care of it. Give it to me – God, it really has . . . hasn't it? Leaked a bit. I've got it, I've got it. Now lead me out and

smile the big one at everyone as we go and no one'll look at me.
Think *The Great Escape*. And . . . *action!*'

vii

As the black Volvo carried him back to Blackheath, Alan Parks
waited − like Eliot's anaesthetised patient, he could not help
thinking (even his similes kept A-list company) − for pain, or its
substitute, to strike him. While they drove round the broad,
silent Green, he realised that to write the commentary on his
own feelings might always be the closest he could come to
feeling them. There was a two-thousand-word piece in that, but
he was never going to write it, was he? Not yet anyway. He got
out of the car and leaned down to say, 'Good run, Sanjay, thanks
very much.' Fiona's sharp profile was eyes front, straight-
mouthed. 'Thanks for everything, Fiona. Smooth as ever.'
     'Goodnight, Alan.'
He walked up the gravel drive with careful feet, past the
Mercedes 280SL which he had given Shirley for his birthday; the
same model had figured in her favourite film, a subject on
which, like many, they had agreed to differ. The house was a
double-gabled, 'Regency-type, defrocked rectory' as he
described it in interviews in which he found it prudent, but in
character, to confess that, apart from his books, he had
accumulated the symptoms of success by 'a process of
premeditated absentmindedness'.
He took off his suede boots before he opened the door.
Shirley had left the light on, as usual, in the hall, where he had
to check the best of the stacked deck of mail before he went
upstairs, avoiding the creakier steps.
     'It's all right,' Shirley said. 'I'm not asleep. I never am. It
seemed to go very well, didn't it? You were on very good form.
Donald and I laughed like anything when you imitated the
incomprehensible airport announcer saying something really
important.'
     'Peak of my powers,' Alan said. 'Even Enoch cracked a thin

165

Nietzschean smile. Suitable for a man who led to the whole place being surrounded with police dogs and yapping lefties.'

Shirley said, 'Did you speak to her?'

'Speak to . . . ?'

'Oh for God's sake! How long have we been married?'

'Yes, I did. I had to. She's a funny woman, Joyce.'

'Is she?' Shirley said. 'I never got the joke personally.'

'I've done profound apologies, Shirl, and that's the best I'm ever going to do. You know he's dead, Peter, don't you? It's been confirmed, as if we didn't know already.'

'I saw the late news,' she said, 'and I'm very, very sorry. It's horrible. I wish I felt more.'

'You're not alone. I wish I did, to tell you the horrible truth. I feel – OK – sick, but . . . oddly, not for me. Sick because . . . I just want to . . . have it be in the past as soon as it can be. On with the bloody motley, because the motley just mottles and mottles and . . . leaves no time for anything else. All the world's a stodge and all the men and women in it merely payers.'

'That sounds worked up,' she said, 'so presumably it wasn't.'

'Top of my head,' he said, 'plenty of space for development there. I'm glad Don laughed. Answer all the questions, did he, and question all the answers, as usual? I don't know where he gets his stock of prattle from.'

'Can't imagine. Did you see the post?'

'I gave it a stony stare. As you doubtless rightly guessed, or why would you ask? Includes a request from the University of Slightly South of Huntingdon Beach, California: would I go and teach Communication Studies for a semester next winter? In a word: Professor Parks at last. What do you think?'

'With lots of California girls sitting at your feet while you look down their well-developed fronts? I can't imagine you grabbing a chance like that.'

'I leave England, even for that long, when I get back they won't know who I am.'

'Will you? How much sheet do you actually need?'

'Sorry. When I turn over, it turns over with me.'

166

'Everybody does,' she said.

'I've not been what I should have been, Shirl.'

'And there is no truth in us, isn't that how it goes?'

'To you, I mean.'

'You can't help not loving me,' she said. 'Go to sleep. It won't be any different in the morning.'

'I still fancy you rotten sometimes, and you know it. A spot of Chanel in the upper and the nether grooves and I'm back being yours till the stars lose their glory.'

'Funnily enough,' she said, 'if it's your idea of fun, I do still rather love you, sometimes. When the shoulders drop and the bald patch glistens.'

'It's the sad inner shit that does it, isn't it, sometimes? The tracksuited zeppelin, Joyce called me one time, in a rare moment of tenderness.'

She sat up and turned to him. 'I didn't know Peter. I saw him those few times, but . . . because I didn't, I'm . . . really sorry for you, Alan. Just don't be angry with me about it.'

'It's nice when you know my name. He was an odd boy, in truth. Pete. Shut himself into his own world, you know? The sound thing suited him. He just listened. All he had to do was say that what was happening was OK or that it wasn't. Invisible men, soundies, when they're good at it. Living in a world of one. Just them and a box of batteries.'

Shirley said, 'You got him that job, didn't you?'

'I got him the interview,' Alan said. 'He got the job. She's flying out tomorrow. Smiling, intelligent, but . . . alone. Reserved, as they say, Peter.'

There was a howl of late tyres on the road outside their window, and then the wince of brakes.

Shirley said, 'Seems to be all right. No breaking glass. Just a loud silence.'

'Things happen,' Alan said. 'And things don't.'

Shirley was lying down with her back to him again. 'You think he's ruined your life,' she said, 'don't you? And you think it's my fault.'

'I ruined his. He didn't do anything much to mine. Casualties of peace. He's dead, I'm alive. Yet they speak of a just God.'

'You know very well I'm talking about Donald.'

'He's a character though, Don, isn't he?'

She twisted towards him with sudden energy. 'Oh don't – don't *broadcast* at me, Alan. I'm not your bloody public. I'm the wife you had the idiot child with, she spends all her time looking after even if he is now a shambling six-foot dribbler.'

'You see how easy it is to take the sheet with you, when you . . .'

'Yes, yes, yes. As if I was ever allowed to say anything else. Bugger the sheet.'

'He loves you the way . . . I should, and can't.'

'And shouldn't. Imagine if he was dead. Imagine if that was the news you'd heard. Think how *wonderful* you'd be about the game little blighter in the two thousand words, minimum, they'd be bound to want you to write by Friday at the latest.'

'I wouldn't do it. You're not being overly kind, Shirley. I don't blame you for it, but . . .'

'Goodnight, Alan. Grooves! Thanks a lot.'

'It was a compliment.'

'I know. That's what hurts.'

viii

At half past eleven, when the boys started clearing up, Giancarlo sat sideways on a kitchen stool by one of the work surfaces, tunic unbuttoned, serious glasses on, making a list of things he would need later in the week. He was too busy to look up when Denis came in.

'How many covers tonight, Gianni?'

'I didn't count. A hundred and two, was it?'

'Any complaints at all?'

'Put it in the cold store, Riri, not in there. I didn't hear any, did you?'

'No? Not even from table six, didn't you? Where my friends were sitting I asked you to do something special for. Nothing got sent back to you, did it?'

'Not that I know of. Why-ee?'

'Because they couldn't, could they, send anything back, and still be my friends?'

'What the fuck you talk about?'

'You always go all Sicilian when you're cornered.'

'I'm not Sicilian. What is your problem? It's late.'

'One of the busboys showed me the floor by where they were sitting. Guess what was on it.'

'People drop their food, it's notta my fault.'

'It's notta? Nobody dropped their food. They spilt it.'

'Same difference.'

'Where did you learn that awful phrase? They spilt it, on purpose, because it was inedible. As you bloody meant it to be.'

'I've got a kitchen to run, for God's sake. Or don't you want me to do that any more? Just tell me.'

'That fish you gave them was stinking. And you knew it, didn't you?'

'With the sauce on it, sometimes it's hard to tell. Food goes out of the kitchen so fast –'

'As if you didn't push your whopping great proboscis into every single dish as a matter of principle.'

'I must tell you one thing: you let everybody make a fool of you.'

'Do I just? Well, I must tell *you* one thing: everybody isn't going to include you, ducky. Stinking fish is stinking fish and what happens once can happen again.'

'Yes, it can. I'm talking about *carissima*. She's cheating on us like hell.'

'I don't care what Jill does and I don't want to hear about it. This restaurant has a reputation, and whatever has a reputation can also lose it. *Comme ça!*'

'To me it matters. What she does. Maybe because I'm Florentine. Maybe because I am also a man.'

169

'I don't think of Jill as cheating anyone, and I never shall. She gave me Septimus and she loves him and, in a way, she loves me. It's more than I ever asked of her.'

'There were going to be the three of us and that's what we agreed. Now there's Norman Segal, in case you didn't know.'

'Oh ducky, so what?' Denis said. 'Shag and shag alike, it's the way of the world. This is all a change of subject routine and don't think I didn't notice.'

Giancarlo tore up the list he had been making and posted it in the bin by his knees. 'All right, you want to know what? I'm going back to Firenze. My uncle has a restaurant, Buca dei Medici, already in the Michelin, he's thinking of retiring and he asks I go in wiz him. Now I do.'

'What you did to my friends was giving in your notice, then, was it, to me?'

'You take my advice, you divorce that whore of an actress and take Septimus away from her.'

'You can be such a silly spiteful little Eyetie sometimes, Gianni. I don't care if Jill wants to go to bed, and breakfast, with the entire membership of Equity, *and* the massed bands of the Scots Guards, if she feels like it. I have something with her – some*one* with her – I could never have had otherwise. And if she only wants to come and spend weekends and Christmas with me and Septimus, I shall count myself a very lucky little fairy indeed. All or nothing has never been my kind of thing.'

'She cheated you from the beginning. With me. In case you didn't know.'

'Cheat is a silly word. And very suburban, for someone discovered, *sans* basket, in the rushes under the Ponte Vecchio.'

'How come you're so sure that Septimus is yours, you bastard?'

'Malice does always seem to take the same sad form, doesn't it? Because, in her curious female way, Jill loves me and she told me so. And because he has my left big toe. I used to suck it when I was a baby. My own, I mean, so I know it very well. I loved you once, Gianni, a great deal. Now I don't. The next time you serve

Paupiettes de Crotte à la crème, I hope some big bully makes you swallow every last mouthful.'

'See how many covers you do without me.'

'The curse of the great chef is that every one has his dauphin, whether he notices it or not. Lorenzo's been with us for six years, watching you like an auk the while. He's all set to cry his eyes out when he hears you're going.'

'I was Sicilian, I'd kill him. I'd kill you.' Giancarlo took off his Yves St Laurent glasses and snapped them across the bridge and threw them into the bin. '*Bischeraccio tu.*'

'That'll teach them,' Denis said.

ix

When Adam and Barbara got home, there was a message from Mike Clode's office saying that a copy of *Fatso*, by Fay Pope, would be arriving by special messenger first thing in the morning. They had only just gone downstairs for breakfast when there was a double rap of the knocker.

'God,' Adam said, 'first thing really is first thing sometimes. Why is knocking always more special than ringing the bell?'

There was another knock before he opened the door. 'I know, I know,' he said, 'you've got a book for me.'

'Hullo, Dad.'

Adam said, 'You haven't got a book for me.'

Tom said, 'Can I come in all the same?'

'All the same? Yes. Yes, you can.'

'How's Mum?'

'She's in the kitchen,' Adam said. 'You remember the way.'

'Do you hate the beard?'

'I don't hate anything. But apparently it isn't easy to say so. Sorry.' He sniffed hard and breathed out and then he had his arms around his son and was staring into the hall mirror at the two of them. He had his arms around Tom, but Tom did not have his around Adam. When Adam let go, Tom went down

171

the stairs to the kitchen. Adam stood looking at himself, as if at a curiosity. He could imagine Tom and Barbara together, as if they were lovers who had only a moment before he interrupted them. He stood in sweet pain and gave them longer than he wanted to. When at last he did go slowly down to the kitchen, he saw that Tom was sitting in his usual place, with a thick cup of coffee in front of him. He was dislodging two Weetabix from the packet. Barbara sat opposite him, tearless, chin on both hands, as if her head was too heavy to rely on one.

Adam said, 'Do I have to say – ?'

'No, you don't. Better that way.'

Adam said, 'His voice is slightly . . . isn't it? Older? Wiser?'

'That's what I just said,' Barbara said. 'The older bit.'

'Then it must be true,' Adam said.

'You haven't changed much then, you two.'

Adam said, 'How long have you been back, in the UK?'

'Does it matter? A few days.'

'Really?'

Barbara was looking at Adam. He nodded as if she had spoken.

'I was in the street last night,' Tom said. 'I saw you both come home. Taxi as usual.'

'After a crap dinner.'

'You seemed happy. You were laughing and laughing.'

'It was *such* a crap dinner,' Barbara said.

'You saw us? Why didn't you . . . come over – then?'

'Didn't have the bottle. Sorry, Dad. Found it later!'

'You know we want to know everything, don't you? Everything you want to tell us. When you do. If you do. And if you don't, don't.'

'Sure.'

'Do you want some eggs?'

'Two, if I can.'

'And a slice of fatted calf with that, would you like?'

'He had to say,' Tom said. 'How's Raitch?'

'I can do where,' Adam said. 'Almost certainly the university

172

library. Footnoting her thesis. She's at . . . our old college, I don't know if you heard. I think she's fine.'

'Thesis! You must be very proud of her.'

Barbara said, 'You haven't spoken to her then?'

'I haven't spoken to anyone.'

Adam looked at Barbara. Were they both wondering what Tom had been doing during the days he had been in London, if he had not spoken to anyone? 'You're . . . ah . . . alone, then,' he said.

'In London I am, yes. Until . . .'

'What's happening?'

'You tell me,' Tom said. 'With you.'

'Here we are. Except when we're in France. We've bought this cottage you don't know about. In the Lot. Otherwise I'm still . . . doing the things I do.'

'And I'm still doing the things he doesn't,' Barbara said.

'How's the new book then?'

'Coming. Not bad. About a month to do.'

'I read *The Disappearance* while I was . . . on my travels.'

'A bit dated?'

'I liked it. Mum looks wonderful.'

'She is. Since you got here.'

Tom said, 'You'll never guess where I read it. *The Disappearance*.'

'It was published when . . . you weren't even at school yet.'

Barbara said, 'Where did you? Read it?'

'Right,' Tom said. 'B.A. actually. Buenos Aires. I was in a bar in the Boca and there was this man reading this book and I couldn't believe it. *The Disappearance* by Adam Morris. I sat and watched him turn the pages.'

'More than I ever have. I've never ever seen anyone reading a book of mine in any public place.'

'He caught me looking at him. Fair-haired man, about your age, silver in it, the hair, and he smiled at me. Strange smile. Not what you think though. I've known some of those too. I didn't have the beard then. But it wasn't . . . one of those smiles. I know

173

those. Anyway, he smiled, this man in the bar, and we had a drink. He worked in B.A. for a man called Levin. Raul Levin. He was in property and Robert – this man's name was Robert Carn – was working for him, as a sort of minder, I suppose. I worked for him myself a bit, thanks to Robert.'

'Robert Carn? You don't mean it.'

'That's right: he was at school with you.'

'You do mean it. You met him once, Ba. We were in the same house at school.'

'Robert Carn?' Barbara said. 'I don't remember.'

'He did you, Mum,' Tom said. 'He remembered the way you looked at Dad when you got on your bus. As if . . . you might never see him again. Then you looked at him, he said, Robert.'

'You got on quite well, it seems,' Adam said. 'What's he like these days?'

'A dandy who couldn't quite afford the clothes, he looked like to me.'

'Perfect!' Adam said. 'Always did.'

'Handsome, but he didn't seem to fit his own skin. He was who he said he was, obviously, but it was as if it wasn't the part he really wanted to play.'

'He was quite a good actor, Robert, at school.'

'He got a part in a play that you wanted to have. He told me.'

'He did too. Hamlet. I couldn't have done it, I realise now. But Osric was a bit of a comedown. Is he married?'

'Had been. I think twice possibly. We're talking a few years ago now. I remember he was having a heavy affair with this rich Porteña. Her husband was connected with . . . you know . . . the Junta. A few years ago, this was. Robert thought the husband had found out and wanted to kill him. Have him killed. I'm not sure he liked her all that much, Melissa, Robert. He did like the danger though. The husband coming after him. That excited him. He was always on the watch for unmarked green Ford Falcons.'

'Why green Ford Falcons particularly?'

'It's what the secret police used when they took people away.

174

Happened all the time only no one noticed, not if they didn't want trouble. And who does usually?'

'What happened to the people they "took away", you said?'

'You don't want to know over breakfast, Mum. Or ever probably. You only had to be suspected of being a *subversivo* and, didn't matter if you were or not.'

'They threw them out of aeroplanes, didn't they?' Adam said.

'Navy helicopters mostly. The lucky ones. Because at least it was quick, and they often drugged them first, probably so they didn't resist. The others they . . . did things to. Pregnant women, didn't matter. Nothing anyone could do. Or wanted to much. Except the mothers. Only the mothers had the guts to protest.'

'We saw a programme about it, Ba, didn't we?'

'The Americans had this college where they trained the people who . . . organised it all. Same with Chile. No one ever complained, not the Americans, certainly not the Brits. The Junta was only bad when it tried to grab the Malvinas, wasn't it?'

'Nothing ever brings out the morality in people quite like a chance to play the patriotic card. And win elections.'

'The Reverend Sung used his . . . connections to spy on people and report them to Navy Intelligence. Is what I found out, from Robert. Which came as a . . . I expected you to smile.'

Barbara said, 'How long – am I allowed to ask? –'ve you been in Argentina?'

Adam said, 'Did Robert . . . ? Sorry.'

'Argentina and Paraguay. Quite a while. Gods, must be going on five, six years. Did Robert what?'

'Silly question. I've started so I'll . . . Recognise himself? As the character in *The Disappearance*?'

'Why else was he reading it?'

Barbara was at the cooker, scrambling eggs. Adam read a kind of anger into the turn of her shoulders, but anger with whom?

'The narcissist who didn't *entirely* love himself. That was Robert Carn when we were at school.'

'He thought he betrayed you once. Did he?'

'I never held it against him.'

175

'No. I think he was sorry. That you didn't. It stood between you, he said, that you wouldn't ever talk about it. Which is why you were never friends.'

'It's why I was never friends with anyone,' Adam said. 'I can scramble eggs.'

'You can scramble everything,' Barbara said. 'But I'm scrambling the eggs.'

'I hardly ever saw him after we'd left school. I don't know how we happened to meet up that evening, the three of us. Having a drink, I suppose, not that that sounds like us.'

'You wanted him to see Mum, he said. You wanted to show him what you'd got.'

'That's not my memory,' Adam said. 'Is it yours, Ba?'

She was dishing out the eggs. 'I do now remember the way he looked at me. Like that. Perhaps that's why you decided to marry me.'

'And perhaps it isn't,' Adam said. 'I never even noticed how he looked at you. Like *that*? Like what? Oh. What did you think when he did?'

'Things,' she said. 'He had a nice chest.'

'Chest, did he?' Adam said. 'You've done quite a lot of living then, Tom.'

'He's how I came to read *The Disapperance*: Robert. He gave it to me, all except the last forty pages.'

'Meaning what?'

'It was a paperback. He tore off the part he'd already read and gave it to me. That's the reason I came home, isn't it, so I could find out how it ends? Sorry, Dad.'

Adam's scrambled eggs tasted saltier than usual. 'I'd never do that to a book,' he said. 'Tear it in half. Never. Have you heard about what happened to your . . . to that Dr Miguel Sung character? I could never do that to a book.'

'I dropped out of all that. I can't even remember now why I ever got into it.'

'Jesus Christ,' Adam said.

'I expect I needed something to get me out of being someone

176

I wasn't. Unless it was someone I was. Went to jail, didn't he, I hear, the old bastard? You cheered presumably.'

'We thought about you,' Adam said. 'And, yes, we did rather, I'm afraid.'

'Mesmerising old shit, Miguel. I don't think he really raped anyone. They loved him. Good eggs, Mum. Young girls.'

'Statutory rape this was, I imagine.'

'You could've had them every day,' Barbara said.

'They wouldn't have been this good then. Robert told me about Miguel being in with the Junta. I think that's what finally did it, as a matter of fact.'

'Robert Carn,' Adam said. 'Incredible!'

'Someone at the door,' Tom said. 'Want me to go?'

Adam said, 'That'll be *Fatso*. I'll go.'

'Who's Fatso when he's at home?'

'It's a book,' Barbara said, 'they want him to make a film of.'

'Still doing that stuff, is he?'

'Only when they ask him. Where are you staying?'

'Do I still have a room here at all?'

He turned and looked at his mother and she was hunched over him as he tried to get up and embrace her. He almost carried her away from the table and then he could straighten up and they held each other, heads over shoulders, looking opposite ways.

'I'm sorry I did what I did, to you, but – I'm sorry – I'm not sorry I did it. I had to. I must've or I wouldn't've.'

Adam took the packet marked RUSH from the courier and stood in the hall, listening to the quiet voices and sounds from downstairs in the kitchen. Nothing now seemed less surprising than Tom's return from the unknown. Adam wanted to find it strange, or moving, but it was as if things had reverted to normal and no sharp emotion matched the circumstances. He peeled the tape from the envelope with the fat book in it and glanced at the gaudy cover and the big type and smiled at an early joke, as if it amused him. Tom's return was the most important thing that had happened to him for years, but he could not keep his mind

177

on it. Why did he not go back downstairs immediately? Tact, indifference, masochism? It was Tom's scene, with his mother, not Adam's. The boy was a stranger and his son; he was grateful that he was back, but gratitude too put distance between them. He was grateful in order not to be angry. He had to decide what to tell Mike Clode, and Ronnie Shapiro, when they dangled the dollars that would lure him to California. He went back down to the kitchen to kill the prospect of the dread that would come when he said 'yes' to them; or when he said 'no'.

Tom said, 'Do you still work as hard as you did then?'

'He works harder,' Barbara said.

'Robert said I should write a book.'

'Very vivid memories you have of him! Do you want to?'

'This was when I saw him again, more recently.'

'He could've given you the last forty pages,' Adam said. 'Do you want to, write a book?'

'He'd lost them, I think. I'm more into film really.'

'Oh my God! And all because I've eaten sour grapes.'

'I met some people in B.A. on the way through, they were working in super eight, you know? Because there isn't any money to do anything . . . unusual otherwise.'

'No need to go to B.A. for that to be true. They didn't mind you were English?'

'Because of the Malvinas? They were more sorry for me, actually, some of them. It did them more good than it did us. They were almost grateful, some of my friends, because losing the war at least meant the end of Galtieri and co. Actually, I don't think they thought of me as all that English. *Mi Español* got pretty good while I was there. Anyway, I was in Paraguay most of the time all that was going on. They hate the Argies up there. At least a cheer and a half for the Brits was how the Paraguayans looked at it.'

'Weird,' Adam said. 'I always wanted to go there. Paraguay.'

'Fantastic people. Tough, brave, humorous, some of them.'

'With their history . . . Bruno wanted to do a film, do you remember, Ba, about Francisco Lopez, the dictator who got them into a war with Brazil and Argentina and Chile all at the same time? Killed almost the whole of his own population. Finally he only had children left to fight for him. Like the late lamented Adolf. He had this opera singer, didn't he, that he found in Paris and took back and married?'

'Madame Lynch?'

'Eliza Lynch is the lady. She was going to be the big blue-eyed female part.'

'I don't know about opera singer. They built an opera house, but that was so Asunción could be the Paris of South America. Which everyone says B.A. is. He never married her, by the way, Eliza. She gave him four kids, as they say, but he never married her. She's got a street named after her. The Marshal's still a national hero. With a tomb like Napoleon's. Guarded day and night. The British started that war, by the way, basically. Not Lopez.'

'Really? Not in the books I read.'

'The British and the Rothschilds. The Rothschilds backed Brazil and the Argentine with millions of pounds of loans. I got to know this local historian, Carlos Montijo. The Paraguayans wouldn't let foreign capital into the country. That's what it was all about. It was the one genuinely independent country in South America. After the Spanish had gone, they closed the boundaries. A character called El Supremo, just like in your book. No one liked them because Dr Francia, his name was, had the balls to stick two fingers up to the rest of the world. Poor but honest, that was Paraguay, and who could tolerate a place like that?'

'All I remember was this one novel about Lopez and the War of the Triple Alliance.'

'You wouldn't believe the things that happened in that war. The Brazilians killed everyone, men, women, children. Genocide. Really. Like clearing the jungle of wild animals, the Argentine President said. Ninety per cent of the male population were slaughtered. Then the British came in, cheerful Charlies one and all, and built the railway; and started the rugby club. As

179

if they'd had nothing to do with the war. The railway carriage I went to the zoo in was made in Birmingham, 1910.'

'What did you live on, if I may ask, while you were – ?'

'Tennis, partly. I was the coach at El Club de tennis de Asunción. Also founded by the British. Half the backhands in Asunción are now British made.'

'What did you think of . . . the regime?'

'Old Stroessner? El General was already on his way out. The way things were was the way things were. I played tennis with his son a bit. I didn't think about it because there it was. To tell you the truth, I felt very free when I was in Paraguay. If you never feel safe, you never feel afraid.'

'Sartre in the Occupation, so he said.'

Barbara said, 'What was the . . . danger exactly?'

'Someone who mattered took a dislike to you. You looked at someone, or his lady friend, the wrong way, that could be that. You might get beaten up, you might get killed, then again you might get asked to dinner. Same when you went into the jungle, you could see fantastic things, ruins –'

'The Jesuit ruins must be amazing,' Adam said. 'I bought this book.'

'There's this church at Yaguaron, Franciscan actually, that you really have to go and see. But then at the same time, you could get bitten by a snake – they've got all kinds – and that would be that. Rattlers, fer-de-lance, the works.'

'You didn't catch . . . malaria . . . or anything?'

'Not malarial where I was. But I knew this guy, José. Uncanny. He knew all these herbal remedies. The Indians taught him. Something got infected, a cut or a bite, he'd beat up some root or find some mushroom or other . . . Met some weird people out there. Dad'd probably've hated most of them. I'll tell you something funny. Fairly. First blue-eyed, fair-haired refugees went out there, after the war, were Poles. *Polacos*. The Germans didn't turn up till a bit later. Blue-eyed, fair-haired, so they all got called *Polacos* too. My friend Wolf, everyone called him *Polaco*. Pure Kraut!'

180

Adam said, 'God's better at irony than He is at justice.'

Barbara said, 'Shall I make some more coffee?'

'I'm coffeed out, Mum, honestly. You got quite a few things right, you know, in *The Disappearance*. Robert thought you must've lived in South America. In another life, I told him, possibly.'

'Spain,' Adam said. 'Near Malaga. *The Disappearance* came before you were born. In good king Franco's golden reign. Only place I could afford to be a proper writer.'

'There were quite a few Jews in Asunción.'

'And Nazis?'

'Plenty. Stroessner didn't give a damn. Let 'em all come. He needed the *cabezas*. Brains. And muscle. What did he care? Long as they paid up. The Germans kept to themselves mostly. They had this town out there somewhere, was pretty well exclusively theirs. You'd sometimes see them in the city, the younger ones especially. I played tennis with quite a few of them.'

'How did you feel about doing that?'

'They had the dollars. I told them to bend their knees and keep their eyes on the ball. I didn't feel anything, unless it was a bit sorry for them. Growing up in the back of beyond. Nothing much to do. They rarely talked about their parents. The older generation mostly stayed in their . . . well, it was a camp really. Which was pretty well protected. As a matter of fact, I was one of their bodyguards for a month or two. Which was a gas.'

Adam said, 'Whose exactly, were you, bodyguard?'

'Never saw them. Old guys. They had this place, the Hotel Tirol. Miles from anywhere. Gave me this shack, up by the main road. All I had to do was ride round, make sure no strangers came on to the property. They were all scared Mossad would show up and put them in packing cases and ship them off to Israel, like they did Eichmann. My friend Wolf said his dad had told him that the Jews had won the war and they could do anything they wanted now. What's Rachel's thesis about exactly?'

Adam said, '*Fame and Fortune: Poets and Power in Ancient Rome.*

181

About covers it. Did they have any idea who you were?'

'Nor did I really. Because who am I? Who's anyone? Know what I'd really like to do? That's have a bath.'

'Well, it's included,' Adam said. 'At a small extra charge.'

'I'll come up and find you a towel,' Barbara said.

Adam stood in the kitchen, wondering whether to go to work as usual. Why wouldn't he? The routine of accumulating pages, of writing in his notebook, of being lost in writing, had for so long been his defence against thinking about Tom that his son's return seemed both a blessing and an intrusion.

'Still here?' Barbara said.

'Seem to be. I was making some more coffee, and pretending I wanted it. How do you feel?'

'I could try "Odd". Very. And also . . . fine. Fine.'

'Me too. Exactly. Bit of a relief, that, you feeling the same.'

Barbara said, 'You should go to California.'

'You've been thinking.'

'It'll do you good. And why wouldn't you now?'

'Why wouldn't I before? Does this mean you don't want to come?'

'And sit in a rented place while you work at a script you'll very soon be saying you wished you'd never agreed to do? Why wouldn't I want to do that?'

Adam said, 'Tom coming back makes you . . .'

'On the contrary. Makes me nothing. I was thinking exactly the same thing before he . . . arrived.'

'Everything changes and nothing changes. I'm afraid of being a coward. The trouble is, I don't know which is cowardly: going or not going. Possibly both. Because either way I'm afraid of something. You? Me? Failure? Success? Mix and they don't match. I wonder what Tom'll do now. "Into film". Jesus. Perhaps *he* should go to California.'

'He didn't have to come here if he wanted to do that.'

'Why did he? Come here?'

'You'll have to ask him.'

'I'll have not to. But I'd still like to know.'

'We are his parents,' Barbara said.

Tom came down in Adam's new white bathrobe. 'Practically nothing still fits that was in my cupboard,' he said. 'Coffee! Can I change my mind? Smells great.'

'That's because I always exceed the stated dose.'

'Even the sweaters are a bit tight.'

'None of my business, Tom, but how come you got out there in the first place, South America?'

'OK, I swung this job as a sort of steward slash entertainment jock slash gigolo on a cruise ship.'

'I had visions of you as a missionary somewhere in Africa.'

'Yeah? Not my bag finally. I did it for a few months and then I jumped ship at Montevideo, went down to Punta del Este . . . got quite a few things to tell you I still haven't. And never will, probably, some of them. I went over to B.A. with some people had a boat and after a few months I took the steamer up river to Asunción. Only fifteen hundred miles or so. There's your nutshell for you. Is this the time possibly to say how pleased I am that you . . . survived?'

Adam said, 'You at the door was the biggest . . . best surprise that we could imagine, and now you're here, it's no surprise at all, isn't that right, Ba?'

'For instance, Juliana,' Tom said, 'I haven't told you about.'

'True. Who is Juliana? He asked casually.'

'OK. Girl I met in Paraguay. We . . . got out together.'

'Got out? That sounds . . . Didn't they used to say "hairy"?'

'It was a bit. Once we made it over to Posadas, that's across the Paraná in Misiones, Argentina, the rest was easy really. We caught a bus down to B.A. . . . . Seventeen hours later, there we were.'

'Juliana. Local girl?'

'Sort of. Was then. German origin. Doesn't speak Alemán though. Born in Paraguay. Grandparents escaped from Germany. Swam rivers, hid in monasteries. Don't ask me what the hurry was, because . . . I didn't ask because, yes, I didn't want to know. But I could imagine. Not as well as you, because I was there and I messed around with those people. They don't spook me like they do you.'

'After the war, they escaped, the grandparents?'

'Grandmother was raped in Berlin, a lot apparently.'

'What was the grandfather doing when the going was good?'

Barbara said, 'Adam . . .'

'Ancient history's not my subject. I'll leave it to you and Raitch. Juliana was born in 1963, OK? Father runs a cheese factory. Viktor. Mother's Belgian. They weren't even in Europe during the war, not after forty-one or forty-two. Don't ask me why or how because I never asked them. Jules's grandpa got his kids out early, I assume. He was some kind of a businessman and he could travel when he liked, as long as his wife stayed in Berlin.'

Barbara said, 'This girl . . .'

'Jules is very beautiful. I hope you'll meet her.'

'She's still . . . around?'

'Very,' Tom said.

Adam said, 'Nice name. Somewhat regal. Where is she now then, Juliana?'

'OK, let's get to it. She's in Germany. She's got a brother went back there to study, Gunther, who's a top obstetrician now. So she's sort of . . . also going to see the best man she can.'

'That's why your sweaters don't fit,' Barbara said. 'You're pregnant.'

'It had to come out, as they say.'

Adam said, 'Is everything all right?'

'If it is with you, it is.'

'What do we matter?' Adam said. 'With the baby, I meant.'

Tom said, 'What is it, Mum?'

'Need a Kleenex,' Barbara said. 'Jealousy probably. When's it due?'

'July, they think.'

'Dear God,' Adam said, 'a German daughter-in-law who can't even teach me German!'

'The thing . . . the *next* thing . . . is she's coming to London.

184

We're not married incidentally. Lynch and Lopez ride again, right? She flies in this evening actually. I have to go out to Heathrow at six and . . .'

'I'll take you. In the Mercedes already.'

'What happened to the Alfa?'

'Mine turned out to be Beta. Not enough room in the back and too many horses in the front.'

'That would be wonderful,' Tom said. 'If you came. Both of you.'

'Too much, too soon,' Barbara said. 'Can't you drive?'

'Come on, Barbs,' Tom said, 'of course I can drive.'

'And ride horses.'

'Then he can take the car,' Barbara said. 'He's insured, isn't he?'

'If he's got a valid licence.'

'He has,' Tom said. 'German actually. I was there before I came over here.'

'Then take the Merc,' Adam said. 'Germany, were you?'

'Meanwhile . . . what does she like to eat?'

Adam said, 'I should've warned you. Your mother's Jewish now.'

'One thing no one ever called *me* by the way out there, and that was *Polaco*. I was always *El Moro*. The dark one. The hair.'

Barbara said, 'What is it, the baby, do you know yet?'

'Kind that comes with a spout apparently. Heard last night.'

'Welcome to the club,' Adam said.

When the telephone rang, the two fathers looked at each other and smiled their different smiles. Adam indicated to Tom that he should answer. Barbara turned away and opened the door of the fridge.

'No,' Tom was saying, 'this is his son. Well, he does. He's right here. Bruno Laszlo. He's still around?'

'Bruno! Hang on, I'm just going to go and take it in the other room. Because that's what I want to do.' Adam looked at Barbara. 'He always has to say "why-ee?" Why-ee? I shan't be long.'

185

Barbara said, 'Means goodbye for the foreseeable future.'

Adam went into his study. It was almost eleven o'clock. He was ashamed to think that he had wasted half the morning; ashamed because he should have been happy that Tom was there, and also because he had not written a word.

'I talk to your agent and he tells me you are not available possibly.'

'There's an offer being made, it's quite true, that I may not want to refuse.'

'I make you an offer at once. You can direct it if you want to.'

'Love's old sweet song. I don't even know you've got the rights for *The Big Time*.'

'I swear to you on the head of my son . . . I have the rights, I get you the money from Nat, from Red, from someone, it's not a problem. You go to Hollywood, I'm sorry for you. You know what Michelangelo said?'

'"I don't want to be in the pictures," didn't he? But the Sistine Chapel was a big hit just the same.'

'Antonioni. About Hollywood. "It's like being nowhere and talking to nobody about nothing".'

'I know. That was only after he'd had a flop, wasn't it?'

'Flop like hell.'

'I liked it,' Adam said. '*Zabriskie Point*less.'

'He should never have left Italy.'

'He comes from Ferrara too, doesn't he?'

'Look, *The Big Time*, you are the one man, because the book, to be honest wiz you, I don't care how many copies it sells, it's not witty, it's not – what can I say? – not hard-hitting enough. It's, a lot of it, I have to say, nya-nya, you know?'

'You do have that habit. And you could be right.'

'You have to make it witty like hell, you know. It needs to take bites out of England today.'

'That's exactly what I told you.'

'It's still true.'

'Bruno . . . I – I can't talk now. My son's just got back from

186

South America. With a pregnant girlfriend we haven't even met yet.'

'You're going to be a grandfazzer?'

'That does seem to be the . . . good news.'

'In dat case you know de bad news? From now on, you have to sleep wiz a grandmother. Listen, I call you later . . . because first I call de Ron Shapira again, as soon as California is open, and this time I don't take "maybe tomorrow" for an answer. Because tomorrow . . . who knows? Tomorrow maybe I am dead. Maybe you are. I hope not. I tell him you can be the writer *and* the director. How about I do that? I would still like to discover you as a director.'

'Talk to him by all means. Shapiro not Shapira.'

'Same thing.'

'Just don't tell him that I've agreed not to go to California, because I haven't.'

'You would be an idiot, I must say.'

'At least I'd be a *paid* idiot,' Adam said.

'That is not de right way to sink, if you don't mind me saying so.'

'Bruno, I have to go, OK?'

x

Joyce was lying, ankles crossed, on her newly reupholstered chesterfield reading a mint copy of *Le Big Time*, the French translation of her current bestseller. She had read French at Cambridge, but she was puzzled by several of the expressions that (she looked back at the cover to check his name) Max-Olivier Basso had used to render English slang into its Parisian equivalent. It was as if she were reading a book she had never seen before, in a language she thought she knew, but now feared she did not. How long ago it had all been, Sartre, Camus, Mauriac and all that *galère*! No one in the fifties syllabus had said *Magne-toi* or accused anyone of having *des yeux en trou de bite*.

187

When the phone rang, she laid the open book across the arm of the chesterfield, like a thick white circumflex.

'Hullo.'

'Joyce?'

'Yes.'

'It's Daniel. Dan.'

'I know,' she said. 'You're supposed to be in Italy.'

'But I'm not. Can I come in, please?'

She pressed the buzzer on the entry phone and heard the street door click open. Then she went back into the living room and took *Le Big Time* off the arm of the chesterfield and slid it, horizontal, among the books on the shelves. She looked round as if for other incriminating evidence (of what, though?) before she went to answer the knock at the flat door.

'What're you doing here?'

'I couldn't think where else to go.'

'You do have this knack of saying the sweetest things, don't you? No, you don't.'

'I'm just trying to excuse myself for . . . putting my foot in it. Sorry if . . .'

'You needn't be. You look . . . different.'

A neat, bronze-coloured beard emphasised the strong jaw and the high cheekbones and made the pale brown eyes seem deeper. In his longish fly-fronted yellow corduroy jacket over a cinnamon-coloured sweater, he was quite the actor again. Joyce smiled at the bold buckle on his broad leather belt. He seemed slimmer.

'I got to Heathrow,' Dan said, 'and I suddenly realised . . .'

'Take your coat off. Realised what?'

'I don't live here any more and I don't know anyone. I was going to go somewhere and call you first, but . . . seems I didn't.'

'If you came to London to see me, you didn't have to.'

'You know me,' Dan said.

'Do I? I suppose I do. Yes.'

'I saw your new novel on sale at the airport. Big stack.'

'Proves what tripe it is probably, doesn't it? Novels! Where are you going to stay?'

'Doesn't matter. Hadn't thought. I'll find a room. I've got money.'

'Stay here. Please.'

'I haven't any words. About Petie.'

'There aren't any any more,' Joyce said, 'not worth saying. They've all been used in shit books and lousy movies, haven't they, by people like me?'

'For quite a long time after I heard, I pretended I didn't know he was dead. No one else knew that I knew, so why should I . . . be different? I felt more . . . bruised than anything else, by him almost. He was . . .'

'I know he was,' she said. 'Was, was, was. Please don't spell anything out. I know you . . . feel what you do, and I'm sorry about everything.'

'There isn't anything for you to be sorry about.'

'Maybe I wish there was. Then I could be angry as well. Then I could be something. Oh hell, Danny, let's have a drink.'

'Danny!' he said. 'How long since you called me that?'

'The night we made Hannah,' she said. 'You were so sexy in those days. I don't know what happened. You got good probably. Or I got bad. Or neither. You don't not drink or anything conscientious like that, do you?'

'I'll have a drink.'

'I never know what drink I'd really *like*. Are you still making shoes, is that what somebody told me? Whisky OK? You didn't make those, did you?'

'These, no. A funny thing happened actually. It was funny at the time at least. It wouldn't be now necessarily. Whisky's perfect.'

'For instance? Do you want ice?'

'Straight. A man came into the shop where I was . . . making shoes, which I'd got rather good at actually, women's, and he . . . he noticed my *accento molto inglese* and − believe it or not − he asked me if I'd ever been an actor. They were making a movie

189

and this Englishman hadn't turned up, Hector somebody. In other words, probably, they hadn't paid him – and was I interested? I said no.'

'Of course.'

'And then I thought –'

'Fuck it, did you?'

'I did rather. So I didn't stick to my last. I reverted to my first, more or less. And . . . never went back.'

'I thought when you came in you looked oddly . . . shiny. No, you do: you shine. You're what you want to be. It's all right: I know you feel what you do, but . . . you still have this . . . *aura*. You look . . . like you used to at Cambridge, except for the grey in the beard. No, it's . . . nice.'

'Anyway, I did this part of a . . . British Tank Corps captain who gets involved with the partisans who're planning to hijack Mussolini . . . and . . . I rather enjoyed myself. Three weeks being brave and laconic. And very good catering they have on films. I met a woman too. That I . . . liked, quite a lot, as a matter of fact.'

'New experience for you, that!'

'Half-Hungarian. And they've asked me to do something else. Rather big. And I am tempted. Or was. Because this was before – what happened.'

'What difference does it make? You should do it. You must.'

Dan said, 'Can I talk about him, please, briefly, can I?'

'But not about the funeral, Danny. About him. The funeral won't be him.'

'It's that he was so . . . quiet, so clear, so utterly . . . the person he was, unpretentious but . . . somehow very sure of himself. No one else. Himself.'

Joyce said, 'He was your son.'

'Thank you. He was ours.'

'Yours. Yes, he was. He had three parents and the only one he was really like was the one that wasn't his . . . natural parent at all. I know it and you know it and that's why you're shaking your head.'

190

They stood there, not crying but weeping, each slightly angry as well as whatever else they were. They sipped at their whisky glasses until they were dry, and Joyce reached to refill them and he put his hand on her hand.

'Will you do something for me, Daniel?'

'Why else would I be here?'

'And promise you'll never tell anybody?'

'I don't tell people things,' he said. 'Never tell them what?'

'That you took me to bed. Now. That you fucked me and I fucked you, a lot, and it didn't mean a thing and that's all anything means. Anything you want to do, do. Except be nice. Please, will you? Because whisky isn't what I want. You were shining and don't say you weren't.'

'I won't say anything at all.'

'Be a stranger. A stranger's what I want. With a beard; and the boots.'

'The Big Time,' he said. 'That what you want?'

'Must be,' she said. 'Always did.'

V

On the day when he was to appear on the panel of Alan Parks's television programme, *That's Asking*, Adam drove up to Cambridge in his pale blue Mercedes 280 in time to have lunch with Rachel. Her thesis had been received with untypical enthusiasm by her supervisor. Sheridan Reece, who had also been Adam's tutor, was not a distributor of easy compliments. Adam was pleased when he went through the main gate and into the Porters' Lodge and was recognised by one of the bowler-hatted older men. Was it still all right that he had parked in the forecourt in the shadow of the chapel? 'You're a senior member of the College, sir, in a manner of speaking, aren't you?'

'I paid a fiver for my MA twenty-five years ago, Mr Follick, if that's what you mean.'

'Must be, sir.'

As Adam walked through Second Court, his smile was flavoured by the sweet taste of small privileges. Rachel had rooms in what members of the college called '*Very* New Court', to distinguish Collins Court's centrally heated, well-plumbed, steel and off-white brick modernity from the Gothic revival edifice which, despite being more than a century old, was still called New Court. Adam climbed the stairs and stood for a moment outside the door of 15C, with Rachel's name on it, before he knocked.

'Who could that possibly be? Come in, come in, whoever you aren't.'

'It's me. But you never guessed.'

'How are you, Daddy?'

'I am as you see me. The same as before, only later. In a word, "senior". I fear.'

'For a frightened man, you look fine to me.'

'I walked through college. It's full of young people and I'm still surprised, and alarmed, not to see any faces I recognise.'

'I'll bet quite a few of them recognised you.'

'Two did wince and looked away. So probably.'

'The T.E. Hulme Society guy asked whether I thought you'd come and talk to them.'

'On how to combine screenwriting with the finesse of fiddles, no doubt.'

'What else?' Rachel said. 'Well come on, what she's like?'

'What's she like?'

'Tom's . . . she's not his wife, is she, yet? Lady.'

'May never be, for all I know. You young people now-adays . . .'

'Do you want a glass of wine or anything? I haven't booked lunch anywhere, but . . .'

'We can go to The Whim or somewhere,' Adam said, 'can't we? In Trinity Street?'

'It'll have to be somewhere, because I don't know any whims in Trinity Street.'

'*Où sont les niches d'antan?* Tons of new places though, I noticed. Thank God we can be spared the Taj Mahal. The Whim used to be where the Gaiety went. The college theatricals' name for themselves. When "Gay" didn't mean *gay*, as far as we knew, or I knew; but what did I know? What do I?'

'I *know*,' Rachel said.

'OK. My daughter the doctor. I don't care where we eat. I'm so glad to see you.'

'It's put you off your food? Then answer the question. Juliana.'

'She is indeed the question. Blonde, slimmish, apart from the obligatory bulge, blue-eyed, medium to tall . . .'

'I'm not a policeman, Daddy. The way you describe her you'd think she stole your handbag. Get human!'

'Nice ears, I noticed. She's a pregnant Aryan-eyed stranger, looks German, doesn't talk it, excellent English. It's as if she was

193

dubbed, very, very well dubbed. I assume she loves Tom. I assume Tom loves her. Or don't people do that sort of thing any more? Your mother –'

'Ah my mother!' Rachel said. 'I did wonder when she'd come in. Thinks what?'

'– thinks she has something over Tom, Juliana, but she doesn't know what it is. I expect she was very nervous with us, which is something I never take into account. Then again, I look at her and I think of –'

'– the things you always do when there's a German in the month. Try reading their bloody scholars, mit de footnotes, and all you'll end up thinking is boredom and verbosity.'

'They should've stuck to that, *nicht war?*'

'And what do you think, about who's got what over whom?'

'I suspect Tom's been a bit of a hero . . . i.e. I think she's made him one. I don't know what, but he did something, to get her out of where she was. It made him strong and it's also made him . . . not weak, it's made him . . .'

'Grateful to the person who is grateful to him. He got her out of something, and she did the same for him.'

'Except –'

'– that it wasn't the same thing,' Rachel said.

'Could well be the truth, and may well not be. They have a joint secret, but perhaps it's only that they're together, against the odds. God, I wish I'd never agreed to do this damn television thing tonight.'

'Then why are you doing it? I have the answer right here as it happens. They twisted your arm, and you do love it when people do that.'

'Are you getting wise on me, Rachel Morris?'

'To you, possibly. You had a girlfriend called Wise, didn't you, once?'

'Depends what you mean by "had". In the modern sense, if it still is, I did not have that honour. I knew her, but not in the ancient sense. Sheila, yes, I did. Why?'

'Her daughter's up here, reading Classics. Olivia. I supervised her last term when Sheridan was laid up. Shingles. Did you like her?'

'Sheila? She had breasts like gift-wrapped presents, dare I say? And Christmas never came. I probably would've married her if she'd ever let me unwrap them. We never got further than the sofa . . . luckily. Not that I thought so at the time.'

'Juliana,' Rachel said. 'Tell me more.'

'We were all rather nervous and very polite and that gets in the way of knowing anything, even what you feel yourself. It was such a relief to see Tom that . . .'

'She was in the way.'

'The family way, even, he could not fail to jest – I think that was probably it. Two strangers, Raitch, is the truth, being kind to two others, is what we were, the four of us. Don't misunderstand me –'

'No? When that's the only way *to* understand you, isn't it?'

'*Hey!*' Adam said. 'She looked wonderful, Tom's . . . lady, the way pregnant women do: the flesh glazed with triumph, brilliant teeth, the electricity fully switched on, surgingly pneumatic, of course. It's going to be a boy apparently.'

'Are you pleased?'

'Between ourselves?'

'I don't see anyone else in the room.'

'No? I do,' Adam said. 'I see the recording angel with his stubby little pencil, or is it hers? Its?'

'If it was a girl it wouldn't be Jewish. Could that be what the rueful smile means?'

'Nor will it be, nor *need* it be, by whatever necessity makes these things necessary, even if it's a boy. The Semitic streak is getting thinner as the generations – what do generations do?'

'Generate, it seems.'

'Succeed to each other, don't they? But I'm a kicker and screamer, you know that, when it comes to that good night. Listen, poor Tom had to do what he had to do and now he's done it. What's it got to do with me? Not a lot. I'll give presents, if I can afford them, and I'll say oochie-koochie if the photographers insist, but for the rest . . . Oh listen, there's nothing I haven't told you.'

'And nothing much you have.'

'She was a pregnant blonde woman. Polite, beautiful, if you like vanilla; she helped with the washing up until your mother forcibly restrained her. She came as a stranger, and she left as one. She didn't want to have to meet us, did she? And why should she? I kissed her goodbye and she kissed me and each of us probably thought we were doing what the other one expected. Why did he bring her to see us after all this time? Who knows?'

'I can guess: they haven't got any money.'

'You're such a romantic, Raitch. She's fine. Don't dislike her before you see her. Nothing to dislike. I'm so glad to see you, darling.'

'Buy me lunch then, Dad? Said you would!'

'I'd buy you the moon, if you wanted it, but you must never know that, must you? You've even got wonderful hair. Where does it come from?'

'The usual bottles. What do you want to eat?'

'Anything but kosher or curry.'

They walked across the covered bridge over the Cam, below where Adam had shared rooms in his first year with Donald Davidson. Donald had been dead for more than thirty years. Adam thought of Francesca and how he would never tell anyone exactly what happened, or might have happened, when he went to her house. Rachel led him through Chapel Court, past the new library with its improbable door, and out of the side gate which he had once had to climb after a late night bridge game in Clare. A whole new parade of shops and eating places had replaced the low buildings that had been there in the Fifties. Adam and Barbara had spent many nights together on the floor of 5, Jordan's Yard, where the landlord was a ballistics boffin who liked to watch pretty girls dress, and undress. Access to the house was granted, and could be withdrawn, with capricious decisiveness, but Adam and Barbara were always welcome. Being given a place at Sunday lunch in Jordan's Yard was the bohemian equivalent, someone once said, of being invited to join the Apostles, a society of which Adam had never heard at the time.

'This is basically a fish place in here,' Rachel said, 'is that OK?'

'Fish and Friday,' Adam said, 'just the job. Tom's interested in film. Did I tell you?'

'Aren't you?'

'It's the way I make my living. Dare I say "our living"? I dare. In theory, it's the art form of our time. In practice, the cinema is third-rate people pretending to be second-rate, and second-rate people pretending to be *auteurs*. All human life is there, alas. And so is Mike Clode, the Maecenas of Beverly Hills, or so he would have me believe. I went into it thinking I could change it into something it had never been; but I never reckoned with the Russian winter, did I? It did for me before I could do anything much for it.'

'I'm not sorry for you.'

'Quite right. Leave that sort of thing to me.'

'OK if I have the turbot?'

'Let's both have the turbot,' Adam said. He smiled at the tall waitress. 'We'll both have the turbot, if we may.'

'Only one turbot left, I'm afraid.'

'Really? Poor thing. Right. *She*'ll have the turbot. I'll have the grilled liver and lots of disgraceful onions which is what I wanted anyway. With mashed swedes. Raitch?'

'Spinach?'

'And spinach for Dr Morris.'

'Any wine at all?' the girl said.

'Wine,' Adam said. 'Of course. How about a bottle of red? House red? Is that possible?'

'Carafe,' the girl said.

'Why not?'

'Red.'

'Red. I thought she'd never go. Where was I?'

'Nowhere we have to be.'

'Oh yes. A doctorate, I was all set to say, may not be as good

197

as being pregnant – in your case it may well be better – but it makes you equally beautiful, if not more so. What's happening with you and men? If anything is, on no account tell me the details.'

'I'm not –'

'You're not going to say "seeing anyone", are you? *Are* you?'

'You know what you are, Daddy? You're a verbal prude. But no, I'm not seeing anyone; I'm not even fucking anyone, as they all say up here these days, some of them. Did you flinch?'

'I flinched, but you didn't see. Verbal prude. You're right, aren't you? What a bitch though!'

'You have no idea how hard I've been working.'

'I do actually, because I never worked that hard, and I wish I had. Probably why I do now.'

'Sheridan wants me to apply for a junior fellowship.'

'Sheridan behind you, you should be a shoo-in.'

'But then what's in front of me? Teaching? I'm tempted, but I'm not sure.'

'The human condition, welcome to it,' Adam said.

'Is he going to marry her? Tom.'

'A neat *glissando*. He may have to, he told us in the modern style, so that she can stay permanently in the UK. Such is today's bureaucracy-driven passion.'

'Meaning you suspect –'

'I suspect only myself,' Adam said, 'of feeling too little and thinking too much. The fault of the Dutch, you may remember. *Mutatits mutandis.*'

'You give me too much credit.'

'What happens when men try to keep up with clever and beautiful daughters.'

'I am *not* going to call myself Dr Morris.'

'Leave that to the *goyim*, as we must never say.'

'Who's the turbot again?' the waitress said.

'You've been the turbot before! And you never told me.' Rachel said, '*Daddy* . . .'

'Verbal prudery, I remember. She is.'

'And you're the liver and onions.'

'There's no hiding it,' Adam said.

'Sheridan'd love to see you if you've got time. He said to tell you.'

'*Love*, did he really?'

'Try "rather like".'

'Fits like a glove.'

'He's quite shy about you actually. Slightly proud.'

'Is as far as it goes, if it goes that far. I gather the Master's retiring quite soon.'

'Any minute. But who knows when that'll be?'

'You should publish your thesis as a book.'

'Oh, I'm going to,' she said.

'Oh. Good. Any idea who might do it?'

'I was hoping you'd tell me.'

'Jason Singer'd look at it if I asked him. My agent. If he claims to understand a word of it, you should be clear for take-off. He'll probably want to call it *Sex, Blood and the Caesars*.'

'Fine by me,' she said.

'Sheridan's going to get it this time, isn't he? The mastership.'

'That seems to be the general assumption below stairs.'

'Bound to. He only just didn't get it last time. It's the one thing he's wanted ever since I used to call him "sir", thirty years ago. Please don't say "more". God help us, he wasn't much older than you are now. What's the betting?'

'Isn't any that I know of,' she said. 'The bookies're all rather assuming he'll be a — what's it you say all the time? — shoo-in, isn't it?'

'*All the time?* Seems rather a lot. Won't happen again. He is the Senior Fellow. It's only logical . . .'

'But then again, this is only Cambridge!'

'He'll get it. This time he has to. How's Trish?'

'Trish?'

'His wife.'

'Oh. Patricia is the preferred reading these days. Domesticated, very.'

199

'She always was very large for a little lady. She jutted.'

'She doesn't do that any more that I know of.'

'You like him, don't you, Sheridan?'

'I swear by him. And occasionally at him; when he's not around. Never lets me get away with a thing. Do you? Like him?'

'I always craved his purse-lipped approval, if that has anything to do with liking. You don't have to like people, do you, is the truth, and still . . . want them to like you?'

'I wouldn't say I *dis*liked him,' Rachel said.

The slightly Americanised Scouse voice said, 'A certain Adam Morris, can it be, a sometime scholar of our common college?'

Adam said, 'But what is this, what thing of land or sea that here approaches? How are you, Bill?'

'Throwing my usual girdle round about the earth. What is that, Shakespeare: what thing of sea or land . . . ?'

'Milton,' Adam said. 'About Delilah. You don't know my daughter Rachel, Bill, do you?'

'And what is much worse, she doesn't know me.'

'This is a certain Bill Bourne, tenured professor, no less, in Austin, Texas . . .'

'No less, but also no more: I am not Bottom, or so I like to believe, but I have been translated. I've removed to U.C. at Los Angeles, by popular demand.'

'Where was the demand exactly, in Texas or in L.A?'

'He felt obliged to quip,' Bill said.

Rachel said, 'I've read you on Catullus.'

'I should much sooner – but must never say so – that you read Catullus on me.'

'Rachel's just got her doctorate.'

'So Sheridan was boasting to me only last night under the famous Senior Combination Room's sagging ceiling. Which threatens, like the whole western world, to fall upon our heads, if not tomorrow, then by the weekend.'

Bill turned a chair and sat at their table.

'Sit down, Bill,' Adam said, 'and join us.'

Bill leaned towards Rachel. 'Might you and I meet in harmless colloquy one day when your father has been lured yet again along the yellow brick road that leads to the everlasting gong-fire?'

Rachel said, 'Why does everyone of your generation – ?'

'Cruel words, fair *doctoressa*,' Bill said, 'sealing us into a formaldehyde-filled amphora labelled Fifties Man.'

'– have to be so . . . *elaborate*?'

Adam said, 'Can it be because words were the only things not on the ration in our formative years?'

Bill said, 'Your parents were very nice to me and my then significant other years ago when we were all unknown, except for Adam. Are they still together, your parentals? He inquired confidentially.'

'At the last count,' Rachel said. 'So I'm innocent enough to believe.'

'*Very* together,' Adam said, 'is what it says in my text. And if my daughter wasn't here, I should make bold allusion to the erotic symphony – or should I say paw-de-deux? Probably not – which you and your dark lady conducted on our sitting-room couch. Upper Addison Gardens. Have a glass of wine, Bill.'

'Thought you'd never ask,' Bill said. 'Sheridan tells me you cavilled at my psychoanalytic reading of Catullus.' He sipped and coughed, and coughed again. 'Forgive us if we talk well above your head, Adam.'

'I can always remove myself tactfully.'

'Dubious. The slam of your father's doors is always audible for miles.'

Rachel said, 'I don't know that I *disagree* – about Catullus – but I do . . . question your –'

' "American-style reliance on a dated psychic *schéma*". So one of your more trenchant footnotes is reported to allege. That's s, c, h, e acute, m, a, Adam, if you're still with us.'

'He was here a minute ago,' Adam said. 'He left this note: "Up yours with a hay rake, Master Bourne".'

'Pleasures to come department,' Bill said. 'If you were still here, Dr Morris and I might embarrass you with reference to the back-entrance use of radishes in Roman erotic cookery and allied arts, but will gallantly refrain.'

'How long are you in England, Bill?'

'I'm the same length here as I am elsewhere. A month or two. I'm working on Martial and his under-rated arts. Then back to the City of Angels. They can't afford me here. Going west is the only way to go.'

'I'm supposed to be going myself, any minute.'

'First class.'

'Only way to go.'

'Then you'll be there when I get back.'

'Unless I'm not.'

'Covers most cases, I think,' Bill said. 'Are you living in college, um, may I call you Rachel?'

'I am. 15C, Collins Court.'

It was strange, Adam noted to himself, how Rachel giving Bill her address, which was hardly a secret, primed a wince of jealousy in him.

Bill said, 'Then I may call you, Rachel! See you on Rodeo Drive, Adam, or preferably Westwood Bullyvard.' Bill stood up, drained his wine, coughed and cleared his throat. 'Exit, as I was about to say, unpursued, but never bearish.'

Adam waved and then he picked up the chair that Bill had turned to their table and replaced it where it had come from.

Rachel said, 'The difference is always amazing.'

'Between cup and lip?'

'The man you read and the man you meet.'

'The man you read is often meatier. He thought you were very attractive. You couldn't tell?'

'A hawk from a handsaw? Of course I could tell.'

'He has quite a reputation, I'm promised, in the satyr role, and a trail of ladies to prove it.'

'Or disprove it.'

'As I was leaving it to you to say. I shouldn't really go to

Calif.,' Adam said, 'but I have this awful feeling I shall, because
. . . fool's gold is still the stuff to give the droops, I suppose.'

'Do you want me to say that you shouldn't go?'

'I was rather hoping you might plead with me, the tears in the
wide ancestral eyes backed with excellent reasons why I should
cast myself adrift from the good ship lollyplop and do something
worth doing, if I knew what that might be.'

'Jews and Jews,' Rachel said.

'A title to sink without trace.'

'That's really your subject, isn't it? Why we provoke them so
much? Doesn't matter who we are, they want to kill us, all the
time. How dare we not think the way they do? And yet for
centuries, we never tried to kill them. They had to make it up:
we poisoned the wells, we ate their children –'

'Never forget the Amalekites,' Adam said. 'All my
anonymous informants remind me about the Amalekites and
how it's been payback time ever since.'

'I wish you'd take a selection of eminent Jews – like Strachey
and the Victorians – including a crook or two –'

'Sidney Stanley would be the one. I'm truly not qualified.
Spinoza and Primo Levi, maybe; Trotsky, yes; but Nachmanides,
Jabotinsky, Rathenau? Meyer Lansky? Not my bag.'

Rachel said, 'It's Mummy, isn't it?'

'Is it? Bound to be. What is?'

'That you're afraid of.'

'I hadn't noticed. You have though. What do I fear? Remind
me. The French for a prompter is a *souffleur*, isn't that nice?'

'I know,' Rachel said. 'Her knowing. Is what you fear.'

'She knows already. Knowing what?'

'How . . . black you are really, and how deep.'

'Deep and black; can we keep it out of the papers, do you
think? She does know. And I'm still trying to keep it from her.'

'Is Tom going to stay in England then?'

'He's more likely to tell you than tell me. Stay or not, they're
still going to need somewhere to live. Why are you looking at
me? Why are they, in the corner?'

'Why do you always think people are?'

'In case they're not, probably. I've got a feeling they're actually looking at you. Why would they do that? I should go and see Sheridan. Are you coming?'

'I shall peel off, like any tactful banana. He'd like to have a talk with you, I know that.'

'Because he didn't say so! Are you coming to this broadcast of mine this evening?'

'Do you mind terribly if I don't?'

'Just what your mother would say. Very wisely. You've heard it all before, both of you. I shan't mind at all.'

'Promise.'

'No, I mean it.'

'I love you. You do know that, don't you?'

'Thank God,' he said. 'And thank you. I shall probably drive back to London immediately afterwards, doubtless with the howls of the mob echoing in my ears. So you're going to end up a fellow of the college I once climbed into, and still have the scars to prove it. Pulls up trouser leg. Reveals ugly hole in left calf.'

'I read "Start off". It's a bit soon for ending up.'

On the way out, Adam said, 'I don't know who you're seeing or not seeing, and it's none of my business, still less of my pleasure, but don't let Bill Bourne be one of them, will you?'

'You must be joking.'

'It is my ugly habit.'

They stood on the corner of St John's Street, waiting for a bus to clear the zebra crossing.

'He wasn't the basis of the character Patrick Clegg, by any chance, was he,' Rachel said, 'in that telly play you did about that red-brick university where someone had a cat called Chairman Miaow? He was.'

'But he must never know. Is my secret safe with you?'

'You made him rather attractive.'

'That's the salt I sprinkle. Indistinguishable from sugar, some might say, given the chance. Meaning he isn't? Bill. Attractive.'

204

'Meaning I bet he knows it was him.' Rachel kissed him and walked on towards Trinity Street. Adam waited for her to turn and wave. Just when he had given up hope she raised her right hand, without looking back, and twisted it a few times.

ii

As he walked across Chapel Court to Sheridan Reece's rooms, he felt as if he were regressing into the underprepared student who still hoped that a glib tongue would cover the gaps in his scholarship. He had looked forward and not looked forward to his weekly sessions with Sheridan Reece almost exactly as he now did to seeing his one-time supervisor. Reece had been difficult to impress, though not impossible to amuse. His amusement was declared in an involuntary simper, which might become giggles after an out-of-school glass or two. Reece had been at a grammar school near Carlisle from which no one had ever previously won a Cambridge scholarship. Having come alone from so far away, the ex–Bevin boy academic had willed himself to be what he was, and also what he was not. Only in the decade or so between the end of the war and the Suez affair had people such as Reece, and Adam, imagined that Cambridge was still that great, good place which it had been between the wars, if that was what it had been. Their ambitions, and their style, had been shaped in a mould that had been broken in the Sixties and which Margaret Thatcher's government, however blue, made no move to repair.

Adam climbed the coconut–matted stairs to Reece's rooms in the renovated part of Chapel Court, which was now neither ancient nor modern. Was that a Bach partita? Reece was a flautist in the college orchestra. His voice had something in common with the reed he played with such timely labial application. He stopped the record-player when, after a minute or two, Adam knocked on the door. Reece opened it, his usually sallow face slightly flushed, as if discovered doing something he wished to keep private.

'Ah, Adam!'

'Hullo, Sheridan, how are you?'

'I am . . . well, well.' Emphasis sounded like temporising with Reece. 'And you?'

'Fine. So . . . Rachel's . . . done well.'

'Your daughter, yes, she's quite a remarkable scholar.'

Adam said, 'Nothing to do with me, Sheridan, as you were almost certainly about to remind me. Or refrain from reminding me.'

'She sees across boundaries. Isn't that something you've been known to do, albeit perhaps in an unscholarly sense?'

' "Perhaps" is kind,' Adam said. 'What D.H. Lawrence called the Jewish genius for disinterested speculation. I hope he meant it nicely. The Jewish part. But then again, why would he? Is that what you're thinking of?'

'Didn't Lawrence have a friend called Kotelianski whom he admired very much?'

'Kot, he called him. Right as usual, Sheridan.'

'I wasn't thinking of a Jewish connection actually. But I was remembering the way you once analogised the conjunction of ethical statements and commands with that between Caryl Brahms, wasn't it, and S.J. Simon?'

'Was it? Dear God, trying a bit hard, wasn't I?'

'Flash and filigree,' Reece said, 'they have their place, they have their place.'

Adam said, 'The ironic and the matter of fact grow ever closer with you, Sheridan! One can be grateful and take offence at the same remark.'

'Thank you and no thank you,' Reece said, 'both can be covered by *merci*, and in some cases *gracias*, I believe.'

Adam said, 'Am I allowed to mention the topic of the moment?'

'And what might that be?'

'We're all hoping – not to say assuming – that you're going to be the next Master of the college. Not like talking about the Scottish play in the dressing room is it, I hope?'

206

'It's on the knees of the gods. No reliable perch. For the present, we still incline to the Master you first thought of. I should be false to deny my ambitions in that direction, and foolish to discuss them.'

'Right. You know, Sheridan, I can't help feeling that Rachel has done precisely what I should have.'

'And what precisely is that?'

'All right. Stayed up in Cambridge, I meant, and done some serious work. You can't imagine what it's like having people never really wanting you to say the things you want to say. They put money in your mouth instead of a gag, but the effect's still the same.'

'I suspect you rather like it that way. And do you suppose that that never happens here? It's just less money, some might say. We too watch our steps. We simply take shorter and more careful ones. Why would anyone choose to be a third-rate academic when he can be a second-rate novelist?'

'You didn't really say that, did you?'

'We're all rather hoping you've yet to write your best book.'

'That's very . . . I must rummage in my adjective box. And what about you, Sheridan? How long must we go on eagerly expecting your *magnum opus*?'

'On what topic are your expectations centred?'

'*Off*-centred,' Adam said. 'How about "The Unresolved Equation, colon, Wittgenstein and Politics"? The colon establishes your academic credentials. I'm serious. It would put you where you deserve to be.'

'It's very good of you to be so concerned with my career prospects, Adam.'

'Look, I know you were offended, weren't you, by the character in *An Early Life*? Brendan Armitage?'

'Offended? Was I? Surprised. It's not often that one catches sight of one's "purse-lipped" self through someone else's eyes. Fortunately, perhaps. Good for the morals, however; also perhaps. In small doses one wouldn't often choose to have repeated.'

'There's nothing like a heart-felt tribute,' Adam said, 'to rend the veil from end to end.'

'Heart-felt I question,' Sheridan Reece said. 'But even veils can be repaired. Supervising your daughter has been my best revenge.'

'Which is what I came up here to thank you for. Heart-felt shouldn't be disputed in this case. You were just the doctor I would have ordered when Rachel needed your help.'

'It was a pleasure.' Sheridan Reece had not followed Adam to the door of the room. He was straightening the chair in which Adam had been sitting, and which had rucked the carpet. He looked up and said, 'Trish, on the other hand, was very distressed by what you wrote about her in your novel.'

'*Trish* was? I didn't writer about her.'

'"Brendan Armitage", I think I quote correctly, "had married a woman that he made sure remained beneath him".'

'That wasn't meant to be Trish. I wasn't thinking of her in the least.'

'Ah. Perhaps that's what upset her.'

'I'm terribly sorry, Sheridan. Please tell her. Truly.'

'Tell her yourself,' Sheridan Reece said, 'if you want to. She's coming to hear you tonight. Your broadcast.'

'Good God, is she really? Why does she want to do a thing like that?'

'Perhaps she has a question she wants to put to you.' Reece contrived to remain at a distance from Adam.

'Thank you again for what you did for Rachel.'

'My job, you mean.'

iii

Adam went to Heffer's and loitered among serried texts he should have read long ago or might now choose to read, were he the man he thought he still might be. He bought four books, one of them Max-Pol Dobrinsky's *Les Juifs et L'État*, a conspectus of European attitudes to Jewishness, 1800 to 1948, which looked bracingly tedious and which he would almost certainly never have bought, least of all in England, had he not been told, the previous day, that Samuel Marcus Cohen (cited from *Débats*, at length, on the back cover) had been impressed for the A.N. Other role on that evening's panel of *That's Asking*.

Adam felt so disturbed by what Sheridan Reece had said, and by the falsity of his own remarks, that he had an urge to get into his car and drive home. As a result, for fear of being late, he arrived earlier at the Arts Theatre than the other panellists, whose smiles he expected to be as false as – good heavens, he suddenly realised – Sheridan Reece's teeth. He wished that he had arranged to see Rachel again; it might have restored him to himself. He wanted to confess the shame he felt at his tone with Reece, that mixture of aggression and deference which he most disliked in himself. He was abruptly aware, as if of his own age, that he and Rachel would probably never again live in the same house.

Adam went upstairs to the bar and sat there, with a cappuccino, reading *Les Juifs et L'État*. When he heard sufficient sounds of activity, he went down to the greenroom and introduced himself to Fiona Maclean in a more diffident manner than he had adopted on the telephone. She had the dark, trouser-suited assurance of a woman who had no difficulty in slipping through the strait gates of power and to whom all celebrities were mere probationers.

'I don't know whether you know Susie Beaumont . . .'

'Largely by her manifold works and wickednesses,' Adam said. 'How are you, Susie? I'm still Adam Morris.'

'I know. I was warned. I still came.' Susie Beaumont disdained looking merely beautiful in favour of the handsome anguish which was her durable, and dateless, accessory. She was an intellectual Queen of Sheba who intended to yield nothing to any Solomon in the way of wisdom. The black curls on the bold head seemed to be a natural eruption of the dark rage which marked her many public denunciations of post-capitalism culture. In one of the mythologies on which she was a comparative expert, the blaze of white hair above her forehead might have been evidence that she had wrestled Zeus to a draw.

'Which of you are you going to be tonight,' Adam said, 'the steel-tongued critic who hated my last movie, and the one before, or the bare-breasted advocate of Amazonian she-gemony?'

'I had a mastectomy two months ago,' Susie Beaumont said. 'Are you blushing?'

Adam said, 'I was speaking metaphorically, he parenthesised lamely. How are you now?'

'I am like poor Kitty in the rhyme,' Susie said, 'with only one titty, to − bump against the wall − isn't that how it goes? But otherwise . . . in shape, shall we say?'

'You're here to publicise what, Susie?'

'*Initial Promise: F.D.R., J.F.K., L.B.J.* Essays in presidential ingratiation and self-imagery.'

Samuel Marcus Cohen stood for only a second in the green-room doorway, assessing the company, and then came straight towards Susie Beaumont. '*Cher maître!*' he said. '*Chère* . . . I think *Madame* will have to serve, though it hardly carries the *full freight* of your at once polemic and polyvalent personality.'

'What a rare capacity you have, Samuel Marcus,' she said, 'for speaking *entirely in italics and with an alliterative vocabulary that only a foreigner could mistake for stylish!*'

'*Initial Promise* is, if I may dare to slip a compliment between your fangs, a title entirely congruent with your genius for incisive iconoclasm.' In double-breasted blue blazer and white shirt, Samuel Marcus had the gloss of a bowls champion about to go to the mat. 'Might I mention, however, in advance of a no doubt imminent reprint, that Yamamoto was no less a gambler than Franklin Roosevelt, and was indeed an addictive *joueur?*'

'I knew that,' Susie Beaumont said. 'Everyone does.'

Fiona had been standing slightly aside, with a transistor to her ear. She turned it off and put it into her black leather bucket bag. 'Has everyone got what they want in the way of drinks?'

Susie Beaumont said, 'What kind of questions are they liable to ask us?'

'No telling!' Fiona said. 'Surprise is of the essence.'

'Likewise predictability,' Gavin Pope said.

Adam said, 'Gavin has a capacity for arriving as though he's been here all the time.'

'The great British pubic,' Gavin was saying, 'only ever wants to talk about sex and what was on the telly last night, which hardly changes the subject.'

'This is Gavin Pope,' Fiona said, 'as I'm sure everybody knows.'

'And if not, it's never going to be for want of his trying.'

'Always nice to be among friends, Susie, but failing that, how cautionary to see your modest self! The blushing violet is so rare at this time of year.'

'Still coping and groping, Professor?'

'Not for a living. I'm advising the government with one cerebral lobe and practising at the Bar, with a big B, with the other. Better gilded than plastered, I've decided. As between now or never, I've opted for the former. Money-making, I have discovered, late but not too late, is the only honest form of intellectual activity.'

'Well, that's cleared that one up.'

'Ten to,' Fiona said. 'I think we could all make our way upstairs . . . Alan's been warming up the audience.'

'We'd better be careful not to touch it with an ungloved hand,' Adam said. 'Why ever do we do these things?'

'*Chez les putes on monte,*' Samuel Marcus said, '*chez les intellos, c'est plutôt la descente, parfois vertigineuse.* Michel Pic.'

'Should cover it,' Adam said.

Susie Beaumont was saying, 'Do I hear you're eventually planning a spectacular return to academic life, Gavin? Via the high road, could it be?'

'You know so much more about people than they will ever need to know about themselves, Susie dear. I simply let the chips fall where they may, but I do shake a little salt on them, and then gobble while the gobbling's good.'

As they climbed the wooden steps towards the stage, Samuel Marcus held Adam back by the sleeve. 'You've heard, no doubt, that ex-professor Pope is soon not only to be ennobled as Lord Turncoat the First but, so I gather, from peachable sources, is also slated to be the next Master of the college to which some clever travellers manage to return. To wit, your own fine, if never scintillating, foundation.'

When Adam was called out from the wings and took his place, to more applause than he expected, he felt, yet again, as if he had volunteered to be examined in a subject of which he knew markedly less than the other candidates. A minute before transmission, Alan had to ask panellists please to pour themselves glasses of water if they wanted them, since to do so 'on mike' sounded like (as his demonstration proved) 'someone having a tinkle'.

Since Alan Parks was a question master who often chose to be the answer master as well, sustained speech was rarely required of the panellists. Listening to his own answers, Adam was surprised by the modest fluency with which he impersonated himself. He looked down at the pad of paper in front of him when, more often than he expected, his contributions provoked the applause to which the audience had been encouraged by Fiona. Adam remembered how, when Winston Churchill was still Prime Minister, he had written and taken part in a Footlights sketch performed on that same stage. He had parodied a Labour politician to whom he ascribed the gruff line, 'We in the Labour Party will do everything in our power to get everything in our power.' The roar of blue laughter and applause which greeted the remark had gratified and slightly unnerved him: until that moment, he had taken it for granted that everyone of his own age was a Socialist.

'And the next question,' Alan Parks was saying, 'is from . . . Bryan Lacey. Bry'n'Lacy, sounds like a country and western couple rolled into one, which I'm told they often are. But enough about me, yes, Bryan? Your question?'

'Come to that,' the plaid-jacketed Lacey said, 'Al'n'Parks

sounds like a pair of old-fashioned comedians rolled into one, and he looks like them too.'

The laughter and applause from the audience (Adam noted how they looked at each other as they clapped and then laughed even louder) made Alan nod, like a boxer who smiles to show that he hasn't been hurt, when he has. 'I think I can fairly be said to have asked for that,' he said. 'And now – while I wipe the custard pie out of my facial orifices – kindly put your cleverly premeditated question.'

'Should there be more sex education in our schools and if so, what and how much should schoolkids be taught about what?'

'Not much sign of country or western there, unless we take a Shakespearian view, which is, of course, liable to have this programme kicked summarily into the long grass and other places where wild colonial boys used to pick up the rules of the mating game. Samuel Marcus Cohen, you're a man of parts . . .'

Samuel Marcus tapped his pencil until the laughter subsided. 'May I intrude a discordant note of what may well seem supererogatory seriousness in the present circumstances?'

'Why else have we come all this way to hear you, Samuel?'

'Education in this country has suffered, in the last thirty years, from the doctrinally driven delusion that schools should be places not where the young learn difficult subjects and are, if necessary, drilled into awareness of something beyond what they can as easily obtain from the television – the greatest pedlar of vulgarity yet to be devised . . .'

'Indeed!' Alan said. 'Why else are we all so keen to be on it? But have no fear, even as we squeak someone somewhere is working to bring us something much cheaper and, no doubt, infinitely nastier.'

'May I revert? Education is not, in my view, a matter of nuts and bolts.'

'That's socking it to them.'

'You are nervous, Mr Chairman, lest inadvertently something unamusing should happen to be said. Let me be alone in trying not to be funny or popular. I confess to the heterodox view that schools are there to provoke the young to think and to excel, yes, to excel, rather than to remain in loyal and empty-headed subservience to the lowest common denominator.'

'LCD is another term for sex, is it? I was never taught that. Wish I'd known. What about HCF?'

Samuel Marcus said, 'At the risk of ridicule, I would argue again – as I did in my book *Art, Obscenity and Media* – and even more forcibly with the lapse of years, that with the young, as with so-called adults, sex and sex talk now furnish the opiate that religion once supposedly did.'

'And hallelujah, some might murmur,' Susie Beaumont said, more to Gavin than to the audience.

'You are wrong, madame, and – if I say so – damnably wrong. *La trahison des clercs* is not only a matter of bearing false witness but also of saying what procures factional applause. The best *educational* instruction in matters of the heart lies in the study of poetry, not anatomy, and you know it, Miss Beaumont. I also expected – indeed knowingly solicited – this audience's derisive hilarity, since that is what they are commissioned to deliver when anything serious is said.' Samuel Marcus glared not at Susie but at Adam, who smiled at the scrap paper on which he was doodling.

Alan Parks said, 'Gavin Pope, you're rumoured – accurately for once, I believe – to have the Prime Minister's ear. Not with you, of course, but . . .' He waited for the release of laughter. 'What has her majesty vouchsafed to you about her thinking on, um, country matters, or should I say the ins and outs of affairs concerning the country?'

'You have a rare capacity, Master Parks, for cracking the same jokes into the same omelette more often than anyone else in captivity.'

'Enough of this love-making, Gavin. Sock it to me.'

'"Her majesty",' Gavin said, 'is a term which, in my sweet old-fashioned way, I apply only to my Queen.'

'Well, that's between the consenting two of you . . . I should, of course, have said "her almightiness", as will appear in later

214

editions. Mrs Thatcher in other words, if there are any.'

'I'm only slightly embarrassed to say that I agree – perhaps for the first time – pretty well entirely with Samuel Marcus Cohen. There are two sides to sex –'

'And counting,' Alan said.

'You know the trouble with this programme, Alan? You know what it is?'

'I only know it can't be me.'

'Like English education, it's not sure if it wants to be serious or whether it's just a way of keeping oiks off the streets.'

'In a word, it's likely to run and run, you're telling me?' Alan turned abruptly from Samuel Marcus. 'Susie Beaumont,' he said, 'in your time – which I am in no way suggesting has passed – you've disrobed very becomingly for a range of adult publications, I'm told by my diligent researchers, so what's your open, wide answer to "What shall we tell the children?"'

Susie did not smile. 'Everything and nothing,' she said. 'I agree and I also disagree with what everyone else has said. Because yes, it's a waste of time to teach kids how little wiggly things –'

'That's not a covert reference to Gavin Pope, I trust.'

'Alan, how about you go into a welcome period of quietus for the foreseeable next ten seconds? To you it will seem interminable, to us an oasis.'

Alan nodded at the laughter. It was what the programme needed. '. . . eight, nine, ten. Go, Susie, go! How little wiggly things, you were telling us –'

'– bully their way into eggs and, given time and luck, lead to people like . . . our chairman. Because that's not what they want to know.'

'Which is?'

'When and where do I get some?'

'A problem for the ages,' Alan was nodding at Fiona, who was pointing to her watch. 'Adam Morris, in the couple of seconds we have left to us? Sex education: how much, how little? What shall we tell the children?'

215

Adam said, 'Well, it's worth remembering that a certain amount of instruction does come with the kit, doesn't it?'

He had played to the gallery and it responded with the same gush of laughter and applause that had greeted him on the same stage thirty-something years before.

'Says it all, Adam,' Alan said, 'and that's all I can say, because . . . that's all from *That's Asking* till next week in – hurried glance at notes – unspoiled Stoke-on-Trent. Thank you, and . . . g'night!'

The usual applause, sustained until they had a 'clear', enabled Fiona to say that it had all gone exceptionally well. Adam alone, out of courtesy or relief, applauded the audience, soundlessly, as he left the stage and followed the others back to the greenroom, where sandwiches and fruit were revealed from under crinkled cellophane. The bottles were already open. Gavin Pope asked for fruit juice.

Samuel Marcus came close to Adam. 'May I ask you something?'

'As long as it's not in the original Hebrew.'

'What emanation of the *zeitgeist*, I wonder, impels you to make that kind of wantonly self-distancing response?'

'Put it down to proximity to "possibly our greatest living intellectual", if I read your blurbs correctly. Which, of course, I have no reason to suppose that you yourself composed.'

'Never, albeit I am known to have pleaded in mitigation of the superlatives. Are you conceivably returning to London this evening?'

'Am I ever? Like a shot.'

'In your own vehicle?'

'Paid for out of taxes. Yes. You want a lift?'

'Whisper it not in Gath, but I do not greatly wish to share the communal conveyance that brought me up here with our unrelievedly entertaining chairperson and his sycophantic cohorts.'

'Cohorts seems a lot,' Adam said. 'Hyde Park Corner do you?'

'I seem to provoke you to a certain . . . how shall I best express it?'

'God, if you don't know, who else is likely to?'

'All right: regressive facetiousness. It does you less service, and honour, than perhaps you imagine.'

Alan came up with a polite plate. 'Any more sarnies anyone? You excelled yourself, Master Morris! Need I say? Your favourite activity! Sorry I had to cut you short.'

'The badge of all our race,' Adam said.

'I wish you'd been as good on the programme as you are off it, I must say. No, I don't though. Thanks a lot. Come again. If invited.'

A small, stout woman in a longish brown floral dress with a gathered top was standing in the doorway. Adam noticed her before he recognised her and then she was coming towards him.

'Hullo, Adam. You don't remember me?'

'Of course I do. Sheridan said you might be coming. You never got to ask your question though, Patricia! Sorry about that.'

'I want to ask it now,' she said.

'By all means.' Adam braced himself, with a smile, for some reproachful inquisition. 'Which doesn't mean I can answer it.'

'The S.C.R. ceiling,' she said.

'I'm sorry?'

'Sheridan mustn't know that I even mentioned it.'

'Right. In what connection?'

'What it could mean for him if there was something you could do.'

'The S.C.R. ceiling, what would I be doing if I could?'

'Finding the necessary money to stop it falling in.'

'Forgive me, Trish – Patricia - but . . . as we Jonahs tend to say when faced with a whale of a question: why me?'

'You seem to have done very well.'

'I'm a writer. The rumours of my millions are, I assure you, much exaggerated.'

'It would mean so much to him,' she said.

217

'Look, I'm very willing to . . . contribute in a . . . modest way, but . . . what exactly is this going to do for . . . um, Sheridan?'

'Isn't it obvious?'

'Must be why I missed it.' Adam looked towards Samuel Marcus but he and Susie Beaumont seemed to be exchanging references.

Patricia Reece was saying, 'If Sheridan were to be associated somehow in procuring the means to save the ceiling . . . If the money were to be – I don't say conditional on . . . anything but . . .'

'I understand. I wish I could write you a cheque. Or him. Or the college. You seriously think it might – what's the word?'

'I'm sure you know it.'

'Redound's the one, I think. As in redound to his credit. Are you sure?'

'It has been . . . indicated. Without anyone saying so in so many words of course.'

'Or in too few, I trust, if trust is quite the word. I can talk to some people, is all I can say for the moment.'

'He has no idea that that's why I came tonight.'

'Just as well.'

'I'd better go. Thank you for seeing me.'

'Oh for heaven's sake!' Adam took a step towards the door, but she did not follow.

'It might make all the difference,' she said.

'Patricia . . . may I just say . . . I never had any intention of hurting you, or Sheridan, you know, with that character . . . in my novel.'

'You didn't,' she said. 'In the least. You were very good on the programme just now. I wish you'd been able to say more. You were too modest.'

'Thank you. A rare charge. And thank you for coming. Truly.'

Susie Beaumont said, 'Who was little Mrs Dowdy?'

'An old friend of mine actually, Susie.'

'Can I ask you something I have no right to?'

'Those are the ones it's a pleasure to answer. Sometimes. Shoot.'

'I've written a screenplay.'

'Not much of a question there. So far.'

'It's coming. I'm having some problems.'

'Morning sickness goes with the territory. Hot flushes are to be expected. And a sudden appetite, possibly, for humble pie in selected cases.'

'Have your fun, Adam, but don't be a smart-ass all the time. If I send it you, could you possibly bear to scribble in my margin?'

'I can save you the postage right here and now, if you like. What you need to do is take twenty pages out of the first fifty, strengthen the main female character – i.e. make her more pro-active and write her with bigger boobs – and accelerate a whole lot more towards the end. Keep your eye on the plot. That'll be five bucks and you don't even have to bend your knee.'

'I'd still like to send it. I asked Jake Leibowitz who I should talk to about it. He said you.'

'Meaning he didn't want the job.'

'He said you were the smartest man he knew. In the field.'

'And I don't even know him, which might account for it. Jake's the only ranking director who I seriously . . . take seriously. You didn't like his Byron movie. I did, a lot. And even you can't argue with *Roses, Roses . . .* can you?'

'I can argue with anything, because anything is arguable. That's the nature of language. But I thought it was pretty good. The mutability of the female character was rare in male-dominated cinema.'

'Wigs aside, I also thought it was a hell of a good thriller. You probably didn't notice that part.'

'Sure I did. I'm not entirely the person you think.'

'But then again, who is?' Adam said. 'What's it called, your screenplay?'

'*A for Omega.*'

'*Cum cantibus in choro?* Had to be.'

Alan was calling, 'Susie . . . the barouche is at the door.'

'Send me your script by all means,' Adam said. 'I'm sure I'll be humbled and instructed. You'll almost certainly think you're on the wrong track because I'm so kind and encouraging.'

Susie did not have to stand on tiptoe to kiss Adam on the cheek. When her hand held his against her breast, he was ashamed to be wondering if it was the real one.

iv

As they walked towards the multi-storey car park, Samuel Marcus Cohen said, 'Have I distracted you possibly from an incipient *rendezvous gallant?*'

'(a) I don't do those things, and (b) making love to Susie Beaumont would be, *grosso modo*, like trying to put your hand up the Statue of Liberty's skirt.'

'A pun too far can sometimes make its point, as – I grant you – in this instance. Who was it who said that she "treads the narrow line between the feminine mystique and the mistaken female"?'

'I must ask her,' Adam said. 'Mentioning your name, of course.' He unlocked the driver's door of the Mercedes and, once inside, leaned across to allow Samuel Marcus to get in.

'Are you possibly unaware that Susan Beaumont's maiden name was, and underlyingly remains, Mona Feinemann?'

'Underlyingly remains, does it? What's that in the original Hungarian again?'

'There was tonight, I cannot but sense, an inadvertent plethora of Jews, which may – but only *may* – account for the frantic frivolity and – if I have my jargon right – camera-hogging antics of the antipodean humorist at whose behest we were convoked.'

'I don't believe anyone even noticed apart from you who was or had been Jewish and who wasn't.'

'We shall, nonetheless, stand together in the same tumbril, or cattle truck, at the last trump. Tolerant provocation – or might it better be provocative tolerance? – is an aspect of the undying cultural dichotomy to which a Marcuse might have appended some useful insights.'

Adam said, 'Your problem, if I may say so, and I may, since this is my Mercedes and we're not even sharing the petrol – oh my dear fellow, pray take your hand out of your pocket, I was only joking – is that you can never quite decide whether you mean to be the noblest Hebrew of them all or wish the rest of us in perdition while you yourself – by virtue of having guessed what was coming – avoid the inevitable. In a word, a twentieth-century Josephus. As between God and Caesar, Caesar has the hotter tickets, but only just, of course.'

'Your performance tonight, like your best work, reflects if *I* may say so – with rare luminosity – the singular duplicity of, in particular, emancipated British Jewry.'

'That sounds like the end of the good news to me. Now for the weather?'

'Your superficial brilliance is the symptom alike of an illusion of facile assimilation – the accent, the glib tongue – and of an egregious sense of inescapable alienation. You draw attention to your Jewishness the better, as you imagine, to escape its reality. As for the famous Oscar, it is at once the laurel on your brow and the millstone around your neck.'

'Would it spoil your evening if I said you were quite possibly right? Not that I forgive you.'

'You will remember what Theodor Adorno said.'

'Not all of it, honestly.'

'"After Auschwitz, no more poetry." Meaning what precisely, do you suppose?'

'Pass.'

'He expected, I suspect, and he did somewhat confirm this to me on one informal occasion, a radical revision of the modalities of western art, the whole language of romance and moral optimism. On the face of it a magisterial misreading, yes, but did his apophthegm not perhaps imply that parody would become indistinguishable from what was once, as they say, the real thing?

Drama becomes collage; its characters do not express themselves in words but are embargoed by words from self-expression: the self cannot any longer be said. Tragedy, in such circumstances, impersonates comedy, without the laughs, and vice versa. We live, in short, in a meta-culture of categorical confusion. Tomorrow can never again be another day.'

'But then, of course, it always is. The bloody thing. And many people have honey still for tea. I omit the American breakfast, as in "a roll in bed with honey", a jest beloved of dated schoolboys of a certain *tranche sociale*.'

'Even in the circumstances of privacy, I note, you play to the unseen audience, your English constituency, which will give you no loyalty in return for your – dare I say? – *collected smirks* than it would for the authenticity that you withhold from it, as from yourself.'

'Whenever I listen to you,' Adam said, 'I'm left with the feeling that you think you're the only real Jew we've got in this country. As perhaps the most famous man in the world more than once said, "-ish is what we are, some of us".'

'You have gone as far in your fictions as equivocation can carry you. I ask you, purely as a passionate admirer, where can you go now?'

'Right at Gant's Hill and up through Tottenham.'

'The *réponse obligatoire*; it not only turns away wrath, which is venial, but respect too, which is not.'

Adam said, 'It's no great scandal, S.M.C., and no great treachery, to see both sides of a question. And both sides of an answer. Ish lacks all conviction, you, and Yeats, may say. That's what I like about it. Your problem is that you wanted to play the Grand Inquisitor and be burnt at the stake at the same time.'

'One of your eminent contemporaries once said of you that no one should underestimate your "piranha-like ferocity" when crossed. I now see his point.'

'Wait till you cross me. Meanwhile, save your insights, I should, at least till we get to a taxi rank.'

'This gleeful, perhaps merely playful, exercise of vulgar

muscle is not remarkably to your credit. My message to you could be put very simply –'

'But then no one would know it came from you.'

'You have a gift, God-given or Caesarian, *peu importe*, and you are in the process of wasting it.'

'A monosyllabic Anglo-Saxon retort bounds, as you might say, into consciousness. Which doesn't mean you're not somewhat right. But then again, S.M.C., wasting it and wanting not have unexpected affinities. I deplore them, as you do, but families must be fed; and housed. One day may indeed never come, but when it does, who knows what nastier piece I may not write for you.'

'In art there are no excuses,' Samuel Marcus Cohen said.

In the hope that it would seem a reproachful courtesy, Adam went out of his way to take his passenger to the bulky, red-brick Finchley house which he shared with his lawyer wife, Tanya Kahn, who lectured on Human Rights at the LSE. As Adam drove on towards Fulham, a series of expressions, dismissive and chastened, angry and amused, paraded across his face. All seemed appropriate.

The light was on in the bedroom window when he drove up to the house.

'You're awake,' he said.

'As if I'd dare not to be,' Barbara said. 'Yes, I did watch it. You did very well. When they let you get a word in.'

'You were quite right. I should never have done the stupid programme.'

'I never said any such thing.'

'And you were quite right. I speak your body language, sometimes. So be careful. Too many Jews is the truth, on it.'

'Imagine if I'd said that.'

'Certainly not.'

Barbara said, 'In case it's what you want to hear, the deal's made.'

'Excuse me? Deal?'

'When you act innocent and aren't, I can see why you're not on the stage. You overdo it. Shapiro called, and deigned to speak to the little woman. They've agreed what they wouldn't agree to. Master Shap has the deal letter in front of him, I am to tell you, and the tickets will be messengered here momentarily. Mike wants you there next week, latest.'

'Shit.'

'I knew you'd be pleased. But then imagine if Mike had decided he didn't want you to write the movie after all, and Harold was going to put his muddy little pauses all over it. Happy now?'

'You're coming with me, aren't you, to Calif.?'

'You know I'm not.'

'I won't stay more than a few days.'

'You won't *want to*, but . . .'

'Two weeks at the outside,' Adam said. 'There's now talk of dumping *Fatso* in favour of a hotter number. Cumquat what may, I'll bite on the bullet-points and then I'll flounce out. OK?'

'Have I conveniently said something I shouldn't?'

'It's not convenient. At all. Any of it. But one is always lucky to find oneself in a comedy. Not everybody does, God knows. Rachel sends you lots of love. She's the real reason I did the bloody programme, you know that. We had a lovely lunch. Jesus, Ba, when you look at me like that —'

'You think of all the tarts you never had.'

'Do I? Not tarts necessarily. Do you ever dream of handsome blond oarsmen taking their serial pleasure with you?'

'One's enough, eaten slowly. You did ask. No, actually, I just tend to get to feel . . . *superfluous*.'

'Not to me. To me you're . . . at once contingent and necessary, as the appalling Samuel Marcus would say, but at even greater length and with a lot of emphasis added. The little shit thinks I'm wasting myself on unworthy trivialities. So do you, don't you?'

'Are you planning to come to bed at all tonight?'

'Ah! That's what I came home for. Thanks for the prompt. Truth is, you get so keyed up doing these silly shows . . . I can dump California, you know, if –'

'You can't, and you won't, and Tom and Juliana have found a flat.'

'All in the same breath, and I'm not in the least surprised. How much?'

'Eighty thousand. It's a very long lease.'

'That's more than we paid for this place.'

'Progress,' Barbara said.

'There was supposed to be a slump. We missed the bottom. How?'

'That's what the bottom is, isn't it: what people miss?'

'That's also the top. What's Tom actually going to *do*, has he said at all?'

While Adam was brushing his teeth, Barbara said, 'Oh, Derek called.'

'To say?'

'To ask. How was Tom, which was nice of him. They're having lunch on Thursday, the two of them, at Stags.'

'What about Juliana?'

'She's having lunch here as far as I know. She saw the flat in Roland Gardens and she seems . . . more than happy.'

'The far side of happiness, what lies there, I wonder?'

'Oh do come to bed before it's daylight again.'

'We shall never know, shall we?' he said.

'I don't know. What?'

'The secret. Only that there almost certainly is one.'

'Suits me,' Barbara said. 'I don't need to know other people's secrets.'

'Got enough of your own, have you?'

She turned towards him. 'Whenever you're ashamed of yourself you talk to me like a stranger.'

'Eighty thousand for a flat! Lucky there's still a California gold rush; look at it that way. Try and think of me as a forty-niner. And not a day over. With the light behind me.'

225

'I'll do my best. Don't worry: I shall be fine while you're away.'

'Probably what I'm afraid of.'

'I shall hate it,' she said. 'But you must never know.'

'You know what's wonderful about women, don't you?'

'Of course,' she said. 'Do you?'

'Secret heat,' he said. 'And now take this bloody thing off, will you? Ashamed of what?'

v

The day before he was due to fly to California, Adam was invited to lunch at his office by his brother Derek. He took a cab to Mount Street and walked, smiling to himself, the few yards up a paved cul-de-sac to where the three top floors of a plain-faced building housed what it pleased Derek to call his 'modest operation', A.O.M. Inc. The small grey lift took Adam up to where Derek was waiting. The luxury of the decor was at odds with Derek's shoeless feet (in red socks), brown twill trousers and open-necked white shirt.

'You don't mind if we eat here, do you?'

'Happy to,' Adam said. 'Quite a view you've got. That's not the Kremlin I can see in the distance, is it?'

'Terminal problems, I gather, they have there. They don't know what to do.'

'That sounds like the Goon Show.'

'Very much what they've got running the place,' Derek said. 'They've been asking for advice, you know.'

'How would I know that? Whose? Yours?'

'The Americans mostly. Schultz in particular. Things fall apart very, very slowly and then all of a sudden. I had lunch with Tom.'

'So I heard.'

'He's not all that like you, is he?'

'If you say not. I'm never too sure what I'm like, if it comes to that.'

Derek led Adam into the back room, which was furnished in Old Times style, with two buttoned chesterfields facing each other across a low, polished Regency-style table. New flowers were arranged in a thick Venetian glass tub. A muscular Ayrton Minotaur crouched in the fireplace, taurine head tilted to quiz its human hand.

'Has Tom told you what I've proposed to him?'

Before Adam could answer, a girl in slim black trousers, fine gold hoop earrings and a white shirt wheeled a trolley into the room. 'Would you like me to stay and serve it, Mr Morris?'

'No need for that, Davina, thank you. Just leave it there . . . and we can help ourselves.'

'Shall I open the Sancerre?'

'If you would. And then go and have your lunch, Davina. Jennifer's there if I need her, isn't she?'

'Of course. The sorbet's in the thermos thing.'

'Exactly what it deserves,' Derek said.

'Shall I close the door?'

'Please. And no calls, tell Jenny, unless . . . the usual.'

Adam said, 'Do you sometimes wonder if it's all true at all?'

'Not really. Why shouldn't it be? The horrors are all true, God knows, and they're no more or less believable than you and me sitting here and . . . eating – oh she found some lobster. Here's the thing, Ad.'

'Ah the thing! I was wondering what it was. What is it?'

'Tom. You're getting ready to be . . . you, about it, aren't you?'

'I don't even know what it is, do I?'

'You know he's got fluent Spanish and Portuguese, don't you? Tom.'

'That he managed to tell me.'

'Thing is, A.O.M.'re in the process of doing two, maybe three, big developments in Iberia: houses, supermarkets, hotels, two or three golf courses. You don't like golf.'

'Oh, don't let that stop you,' Adam said.

'I happened to mention this to Tom and, to my total surprise,

227

I promise you, he was quite interested. He needs money, I gather.'

'Who doesn't, apart from you? With a pregnant wife . . . I'm just in the process – funny the way we talk as soon as money gets involved – I'm buying them a flat.'

'He feels bad about that.'

'No big deal. He is my son. Derek, what does A.O.M. stand for? As in A.O.M. Inc. I've always wondered.'

'No idea. I bought it off the shelf when I was starting out. Any Other Morris, it could be, but it isn't. It's just this shell I crawled into.'

'Sorry. Tom.'

'Right. What it comes to is, I've suggested he comes in, works as my personal assistant on the Iberian front and, if all goes well, and I strongly suspect it will, he can be A.O.M.'s general manager down there in a year or two.'

'What would Ferdinand and Isabella say, I wonder, if they could be with us here today?'

'"What's in it for us?" most likely, I should imagine.'

'Is that it?'

'That's pretty well it, yes.'

'And I thought I was coming to see the dentist.'

'Open wide then. Because how do you feel about it, Ad, seriously?'

'That it's very nice of you.'

'Are you sure?'

'Isn't it?'

'You honestly feel that?'

'What else would I feel? Yes!'

'Never know with you.'

'Of course you do, little brother grown so big and strong! Tom was talking about going into films, which was . . .'

'. . . what he thought would please you.'

'When all I want to do is get out of them? Just shows how little we know people, especially the ones we know best.'

'They haven't treated you so badly, the films, have they?'

'What're you going to pay him, as if it's any of my business? I just like to try and keep up with . . . what's happening in the . . . real world, if that's what reality is.'

'Forty grand a year to start with, and then when he's learnt to sharpen the pencils the way I like them . . . Do you not think it's enough?'

'If anyone had offered me that when I was his age, I would've taken up golf immediately. It's very generous of you, Der. Unduly even.'

'I imagined you'd think that. It's not at all. He's been through a lot of stuff in South America. Worked in property actually for a while, this man called Raul Levin.'

'He mentioned him.'

'Did you know he also killed somebody? You didn't.'

'*Tom?* And now I do. Killed who?'

'I'm sorry. I don't know exactly. I'm really sorry.'

'Are you? What are you sorry about? Something you have to pour Sancerre on in a hurry?'

'You think I told you that because I wanted to prove that he told me things he didn't tell you.'

'Oh Derek, for God's sake, it's very nice of you to give Tom a job. Let's leave it at that.'

'I imagined he'd've told you.'

Adam said, 'Very good lobster. It's all very good. It's delicious.'

'Have some cheese.'

'Trust you to have an Époisse.'

Derek said, 'I wasn't going to tell you –'

'You told me,' Adam said. 'And now I know, and so what?'

'Not that,' Derek said. 'About Carol.'

'Carol. Right. How is she? Is she all right?'

'I don't know. Possibly. Possibly not. All right, she's walked out on me. No slammed doors, no angry notes. She just said "I'm going now, Derek," one day last month, and I said, "When will you be back?" and she said, "I won't. Nothing to do with you particularly," she said.'

229

'She has put on a lot of weight, hasn't she?'

'And you never noticed until today.'

'You never did show very much, did you, Derek?'

'I didn't want to be like you, did I?'

'Is there a connection?'

'Between what and what?'

'Carol leaving you and you giving Tom a job.'

'Connection? None whatsoever. That I know of. She said she'd read *Fatso*, this novel –'

'*Fatso*, Jesus! Don't tell me. I know all about *Fatso*, from way back. Whom did he kill, did he tell you that?'

'I've said enough,' Derek said.

'You've said too much. But not enough. He did. Tell you.'

'You're making way, way more of it than you need to.'

'Have you ever killed anybody, Der? Nor have I. So it does seem to be quite something. A bit more than, well, having girls all over the place, which I gather is not wholly foreign to your manifold activities.'

'I like women. Don't you? And cars. I do like cars.'

'Must be nice what money can buy.'

'Are you playing the pauper, or the moralist, or both? Alternatively, as you might say in your robuster moments, fuck you.'

'Takes a little digesting,' Adam said, 'this kind of thing.'

'It does. But I'll get over it.'

'About Tom, I meant. Sorry. Carol, tell me. What's she doing? Where's she gone?'

'Her business. Her pleasure. Whichever, wherever.'

'I thought she was the most delicious thing I'd ever seen when I first met her.'

'Me too, brother. I thought she'd keep me playing wind-screen wipers for the rest of my life. Don't look like that. You taught me that expression.'

'Ay have no mammary of that.'

'Then kindly leave the stage,' Derek said.

'So . . . what're you going to do, Der?'

'This. And that. And the other, if time allows. Any other business?'

Adam said, 'As a matter of fact . . .'

'Have some more of this whatever it is. Pavlova. You like meringue, I seem to remember. Have some Époisse on it. What fact is there a matter of?'

'The S.C.R. ceiling.'

'S.C.R?'

'As in Senior Combination Room. Literally. In our old college. It's threatening to fall in, the ceiling. Jacobean plaster only lasts about three centuries apparently. Trish Reece – you remember Trish – she thinks that if some of Sheridan's . . . supporters . . . for the mastership –'

'– also supported the ceiling . . .'

'You've rumbled her ruse. Which is not . . . disgraceful.'

'At all.'

'Masters of colleges are basically fund-raisers these days, so . . . as long as nobody actually *says* anything *ouvertement*, as Samuel Marcus would say . . .'

'Samuel Marcus being . . .?'

'Never mind. It'd be nice to see Reece become Master, wouldn't it?'

'I never actually liked him all that much.'

'Reece? Nor did I, but . . .'

'You never know though,' Derek said, 'if he gets it, they might even make you an honorary fellow.'

'I sometimes think you don't like *me* all that much, Derek, you know that?'

'I love you like a brother. You know damn well. How much do they need?'

'Quarter of a million probably altogether.'

'A quarter of a million'll have to do,' Derek said. 'I'm not going higher.'

'Jesus Christ, I never – that's incredibly generous.'

'Jewily ostentatious, might someone say?'

'He or she might well.'

'Let 'em. And fuck 'em. Doesn't matter what we do, does it? Tell me when you want it, and you might even get it. The money. It was a woman.'

'It was a woman. What was?'

'He killed. Tom. As I understand it, she threatened him when he and . . .'

'Juliana.'

'Correct. When they were trying to get out of wherever they were.'

'Paraguay. Presumably. Threatened him how? With a gun?'

'He only said he had no choice. And he doesn't feel guilty.'

'Nor should you, Der. Nor should you. Seriously. I've digested it now. Mixes really well with the Époisse. Not to mention the Pavlova. You seriously don't know who Samuel Marcus Cohen is?'

'I don't read those people. I'm a bees-kneesman, remember? As in "mere". Forgive me, Ad, will you? Please. About Tom.'

'You didn't do anything that needs to be forgiven.'

'All the same.'

They embraced as brothers should. They held each other close for a long moment, as if it was not evidence of how far apart they were, though Adam knew that he was farther from Derek than Derek from him. He might think – as he walked along Mount Street not knowing whether he wanted the taxi he was looking for, nor where he wanted to go when he had it – that Derek had acquired the son he and Carol had never had, but at the same time he was sure that his brother was innocent of any such intention.

vi

Adam had not used his headphones when they came to collect them. For half an hour of the flight, he had lip-synched the predictable dialogue in a film he had once been asked to write, and for the rest of the time he had slept and read *Les Juifs et*

L'État, as a specific against what would be required of him when he went to the studio.

'Welcome to Los Angeles, ladies and gentlemen, where the local time is 4 p.m. in the afternoon. The ground temperature is 75 degrees.'

Alone, Adam was amused by his successful impersonation of the fifty-eight-year-old whose passport he carried and whose qualities were presumed to merit the privileges of first-class travel and the presence, on the far side of the automatic door, of Ron Shapiro, in wrap-around shades, check pants and a seersucker *blouson*.

'Hey, Addo! Good flight?'

'I was there, Shapiro, and now I'm here. So what could be wrong with it? Nothing like unaccustomed luxury to persuade you you must be doing something wrong.'

'I never find that,' Shapiro said.

'Never go to school in England.'

'Unlikely to happen. Car's this way.'

'So tell me, Ronnie,' Adam said, 'what's gone wrong since everything was all set?'

'Pass. You tell me. I didn't hear anything had. But what do I know? What's for sure is we have the deal letter. Pay or play is how it is. You also have a mini-suite, if you can live with the ongoing indignity, at the Beverly Wilshire as was and you're seeing your old best friend Mike Clode at the studio eleven o'clock in the morning. They're sending a limo, ten-thirty, but you're free to rent a car any time you want one.'

'That all sounds terrible.'

'It gets worse, if you're patient. I've been getting calls about your availability for something else.'

'Something else is always better than what you've already agreed to. Such as what?'

'Can you believe there's anyone in this town that can really keep his or her mouth shut? There is. One. This guy over in the Valley who totally won't say why he's calling, but he keeps doing it, about you. All he'll tell me is "somebody" wants to know, we won't be sorry when he tells us who, assuming he ever does.'

'What do you tell him? Nice wheels, Ronnie.'

'The usual lies, which happen to be true in this instance. Lamborghini steering takes getting used to. Jeannie hates it. She wanted a Porsche. Everyone has a Porsche. Maybe that's why. In principle you're busy, busy, but . . . there's always next time.'

'Until there isn't.'

'I will omit to say. What're you doing tonight?'

'Gasping for air, probably. Might catch a massage at the pool.'

'Great Chinese guy they've got there. Goes off at six though. If you want to come by the house, hang out, Jeannie says you're the exception that proves the rule. I hope that's good.'

'It's certainly nice of her, but tell you what, I think I'll just mope around the hotel and try and get overtired enough to get to sleep just in time for the alarm call to wake me up.'

'Gotcha. We'll get together later in the week.'

'How long do they expect me to be around?'

'There's a house way up on San Ysidro someplace that Mike was saying they could rent for you, Oak Pass Road, belongs to some chick he knows, he thought you could maybe work out of there . . .'

'I agree with William Faulkner: I'd sooner work at home.'

'Faulkner was Faulkner.'

'And I'm not?'

By the time Adam had checked in and was taken to his suite it was three o'clock in the morning London time. He was too tired to read; the television was boring; so although he had no desire for a drink, he went down to the bar, with his book. He sat in a corner away from the bar and ordered a margarita, if only for the salt around the rim of the glass.

'Adam Morris, can it be? All by yourself?'

'I knew I was waiting for someone. Had to be you, Jill, didn't it?'

Jill Tabard was standing there in black high-heeled shoes, thin straps over the instep and round the ankle below loose white

234

linen trousers. A gold necklace had a knuckle of amber tilted between her neat breasts in the vee of her pale blue'n'green silk shirt. Her hair was shaggily shaped and had gold lights in it.

'May I sit down?'

'You look to have all the necessary equipment,' Adam said. 'Will you join me in a margarita?'

'I shouldn't, should I?'

'One more margarita, could we, please, over here? So, tell me everything, some of it. What can you not possibly talk about that brings you to this happy oasis?'

Jill said, 'You know Norman, I'm with now.'

'Segal. I know of him. His little candle throws an increasingly powerful beam. *Plain Crazy* is tearing up trees, they tell me. And I even believe it.'

'Thank you,' Jill smiled at the waitress and then at Adam. 'It's a little picture but people seem to like it. Carlo Pavlides over at Albatross has brought us out here to do a biggy, which is only amber-lit thus far: script problems, what else? But Norman's all set to direct it. Cheers.'

'With you? In it, I mean. Cheers indeed.'

'That's the lie they're telling at the moment.'

'Then it has to be true. What's the subject?'

'No one's supposed to know.'

'And what is it?'

'Period piece. It all happens in Paraguay, most of it.'

'You're going to be Madame Lynch!'

'Who told you that?'

'You did. Two seconds ago. You'll be perfect. You've got the eyes.'

'You don't think I'm too old?'

'Terrific subject. Too old? You'll never be too old. Not for me anyway.'

'Ha! Seriously, did you read something? About it?'

'Years ago. Everything. I got very interested in Paraguay at one point for some reason, Madame Lynch and Francisco Lopez and all that, and only recently I found out what I didn't know,

235

which was that my son Tom had actually gone to Paraguay and was living there for quite a while.'

Jill said, 'What do you hear?'

'"Our Love is Here to Stay", don't I? Not that you'd guess it from the way he's playing it.'

'You know why we're here, don't you?'

'To allow God to work his purpose out, as year succeeds to year, aren't we? Did you hear different?'

'Norman and me. Because Carlo knows it'll wind Mike up.'

'Good old Carlo, as some say. That's not the only reason.'

'Mike cancelled Carlo's multi-picture deal with Transworld. One of the first things he did. Then Albatross brought Carlo in from the cold . . . well, from Palm Springs actually.'

'Freezing at this time of year.'

'And just about the first thing Pav did was suggest we come out.'

'Very wise. Very flattering. But not unduly, when I look at you. Good old Pav, some say; not all that many though.'

'We love him at the moment. He'll do anything he can to bug Mike. Is what it's really all about. The more publicity I get as Mike Clode's ex-wife working for his new best enemy, well, the more it stirs things up.'

Adam said, 'People like Carlo Pavlides don't make movies just to bug other people.'

'No? Then again, that could be why we're not making it yet.'

'Meanwhile, he is looking after you nicely, I hope.'

'God, yes. He's toted Norman off to Costa Rica. They're thinking of shooting it for Paraguay. Cheaper.'

'So they've flown down in the private jet to save money.'

'You're terrible. Are you always like this? You're not.'

'This is the export model. Left-hand drive. You noticed.'

'I'm just so glad I bumped into you. What're you doing here?'

'Nice of you to ask. You probably shouldn't have.'

'Working for Mike in other words.'

'Under protest.'

'Which always raises the price. Do you know lots of people out here?'

'A few. I always think I'll give them a call. And end up having a solitary margarita, waiting for Jill Tabard to come sit at my table. Presumably you're staying in the hotel.'

'Meaning I wouldn't be cruising the bar if I wasn't.'

'You look terrific. Is that amber?'

'So what is it? That you're working on. Not *Fatso*?'

'Is right. I got out of doing *Fatso* . . . which is probably going to be a major, major hit, and I'm doing . . . something else.'

'Which you're not supposed to tell me about.'

'I'll give you a clue: it's the greatest American novel published this week. Mike spotted it — i.e. one of Mike's underlings who can read spotted it — when it was no more than a helpless little typescript. And here I am, to alter it out of all recognition so that people can say it's just like the book.'

'*Fortune's Fool!* Has to be!'

'How can I say no to you, Jill? I can't.'

'Loved it. I read it on the plane from New York. Have you seen Mike yet?'

'Pleasures to come. I got here two hours ago. I need a good night's sleep first. If I wake up and find this is all a dream, I can get up in my own home and write something worth writing.'

'You love it really, don't you?'

'Whoring? Don't we all? The lovely moment when the rich, ugly bastard crooks his finger. And the old tart says, "Who? Me?" Irresistible. How's . . . um, Septimus?'

'Denis has got him. He loves having him. He's at school all day, of course. Denise wouldn't care if I never went back, I don't think, if he could keep Septimus.'

'Everybody's happy then,' Adam said. 'Do you want another one of those?'

'Better not. I've got this trainer I work out with and he guesses things.'

'You're looking at me as if you know something I don't.'

'Oh darling, don't take it personally.'

'None of it? That hurts.'

Jill said, 'What floor are you on? Your room.'

'Third, in the new building. I have a mini-suite. Non-smoking. Something wrong with it?'

'Not that I heard. I'm over there too.'

'How about we do breakfast together?'

'You always break out in American dialogue when you get over here?'

'Eliza Lynch, you really do have the eyes all right.'

'We should get you to do this rewrite.'

'I've been waiting for you to say that.'

Jill said, 'Are you someone who keeps his promises?'

'Absolutely. If it doesn't interfere with my career.'

'To your wife.'

'Yes, actually, I do.'

'Why is that?'

'So that I can live with myself, I suppose, when I have the time.'

'Only, I'm in 373, if you wake up in the night and find you're not asleep. No one need ever know.'

'Not much point then, is there?' Adam said.

'Just checking,' she said.

'Love your work, Miss Tabard.'

'What is it that girl always said, the one that was on drugs? *Saturday Night Live*.'

'"You're no fun any more." That one?'

'That was the one.'

vii

'Good morning everybody! Today's weather, looks like being fine, 73 degrees in Hollywood right now, going up to 78, 69 degrees at the beaches, but that should get to 72, 3 later today.' Adam tried to discover how to turn off the radio in the back of the stretch, but succeeded only in first closing the glass screen between him and the distant driver, and then turning on the television.

'Gentleman's here to see Mike Clode. Adam Morris?'

'Park it right over there, Clyde, in front of the fountain.' The cop on the gate leaned down and the driver rolled down Adam's window. 'Go straight into the main building, Mr Morris, to your right and up to the fourth floor.'

Adam walked into the grey and white lobby of the Harold T. Gampell Building, where a black girl in a black suit, with strictly plaited hair and no blouse that Adam could see, smiled at him.

'I've been told to go to the fourth floor. I hope you have one. With Mike Clode on it.'

'Last time I looked,' she said. 'Elevator to your left.'

Adam came out of the elevator and was faced by heavy double doors, with strengthened glass panels. They swung open easily. Inside, there were wide desks on either side of a closed inner door, a grey-suited secretary behind the one on the left. To the right was an area with two deep armchairs, a couch and a glass table with a fan of trade magazines on it; and the new flowers.

'Hi! I'm Adam Morris.'

'You made it! That's wonderful. Good flight?'

'Unbelievable flight. You have to be . . . Hannah.'

'Not really. Hannah is in with Mike. I'm Tamara.'

'I don't doubt it for a second.'

'Can I get you something?'

'Is that local language, possibly, for he's not here yet?'

'Mike? He's here. He's here seven o'clock in the morning. How about some coffee? Anything else I can get you?'

'I'll be fine. I have this . . . I have to read. He is expecting me though, isn't he?'

'Is putting it mildly.'

'Then that's the way we'll put it.'

'Unfortunately, and I know it's not Mike's choice . . .'

'When he's ready,' Adam said, 'I'll be the guy over there in the corner, the one with the dust on him.'

Adam sat on the low couch and read Susie Beaumont's

239

screenplay, which was now entitled *A Choice of Motives*. Having determined to be scrupulously pitiless, he found that he took more pleasure in his approving ticks than in scoring his dismay at clumsy dialogue or wriggling dubious lines under pretentious camera directions.

After a while, two men in dark silk suits came through the heavy doors from the elevator. Both carried slim briefcases. They walked past Tamara and straight into Mike Clode's office. A few minutes later, the younger one came out, listening to his cell, and held the door open for two more people, one a woman with big hair, in a dark grey strictly business suit, black patent-leather shoes and intelligent glasses. When she had looked at Adam and he at her, he checked that he had not been turned to stone.

They all went back to Mike's office and the door closed with what Adam read for finality. He finished Susie's script, which fell into the beta-alpha category which his Greek master in the Remove amused himself by awarding to second-class first-class work. Adam flicked through the Trades, sighed, drank some water and then got up.

'OK, Tamara, this is getting a little silly, isn't it? Almost noon, right?'

'Twenty of. I feel terrible.'

'Perhaps we should both go home, before I catch it.'

'About this.'

'What's going on?'

'I totally do not know.'

'That sounds like a lot,' Adam said.

He sat and reread Susie Beaumont's solemn script, in which almost every scene, he realised, contained a *hommage* to some key movie of the last two decades, apart from *The Woman in Question*. The more annoyed he was, the more suggestions he pencilled in the margin and on the facing page. If he was kept waiting much longer, he realised, he would have done a complete rewrite. Next to the (dated?) title, he wrote *Remember Me?*

'Adam!'

Adam continued to write on Susie's script and then he looked up and there was Mike Clode, in the door of the office, with his arms apart in welcome.

Adam said, 'Harold T. Gampell? If you say, "No one told me you were here", I will . . .'

'I knew *bloody well* you were here, old son. That's partly why I'm so angry. Come in, come in.' Mike stood there, feet apart, in black cotton trousers, a little fuller than Chairman Mao's, and a patterned black and white cotton over-jacket, with no buttons and big pockets. 'Thank God for a friendly face.'

Adam said, 'You're in real trouble, aren't you?'

'Tell me about it. Hotel all right?'

'Hotel's fine.'

'Anything you need, now's the time to say so. You've heard about this house on Oak Pass —'

'Mike, listen, I truly don't want to stay longer than a few days if I can help it, if *you* can help it, actually, which I'm sure you can.'

Mike said, 'You haven't heard.'

'An enormous number of things. For instance what?'

'Put it this way: never come out here and work, Adam. Ever.'

'Right.'

'The house fell through. I don't want to talk about it, but that was the moment when I . . . These people are unbelievable. They're unbelievable. You cannot imagine what's going on in this organisation.'

'I won't even try.'

'Not OKing the house, on Oak Pass, is the least of it. But typical. You would never believe how petty these Americans can be. I cannot tell you what a relief it will be to be back in England.'

'When you can, do. Tell me.'

'They pretend to be your friends, they pretend to be behind you, they promise they'll back you up to the hilt, and then they stab you in the back.'

241

'That's academic life all right.'

'You are *so* lucky.'

'So I keep hearing.'

'Not really to be in the business at all. One thing I can tell you: your deal is safe, solid, signed and sealed, nothing they can do about it.'

'Do I possibly gather that they're changing the guard and no one told you until a few minutes ago?'

'You know me, Ad. I'm someone who believes in loyalty. We go back a long way, you and I, it's beginning to be. Do you know that total prize shit Carlo Pavlides?'

'Not a lot,' Adam said. 'He kisses me on the lips, but that's as far as it goes.'

'His mother was a camel. I thought at least Lou would keep his word to me. His solemn word, he gave me. Just so you can know what kind of people we're dealing with here, they've asked me to be off the lot by noon. They're painting out my name on my parking slot even as we speak. Nice people.'

'I have the picture. Think my limo'll still be there?'

'Never again, Adam, never again. England's the place for me from now on. I wasn't going to stay here anyway. What I really want to do more than anything in the world is get into the opera house. One thing I promise you: your deal is safe.'

'You said that before,' Adam said. 'Does that mean it isn't?'

'You play this game brilliantly, Ad. Don't think I haven't noticed. No one better. But I'm not playing it no more, no more. I'm only going to do things that really resonate with me —'

'Nothing like resonating.'

'Soon as you get back to London, we should meet up.'

Adam said, 'Back to London?'

'I'm sorry about *Fortune's Fool*. Which is of course exactly what I am at this point.'

'Dramatic irony, lovely stuff, always was. In what way are you sorry?'

'The new head honcho, my old ex-friend Sidney Swerling,

242

he's never ever going to go ahead with anything that I set up. You'll get your money, because having to pay you for doing zip will prove to the board what a spendthrift I was buying the novel in the first place, but . . . forget about ever actually having to write anything.'

Adam said, 'How am I going to live with myself, Mike?'

'Carlo's revenge, that's what this is all about. He's only going to be chairman and CEO.'

'I saw Jill last night.'

'They'll never make it,' Mike said. '*Eliza Lynch*. Not these people. Period? Forget it. She's too old anyway. Much. Those refrigerator eyes? She'll never be a star. Not a star-star.'

Three days later, Adam flew with Mike Clode to New York, where they caught the Concorde to London. The following day, Mike flew to Milan to see the people at La Scala. A week later, Adam and Barbara drove down to their cottage in St Julien-la-Forêt. He resumed work on his novel while a local architect was measuring up the big barn which they planned to turn into an apartment for visitors.

VI

The day before *Life and Loves* was to be published, Adam
Morris was the guest on Alan Parks's new weekly radio
programme *Book Now.* 'I've moved up market,' he told Adam.
'Time I did. Once you've gone far enough down, up is the
only way to go. So listen, the way I'd like to do it is, you read
a chunk of the book – which I actually think has to be your
best – and then we talk about it, and then you read some more,
and then we talk again and like that until the last syllable of
recording time, OK?'

They tested their voice levels and Alan did his introductory
piece, which was neatly leavened with his usual deferential
condescension, and then Adam took the recommended deep
breath and started to read. 'I was a young man on his travels in a
Europe which, only ten years before, had been butchered and
brutalised in ways I had read about in the safety of England. I had
already met the woman who, I assumed, would be my wife. I
loved her and she loved me; what more could I want?

'Modestly enriched by a bursary that required me, as a
promising writer (the promises entirely my own), to travel until
it was exhausted, I left Kate with tearful heartlessness (the tears
hers, the heartlessness mine) and set out for Greece.

'Travelling alone, the first thing I discovered was that, clear of
the England in which I had been cloistered, I was no one very
much or in particular. I went to galleries and museums and I
visited temples and studied a modern Greek grammar, but I
lacked any vivid sense of myself or of what to do with the
freedom I had been given.'

Alan said, 'The first thing that strikes me, Adam, is how slap
bang down the middle, in narrative style, you choose to be. Dare

244

I call you "conventional"? I seem to have managed it. Self-consciously prosy, is that a compliment too far?'

'The more unusual the story you're going to tell,' Adam said, 'the wiser it is, maybe, to begin in the usual way. I wanted to convey something of the ordinariness of my hero –'

'Who, as so often in your work, seems pretty well indistinguishable from his author.'

'Rembrandt's self-portraits aren't Rembrandt, are they?'

'I didn't know that.'

'Yes, you did,' Adam said. 'The first-person narrator in my novel –'

'Who, incidentally, is the only character who never gets called by a first name, or a last one, come to that –'

'– he's almost a space which I invite the reader to occupy. Or share.'

'In your book, we're all in this together, so to speak.'

'You take the point perfectly.'

'He's having one of his good days,' Alan said. 'So: our unheroic hero who shall remain nameless goes to Thessaloniki, with no particular sense of mission or purpose –'

'All he knows, or I knew at the time, about Greece is ancient dust.'

'Duster in hand, twenty-something years old, as we all still are, of course, he sets out in search of what you call "reality". Might that be what the rest of us used to call "sex"?'

'Not entirely. At all.'

'But you do get some, doesn't he? And then some.'

'It's not "sex" in the sense simply of – what's the term we're allowed to use these days?'

'You could try "healthy exercise",' Alan said, 'and we'll see how many indignant letters we get. Time you read us something more from – dare I say? – deeper into the book.'

Adam opened his novel at the next flagged passage. 'I walked down to the ruined docks and into the tight streets of a city that was, for a long time, more Jewish than Greek or Ottoman or Christian. Anxious to drop old habits, I made a new one of going

245

daily to the café Byzantino in Plateia Aristotelou and sat at the same table. Radiant cracks in the wide window had been patched with brown tape. I ordered *ena cafe, metrio*, which came with a tall glass of water, and scanned the dusty square as if waiting for something or someone.'

Alan said, 'Nice scene-setting, but it's a bit pretentious, isn't it, expecting us to know what the hell all those little bits of Greek mean?'

'It's a little pretentious, isn't it, Alan, pretending that you can't understand them pretty well? Because they're quite brief, and almost always clear from the context, and . . . well, the story does take place in Greece.'

'I couldn't be being put in my place, could I?'

'*Veveos!*' Adam said. 'Greek for "if you say so".'

'*Veveos!* Let's get to the female interest here, can we?'

Adam read on. 'She came first with a tall, thin man, in a black coat and thick spectacles. When he lifted his chin, signifying "no", in the Greek style, his glasses became silver coins on seemingly sightless eyes. The girl, in a black high-necked sweater with stretched sleeves, talked in lisping Greek which I strained, vainly, to decipher. They never glanced towards me. After a while, I walked back to the pension and worked at the comic novel of which my imposture, as a proper writer, required me to write a thousand words a day, sometimes more, never less.

'One morning when I saw her approaching with a quicker step than usual, I saw myself, in the bent window, smile as she approached.

'I said, "*Kalemera*." '

'She said, "*Kalemera*" and frowned with a downward glance as if at a memory. Wishing that I was the someone in her past, whom she remembered with that clustered brow, I said, "*Meepos thelete ena cafe?* Feel like a coffee?"'

'Right, so you have this coffee and you try out your Greek and then she . . . pretty quickly actually, she . . . gets very friendly.'

'She gets very,' Adam said, 'but I'm not sure it's friendly exactly.'

'I set that up for you, and you hit it very sweetly. Because this girl's an enigma, right? Without giving the plot away, it turns out her name is Katerina – which just happens to be the same name, pretty well, as the girl your hero left behind in Jolly Old. A bit of symbolic fancy footwork in there, is there? Look at me I'm dancing?'

'You often know people with the same names in life – you may well be amazed to know that I know several other Alans apart from *the* Alan –'

'You're too kind.'

'I know. I thought it would be nicely confusing to have a Kate and a Katerina, and make them as different as I knew how. At least superficially.'

'Your character pretty soon finds himself in the sack with this Katerina. Impressive, the speed with which a cup of coffee can get a completely strange woman radically overheated. Your frequent experience, has that been, in life?'

'They have quite long talks actually. She tells him how she is trying to get her family house back from the people who, she says, have stolen it.'

'You get lucky.'

'I is not I, as Evelyn Waugh said.'

'*He* gets lucky. Unlike Evelyn. Deny that. With the heroine.'

Adam said, 'I guess people of my cloistered generation, who never went to war, and didn't have the luck to be educated in the gutter, can never quite believe their luck when women don't . . . make difficulties.'

'Which Katerina does not. Read us that bit.'

'In my room, I watched as she pulled the black sweater, with the stretched cuffs, one with a long loose thread, over her dark head and there were the unguarded white breasts, bigger and whiter and softer than I had imagined. She undressed without haste. She could have been getting ready for work. I chose to forget my shame and fascination when she told me the lessons she had learned while I was studying *ho, hee, toe* in my evacuated prep school. I realised now that she was not as young as I had

247

supposed. I wondered how she would taste, when she last had a bath, and how safe it was to proceed.'

Alan said, 'We won't go into the anatomical detail that's there in the book since, as you know, the BBC has to assume that very few of our listeners have ever seen another human being in a state of even modest sexual enthusiasm, and if they have, they don't care to be reminded unnecessarily of that kind of embarrassing experience.

'One more extract is all that we can afford from the multi-layered, polyphonic – if I dare to say so – tragic-tragi-commie-comedy of Adam Morris's *Life and Loves*. My premeditated choice would be the scene where he sees Katerina for the last time.'

Adam cleared his throat. 'All my life I should have this imperishably shameful memory. More than my great love, Katerina would be my secret crime. She had said that I should go; her life carried too many scars for me ever to share it. What had been terrible to her had been exciting to me. My desire was tinged with callousness; my love was salted with disgust, that a woman who had endured such things could still gasp as if with pleasure when I took her. As I was leaving, I said, "*Lipoumeh polee*". Sorry, sorry. Regret and relief were tearful twins.'

Alan Parks left it a second or two and then he said, 'Adam Morris's new novel, *Life and Loves*, is published tomorrow. I'm Alan Parks, and that's the end of *Book Now* for the foreseeable future of this week.'

They waited for a 'clear' from Fiona and then Alan said, 'You're a prickly bastard these days, Adam. I was as nice as I could be.'

'You were a sweetheart, Alan. I appreciate it, truly.'

'Susie Beaumont's movie, have you seen it, *Remember Me*?'

'I've seen the title,' Adam said.

'Got quite a few lines in it you might have written yourself, if you'd had the time. You know who's fantastic in it, apparently, that's Dan Bradley.'

'Dan? Is he really? Oh my God.'

'What?'

'Of course. He's playing the Englishman who's falsely accused of having sex with an underage girl and when he's acquitted, he goes into exile and then, years later, the girl comes and finds him and says –'

'I thought you hadn't seen it.'

'Remember me!'

ii

Adam wondered whether he should tip the BBC cabbie and decided, in the public interest, that he should not, and then did. He walked slowly to his front door. There was no one in the hall, and no post on the table.

'Hullo? Anyone around?'

Barbara called up from the kitchen. 'Hullo.'

Adam said, 'What's wrong?'

'Nothing, is it? You came across very well. Very . . . laid back, very Adam Morris.'

'You didn't like it.'

'He knows how to do it, doesn't he?'

'Bring out the worst in me?'

Rachel came down the stairs. 'Daddy!'

'Raitch! You never said Rachel was here.'

'And now I don't need to, because here she is. Do you want something to eat?'

'If you're making something. How are you, darling?'

'I'm terribly well, really.'

'Are you eating with us? We can go out . . .'

'Actually, no, not tonight.'

Adam said, 'You look . . . what do you look, apart from beautiful?'

'Shifty perhaps?'

'You've got a secret.'

'I'm going to California.'

'California? They're going to make you into a movie? Don't

249

let them.' Adam looked to see if Barbara was smiling, but her back was to him, and he knew she was not.

'With Bill,' Rachel said.

'Bill.'

'Bourne,' Rachel said. 'He said you'd be . . . unamused.'

'"With him" with him, is this?'

'I thought I would.'

Adam said, 'He's a lot older than you are. I mean . . . a *lot* older.'

'That's probably part of it.'

'Ah.'

'He's very clever and we have a lot in common, except that he has more of it than I do. You could say I was on the take.'

'And what's he on?' Adam said.

Barbara walked out of the kitchen, quietly.

'I should just have gone, shouldn't I?'

'I like Bill,' Adam said. 'He's a proper scholar . . .'

'. . . but you did warn me. About him.'

'Should I have known better? Is that what your mother's upset about?'

Rachel said, 'You're the cleverest man I know, sometimes.'

'But this isn't one of them.'

'Could be my point.'

'She's not upset about you, she's upset about me.'

'You are, as Bill would say, back on track.'

'Do you love him?'

'Don't know really.'

'That used to mean you didn't. What does it mean these days?'

'I admire him. A lot. I shan't be with him all that long.'

'I see. Do I?'

Rachel said, 'He wants me to work on something with him. He's prepared a lot of material, some of it quite close to some things in my field and . . . we seem to have converged to the point where . . . collaboration is the obvious answer. I can teach some courses out there, he says, which'll pay some bills and . . .

That time you took us all out there, when I was . . . I don't know
. . . eleven or twelve, I thought it was terrific. Hamburger
Hamlet. Bob's Big Boy. I love those places.'
'It's not a . . . passion then,' Adam said.
'Passion? No. Do you mind?'
'None of my business,' Adam said.
'Not my question.'
'It's still my answer. It'll take a little getting used to. Like a bad
review. Twenty-four hours and you feel better. He lied.'
'You always used to be in favour of people . . . doing what
they want to do, if they want to do it. Or am I wrong?'
'You're a very strong person, Rachel.'
'Everyone else is always strong. We fear. They rarely are.'
'Barbara hates the book, doesn't she? And she hated me being
on the radio and talking about it the way I did.'
'That's between you and her,' Rachel said.
'How do you know you won't be with him for long?'
'Because.'
'So when are you going?'
'Friday. You think he's doing it to you, don't you? You think
he's laughing at you.'
'As long as he doesn't laugh at you, it really doesn't matter.
Have you got time for lunch or something before you go? The
two of us.'
'Of course! Cheer up. Nothing terrible's happened.'
'Yet,' he said. 'Did you listen to me on the radio?'
'I caught the end,' Rachel said. 'Sounded good.'
'What did your mother say?'
'She said you seemed to be having a good time.'
Adam went up to the bedroom, listening to the silence. The
bathroom door was shut. Adam sighed, took one arm out of his
antelope suede jacket and then put it back in again. He did not
try the bathroom door.
'Ba? Can I come in?'
'I'm having a bath. If you want to come in, come in.'
'Madame Bonnard, I presume.'

251

'Oh do stop.'

'Have I started? If so, what?'

'She told you. Being unduly . . . fancy. What do you think? About Rachel, and Bill Bourne?'

'She's a grown woman. And he purports to be a grown man. I have no right to think anything.'

'Nor do I,' she said, 'but we both do, don't we?'

'Between the two of us, I don't much like the idea of his hands on her. I'll get over it, but I don't like it. As for the rest of the . . . operation, I don't . . . it doesn't seem to . . . be something I'm going to think about. What about you? You truly are a lovely woman, but what else is wrong with you?'

'You're so angry with me sometimes.'

'And you're so "not angry" with me. Sometimes. Which can be worse. For instance now. Why? Ba . . . It's a work of fiction. *Life and Loves*. By definition. I is not I, I meant it.'

'And aren't you?'

'Aren't I what?'

'You know exactly what: a work of fiction.'

'God, yes. Every time. Not a word of truth in me.'

She stood up and the water slipped back off her into the bath as she reached for the towel he was holding out for her.

'As for Susan Hayward, in *Samson and Delilah*.'

'It was that girl in Venice, wasn't it?'

'Was it? What was? Who was?'

'OK.'

Adam said, 'That's the least OK OK in the history of OKdom.'

'You bloody well know,' she said. 'Her that you based it on. How did you manage to see her again?'

'See her again? I never saw her again.'

'So it was her.'

'Not so much Madame Bonnard now,' Adam said, 'more Inspector Barbara of the Yard.'

'They're all going to believe that she was the great love of your life.'

'Not if they were standing where I'm standing, in the standing sense of standing. Look, Ba, you read it in manuscript, you corrected the proofs, and suddenly it all comes as a big surprise.'

'You did go to Greece though after Cambridge, didn't you?'

'Six weeks of heat, blisters, *ouzo* and wishing you were there instead of Bill Bourne, who was. It was while you were – what were you doing?'

'Getting teaching experience, wasn't I? In Brixton. The kind of experience that leads you to give up teaching. And you never looked at a woman all that time.'

Barbara hung her towel on the rail and walked naked into the bedroom.

'If we must take inventory, we did talk to some girls at several points, and Bill may even have had his abrupt way with a particularly plain Swede, with black hair – and teeth – as I remember.'

'You were too virtuous, were you?'

'Squeamish would be crueller. And truer. If you're thinking of a rewrite. I never met the right class of temptation. Let's say. If that's the kind of salt the wound requires.'

'You should never have married me,' she said.

'Nobody should ever marry anybody, as is now generally known. Too late in my case. I don't know about yours. You'd better put some bloody clothes on before I belie my years.'

'Not to mention mine. I think it's a wonderful book.'

'Thank you. Wait till you see what Samuel Marcus Cohen has to say about it. I'm threatened with his imminent attentions in the *TLS*, so Jason Singer is pleased to promise me.'

'I don't give a shit what that venomous little monster says about it. It's . . . extraordinary.'

Adam hunched himself into a facsimile of Samuel Marcus's gleaming and emphatic persona. '"But is it extraordinary *in the right sense*? Does one not perhaps have an *intimation* that *too much is at once not quite enough*?" Is the medicine he's widely predicted to be *concocting* for me.'

'He's a warped little shit.'

'But not stupid,' Adam said. 'The thing about writing is, one never quite says exactly what one means to say.'

'If you could, it wouldn't be worth saying, would it?'

'That's beautiful! Plus, *you're* very beautiful. I'm glad I married you. I can't say why, because if I did it wouldn't be worth saying. Because I can't say it, is why.'

'End of commercial?'

'*Life and Loves*, for better *and* for worse, it seems, is what I wrote. I'm sorry if you're – how about . . . piqued?'

'But you don't give a damn.'

'And I love you.'

They were still kissing when the telephone rang.

'Had to happen,' Barbara said. 'Don't pretend you're not going to answer it. Or do you want the little woman to?'

Adam said, 'Hullo.'

'Hey!'

'How are you, Shapiro? It's Shapiro.'

'See you later,' Barbara said.

'How am I is quite impressed as a matter of fact.'

'Anything I could empathise with? Or that might resonate with me?'

'What do you think of Jake Leibowitz?'

'Our greatest living director? *Roses, Roses* . . ., *Samarra*, *The Land of the Free* . . . to name but a few. *That* Jake Leibowitz? He is, as they say, the business, which is more than the business is. But who am I? S.J.Perelman? Why?'

'It only turns out he's the mystery man they've been asking about your availability for.'

'He also swallows people alive, doesn't he? Doesn't even spit their boots out.'

'Lucky if you get an unmarked grave,' Shapiro said.

'So what does he want?' Adam said.

'They should tell me? An agent? He never talks to rodents. All I know is, he wants to send you a piece of material. You read it, and if it interests you, he'll call you, and then . . . if there's a meeting of minds . . .'

'He is at least one of the few people in the movies who actually has one. Would this be for money?'

'This would have to be for money. You don't need it, but I do. This would be for money money.'

'Then he'd better send it, not for that reason, the book; whatever it is. Probably crap. They have a nose for it.'

'You never know with Leibowitz.'

'That much I know. Is that it?'

'That's it. It's on its way soon as I put the phone down.'

Adam hung up and looked at Barbara. 'Jake Leibowitz, how about that?'

'Somebody somewhere still wants you.'

'Even if you don't, do I read between your lines?'

'That's not nice. And it isn't true.'

'Until I said it, which I didn't. You know very well what I meant. You still wanting me is what matters, if you do.'

'Oh shut up about it,' she said. 'Jake Leibowitz! God calling would now be an anticlimax. Have you ever actually met him?'

'Once. At a dinner party in 1972 you wouldn't come to. I put him right about the emperor Nero. After, as it happens, Bill Bourne had put me right on much the same point. About twenty years previously. The small change of scholarship. Useful for tipping directors. About Nero and his brazen beard.'

'How did he take it?'

'On the chin. Did you know that when the Bible talks about a boy's first beard, it refers to his nether beard? Nor did I till today when I read it in a footnote. Dear little things. What're we doing tonight?'

'Making sure it's all shit on television, aren't we? And then turning it off when it's too late to do anything else.'

'Want to go out to dinner? Denis Porson's opened a new place. The Brasserie St Pierre, otherwise known as the Rendezvous des Tantes. Biggest buffet in London. Place where people go and eat very little just to prove how rich they are.'

'Maria left one of her special lasagnes in the oven.'

'Do me fine. What're you going to have?'

'You were hoping he wanted to do *Life and Loves*, weren't you?'

'Leibowitz? Of course I was. And of course he doesn't.'

'It'd make a hell of a movie though, wouldn't it?'

'Are those clenched teeth you said that through? Thank you all the same.'

'You are capable of being a very silly man.'

'When at the peak of my powers,' he said. 'You smell wonderful.'

'That's what money can buy.'

'Must be why it's caught on. What would you say to an early night?'

'Where does he live exactly?'

'South-west France somewhere, I gather. Someone on the coast asked me if our cottage was anywhere near his place. As if I'd know.'

'You soon will,' she said.

'Depending on what god-awful piece of material he's decided he wants to make into a movie.'

iii

A courier in a crash helmet arrived the next morning with a large envelope. A smaller inner envelope contained a printout of a long short story called 'The Siren's Song'. The author's name had been excised from the title page. A card headed '20142 Productions' was pinned to the text. There was no message on it. By the morning post had come a copy of the *Times Literary Supplement*, containing the review of *Life and Loves* by Samuel Marcus Cohen, whose name entailed Adam's front-page prominence.

Barbara had to go to a meeting of Shirley Parks's charity committee. Adam took Rachel to the Brasserie St Pierre for lunch. When they were back at their table with plates loaded from the buffet, Rachel asked Adam, in a voice that seemed just a shade deeper than usual, what it was that Leibowitz wanted him to do.

'Something called 'The Siren's Song', you ever heard of it?'

'Have I? What's it about?'

'The opening sentence was, "One cannot always like the unfortunate." I have to say it was like . . . ouch! The minute I read those words.'

'So you're going to do it.'

'It's pretty . . . impressive. Nasty of course. Dark. Listen, I haven't even spoken to him yet. Who knows what he wants to do with it. Maybe he wants to make it into a musical. It's all about a Greek, which – well, it's not my problem, but who's going to care?'

'The *Iliad*'s all about a Greek.'

'See what I mean? It's a downer. It is, in fact, literally a downer because it's about this shipload of Jews that've escaped from occupied Europe and no one'll let them land anywhere, especially the British won't let them across into Palestine, and . . . finally the Turks tow the ship out into the Black Sea . . . and it gets torpedoed. By the Germans. Or the English. Who knows who by? Maybe it just breaks up. They all die and no one did it, because who cares? Everyone's out of trouble.'

'It's based on a true story,' Rachel said. 'The *Struma*. And in the story only the captain and this character – Iakobos, isn't that his name? – the first mate, survive.'

'Jesus Christ, you have read it. You've read everything.'

'Rings a ship's bell, as you might say. Sort of a *Lord Jim* in modern dress. Read it in one of those American fat and floppy college mags, I think. Can't remember who it's by.'

'He doesn't want me to know, it seems. The great man of mystery probably doesn't own the rights yet.'

'Are you going to do it? You hate adapting things, don't you?'

'Jake Leibowitz is different, at least until he turns out to be the same. I'm going to talk to him. Half-hoping he's wanting to do enough horrible things to it to make me turn him down.'

'And the other half hoping he won't.'

257

'You have me to the life,' Adam said, 'if that's life. So they're going to give you a fellowship.'

'Starting next year, the word is.'

'Sesame, it seems.'

'Which makes this a good time to get some sun.'

'I suppose I should've asked Bill to join us. I never thought. Let's not analyse that, shall we?'

'He had to go to the doctor actually. Can't seem to shake this throat thing he's got.'

'By the time you get back to Cambridge, Sheridan Reece ought to be Master of the college. Get him to make me an honorary fellow, will you? It's the only honour that'd really mean anything to me. So don't mention it to a soul, obviously.'

'I won't. But when they make *me* Master, it's the first thing I'll do.'

'Take it easy. Make it the second thing. You're not going to marry him, are you? Bill.'

'Would it matter that much?'

'Of course not. But you won't, will you?'

'I'm not sure I'll ever marry anybody,' she said.

Adam said, 'None of us ever are – or should it be "is"? – until we do. Of course I may feel differently when I get to your age.'

'Or I get to yours,' Rachel said. 'Success is a kind of aspic, isn't it?'

'In the sense that it's transparent and makes you inclined to wobble? Probably.'

'It insulates you, I meant, and it keeps you looking . . . like you look.'

'But what if I only look like this when I'm with you? Success is what other people have. You never do. One person doesn't like your book or, even worse, needs to talk about the script and . . . pop goes the wassail. Which reminds me, painfully, of my soon to be ex-friend Samuel Marcus Cohen, and what he said in the *TLS* this morning.'

'No one rates him at Cambridge, you know, at all. Not since he said in a lecture on the radio that Theseus went to Crete "to rescue Ariadne from the Minotaur". "Over-reach is the way he reaches," is what Sheridan said. And that was nice! What did he say, as if I care?'

'I care, unfortunately. He did concede that my book is, and I quote, "almost major", but he then accuses me of "Holocaust tourism" is the *phrase du jour.*'

'How does he manage that?'

'By denying, *categorically*, that he's doing it, of course. That's what comes of giving people lifts in one's hard-earned Mercedes.'

'Who reads him any more, apart from you?'

'You do, and I do, and so, I suspect, does that smirking bastard over there in the corner. Who's another friend of mine.' Adam waved and smiled. 'Hullo, Michael!'

Rachel said, 'He writes those plays, doesn't he?'

'He does indeed, again and again. He's the man with the Midas formula for turning "smooth" and "abrasive" into synonyms. He claims to be an eighth Jewish, but he makes sure his work isn't. Tell me something, how come you're Jewish and Tom's not?'

'He isn't *and* he is,' Rachel said.

'He is because he married Juliana, or he isn't, for the same reason?'

'He's going to be rich,' she said, 'which heals all wounds.'

'Except the one you first thought of,' Adam said. 'Take care of yourself out there, Raitch. Because no one else will.'

He sat looking at her and she sighed (like her mother at that moment) and looked down and up at him again and then she said, 'You're such a softy really. *Soft* and abrasive, that's you. But I won't tell them.'

'They know,' Adam said, 'they know.'

'Captain, my Captain! No one told me you'd come ashore!'

'Hullo, Denis. You know my daughter . . . *our* daughter . . . Rachel, don't you?'

'Not in the large economy size. Using "large" in the nicest possible sense. Once seen again, unlikely to be forgotten.'

'You've changed your spots rather.'

'*Haute cuisine, je m'en fous, honnêtement!* My new creed's *sauve qui peut*, three sittings in the space of one, and Bob's your auntie! Temperamental chefs, dear, I have *had*. Literally. But enough of me, what of you, both, to name but a happy few?'

'We are as you see us.'

'That will do very nicely. At least in one case.'

Adam said, 'I saw Jill in California. I hope it isn't tactless to mention.'

'We are the best of friends,' Denis said, 'Jill and I. That's how much it hurts, but I shall never admit it, except under duress. When I would gladly also give you the address of my nearest and drearest.' Denis had his hand on Rachel's shoulder as he leant down towards Adam. 'I never hear a word, would you believe it, from him?'

'From?'

'Not one. Since the day he left me. And I can still see – excuse the lacrimose details, Rachel dear, you *are* a pretty girl, woman. Female. I can still see us in Battersea Park, with the fairy lights behind us, Gianni and I, declaring simultaneous orgasms, in the – for the moment – strictly sentimental sense, and plighting eternal troth. As if that sort of thing ever lasts! Except in your case, Adam Morris, of course. Jill, I . . . can understand . . . but Gianni . . . that hurts. But only when I larf. Food go down all right?'

'Loved it, every vulgar mouthful,' Adam said.

'Come again,' Denis said. 'Alternatively, report me smiling the last time you saw me.'

'Septimus,' Adam said, 'how's Septimus?'

'Straight as a die, dear. Gooses the girls in his class as if there was a prize for it.'

'There is,' Adam said.

'Good to know, dear. You're a very clever girl,' Denis said to Rachel, 'don't ask me how I know; I know. *And* who you got it from: give her a kiss from me when you see her.' He looked quickly at Adam. 'She is all right, isn't she, Bra?'

260

'Couldn't be better,' Adam said.
'All my friends are dying,' Denis said.

iv

'Can I have Adam Morris, please?'
'You have him,' Adam said.
'This is Jake. Leibowitz.'
'So far so good,' Adam said.
'Have you finished it?'
'The script?'
'The story.'
'The story, yes. Three times. Who's it by?'
'What do you think? Is there a movie there?'
'There's a movie everywhere, I remember you saying. That was the hell of it supposedly. Of course there is. It's very cinematic in some ways.'
'It's not a copy out job.'
'That raises the price,' Adam said. 'I know that.'
'But I want to keep the beats. The beats are all there. You agree?'
'I love the — I think of them as "panels" — the disjunctive way he tells the story. Leaps and bounds, I like those.'
'So listen, do you want to do it with me?'
'You're about the only person who could do it and that I'd say, sure, it would be a pleasure. I hope.'
'Still Shapiro I talk to?'
'He does numbers. I do words.'
'So when are you going to your place in France? Because I can send a car for you when you get there. We live maybe less than a couple of hours from where you are. Can you be there by the end of next week?'
'You've done some research. Yes, we can. Send me the directions and I'll drive over whenever you want.'
'Tell me when you're going to be there and I'll send a car. I never send directions.'

'OK. I think. Did I say I was excited? I probably shouldn't. First and last time, OK?'

'I'll call Shapiro right away.'

A deal was made that evening, for more money than Adam had received since immediately after he won the Oscar. The first fat payment would kick in after a 'meeting of minds' between Adam and Jake Leibowitz. On the following Sunday, *Life and Loves* appeared on the *Sunday Times* bestseller list, in last place.

Barbara booked the ferry to go to France for the following Wednesday. Adam called Shapiro to pass the word to Leibowitz, who had not yet given him a number to call. On Tuesday morning, Derek called to ask Adam if he had a minute to come and see him, 'Preferably right away'. Adam left Barbara packing and took a cab to Mount Street.

Derek said, 'Thanks for coming. I can imagine –'

'Don't imagine. Leave that to people who need the work. Something's wrong? What? Not with Tom, is it?'

'Tom?'

'Tom, for Christ's sake. My son, your . . . general manager, Iberia, isn't he now?'

'No, no. Tom's fine. We've got a giant new project near Cadiz he's working on. He's on a big bonus this year.'

'Something's up. You're wearing your shoes. What?'

'I shouldn't have called you. I didn't know who else I could talk to.'

'*Faute de mieux* is my middle name,' Adam said. 'Amazing how many calls it gets. Talk about what, Derek? Not broke, are you?'

'It's Carol.'

'Is she back on the scene?'

'Not on mine, but . . . All right, she's living with another woman. You didn't know?'

'How the hell would I?'

'You did. Filthy newspapers. She's a writer. She's with. Fay Pope, if you know her. Did a book called *Fatso.*'

'I almost wrote it. The movie. There but for the grace of Mike Clode, or turds to that effect.'

'There was a picture of them holding hands. You didn't see it? Everyone else did. In one of those gossip mag exposés.'

'The Almanach de Gotcha, someone called them, those bastards.'

'And now what do I do?'

'What can you? And why would you want to? Nothing to do with you. You've got another woman, or three, haven't you?'

'I look like the biggest fool in London.'

'And the richest,' Adam said, 'never forget a thing like that at a time like this.'

'You don't get it, do you? How I feel. Never mind the things she goes around saying.'

'Excellent plan. Never mind them. Taking a loss is like taking a shit, isn't that what the poets say, and you once told me? You feel better when it's over.'

'It's all very well for you.'

'Unworthy,' Adam said, 'and . . . Oh, unworthy will do.'

'What can she really be *like*, Ad? Underneath?'

'Female anatomy; leave it to gynaecologists.'

'All those years . . .'

'Don't they fly by though?'

'I thought she loved me.'

'And who says she didn't? Life and loves,' Adam said, 'as if I knew anything about them!'

'I haven't read your book yet.'

'But you took the reference at least.'

'Can you hear yourself?' Derek said. 'You think less of me, don't you?'

'Less than you think, I think of you. And so do other people. I love you, Derek, and I'll do anything for you . . .'

'. . . and that's as far as it goes. I know you. But be honest.'

'Never ask people to be honest. It only leads to mutual understanding.'

'I'm responsible, aren't I? For what she's turned into. That's what I can't handle. I'd've given her anything she asked for.'

'That's why she didn't ask. I never realised just how rich you were before, Der. You think there's nothing you shouldn't be able to buy and sell.'

'You're still . . . still *something*, because I gave Tom a job. Not quite angry? What's that?'

'Grateful, it could be. Very. Which I am.'

'And ashamed, am I right?'

'If that's what you think, maybe you should be. Tell you what, Der: stick to making money, I should. And leave the psychological insights to me. You were tired of her and then she did the unforgivable, and got tired of you.'

'I turned her into what she is, is what you're thinking. And now she's completely out of control.'

'You don't have to control what's in your wastepaper basket, not once you've chucked it.'

'I always shred things,' Derek said, 'these days. You should too, Ad. She's doing it to me, and you know it. *Against* me, she's doing it.'

'If she is, she is, and if she isn't, how about she's trying to make a life the far side of Derek Morris? You can't shred people, Derry. Not till you're even richer.'

Derek said, 'You wouldn't talk to her, would you?'

'If I met her? Of course, I would.'

'And tell her to mind what she says, ever, about me, to people.'

'No. I won't. And do take that look out of your eye. If you're practising being a hard case, it almost works. But it's not a pretty sight. You look like you're thinking of renting a killer. Don't do it, OK?' Adam clapped his hands. '*Derek*, she doesn't matter. If she's down the swift Hebrus, then so be it.'

'The what?'

'If she's gone bi, she's gone bi. Finish.'

Derek said, 'I only wish I had someone like Barbara.'

'And for all I know, she wishes she had someone like you.

You don't; she doesn't. You'll wish you hadn't said that one day. Possibly later today.'

'I do,' Derek said. 'I wish it now. I'm sorry, Ad.'

Adam said, 'Don't be a *schmuck*, as you people say, I believe. Enjoy the new lady or ladies, and to hell with the old one, I should. You know damn well you're a change-of-potatoes man from way back. It's amazing she stuck around as long as she did. Let her go.'

Derek said, 'I'm thinking of taking her ex on to the board of one of my companies.'

'Her ex is Derek Morris, isn't he?' Adam said. 'Or have I missed something?'

'The *Fatso* woman's. Gavin Pope. Late starter, but he's quite the hotshot lawyer these days. Chancery Division. Million a year man today, I shouldn't wonder.'

'*Gavin?*'

'And he's looking for corporate directorships. Good move, don't you think so? Of mine?'

'Mate in three. No getting out of it. Which, being a humble wage slave, I must. Why aren't *I* on any of your bloody boards?'

'You're never here. And you'd hate it. Business is business, you know.'

'Don't look at the papers for a month and you'll find that nothing has happened that anyone remembers. I wish I could do the same with reviews.'

v

When Adam reached home, he went into his study and had another look at Samuel Marcus Cohen's article. It was, as expected, lofty and spiked with petty accuracies: Adam's 'affectations of cosmopolitanism' were said to 'strike a note of sophisticated gaucherie'. This, Samuel Marcus said, was a pity, since 'the relationship between the SS Colonel and Katerina contained some remarkable intuitions'. As for the narrative, with its 'paucity of solid furniture', it was valid in that it reflected 'a post-Auschwitz world without fixed values or reliable *sacra'*, while the sustained 'dialectical *glissandi*' constituted 'a high wire, bereft of underlying reticulation, between vacillating *mises-au-point*; in disconcerting consequence, Morris's alertness to the nervous provisionality of post-war polarities' was 'at once intellectually *ben trovato* and imaginatively occlusive'.

The further the ferry took him and Barbara from England, the more amused, Adam told himself, he was inclined to be by the critics he had left behind. As they drove south, France was a narcotic that returned him from paranoid vanity to the joy of being an unmarked man. By the time they arrived at *Écoute s'il Pleut*, and found unfrosted blossom on the apple trees, and the telephone in working order, Adam was ready to believe that the last thing he needed was to hear from Jake Leibowitz. But he didn't go far from the house until he did. Jake said that he was sending his local driver to collect him at ten o'clock the following Monday. Adam said that he would look forward to it.

Yet when he sat reading 'The Siren's Song' again, waiting to hear the taxi coming up the lane towards *Écoute s'il Pleut*, he remembered the story of the French aristocrat who stood reading a book as his tumbril approached the guillotine and who, before he ascended the steps, folded back the corner of the page he had reached, as if he expected to resume it later. Barbara was dosing the new geraniums with fertiliser.

Adam said, 'The car's here.'

'Off you jolly well go then. Are you taking a toothbrush?'

'You know I'm not. I'll be home tonight. I know: Moses said the same thing when he went up the mountain, according to texts recently discovered under some tank tracks in the Sinai desert. But I still will. Why is it all such a farce?'

'Be grateful it isn't a tragedy,' she said, 'isn't that what the girl said in the novel everyone's talking about? I need some new secateurs.'

'I'll ask Jake if he'll sell me a pair. See you tonight.'

The taxi driver, who had already turned the car around, did not get out of his grey Mercedes as Adam approached. He agreed to say *Bonjour* when Adam greeted him, but he was not disposed to conversation. Adam had decided not to bring his annotated copy of 'The Siren's Song' with him, lest he seem too diligent.

Only for the first miles did he recognise exactly where they were and in which direction they were moving. The driver took side roads through thick woods before returning to a main road from which he almost immediately diverged. Although not blindfolded, Adam was reminded of the Sherlock Holmes story in which a Greek interpreter is driven, eyes bandaged, to a secret rendezvous which may not be as far from where he set out as the protracted journey makes it seem.

After a long while, the Mercedes crossed a green river. Suddenly, they were in among the grassed ruins, the roasted beams of the murdered village of Oradour-sur-Glane. They passed a dead tank on the way out. Adam wanted to ask the driver if Mr Leibowitz had asked him to make what seemed to be a detour, in order to remind him of what the Das Reich division of the SS had done at Oradour, but he had said nothing for so long that he now felt involved in a silent challenge. They turned down past a long grove of poplars and came to an area covered with wide nets, supported on tall wooden crutches. The grass was long under the nets. Beyond the nets was a low brick building with hutch-like openings along the base. It looked abandoned. Behind the brick building was another wide area of netted ground. Then again there was a low building, this time of corrugated metal. There was a yard on the far side, with a rusting tractor in it.

Adam said, '*Qu'est-ce qu'on faisait ici, monsieur?*'

The driver did not answer at once, and then, in a surly voice, he said, '*C'etait un élevage de cailles, qui a fait faillite.*'

'*Comment ça?*'

The driver shrugged. Either he did not know why the quail farm had gone broke or he was not disposed to prolong the conversation. After twenty minutes of further silence, the car turned off a side road, turned up an unpaved track, past two well-restored cottages with loud dogs. It slowed for the opening of a wide electrically operated gate and continued up into a long alley of green-candled chestnut trees as far as another set of gates. Triple strands of bright barbed wire ran left and right, as far as Adam could see. There were vines inside and outside the wire, arthritic stems cropped and tethered to their *tuteurs*.

The driver got out and announced himself on the entry phone. The gate slid back this time, and they drove on up to the compound. Thick-walled, tawny stone buildings filled three sides of the square. A large, squat tower bulged into one corner. It had a black slate conical roof with a weather vane on the pointed top. A Volvo estate, two Mercedes, a Toyota jeep and a narrow vineyard tractor were parked under the heavy arches of the main building. A terrace, with a roof of flat stones laid in unmortared rows, frowned over the courtyard at first-floor level.

The driver stopped the car and made no move. Adam sat for a moment and then got out as the door of the main building opened. The gravel was thick underfoot. Leibowitz was a man of large medium size, in jeans, blue espadrilles and a jeans jacket unbuttoned over a blue work shirt and black clip-on braces. Grey and black hair seemed to burst from his head and spill down into the tangled beard. He wore thick-rimmed glasses. The impression of bigness must have been a function of reputation: Adam was secretly amused to find how much taller he was than the great man who held out a small, white hand.

'You got here.'

'Finally,' Adam said. 'Close is always further than you think.'

'You're bigger than I expected.'

'I get smaller,' Adam said.

'Meaning?'

'Everybody does, don't they? When you get to know them.'

'I get smaller, you tell me.'

'I don't think so,' Adam said.

'How about we go in here?'

Leibowitz led the way across the loud gravel to a high barn.

'They dumped this gravel, but they didn't roll it yet. They have to come back and roll it.'

268

He opened a heavy oak door and they went into the high barn which was straddled by oak beams, the unconcealed tiles of the broad roof racked above them. The floor was paved with whitish slabs. Their footsteps scarcely sounded. Leibowitz stopped and listened to something which Adam could not hear, and then walked on, as if worried and reassured all at once, up a wide, straight flight of wooden steps on to a broad planked platform where there were several oak tables, stacked with boxes. More boxes stood on the floor, many taped and unopened. Beyond them, four heavy wooden chairs addressed a long table with piles of new and old books on it, some with many flags between their pages. A trestle table against the back wall had several monitor screens and electronic gear on it, a coffee percolator and cups beside them. A camp bed, with two pillows on it was pushed between the trestles.

'Seems to be some coffee up here. Want some?'

'Why not?'

'You read it again? "The Siren's Song"? You want milk?'

'Yes, I did. Yes, I do, please.'

'Doesn't seem to be any.'

'Then I'll go without.'

'Are you married?'

'Yes, I am. Very.'

'This is about a marriage. To me that's the story.'

'Really?'

'I can get you milk, you want milk.'

'I'd like some milk actually.'

'Sweetener OK?'

'I'd sooner sugar.'

Jake Leibowitz walked on his soft feet to the corner of the platform and opened a large armoire. Inside was a refrigerator. From the shadows, he called back, 'There's a place he says . . .' Adam took the milk carton from Leibowitz as he went to the table and took up one of the flagged books. 'Right here: "Their facsimile of passion is more passionate, more reckless (in secret) than passion itself." What do you think?'

'Is that about marriage?'

'Try this: "It almost makes them like each other; it almost generates love." False and true. Which is which? Do we ever know? Hand on heart, do we? Do you?'

Adam said, 'I suspect we do, or you wouldn't ask.'

'You wanted sugar.'

'I'm fine. Iakobos is a special case. He lives with guilt; it's his fuel but it's also his . . . secret wound, isn't it? The flaw that blights everything, except money. It makes money grow.'

'I don't want to call him Iakobos,' Leibowitz said. 'Sounds Jewish.'

'Are you not Jewish?'

'Both my parents happened to be, but that's it. What's Jewish?'

'What's anything?'

'You like to argue. You're afraid I'm going to ride over you. Am I right?'

'Yes and no. Both the same answer.'

'I wish they didn't have to be Greeks, these people,' Leibowitz said. 'How do you feel about that?'

'No Jews, no Greeks, what's left?'

'Oklahoma,' Leibowitz said. 'You want a cookie?'

Adam said, 'Is this lunch?'

'She's doing lunch. My wife. Lisa. She wants to meet you. In the house later. You want a cookie, have a cookie.'

'I'll have a cookie.'

'OK, so it's the man and woman, and – you're right – the money and what it does, power and what it does. The need for corruption. Part of the natural process. You have to be willing to kill.'

Adam said, 'Did you ever kill anybody?'

'I don't do "did I ever", OK? The Jews in the boat that gets sunk in the Black Sea. What did you think about them? *Did* you think about them? Once we got into the story of Iakobos, whatever we call him, and Irini, did you?'

'Think how?'

270

'You didn't. Hitler wins.'
'I did in the end. When he's drowning.'
'We lose them. You're honest enough to admit it.'
'Not an admission.'
'You're fighting your corner. That's what you want to do, go ahead and do it. But once that boat went down, you didn't give them another thought. Now I remind you, you're angry, and you're guilty; makes you aggressive. My point.'

Adam said, 'It's still the premiss of the story. The Jews dying. I liked the way the Zionists threatened the captain. They behaved the way I wish I had the nerve to behave.'

'Unless that's why they died, maybe. They threatened him if he went back into harbour they'd kill him. He didn't; so he had to kill them. Am I right?'

'He didn't kill them. The ship was torpedoed.'

'Doesn't matter. They die. He lives. He plans to get out and leave them to drown. He knows it'll happen; one way or the other, Jews die and no one gives a shit. The captain's going to survive, he and . . . whatever we call him, and that's the story, and we know it will be.'

'OK, if you want to be right.'

Leibowitz said, 'You don't like working with other people.'

'Some I do.'

'Slavery and screenwriting, you talked about that one time.'

'Maybe even two.'

'You were right. Do you love your wife?'

Adam said, 'Don't you?'

'It's a conspiracy, isn't it? Marriage. Either it's a deception or it's an illusion, and then it falls apart. I had a couple of those. You don't answer me because "Yes, I love her" is either a lie or it's not true.'

Adam said, 'He can still be Greek, but he can't be called Iakobos, is that where we are?'

'Meaning "Fuck you".'

'Meaning "Fuck you".'

271

Jake Leibowitz said, 'That's OK. You've said it, you feel better.'

'No, you do.'

'How about we both feel better? The Holocaust. You know what was wrong with it, when people talk about it? Gentiles. For them, it wasn't "holo" enough.' Leibowitz's beard made his cup hairy. 'They wish you were dead, they wish I was. They wish we all were. It haunts them and they don't like that. It makes them false, all of them, having to say they're sorry, knowing they're not. You think they don't include you. They do. I do. We're trouble. To each other even. You don't like me. Do I like you?'

'I have an idea you're playing games here.'

'Oh Jesus Christ, games are what we play. Aren't they what we play?'

'With me. I have to guess how you want me to react, and then either react like that, or not, because maybe even that is what you want. Eternal regression is a long way to go the first morning.'

'Take it easy. You need some sugar, I'll get you some sugar. Because here's what I'd – I was going to say "like" – our story to do. *Not* like, but want: make them realise the pleasure in it. I want to not let them *not enjoy* what they're seeing, and what it makes them feel. Good. Bad as that.'

Adam said, 'Clear something up for me here. It wasn't "holo" enough, you said, the Holocaust. Meaning what? It wasn't complete? Is that something you'd say if we were standing on the platform at Auschwitz?'

'But we're not. Neither is the audience. Get mad, you miss the point. Which was, suppose it had been "holo", who'd talk about it today? As it is, they wish they didn't have to, but only the crazies dare to say so. We embarrass them. Jews. Even the word. By surviving, *any* of us. It means they have to pretend, all of them, all of the time. That they wish it hadn't happened; when they wish it had. But totally. Don't they? This way, they pretend, *you* pretend. You have to or face the truth.'

'And you don't? Pretend?'

'Sure I do. What else? I make movies. What was wrong with *Citizen Kane?*'

'*Citizen Kane?* Not too much, was it?'

'Guy was a big baby. Charles Foster Kane. He played. He strutted. He sulked. He wanted his sleigh back. I do that, you do that. Our man doesn't do that. What can we call him?'

'How about Nikos? Implying conqueror.'

'He doesn't conquer. He wins. He kills, but he doesn't mean to, until after he's done it. He lives with it and he doesn't deny it or not deny it. That way he's the king, *almost*. That's it. How do you photograph "almost"? Tell me that and we've cracked it.'

'I don't do photograph. You do photograph. I'll tell you what I'd do, and then you can not do that. Might work.'

'How about we make the Holocaust – this little piece of it – into something the audience – how about, we make them *want* it? We make them sick of those Jews in the boat, the crying kids, the old guys *kvetching* and *dovening* and *oy-yoy-yoying*. Make them see Nikos – call him that, if you want to – hate them, smell them, wish they'd never existed. *And feel the same thing*. Now the picture is something else. Now we're in the fucking raw of the thing. We're hurting them and they're liking it.'

'And when it's too late to deny it, down he goes, and they go with him. The audience.'

'But they've already paid. Because he's their fucking *saviour* at that point. They worship him because he killed the Jews and he took the responsibility. They can get away with it because he doesn't. You don't like Jews, do you? I read some of the things you've written.'

'A few of them I wrote just to be . . . scandalous, maybe. Which I now somewhat regret. No, I do not hate them and I never said so. Do you?'

'Glad to be Jewish, are you?'

'The truth? I'm not even glad to be here. Entirely. I'm kinda proud to be, I wouldn't have missed it, but "glad", what's glad?'

'Gladiator, what does that come from?'

'Latin *gladius*, a sword. As you probably know.'

'You're not popular, are you, as a writer? I had them run some sales figures on your books. You don't sell too many copies. Why? Because you make people feel bad. Who buys what makes them feel bad?'

'Isn't that what you're risking asking an audience to do?'

'I want them to feel good,' Jake Leibowitz said. 'With him. Surviving. To hell with the Jews. I want Nikos – Nikos is fine as a name – I want him to act *guiltless*. Liberated. How about he *pretends* to be guilty, even to himself? Because then he can do what he likes. He can give Irini pleasure like a kind of . . . torture. He can be fearless when he fucks her, when he fucks everybody. Like a dead man who's alive. Can you write that? A fucking Jesus who knows he's a sonofabitch.'

'I can try.'

'Can you enjoy it?'

'I'm afraid I probably can. Yes.'

'We'd all be Nazis if we could, don't you think so?'

Adam said, 'Do I have to say "yes" to get lunch?'

'Now you're going English on me. Proving I'm hitting on you in ways you find threatening.'

'I don't think I could handle the . . . solitude. Being a Nazi. Would be my answer. The boots are cute, and the hats, but . . . I'm not so sure about the armband.'

'There wouldn't be any solitude. *Ein Volk*, remember? You'd always have brothers, you'd always know who you were and what you believed. No one is more sure of what he is than a fake. Serving a god nobody believes in and doesn't exist. Wholeheartedly. You can't do wholehearted any other way. Only the fake has no doubt. Isn't that the ultimate trip? Think of the Jesuits. Think Rococo. How do we do Rococo here?'

'What's the movie *about*?'

'It's about a man who fucks the world and makes it believe it's because he loves it. That's what *Kane* wasn't about, because Orson wanted to be an artist-slash-tycoon that everyone loved

274

and admired, and also *pitied*. He never lost his virginity that way. He was the clever kid got spanked all his life, and liked it. Remember that fake Irish accent in *Woman from Shanghai*? Proves it! He couldn't fake fake well enough to get away from being the kid with the train set.'

'Every great movie director still has to be his rival.'

'When Nikos gets pushed in the water, assuming that's what happens at the end, by the captain – Rubik, that his name? – the guy who saved his life in the first place, that's the sweetest moment in his life, and our story. There *is* a God, *and* He doesn't exist. Likewise justice. Make that work, it all works. But how? To make it work.'

Adam said, 'The song the siren sings. Is the clincher. At the end.'

'Do we hear it?'

'*Don't* we? OK, maybe not.'

'He does. We don't. Voice-over. Could be the answer. You hate it? I don't.'

Adam said, 'How about . . . we tell them "listen" and we make like *we* can hear it and they can't and what's wrong with them?'

'They're not Jewish!' Jake said.

'Because *we* can hear it fine, can't we?'

'We push fifty million dollars of the studio's money up their asses. You're asking a lot.'

'The song's better. If it's the right one. But what?'

'How about if the sirens sang flat?' Jake said. 'Who said they didn't?'

'Then why did people get lured on to the rocks when they sang to them?'

'Great tits,' Jake Leibowitz said. 'How about they had great tits? A lot of people go on the rocks for those. And then they say it was art seduced them. How do you work?'

'With the door closed,' Adam said.

'Same way you crap. Writing's jerking off, right?'

'And what's directing?'

'Directing is invading Russia. Alone. With an army you can't trust.'

'You answered a question!'

'I see it as a terrible farce. The Holocaust, is how I see it. Tragedy as farce. The end of categories: civilisation is barbarism, nothing stands between anything and anything else.'

Adam said, 'How many of your family did you lose?'

'Not a one, I know of. How about you?'

'Me neither.'

'See? Maybe it never happened.'

'Did Oradour happen? The massacre. In the village your driver took me through.'

'I don't know. Do you know?'

'I hope you're joking. Or do I? Because if you are . . . who are you to do that?'

'Who's anybody to do anything? For *us* it never happened. Like death. Yet.'

'Are you planning to make a movie says it didn't? Is that how cute you mean to get? Because I have no illusions –'

'Sure you do. Like it matters. Like we're alive. They wanted us all dead and we're alive and they're stuck with us, till the next time. When they won't make the same mistake.'

Adam said, 'You know who should write this?'

'Is this a resignation speech you're making now?'

'Samuel Marcus Cohen.'

'He can't write.'

'Apart from that,' Adam said.

'OK. Faking it. That's what everyone is doing now. That's what Nikos stands for for me: the falseness of reality; that's what's real about it. Don't say it, ever, but that's what has to come through. They put the world back together again, and they couldn't, and here we are, if we are.'

Adam said, 'I don't know that I believe in "together".'

'How about lunch? Believe in that? Hope there still is some. Across the street.'

Adam smiled at the idea of crossing the *street* to get to the other side of the courtyard. Did the afternoon heat make the gravel crunch more loudly? They seemed to wade in the hot air. Jake Leibowitz led the way from near the tower up stone steps, set against the face of the building, to the long, moss-badged terrace. He tried a thick door as if it might not open for him, but it did. Then they were in a more formal house, brocaded furniture, Limoges and Sèvres porcelain in a glass-fronted case, Persian rugs on the tiled floor. The large, sticky-looking landscapes on the white walls were elegantly framed. None had any shadows.

'Are you OK with cold cuts?'

'I'm OK with anything, pretty well,' Adam said. 'I can do without tripe.'

'Lisa doesn't do tripe. I try not to. Lisa, this is Adam Morris, been here for a week it feels like to him.'

Lisa Leibowitz had come from the dark interior of the house. Her blonde hair was pulled behind her head into a gleaming bundle, not tight enough to be a bun. The face was pale, the high cheekbones faintly shiny. The unblinking grey-blue eyes did not smile, nor did the pink lips. She wore black trousers, grey slip-ons and a ribbed, turtle-necked white sweater with two broad blue horizontal stripes.

A long walnut table, with four stiff chairs on each side, and similar ones, with polished arms, at each end, had a dozen bowls on it, of various salads and fruit. A majolica platter was striped with cold meats, pâtés, and chicken. There were bowls of pickles, and there was ketchup. A stack of large plates suggested, but did not promise, that other people might arrive.

Jake said, 'What do we do?'

Lisa said, 'Help ourselves. I read your latest book.'

'That makes two of us,' Adam said. 'Thank you.'

'I know her. Your Katerina.'

'Do you? In what sense?'

'She was a liar.'

'Was she? I didn't know that.'

'She told a lot of lies. The girl. She made things up.'

Adam said, 'She was fiction. If you're talking about the one in *Life and Loves*. I don't know what you mean exactly —'

'What I said. When she says she was raped; she wasn't.'

'I don't think so.'

'You don't know women. You don't know what our lives are. The colonel saved her, the SS man. The only way he could. And she meant him to. That was their deal. Deals are what we make. Why else are you here? Why is anyone? Your hero was some kind of an ignoramus, wasn't he?'

'The same kind as I am, probably. He didn't know much. He learnt a few things, or he was meant to.'

'For me, he was always apologising too much. That's what some kind of men always do. They're kinder than they want to be.'

Jake said, 'You want mustard?'

'I already have it, thank you,' Adam said.

'Like you say "thank you" when you don't mean thank you. Politeness — you don't agree.'

'. . . is a form of contempt, were you about to say? I do agree; can be.'

'You'd like to be angry,' she said, 'but you daren't. In case . . .'

'I have to walk home? Possibly.'

'Lisa shoots pictures,' Jake said. He seemed younger when he was eating; he was only six years older than Adam, the books said. 'Her father did it too.'

'And paints them, don't you? I wondered who did those.'

'You were too young for the war,' Lisa said.

'I was too young and now I'm too old. Fortune's fool. Lucky me.'

'*Romeo and Juliet*'s a comedy, am I right about that?'

'You don't like them. The paintings?'

'I never said that,' Adam said. 'What was it Nietzsche didn't say? Whatever doesn't kill me turns me into a . . . could it be a clown?'

Lisa stared at him with unblinking eyes and then she took a

278

clean porcelain plate from the stack beside the dishes of salad, salami and cold meat. She turned it over and looked at the maker's name on the back and then held it over a patch of uncarpeted tiles and detached her hands from it. It smashed into daggers. She was still looking at Adam as her slippered foot pushed the patterned shards under the central bar that ran the length of the table. She raised her body on the flat of her hands on each side of her chair to make long legs longer.

'My father knew her, you know,' she said. 'Your girl. Intimately, as they say. He knew her. She posed for him. I can show you the pictures. She opened her legs. She did what she was told. Would you like to see them?'

'Someone like her, you mean.'

'Girls like that were not rare. They aren't now. They are girls.'

'Your father . . . was he German?'

Lisa said, 'Italian. Was he a Fascist? So were many Italian Jews. Until they couldn't be. Then they were Jews again, despite themselves. Nationalism was a way of not being Jewish. It still is. Look at Israel.'

Adam glanced at Jake, who made eating his serious concern. He might have been a linesman in a rally that made no call on his attention. The huddle of his shoulders and the closeness of the beard to his plate seemed to isolate him.

'Very nice ham this,' Adam said. 'Does what you're saying tell me that he was a Jew, or a Fascist, or none of the above?'

'It tells you nothing. You tell me that you are inclined to make light of things if you can.'

'No shadows,' Adam said. 'You're pleased to be somewhat . . . how about "challenging", aren't you? Are you from Turin possibly?'

'How about Israel?'

'Israel. In what way?'

'Is where I am from. I was born in Trieste and I was taken to Israel. You hoped he was a Nazi, my father. A Fascist at least. Not the same. He was. For a while. As good as. Until he was

279

betrayed. You missed one thing in your novel. In your Nazi colonel. The – what's the word? – *exhilaration*. He suffered too much. I don't think they suffered. I think that was exactly what they didn't do.'

'Exhilaration at what?'

'Mastery. What else? And the shamelessness. Of being right by simply being what you *were*, and chose to be, not by . . . making a case. Appealing. Never by appealing. Beyond question. Without reason. Beyond . . .'

'Good and evil.'

'. . . why and wherefore. In Auschwitz there was "no *warum*": no why.'

'I too have read Primo Levi,' Adam said.

'Nazis were the only people who always *had to be dressed*.'

'But they weren't. Always. Under all those clothes they were stark naked.'

'To be a superman, you have to be dressed. Your colonel took your Katerina with his clothes on. Didn't you see the point of your own book?'

'On a good day,' Adam said, 'I can see the end of my nose.'

'She felt the buttons and the decorations on her breasts, you said it yourself: "He rode her like a horse." Hitler could never be Hitler when he was naked. That's why he never married. Marriage . . . You want some fruit salad?'

Adam said, 'Why not?'

Jake said, 'Can we go on talking later?'

Adam said, 'Soon as you like.'

'Can you stay the night?'

'Can does not entail will. I did tell you I like to go home.'

'It's a long trip there and back every day till we're ready. I never realised how long it took.'

'I don't mind.'

'For the driver,' Lisa said. 'He has to do the journey twice for every time you do it.'

'Give me directions and – I told you – I'll drive over myself.'

'I don't want you getting here tired.'

Adam sat there between them. He drank some water. Suddenly, Lisa and Jake were laughing, quite loudly.

Adam said, 'Excuse me, am I the joke?'

'We're all the joke,' Jake said. 'Like Neat-she said. Doesn't seem like anyone else is coming to lunch, does it?'

Adam said, 'It was delicious, Lisa. The lunch.'

'The girl put it out,' Lisa said.

Jake said, 'I just have to make a coupla calls.'

He went out on those silent feet.

'Who do you like less, me or him?'

'You're both very . . . intriguing, could you be?'

'And what are you?'

'I'm the new help, aren't I?'

'How many scripts do you suppose are dead and buried in this house, of this story alone?'

'It's never very cheering to count the dead. Not while we're alive. And after that it's too late. We always think we're the one bride that Bluebeard won't kill.'

'Now I know, don't I? It's me. You don't like.'

'Can I afford it?' Adam said. 'I'm in your way, aren't I?'

'We're both brides,' she said. 'You're the one he wants. For the present. What was her name? The girl you knew.'

'Anya. Was told about.'

'It doesn't matter, does it? Who was she?'

'That was, as they say, your earlier point, wasn't it? I never met her.'

'But you believed the story.'

'Don't you?'

'I don't need to believe it,' she said. 'I lived it.'

Lisa picked up another plate from the stack of clean ones and raised it high over the hard part of the floor, as she had the earlier one. Adam made some kind of a face and braced himself to be indifferent to the crash. She brought her hands down, but she did not let go of the plate. She put it back on the pile, with care.

'That's today,' she said.

'Do I understand you?'

'That's you. That's me. You understand me. Broken, unbroken; not so different as you hope.'

vi

'How much land have you got here?' Adam said, as they walked back across the now shadier gravel.

'Land? I don't know. Some. Land's not what I do.'

Jake Leibowitz walked ahead of Adam into the barn and on to the platform. Adam stood there while Leibowitz walked to the bank of electronic equipment on the trestle table.

'OK, so listen to this, if I can get it. I can. Listen to this. For me, I have to tell you, this is the song the sirens sing. How about it?'

Adam said, 'Is that what I think it is?'

'Depends what you think.'

'The Horst Wessel song.'

'I'd join in,' Leibowitz said. 'Listen to that. You were blonde, wouldn't you join in? He was right about a lot of things, Adolf, wasn't he?'

'I can't sing. Maybe that's why I'm not a joiner. Altogether boys never appeals to me.'

'Would you go to an orgy?'

'If I was in a strange town and no one knew who I was, maybe. But here's the thing, which has nothing to do with orgies: I admire your work. I like the story. I'm not going to do your script. Can I go home now?'

'What's the matter? Scared?'

'Of you, no.'

'Scared of what?'

'How about wasting time playing games I don't like to play?'

'What did she say to you?'

'She said what she said. You heard most of it. She's probably right.'

'About what, is she?'

'About Katerina and what I don't understand about her. About women in that situation.'

'You ever go with a hooker?'

'Who was it said "I don't do did you ever"? Neither do I.'

'It's more real, you know, with hookers. You know who you are, what it's all about. Nothing. You take things too seriously. Think you can't cut it?'

'I don't think anyone can, with you. I think you do the cutting. I'm too old to find it fun. Not because I couldn't, but because I have only so much time. And not enough for you.'

'You've wasted my time, OK?'

'Oh dear. You played it the way you played it. That's your idea of fun, the *Horst Wessel Lied* and we join in? Not mine. Do you want to call me a taxi and I'll pay? You can do that if you want to have the last laugh. But please do it, right now.'

'You go wait in the yard, I'll get the guy to come. Wait in the yard. It was a good morning, I thought, wasn't it?'

'Memorable,' Adam said.

'You want to shake hands or don't you?'

'Sure. I'm sorry, believe me. But I know it's best.'

The small white hand was also soft, and warm, as if recently washed.

The same driver came, after some time, and drove Adam away from the house. They went back past the empty, netted fields but they did not pass through Oradour-sur-Glane. Even after they had stopped to buy a new pair of secateurs at a garden centre, the return to *Écoute s'il Pleut* took twenty-five fewer minutes than the outward journey. Barbara was playing Mozart's Jupiter Symphony when he came into the kitchen from the patio.

'You're earlier than I expected,' she said.

'Earlier than I did. But here I am. And here are these.'

'You remembered.'

'Thinks: he loves me,' Adam said. 'And so he does.'

'So . . . tell me. How was it? Do you want some tea?'

283

'Tell you the soppy truth, I want to cry. Like some people want to be sick, I want to cry. Because it would be a way of . . . getting rid of something. But I won't.'

'You didn't like him.'

'Kinda.'

'He didn't like you.'

'I'm afraid he probably did.'

'So what happened?'

'Now I'm back here, nothing much. Ten years ago, I'd've hung in there. Today, I . . . didn't feel the vocation. Shapiro's going to be very . . . Shapiro, about this.'

'Then he'll have to be. Did he . . . insult you? Leibowitz?'

'Not at all. He was as nice as he could be. Hateful. I mean . . . full of hate. Not of me, I don't think. Of himself? His body maybe. He was . . . He wasn't . . . deep . . . but he was dark, very, very dark. He wanted me to do something and I don't think he knew what it was. He wanted me to know, but to find out I had to . . . go down with him. Like the guy . . . like Iakobos . . . in the story. Finished. Played out. I'm not doing it. I still want to, but I can't.'

'You need food,' she said.

'I need a bath. I need never to work with anyone else again, ever. I will, I suppose, but I need never to. Not anyone.'

'Then don't. Don't. You can cry if you want to. I'll run you a bath.'

'I'm a man,' Adam said. 'I'll run my own bath.'

They had had the bathroom redone. The walls were covered with pale blue tiles but the original oak beams spanned the room. Adam turned on the taps of the big tub.

'Anyone call?'

'Yes.'

'Anything I need to worry about?'

'Worry? No. Bruno. Laszlo. About your book. Are the rights available?'

'He doesn't give up.'

'But you just have, haven't you?'

Adam stood there naked, one foot testing the water. 'My own book,' he said.

'I agree. Of course I agree.'

'He's very clever,' Adam said. 'Make no mistake. Jake Leibowitz.'

'I don't like him,' Barbara said.

'You haven't met him.'

'I don't need to. I can feel him. I can see him. Oh, and they want you to go and give a reading at the Grantchester Literary Festival. Work in progress is what they'd like.'

'I'd better do some then.'

He lay in the hot bath and listened to the Horst Wessel song as it played silently in his head. The bath filled and he lay and listened to the sirens until, with sudden decision, he slid down and submerged himself in the boxed water. When he came up, with hair over his eyes (nice that it still could be), Barbara was there with a piece of toast and home-made pâté on it.

'Supplies!' she said.

'I was afraid you'd think I was chicken.'

'I don't care what kind of a chicken you are, I like you. I don't think you're chicken.'

'I hate to think of what I'll feel when he makes the movie, with a script by Susie Beaumont or someone. I so want it not to matter a damn. And I'll try not to let it show. But it will.'

'You do know I love you, don't you? Does it need saying?'

'God, yes. What else keeps me straight? I wouldn't've done it otherwise, probably, would I? Walked out. See what you did?'

'Suits me,' she said. 'No more lonely lunches. Are you going to call him, Bruno?'

'What's your guess?'

'It isn't a guess. You should.'

'You know the silly comedy of life, don't you?'

'I know it runs and runs, if you're lucky.'

'But with fewer laughs than you expected. Bruno's going to ask me who I want to direct it. *Life and Loves*. And who is the one man who could do it better than anyone else?'

285

'Give me a split second. Jake Leibowitz?'

The following morning, Adam made a note in his squared notebook about the visit to Jake Leibowitz, who never called again, as he half-hoped he might, if only for the silly pleasure of refusing to change his mind. Then he looked again at the manuscript he had abandoned about a London solicitor, Saul Nathan, who is asked by the Foreign Office to go to an African country to plead for a reprieve for a man who, it would turn out, was at school with him. What Tom had told him about Robert Carn, his schoolfellow all those years ago, was at the root of the character whom he now called Guy Fielden, just as 'Hooky' Nathan stood in for Adam himself. He began the book again, overriding the earlier draft with new confidence. Guy was now shown as *envying* the pain which Saul had endured at school, and which Guy simply observed. By seeking to save a man who did nothing to help him, Saul puts a small trump on Guy's voyeurism. Saul's mission is worthy, and somewhat bravely achieved, but it is conceived in contempt; for himself and for the other. Alienation makes him falsely good, as it makes Guy falsely bad.

When the telephone rang, Adam said, 'How are you, Bruno?'

'Look, I must tell you one thing: I can't pay what your agent is asking.'

'Love's old sweet song,' Adam said, still punctuating the page he was working on. 'Then offer all you can afford and I won't accept it.'

'Look, it's your book we're talking about.'

'Look, I'm now writing a new one, so . . .'

'Adam, for God's sake. Hullo.'

'I'm still here,' Adam said. 'Well, actually I've moved slightly and since no one is listening, I'll say something really unwise: if you really think you can get *Life and Loves* made, I'll do it for scale. The way I think it should be. But not less.'

'We have to have a director they will go with.'

'Nicely put. That's me in the long grass then.'

'What do you think about Mike Clode?'

'I don't,' Adam said. 'Works for me.'

'Being made a lord,' Bruno said.

'Ermine for vermin,' Adam said, 'very much the modern style.'

'He still wants to direct it.'

'Until something better comes along. Bruno, I have to get back to the condemned cell.'

'Wha . . . at?'

'I'm just visiting, as they say. But . . . listen, make a deal I can live with, in reduced circumstances, and I'll be in London in a few weeks and you can start telling me how to write.'

vii

By the time Adam and Barbara went back to England six weeks later, he had finished the new draft of the African novel which Barbara begged him not to call *The Horror, the Horror*, which was still on the title page when he gave it to Jason Singer to read. He drove up to Grantchester, with a selection of pages from the novel, while Barbara went to see her mother in Macclesfield.

Since Cambridge was only a few miles from Grantchester, Adam planned to stay the night in college. The literary festival was being held in the gardens made famous by Rupert Brooke's 'Stands the clock at ten to three?/And is there honey still for tea?'

After his reading, and the expected questions ('Is this based on something that really happened to you?', 'Why are the African characters not more developed?'), Adam went into the greenroom for tea and fruit cake before going to sign some copies of *Life and Loves*. He leafed through the programme of the festival, in which few of the speakers were not journalists or celebrities.

''ullo. You don't remember me.'

Adam looked up at the sound of the cigarette-roughened voice. He saw a small woman, with her short legs in what looked

287

like black bloomers. He said, 'Anna! Of course I do. How are you?'

'As you see. Not much of a sight. I was in your audience.'

'And I shall be in yours. I didn't know you wrote poetry.'

'Nobody does. But I do. Are you alone then? Can we have dinner afterwards?'

Adam said, 'Dinner. Of course. In Cambridge, shall we?'

'I don't care where.'

'How . . . how are your children these days?'

'I don't know. They're ashamed of me. I don't blame them. I don't blame anyone.'

'Don't you? I do. All the time. But you're probably right.'

'I better go,' Anna said. 'You were very . . . fluent. I shan't be at all like that. I'll see you later, if you're still here.'

He watched the dumpy little very nearly old woman with the cropped hair turn away in her beige shorty mackintosh and too wide trousers and scuffed flat shoes and tried to believe that this woman had been, as she had, *the* actress of their Cambridge generation.

He went late into the tent where Anna was to read her poems. There were no more than thirty people on the canvas-seated chairs, but one of them – Adam smiled at him – was the editor of a poetry magazine that those excluded from its pages regularly denounced as élitist. Anna came on to the stage and stood to the left of the lectern, as if the expected speaker had failed to arrive.

She looked at the audience, and then at the door, and then she said, 'This poem is called "Legacy":

> I once had them,
> But I don't have them now.
> I used to have my friend,
> But I don't have any now.
> I once thought things
> I never think today.
> I used to be somebody
> But I've stopped being now.'

288

She stopped and looked again at the door and then she said, 'This one is called "Please Don't":

> Stop me if you haven't heard it.
> I favour repetition.
> I say my prayers and sing
> My hymns. I've nothing else
> To say or sing. I'm glad to say.
> I bottle words and set them
> On the highest shelf,
> That way I know I'll never
> Reach them when I want to.
> I talk to strangers sometimes,
> But not to friends.
> If you wonder where I am,
> And why, please don't.'

She stopped in a way that seemed deliberately to abort surprise. The audience was silent, and still.

Anna said, 'This one is called "The Past":

> I once was someone else
> People still mistake me for.
> I like to please and so agree
> That person once was me.
> They think I miss the miss
> I was, but I was never she.
> I did pretend, and now I don't.
> I should wash my hands
> And comb my hair
> And act as if the past was there.
> But I don't and I won't.
> The past is past; so there.'

Anna recited several more of her terse poems. It was as if she had not written them, but had had them forced out of her. Like

289

some derelict priestess in a defunct oracle, she recited without gestures and, even at the end, when she walked into the alley between the seats as if she were one of the audience, leaving early, she allowed no space for the applause which she did nothing to solicit.

Adam took her to the same fish restaurant in Cambridge where he had had lunch with Rachel, that day when he introduced her to Bill Bourne.

'Amazing performance,' he said. 'It was as if you were . . . dropping pebbles from a great height. On empty heads. Your poems aren't like anything I ever heard before. To think I never even knew you wrote!'

'You have to do something when you're dead.'

Adam said, 'Were they once much fatter, the poems? Like Giacometti's sculpture before he thinned them down.'

'I don't know anything about sculpture,' she said. 'I am a very short person though. I am what I am, they are what they are, and I am.'

'Abrupt even.'

'Curtailed. I read your books, and things.'

'Which are . . . fleshier. Than they should be, perhaps.'

'You're in the world,' she said. 'I'm next door.'

'You weren't always. By any means. In Cambridge you were . . . quite the star.'

'You can't be a star without the twinkle, not for long. I faked it.'

'We all faked it. A lot of us still do, don't we?'

'And then I stopped,' she said. 'I've found God, you know. Of a kind. The kind that isn't there, and isn't kind. How is your wife? Still beautiful, is she? Still your wife?'

'Still both.'

'Do you still make love then?'

'We do actually. Quite often at the moment.'

'That must be strange.'

'Must it? Strangely we don't seem to find it so.'

'No one's been between me legs in years and years.' She spoke clearly enough for Adam to glance at the people at the next table. 'You're hoping no one thinks we're married, aren't you?' Anna said, 'you and I? Other people having dinner.'

'I don't think anyone will think that.'

'Nevertheless,' she said.

'*Nevertheless.* A one-word poem that sounds like, by Anna Cunningham —'

'As was. Very little needs to be said, does it? If it's said right.'

'Very.'

'Did you ever fancy me at all?'

'Didn't everyone?'

'I should've you.'

'You're oddly . . . oracular. Forecasting backwards. I don't think you did that I noticed. Fancy me. And I would have.'

'I have dirty fingernails, did you notice that?'

'Presumably you garden,' Adam said.

'And I don't wash all that much. Can I have another glass of wine possibly?'

'Of course. Of course.'

'God doesn't mind.'

The attention he paid her was a kind of appalled admiration. She had been right: he did hope that no one would assume that they were *together*. And yet he saw in those almost colourless eyes the small genius of serene despair: purity unalloyed by hope. When they had finished dinner, and she went for her bus to God knows where, he was ashamed of how glad he was to shake a mittened hand and say goodnight. He bent and kissed her cheek and knew she knew what she knew.

After the porter had given him the key of guest room B, Adam went, as he had all those years ago, and looked at the college noticeboard. A drawing-pinned card carried a list of new fellows. At the bottom he saw that two honorary fellowships had been awarded. One of the recipients was Derek Morris Esq. Adam tried to smile as he walked across Second Court to his narrow bed.

As a title, *The Horror, the Horror* was, as Barbara said, an invitation to savagery which few of the critics were likely to refuse. On second thoughts, *Into Africa* was less provocative. The text was being copy-edited by the time Adam and Barbara went back to *Écoute s'il Pleut* and he began work on the script of *Life and Loves*. There was odd pleasure in the callousness with which he cut and reordered his own book. One day, just after noon, when he was revising the morning's papers, the telephone rang.

'Hullo?'

'Daddy?'

Adam said, 'Rachel? What's wrong? Where are you?'

'Still in L.A.'

'L.A? What time is it out there?'

'Time? I don't know. Why?'

'I know, don't I? It's three something in the morning. Three-twenty. Has to be. What's happening?'

Rachel said, 'It's Bill.'

'What's he done to you? Raitch . . . tell me.'

'You know that . . . that telly play you did, with the character – Patrick Clegg, wasn't it? – based on Bill?'

'That can't be why you're calling.'

'Yes, it is actually. Because have you got a copy you can send me? Right away?'

Adam said, 'Rachel, what's going on? I don't care what it is. Yes, I do probably, somewhere. But what's happening out there?'

Rachel said, 'OK, he's dying.'

'*Dying?* Who is?'

'Bill. It was cancer. His throat. And they've now told him there's nothing they can do. He wants to see the play. Can you send it? Today, if you can.'

'That's awful. Yes, of course I can. How are you, darling?'

'I'm fine. It's not catching.'

'I know that.'

'Will you talk to him? He'd like to talk to you.'

'Now?'

'Are you busy?'

'It's just it's so late. For you, I mean.'

'We're not asleep.'

'Of course I'll talk to him.'

'*Sic transit gloria mundi.*' Bill's voice was furred and forced, but the ancestral Scouse accent seemed once more to inflect his words. 'Ingloriously, as was to be expected.'

Adam said, 'How are you, Bill? The stupid question always jumps the queue. What I mean is, are you . . . in pain?'

'I'm in morphine heaven, thank you all the same. I wanted to let you know, Rachel's the best thing you ever did.'

'Oh I know that. I know that. Barbara ever did actually.'

'I'm very lucky,' Bill said.

'It's a view,' Adam said. 'And a very brave one, if I may say so.'

'Did you hear the news?'

'News. The great thing about the French countryside is, you don't hear anything except Mozart and the neighbours' tractors.'

'About Sheridan. Sheridan Reece. You know the Master died, don't you, of the college?'

'Oh my dear Bill,' Adam said, 'what does it all matter?'

'All part of life's rich pattern. As you know, Sheridan was favourite to get it.'

'You shouldn't talk too much . . .'

'No risk of that.'

'Meaning he didn't, presumably. Get it. Sheridan.'

'They elected someone called Ronnie Braithwaite, if you know who he is.'

'Ronnie? Did they really? More fools them. To stick a finger in Madame Thatcher's already tear-filled eye presumably.'

'You can't help laughing, can you? I can't swallow but I can laugh, almost. *Capax imperii* and never got the job, poor old Sherry! Ambitions are like wives: you need to have at least a couple.'

'*A débattre*,' Adam said. 'What does it matter finally? Sheridan, I mean?'

'All your fault apparently,' Bill said.

'My fault, did you say?'

'I tried. Word is, you got your brother to give them a bunch of money. To help Sheridan get elected. But it didn't apparently. Rather the reverse.'

'I can't believe it.'

'Yes, you can, my old son. Yes, you can; and you do. Cambridge is still Cambridge. *Sic semper* the best-laid plans.'

'Damn and blast it, Bill. Trish asked me to . . . do what I could. But Sheridan was never even mentioned when Derek sent the donation. Fuck the S.C.R. ceiling honestly.'

'Not up to it in my present state. But who knows what I'll be able to do when I rise on the third day?'

'Who can possibly have told them?'

'And what does it matter?' Bill said. 'The last twist of the paperclip!'

'Damn and blast it all,' Adam said. 'I'm so, so sorry. About you, I mean.'

'Thanks to Rachel, I'm just managing to finish the intro to my translation of Valerius Flaccus. Ask not for whom the bill toils. Posterity gets more than it deserves. I did tell Rachel to leave, but she wouldn't. I fear she's fallen slightly in love with me, now I'm no good to her. I hope you don't mind. I do want to see myself in your play again. *Vanitas vanitatum*, as the vicar keeps saying.'

'I'll pack it up and messenger it to you soon as I can.'

'I think I shall just about manage my final seminar on Petronius next week, and then I may have to go. Voice is going already. I won't imitate the Arbiter and open my veins in the bath, though, don't worry. I've been packed this terminal picnic by my professional friends in the medical department. I shan't leave until I have to, but *tempus* fudge it. I am a bit . . . what was the word you public school people used? *Pushed*, wasn't it? I am a bit pushed. By three fat fates. Or is it pulled?'

294

'I'm . . . so sorry, Bill. Lame words.'

'You know what the Roman general said when he fell on his sword, don't you?'

'Instruct me. You often have.'

'"I am well", is what he said. That's how I am. Thanks to Rachel. I'm glad to have talked to you, Adam. Sorry we didn't know each other better. *Ave atque vale.* Such is life, if you have to go in for that sort of thing.'

'May I have one more word with Rachel, Bill, please?'

Rachel said, 'He was really glad to talk to you.'

'What's going to happen, darling? I know you can't talk much now, but when he . . . when he dies, what're you going to do?'

'He's fixed to be cremated out here. His friends are going to have a sort of vigil, isn't that what they call them? Wake. In his honour. Meaning, they're going to read some of his work and have a lot of drinks.'

'Are you going to be OK? I'll come out, if you want me to.'

'I've got a friend or two out here. One in particular who's very . . . kind to me.'

'Kind. Who's that?'

'Very. He's called Clifford Ayres. Bill knows about him. He's one of his graduate students actually. I shall be fine. You certainly shouldn't come. I've got things to finish out here.'

After Adam put the phone down, he sat for several minutes swallowing his emotion, and wondering what exactly it was, and about what. Then he went back to revising the text of *Into Africa*. He worked more quickly, and decisively, after speaking to Bill, and to Rachel. Clifford Ayres, who was he? Barbara was digging in the garden, with her floppy hat on. He was alone and not alone, himself and not himself, a writer at work; and he was, God help him, a happy man, almost.